THE ROOMMATE "dis"AGREEMENT

LEDDY HARPER

To anyone who has ever loved a child as if they were your own, despite biology.

PROLOGUE

Cash

The sunlight started to fade while I stared at the computer screen, the blinking cursor calling to me like an eager street peddler. I'd assumed the words would come as soon as I started, but once I sat in front of the keyboard, all thought drained from my brain.

Looking for a female roommate...

I hit the backspace, like I'd already done a million times, and tried again.

Man seeking a roommate—preferably female—for companionship.

That one actually made me laugh. I didn't care to sound pathetic. Once I found someone to move in, they'd realize how pitiful I truly was, but I didn't need to advertise it ahead of time. I ran my hand over my face and began the process all over again.

I'm gone a lot for work and need someone around the house while I'm not home.

Well, that did nothing but scream "come steal from me because I won't have a clue until you're long gone." I shook my head, raked my fingers through my hair, and contemplated giving up entirely. I'd had a reason for doing this, but as I sat here, cursing at myself, I couldn't for the life of me remember what it was.

Oh, yeah. Because I was alone, and I hated it.

Anytime you hear of a person catching their spouse with someone else, it's always the woman walking in on her husband, balls deep in his secretary. Well, I'm living proof that it happens the other way around, too. Except for the secretary part...I can't really prove that.

A year ago, I had caught another man balls deep in *my* wife.

My now *ex*-wife.

Colleen and I had been married for just over six years when it had happened. I'd worked a lot out of town, which was ironic that I hadn't caught her any of the times I'd come home early. I wasn't supposed to be out of town, and I definitely didn't have any suspicions about her infidelity. It'd happened one night when she had gone out with her girlfriends, like she had done every month. I'd figured while she was out, I would go grab a rare drink with one of the guys. So it came as a surprise when I found her cozied up with someone who wasn't me in a corner booth of the bar.

I hadn't gone ballistic and started breaking shit. Instead, I'd waited it out. When they left and headed outside, I trailed behind them, making sure they couldn't see me. Colleen had no clue what I truly did for a living, so I couldn't really blame her for not being more careful—especially when she got in the guy's truck.

I'd stood along the wall, hidden in the shadow of the canopy above, and watched as she leaned over the console and touched his face like she used to do to mine. Then they kissed. I couldn't move, torturing myself with the visual of their hands all over each other's upper bodies, her climbing into his lap, the steering wheel at her back. When her shirt had come off, I thought I would vomit. But I didn't leave, not even when her body began to move.

Normally, I would've stormed to the truck and busted out the window, dragged my wife out to prove a point. Yet I didn't. Instead, I'd stood stock-still and waited for their parking-lot romp to end. The entire time they fucked, I contemplated what to do. I was faced with two choices: confront them both, or walk away.

While Colleen had fastened her bra in the passenger seat, and the guy lifted his hips to button his jeans, I hung my head and walked around the corner to my car. I raced home before she could get there and hurriedly packed my bags. I didn't leave behind a note to explain my absence or inform her that I wouldn't be back—ever. Instead, I'd twisted off my wedding band and set it next to the sink in the bathroom.

Now, as I sat on the front porch of my grandfather's old house—left to me in his will—I watched the last of the light fade behind the Gulf and realized how lonely I was. Living by myself sucked, and more than company, I'd missed the presence of a female. I wasn't interested in dating anyone, and I didn't have any friends in town, aside from the vagrant who roamed the beach in the mornings. I traveled during the week and spent my weekends holed up in this tiny beach house that faced the ocean.

Which was what had sparked the idea of going online to find a roommate.

I dismissed the thoughts of Colleen and finished my ad.

Newly divorced male seeking roommate to combat the loneliness. Looking for a woman who's interested in a platonic friendship. Would get your own room/bathroom, and share communal space. House is paid for, so rent can be negotiated. Pets are allowed but subject to approval. Only serious inquiries will be taken.

CHAPTER 1

Jade

I sat on the floor with my knees pulled to my chest, my arms wrapped loosely around my shins, and watched the little angel on the couch in front of me sleep. Her mouth was open, her lids fluttered with the movement of her eyes, and the soft snores flowed like my favorite song.

"It's creepy to watch people sleep...even little people," my best friend whispered from behind me on her way to the kitchen.

Stevie—apparently, "Stephanie" wasn't cool enough when she was younger—had let me crash at her place until I could find somewhere else to go. It'd been three weeks, and I wasn't sure how much longer I had before she would politely ask me to leave. It wasn't that she didn't have a desire to help, but having four people live in her tiny, one-bedroom, studio apartment proved to be too much. With nowhere to put my things, we lived out of a suitcase in the living room, and the couch and floor had become our beds. Most mornings, I was left to brush my teeth in the kitchen sink while bouncing on the balls of my feet to keep from peeing on myself before I could gain access to the toilet. If it were only her living here, I'm sure there wouldn't have been a problem. But she shared the space with her boyfriend, Derek—it was actually his apartment—and he was tired of having guests in his home.

I wiped my eyes and shuffled my feet toward the kitchen. Stevie was in the middle of pouring a cup of coffee while thumbing through the notifications on her phone. It was her regular morning routine. It was amazing how well you knew someone after hijacking their living quarters for less than a month.

4

We'd met in high school and became fast friends. We'd even enrolled in the local community college together and signed up for the same classes. I was the quiet one, while Stevie was wildly animated. Seriously, that girl never met a stranger. When I'd fallen pregnant, she was the only one who didn't disown me.

"What would happen if a cop asked me to prove that Aria is mine?" I climbed onto the small space on the counter next to the fridge. "Like how would I prove that?"

Her gaze slowly shifted from her phone to my face, the bewilderment was obvious. "I'm no mother or anything, but back in my day, they had these fancy pieces of paper with various information on it…such as mother's name. I'm pretty sure that would suffice in the unlikely chance a cop would ask you to show proof."

I waved her sarcasm off. "Seriously, Stevie. What if I'm at the store and someone thinks she's not mine? It's not like I carry her birth certificate with me. Would they follow me home so I could get it? Would they take her and not give her back until I got it? What would happen?"

"I think the more important question is…why are you even asking this?"

"She looks nothing like me."

Stevie stared at me with wide, unblinking eyes, her mouth hung open. "You're kidding, right? She looks *just* like you."

"I don't think so."

"Then who does she resemble? Certainly not her father. So who?"

I shrugged, not having a clue whose features Aria had gotten. "You know how you can look at a kid and be like, 'I know who your mom is'? I just don't feel like people say that when they see us together."

"Honey, no one says that. We may think it, but unless we know the person, we keep our thoughts to ourselves. Not to mention, we don't ever call the cops unless the little kid is screaming or mouthing 'help me.'" She dramatically acted out the last part, which made me laugh and forget all about my irrational fear—for the time being.

"Whatever. What's new in the world of bookface?"

Stevie was my source for all the latest gossip. It was almost unheard of for someone not to own a smartphone in this day and age, but here I was, twenty-two, and the not-so-proud owner of a prepaid flip phone. Texting was a drawn-out affair due to how long it took, and forget about checking email or keeping up with social media—not that I really had a reason to have an account. It wasn't like I had friends outside of Stevie and the group she hung out with.

She unlocked her phone and began to scroll—exactly what she had been doing before my completely valid question sidetracked her. "Jade…" she tsked and shook her head without glancing at me. "If you keep calling it that, people will start to take you seriously. But in the world of *Facebook*, there's some guy looking for a roommate."

I hated it when she paraphrased. "What's the big deal about that?"

"He's only seeking a *female* roommate. Says he's divorced and lonely. He sounds like a creep. Not to mention, there's no picture attached to his profile, and anytime he's been asked about it, he just comments and says they're not what he's looking for. I bet he's a serial killer or something."

"Or horribly hideous and can't get laid. Where did you say he lives?"

"The Gulf Coast. Looks like it's straight across the state. Says he has a house on the beach that's paid for, so either he's a millionaire, or it's a scam. My money's on scam. Although, you have a good point…he could be like that gross slug creature on *Star Wars*."

I shivered at that mental picture. A boy I'd gone to middle school with had some disgusting fascination with Princess Leia and Jabba the Hutt. Puberty did weird things to boys. "Does it say how old he is?"

She scrolled with her thumb, her dark eyebrows knitted together in concentration. "No, just a generalization. It's listed as twenty-five to thirty-two." Her top lip curled like she'd just tasted something putrid. "I bet he's old, fat, and gross. Eww—" She gagged dramatically. "He's probably one of those sick fucks who likes to stick his wrinkled dick in young pussy."

I leaned to the side, checking on Aria. She was still too young to understand what Stevie was saying, but regardless, she didn't need to hear it. With her curious nature, she'd ask someone what it meant, and there was no way I'd be able to explain that. If the cops weren't called for her not looking like me, they'd definitely be called for a toddler going around talking like Stevie.

"Here, check it out for yourself. I have to go get dressed for class." She handed me her phone before taking her coffee and leaving the room.

The apartment was small, consisting of a living room that fit one couch and a TV that had to be mounted on the wall to conserve space, a kitchen only two adults could comfortably fit in, a tiny corner big enough for one table with four chairs crammed around the top, and a bedroom. Even the bathroom wasn't accessible from the rest of the place, proving this apartment was not meant for entertaining guests.

I checked on Aria again before reading the ad that had been shared on someone's wall. It was from a guy named Cash Nickelson—probably a fake name—who claimed to live on Geneva Key, an island off the Gulf Coast of Florida near Sarasota. I'd heard of the town, but had never been there before. From what I'd been told, it was a ritzy place, full of rich people with more money than God. However, there wasn't an address or picture, so he could've very well been lying about the whole thing. Stevie was right—this had to be a scam, a way to take advantage of women or find his next victim.

Just before locking the phone, an idea struck. So I jotted down his name, and any other information I'd been able to gather from the ad and comments attached, and waited for Stevie to leave for school.

If he could play games, then so could I.

It wasn't like I had anything else going on. There was only so much I could do with a two-year-old. I was pretty sure I'd crossed over into insanity about five episodes of *Blue's Clues* ago. So if this Cash Nickelson character was in fact crazy and believed women were easy targets, he'd clearly never met a mother of a toddler.

As soon as the front door closed behind my best friend, I grabbed the laptop off the kitchen table. I couldn't live with Stevie and Derek forever, but in order to move out, I needed a paycheck. And I couldn't get one of those without childcare. Knowing I had no connection to the outside world with my outdated cell, Stevie was nice enough to let me use her computer to apply for jobs—which I had done. Every day for the last three weeks since I'd moved out of my mom's house. But today, I decided I needed a break from reality, and chose to focus on this scandal instead of my own.

I searched his name in the area he claimed the house was in, but I came up empty-handed. I even tried to find a profile for him on every social media site I could think of—including MySpace— but he didn't appear to exist. My stalking abilities weren't the best, so my last-ditch effort to learn something about him was to look up property records. Just to be thorough, I included every county in a fifty-mile radius of Geneva Key, but I couldn't find a single deed or tax record with his name on it. Granted, I didn't have any social media accounts, and if anyone tried to find property information with my name on it, they'd come up empty, as well. The difference was…I wasn't seeking a roommate for a house I claimed to own.

Anytime someone questioned him about personal information—otherwise known as research to make sure he wasn't on America's Most Wanted list—he either dismissed the person or responded by saying they could fill out a request as long as they were serious about it.

Figuring I had nothing better to do with my time, I decided to complete the inquiry, for nothing more than to catch a killer before bodies started washing ashore along the Gulf Coast. What I found most odd was his unusual request for anyone with a picture attached to their email account, to remove it before submitting their response.

He only asked for my name and the age range I fell into, nothing specific. There was a place to add where I currently lived, and a box to list my reasons for seeking a room to rent. Other than my email address, he asked for no other way to reach me. For the most part, it looked legit—other than the complete anonymity on his part.

In all honesty, I didn't expect to hear anything back, but that hadn't stopped me from checking my email incessantly throughout the day. After Stevie and Derek headed off to bed for the night, I refreshed the page one last time before giving up, and to my surprise, I had a new email from Roommates Anonymous.

Dear Jade, thank you for your recent inquiry submission on my post. Let me start out by saying I'm only looking for people who are serious about moving in. I have to be honest and tell you I've received hundreds of emails from people all over the country, some legitimately looking for a room to rent, but most have been curious folks trying to get information on me. It's not that I am keeping my identity a secret for malicious reasons, and once I explain, I hope you can understand my logic.

I'm not interested in a relationship, so therefore, I don't care what you look like, hence the no-photo request. If you're in dire need of a room, this probably won't work out for you. As much as I would like to have the spare room filled tomorrow, I feel it's necessary to get acquainted with one another a little first, so that when you do move in, we won't feel like complete strangers. Before a final decision is made on either of our parts, you will have all the information about me you'll need in order to make a sound assessment as to whether or not this is the right move for you.

I am a thirty-year-old single man who works a lot. You won't see me Monday through Friday, but I will be around on the weekends. I don't currently know anyone in the area, as I've recently moved here after my divorce, and I'm not home enough to meet many people. The house is small, three bedrooms, but plenty of space, so you won't feel like we're living on top of each other, and it's right on the beach. It's a small community (I'm sure you've probably already done your research on Geneva Key) so almost everything is within walking distance or a short bike ride away. I have cable and internet, both of which you are free to use as you'd like, and obviously utilities. Like I said in the ad, rent can be negotiated. There won't be a lease, so you don't have to worry about that, but since I will be gone a lot, leaving my home vulnerable to someone I'm not familiar with, I will ask for permission to run a full background check and screening. Now would be the time to make me aware of anything I might find.

If you're still interested in taking the next step, please reply to this email. If not, thank you for your request, and good luck on the search for finding the perfect roommate.

Best of luck,
Cash N.

I'd expected the hairs on the back of my neck to stand on end, warning me of danger ahead, but I didn't get that feeling. Instead, I sensed sincerity. Then again, "Oh, Johnny killed ten people? Yeah, I always thought he was weird and totally capable of murder," said no one…*ever*. I was pretty sure sincerity was what kept these guys with stockpiles of victims.

I had no plans to move in with the guy—there was no way I'd put my daughter in that situation—but that didn't stop me from responding, if for no other reason than to learn more about this mystery that had blown up and made its way to Stevie's Facebook wall.

Unsure of what kind of response he was looking for, I simply said I was still interested in finding out if we'd make a good team, and signed it with, "Looking forward to hearing from you." Then I closed the lid of the laptop, set it aside, and curled up with my blanket on the pallet I'd made on the floor next to where Aria slept peacefully on the couch.

✦

To my surprise, I had an email waiting for me the next morning. It had come in minutes after I'd sent my response last night, and I kicked myself for not waiting up for it. Having this to entertain me could've saved me from an hour of tossing and turning on folded blankets that did nothing to soften the hard floor beneath me.

It's so great to hear back from you, Jade. I've created a form for you to complete. If you wouldn't mind answering the few questions I've laid out and send it back, we can get started on moving this process forward. Again, I hope you can understand my need for things to happen this way. As I'm sure you might have figured out, my ad has been somewhat elevated, and I would really like to find someone who truly wants this opportunity. Wading through the requests has been a challenge, so I ask that if you're not serious, please end it now.

Thank you,
Cash N.

I clicked the link he provided and pounded away on the keyboard.

Full Name: Jade Duran Robertson
Email: JDR95@gmail.com

Age: 22

When I got to the question about pets, I debated. It wasn't ideal to refer to my daughter as an animal, but considering I didn't plan to ever live with him, he'd never be aware that Aria, the two-year-old "small breed," was in fact a human and not a dog.

I laughed at myself and continued with the form.

Price Point for Rent

He'd given three options: two hundred to four hundred, four hundred to six hundred, and six hundred to eight hundred. Beneath those, there was a spot for "other" and a blank to fill in my own answer. I chose the first one. It wasn't like I could've afforded any of the options I had, but I figured "zero to fifty" would conclude this game, and if I were honest, I was actually having fun with this.

Job: Nanny

It didn't matter that it was for my own kid.

Then came the actual questions, which were different from the ones above that read more like an application for a loan. He asked if I drove, if I owned a car. If I would have a problem being alone in his house for extended periods of time—to which I answered no. I thought it was an odd thing to ask, but then again, there were probably people who would've felt uncomfortable staying by themselves in a stranger's house. Without ever having been in that type of situation, I gave him the most honest answer I could. After that, he went on to ask about family, if I was in a relationship, and if I could foresee the possibility of having overnight guests often.

The only reason he'd need information about my relationships with others was to find out how long I could go missing before anyone came looking for me. But instead of deleting the form and any communication with this guy, I lied...through my teeth. I told him I was very close with my family and even had relatives in his area, which was why I'd contacted him in the first place. The dating question made me hesitate. I assumed if I said I was in a relationship, it'd look odd that I would be interested in living with a guy. I also assumed it'd be strange for me to move away from a boyfriend, and too coincidental if he lived on Geneva Key. So I went with simple and said I'd recently split with my ex, hoping that would give us something in common.

Spinning tales and half-truths could've almost been a full-time job. But the hardest part would be remembering everything I'd told him. Nothing turns a face redder than being caught in a lie.

I hit send and then quickly put the computer away to keep me from another day of obsessing over my inbox. Instead, I took Aria to the local park after her nap. It was obvious Derek had tired of us being there, cramped around the table every night for dinner. So, to give them some alone time, I stayed out later than usual and hit the dollar menu at a drive-through.

By the time I made it back, Stevie was in the kitchen cleaning up dinner dishes, and Derek was on the couch. He craned his head, took one look at me, and then headed off to their room. I couldn't help but grow agitated, realizing Aria and I would have to skip another shower. I'd learned very quickly how to bathe myself in the kitchen sink, but Aria still had trouble getting through it without making a mess.

"You were out late," Stevie said as she put the last dish away.

"Yeah...Aria needed a break from the TV, and while I was out, I grabbed a few numbers to call off the message board at the college." I conveniently left off the part about how I'd already called them and got turned down as soon as I mentioned having a kid.

"It took you all day to get numbers?"

"No. I was just trying to give you and Derek some time together without us being in your way. I'm sure this hasn't been easy on you. Believe me, I'm looking for another solution."

"We're managing just fine. Don't rush out before you're ready."

"Derek hates us being here."

"He'll get over it." She waved the dishrag in my face. "He's aware of how hard it is—he was raised by a young, single mom. So he's more understanding than he acts. Don't let it get to you. First, you need to find a job. You won't be able to go anywhere without one of those."

"I'm trying. I've applied at almost every daycare in town, but it's hard without any certification or degree. And from what they all charge to actually watch Aria for me while I work somewhere else, I'd have to sign over my entire paycheck, plus some. It's insane how much childcare costs. It baffles me how single mothers without family can afford to work."

"You'll get through this. You always land on your feet, and this will be no different. My only concern is that you'll worry too much about cramping our style and rush into something, only to find yourself in a worse situation." She raised one eyebrow to punctuate her meaning, but she didn't need to do that, I understood all too well. That was the last thing I wanted to happen.

I had no desire to crawl back to my mom's house for many reasons, but I'd be lying if I said I hadn't thought about it. Stevie could tell me until she was blue in the face that I hadn't overstayed my welcome, though I'd never believe her. The walls were thin, making it easy to overhear some of the conversations they'd had behind their closed door at night when they thought I was asleep. In fact, the walls were so thin, there was no doubt Stevie and Derek weren't having sex—and he'd pointed that out to her in these hushed, late-night discussions. But I couldn't exactly tell her that I'd been privy to that information.

"Thanks, Stevie." I gave her a hug before she headed back to her room.

By the time I finished bathing Aria and wiping myself down, it was after ten. I'd gotten her settled on the couch with cartoons on the TV, and as soon as I heard the first note of her own personal lullaby, I grabbed the computer.

ᵀᴴᴱROOMMATE ᴅⁱˢAGREEMENT

My heart skipped a few beats at the sight of another email. Except this time, rather than it coming from Roommates Anonymous, the sender was Cassius Nicholson.

CHAPTER 2

Cash

When I'd submitted my ad for Roommates Anonymous, I suspected I'd get dozens of fictitious requests. However, I hadn't expected it to go viral. Rather than dozens, I had to field off hundreds, if not thousands, of people interested in my identity.

It wasn't like I was some Hollywood movie star, or even someone famous. But that didn't mean I wanted every Tom, Dick, and Harry looking me up, either. I'd left quietly in the middle of the night, purposely ignored calls from Colleen, and relocated to this tiny town for a reason. I happened to like my privacy.

I just hoped giving her my personal email address wouldn't backfire.

I fell onto the couch, ready to flip through the channels until I fell asleep. Ever since finding Colleen riding that dickhead in his truck, I had a hard time sleeping. Before that memorable event, I'd come home on a Friday night from a job and crash. There was something about being next to a woman that made it easy to shut off my brain and give in to the world of unconsciousness. But ever since I'd left her, I had turned into an insomniac. On the job, away from the job—it didn't matter. I was lucky if I got four hours a night, less than that if my target was sneaky.

Just before I grabbed the remote from the side table, my phone alerted me to a new email.

Cash…or Cassius? Which do you prefer? I'm sure there's a good story behind a name like that. Hopefully I'll be around long enough to hear it. And what about the last name? Did you spell it wrong on your profile? Sounds like something that would happen to me. Anyway, it was nice to hear from you. I just thought I'd tell you that I don't have email on my phone. (I'm currently using my friend's computer.) So if you email me and it takes a while for me to respond, that's why. I'm not great at texting, but it's probably the fastest way to reach me. If I'm moving too fast, please forgive me. I'm not at all trying to speed things along, just didn't want you thinking I've bailed when it's just taking me a while to get online.

Beneath her name, she included a phone number.

I'd passed on so many women over the last few weeks that I wasn't sure I'd ever find someone to live with. I wasn't picky, I just knew what I was looking for. I didn't need someone to cuddle at night, but I did hope to find someone I could spend time with. I needed conversation, companionship, someone to sit on the couch with and watch movies. I didn't think that was too much to ask, but I hadn't taken into consideration how many weird people were in the world.

The good part about my job was my access to personal information. Most of the time, I could tell by the initial inquiry if it was legitimate or not. Those that fit the bill were easy-screened, meaning I pulled up basic information to determine if I was interested in moving forward with the process. It wasn't detailed, but it was enough to tell me if they were real or not. When I pulled up Jade's, I was surprised to see that she'd given me correct information. That's when I decided to send her the full questionnaire to be able to dig a little deeper. I made sure to stay above the line, so as not to be flagged for running multiple background checks on random women. In my line of work, someone would question it. And still, she came back clean.

I tapped on her number, highlighted in blue, and pressed the option to send a text.

Me: Jade?

Her response was almost immediate.

Jade: Yes…who's this?

Me: Sorry, this is Cash.

Jade: Oh, hi

Me: I didn't wake you, did I?

I laughed at myself, knowing full well I hadn't. She'd just sent me an email less than two minutes ago. But I wasn't sure what to say, and that was the first thing that came to mind. Oddly, this reminded me of dating, and it made me a tad uneasy. But I had to see it through if I had any hope of not living alone forever, so I went with it.

Jade: No

I typed a few things, but deleted them when I realized how forced it felt. Figuring I'd leave it alone for the night and try again tomorrow, I closed out the message app and grabbed the remote. About two minutes later, my phone chirped with an incoming text. I nearly jumped when it vibrated on my chest.

Jade: Were you just checking to see if I stay up late? If so, I usually don't.

Jade: I was out late tonight to give my roommate time alone with her bf.

Jade: If you weren't, then I just gave you information you probably don't care about.

Every time I started to reply, another message had come through. By the last one, a laugh had actually blown past my lips in a burst of air. What surprised me even more, was the smile curling my lips. It'd been a long time since someone other than the guys on my team had been able to give me this kind of reaction.

Me: LOL. Actually, I'm not sure why I texted you. You said you don't check your emails, so I reached out this way, but then I didn't have a clue what to say. Although, I've gotta admit, I'm a little sad that you go to bed early. I'm a bit of a night owl. One of the reasons I went looking for a roommate was bc I miss having someone to talk to at night.

Wow, Cash, way to look pathetic.

After a few minutes without a response, I thought she'd given up and deleted my number—or blocked it—so I set it down and went back to flipping through the channels. But then, over five minutes after I'd sent mine, a text came through.

Jade: I'd prob die of boredom if I suddenly found myself alone.

Jade: And sorry this is taking so long, I have an extremely outdated phone and typing is a PITB, and your text came out of order so it took a min to understand what it said LOL

I stared at her words and laughed, enjoying the rumbles it sent through my chest.

Me: What's PITB???

I worried the age difference had left me confused on her acronyms.

Jade: Pain in the butt.

Then I laughed…*hard*.

Me: No worries.

This time, ten minutes had passed without a response, not that one was necessarily needed, but I wasn't ready for the conversation to end. Rather than send another message, I hit the call button and listened to it ring. I immediately wanted to hang up, but I wasn't given enough time before she answered. It was too late to back out now.

It was strange. She picked up after only one ring, but she didn't speak. There was some rustling on the other end of the line, then a low creak that could've been a door, before she said, "Hello?" almost sounding out of breath.

The first image that came to mind was Colleen, and I couldn't help but wonder once again how many times she'd taken calls while I slept next to her. I attempted to shake off the thought, but it wasn't so easy.

"Jade?" I couldn't keep the deep, raspy trepidation out of her name. "Are you okay?"

"Yeah." It was breathy, like she'd just hopped off a treadmill. "Why?"

"It just sounded like I caught you at a bad time or something."

"Oh, no. You didn't. I mean, I just rescued a baby from a well, thwarted a bank robbery, and saved an old lady from getting hit by a train. But that's nothing new. Now I'm taking a break, so your call came at the perfect time." There was a hint of a smile in her words, and it was enough to wipe away any thoughts I'd had of my ex.

"Wow, all that happened at eleven o'clock at night? How do you ever get any sleep?" Once upon a time, I was a funny guy. Apparently, having a front-row seat to your wife's infidelity kills any chance of humor in your life. This fact was proven by my lame attempt to crack a joke.

Either Jade was a really good person who didn't want to hurt my feelings, or she was sleep deprived, because she laughed. "Red Bull. And cocaine." She paused, and then blurted out, "Oh my God, I was totally kidding. I don't do drugs...of any kind. Which is why saying I do coke was funny. But you don't know me, so you don't know that I don't do drugs, so my joke was lost on you, and I just made myself look totally stupid, and—"

"*Jade*," I repeated for what felt like the fifth time. But at least it worked. She finally stopped talking long enough to let me speak. "It was funny. I actually laughed." A nervous sigh filled the line, and then a horn honked in the background. "Are you outside?"

"Yeah, my roommate's in bed and the walls are thin. The TV is off, so I was scared I'd wake her. What's up? Did you call to find out if I was awake, or do you only do that in texts?"

I hadn't realized until now, talking to her on the phone, how much I had missed simple conversations. Sure, we fuck with each other on the job and get a good laugh out of it, but there's something to be said about the easiness in talking to Jade. I really hoped this worked out with her, because I could tell having her as a roommate would be entertaining and enjoyable.

"Well, you kinda went silent on me with the texts, so I thought you might've fallen asleep."

"So you called? Seems kind of rude." Humor filled her soft voice.

"I already told you I'm a night owl, that I'm looking for someone who can stay up and hang out with me. I figured there's no better way to see if you meet that criteria than talking on the phone."

"That seems like sound logic. So now that you have me, let's chat. Tell me something about you, Cash. You said you're divorced, how long has it been? And what happened? Did she not talk enough for you?"

This wasn't really a conversation I wanted to get into with her, at least not this soon, but we were here. She'd asked, and I had to own it. "It's been a year, and I left because my wife—*ex*-wife—cheated on me, and I'm the one who caught her."

"Oh my God, Cash. That's horrible. I'm so sorry."

"It's fine. Nothing to be sorry for. It's a sucky situation, but it sure beats staying in that kind of marriage, you know? It's also the reason I'm not interested in a relationship. I mean, there are many reasons, but that's the biggest."

"Yeah, I don't blame you."

"What about you?" I didn't want to chance her getting in another question I'd feel obligated to answer. "You said you've recently split with your ex. What's your story?"

"It's complicated." That was all she said, as if it answered all my questions and cleared everything up.

I waited a few more seconds, hoping she'd add something, but still, she gave me nothing. It seemed I'd have to pry information out of her, and it made me wonder if her humor was nothing more than a mask to hide her secrets. "Okay, I'll give you that—*for now*. Was it serious? And how long ago did you break up?"

"Three years ago."

It didn't go unnoticed that she only answered one of my questions. "*Three* years? I thought you said it was recent."

"That's such a relative term."

I opened and closed my mouth so many times, but nothing came out. For the first time in my life, I was speechless. I couldn't decide on what I wanted to ask or say first, so we ended up spending a few moments without speaking.

"Oh, crap. Did I lose you?" Her voice moved further away, and I could only assume she pulled the phone from her ear to check the screen, thinking I'd hung up.

"No, I'm still here."

"Good, I was worried for a second there that the call failed. My phone isn't the best. This old piece of crap frustrates the heck out of me." Her avoidance of cuss words was obvious and brought a smile to my face.

"Frustrates the *heck* out of you? Damn, girl. That must be bad."

Her laugh was soft and airy, genuine if not slightly shy. "Would it be better if I cursed like a sailor? I'm sure other people would have a problem if...if the children I care for started repeating what I say."

"Yeah, that probably wouldn't be a very good idea."

"So, you don't have kids?" Her question was effortless, so easy that if I closed my eyes, I could've believed this woman had been in my life forever. There was a gentleness to her voice, and if I'd let it, it could've carried me away until I no longer cared about her history or background check.

"No. And honestly, if I did, there's a good chance they'd sound like sailors."

She was quiet for a moment, and I started to question what I'd said to make her stop talking.

Another horn honked, and it reminded me of her sitting outside. "Why again did you have to leave your room to answer my call? So far, you haven't screamed like a banshee or made any shrieking sounds. I don't understand what thin walls and no TV has to do with you going outside to talk."

"That's because I didn't want to scare you off yet." She giggled and added, "My roommate, Stevie, is in her room with her boyfriend. I think he's tired of me sleeping on his couch, so I didn't care to give him any more ammunition to kick me out before I find a place."

Now I just felt like a prick. "You're sleeping on the couch?"

"Well, yeah. I mean, it's a small place, and there's only one bedroom."

"Is it at least a pull-out couch?"

"I wish, but no."

I grumbled to myself, hating the thought of anyone not having a bed to sleep on. I guess a sofa wouldn't be that bad, but it was clear Jade needed somewhere to live. "Where were you living before?"

"My mom's house."

Her short answers were starting to feel a whole lot like a game of cat and mouse. "Why go from there to a couch? Did she kick you out or something?"

A sigh flooded the line, but just before I thought she'd brush me off again, she started talking. "My mom has become more and more difficult to deal with. I can't stand her husband, and it seems like he's always whispering in her ear, telling her what to do when it comes to me. It's like she can't even think for herself anymore. I finally got fed up and left. My best friend, Stevie, offered me her couch, so I took it."

"I thought you said you're close with your family?"

"It's hard to explain. I love my mom, and I can get along great with her, but my stepdad and I are like oil and water. And as long as he's calling the shots and interfering in my relationship with my mom, I don't want to have anything to do with them."

"And there was nowhere else to go but to your friend's couch? You said you have family on the island. Who lives over here?"

"Oh, um…my aunt." That was such a lie.

"And why can't you live with her?"

More rustling came through the line, followed by a full exhale. It sounded like she was about to excuse herself from the conversation, but to my surprise, she didn't. "She's old. She doesn't want someone in their early twenties living with her."

I was well-trained at my job and had been doing it for years. One of the things I was best at was reading people, a human lie detector. When she had avoided questions earlier, I didn't push. Her hesitancy didn't necessarily indicate deception considering she didn't know me. Not everyone can open up to a stranger about personal matters, so I'd passed it off with the intention to uncover the truth at a later time. But this…this was most definitely a lie. The question became, what was her reason for it? Most people don't make up stories for the hell of it—it's generally to hide something.

I just had to figure out what that something was without alerting her that I was aware she wasn't telling me the truth.

"I'm sure you'd be her dream roommate. You go to bed early, you're single, and you work as a nanny. What's there not to like?"

"Well…she lives in a retirement home, and they have rules against anyone under a certain age living there. It doesn't matter how early I go to bed; it doesn't change the fact I'm twenty-two."

That made sense, except there weren't any such places around here. "She lives on Geneva Key?"

"Yeah."

24

"Where? It'd be great if it were close so you could visit with her while I was gone. That way, you wouldn't be so lonely. Trust me, dinner for one is pitiful. I'm sure she'd love the company, too."

Silence stretched over the line before she said, "It's late. I've had a long day and have to get up early. It was really nice talking to you, though. Thanks for calling. I'm looking forward to chatting again."

It was an obvious brush off. I'd gotten them more times than I could count through the years, which indicated I'd pushed too hard too fast. It made me clench my jaw and fist my free hand in frustration. I didn't make that kind of rookie mistake. I knew the exact amount of pressure needed to get answers, but apparently, this intriguing firecracker had thrown me off my game.

"I'm sorry, Jade. I didn't mean to keep you up. Do you work tomorrow?"

"Yeah. Shift starts at seven."

"Will you have a job lined up if you move?"

Her hesitation to respond indicated she was hiding something, but it was so hard to tell because her answer, her tone, came across as genuine. "Yes. I'll have a little girl to care for if I move there."

I soaked up her words, desperate for the truth she kept hidden. But I couldn't keep her on the line all night, no matter how badly I wanted to. I tried to believe my need to talk to her was to get all the information I could on a potential roommate, but that wasn't the truth. The thought of getting off the phone with her left me feeling even more lonely than I was before.

"Okay, that's good. I'd hate for you to lose your job. It sounds like it means a lot to you."

"It does. Thank you. Goodnight, Cash."

"Night, Jade."

✤

I'd managed to make it until two in the afternoon before picking up my phone. I'd checked it ever since waking up, hoping to find a text, email, or even a missed call from Jade. But there was nothing. Unable to wait any longer, I touched her name and listened to the line ring in my ear, needing her to lessen the loneliness that surrounded me.

Seconds before giving up, expecting to get her voicemail, she answered, once again sounding out of breath. But this time, there was a hint of laughter in her tone rather than secrecy. It took me a moment to absorb it, trying to block out the images of her running around. For some reason, I couldn't help but wonder what she looked like, what color hair she had, how long it was. I had purposely avoided knowing these things in my plight to find a roommate who would remain platonic. Yet now, without any of that information, it made visualizing her difficult and confusing.

I shook those thoughts from my mind. "Did I catch you at a bad time?"

"No, not at all. I'm at the park and didn't think I'd make it back to the bench in time to answer the phone." The happiness in her voice was undoubtedly genuine, and it proved to be all I needed to lose some of the weight I carried on my shoulders.

"Oh, you're working. I'm sorry, I didn't mean to interrupt."

"That's okay. It feels like I'm always working, but you're fine. What's up?"

"You sure? I feel like an ass for taking up your time when you're supposed to be watching other people's kids. If you'd rather call me back when you get off, I can wait. I just wanted to talk some more."

"No, it's okay. I can do both."

That was a relief, because I had no desire to hang up.

"What did you want to talk about?"

Here went nothing. "Anything. Everything. I don't care. I just figured this is the best way to get to know each other, and since I work during the week, my time is rather limited. I'm a firm believer in trust, and if we end up living together, we need to have that between us. And I understand that's something that's earned, but I guess I just want to make sure you aren't wasting my time."

"Oh," she breathed into the receiver, quiet and completely unsure of herself. It twisted my insides into unyielding knots, a feeling I was unfamiliar with. Empathy. Possibly pity or compassion. Whatever it was, she inflicted it with one, soft-spoken word.

One syllable.

One exhale.

"Shit…I'm totally fucking this whole thing up."

"No, I get it, Cash. And I agree."

"You do?" I was shocked. That hadn't been what I expected her to say.

"Yeah. There definitely needs to be a level of trust between us before we decide to live together, which I think is smart. But I also don't see that being very possible. I mean, I can answer any question you ask, give you my whole life story, but at the end of the day, you'll only have whatever information you find on a background check. I'm not saying I've lied to you or plan to, but that's the reality of it. Not to mention, I don't know the correct spelling of your last name. You spelled it one way on your profile for Roommates Anonymous and another on your email. So it's slightly concerning that you could be some grand con artist, and I wouldn't even be aware of it until you've taken off with my identity or every last possession I own. If I'm being truthful, this worries me."

She made valid arguments, and the last thing I wanted was for her to be concerned with me. I may not have been completely truthful to her, and there would always be one aspect of my life she'd never find out about, but in the grand scheme of things, I hadn't lied. "My last name is spelled N-i-c-h-o-l-s-o-n. I purposely spelled it wrong on the ad because I didn't care to have a shitload of people in my personal business."

"Well…that makes sense." Embarrassment rang in her tone, which ate at me.

"So let's get to know each other."

"What do you mean?"

"Let's talk."

CHAPTER 3

Jade

My throat constricted and I clawed at my neck, desperate to relieve the pressure caused by the invisible noose. There were things I couldn't tell him, things he'd never be able to find out about, information that would never turn up on even the most detailed history report. So I figured I'd go into this blind and pray he didn't ask the tough questions—I wasn't sure how many more times I could avoid them.

"What do you want to talk about?" I leaned back on the bench and watched Aria out of the corner of my eye. She was in the sandbox entertaining herself.

"I don't care. How about we pick up where we left off last night? We were talking about your aunt."

"Oh, yeah." I wondered if he'd believe my phone had dropped the call if I suddenly just hung up. Probably not. And he'd more than likely call back. I could've blamed it on a dead battery, but that would be too convenient.

"So I drove there today to check it out." His words caught my attention, and I realized I hadn't heard a thing he'd said.

"Wait…what? You drove where?"

"To the retirement home you were telling me about."

"I didn't tell which one, did I?" I distinctly remembered avoiding that answer last night.

His rumbling chuckle reverberated through the line. "It's good to know you listen when I talk," he teased.

"Sorry, I had to open a pack of crackers." When in doubt, blame a kid.

"That's fine. I'll start over. I looked into retirement communities here on the island, and there's only one. It's actually not that far from the house. So I went over there to check it out, and you'll never guess who I ran into?" The mock surprise in his voice was thick.

"My aunt?" *Kill me now.*

"Yeah! I walked in and there she was. I didn't even know it was her until I started talking about you. How completely unbelievable is that?"

"That's...*really* unbelievable. Did she happen to tell you her name?"

"Yeah, it's Michelle."

"Oh, then that's not my aunt. Must've been one of those Alzheimer's patients. You can never trust anything they say."

"That's disheartening. She was really nice, too. What's your aunt's name then?"

"Sally. Aunt Sally."

"Sally what?"

"Jessy."

"Her last name is Jessy?"

"No. It's Raphael."

There was a long pause, and I almost told him I was being kidnapped and had to call him back later, but before I could, in the most disbelieving voice I'd ever heard, he asked, "Your aunt is Sally Jessy Raphael?"

"Yup. Sure is. But hey, I'm going to have to let you go." I glanced up to the bright blue sky and added, "It just started to pour here. I'll call you later."

"Oh, that's fine. But when you call me back, can you do me a favor?" He paused, and when he continued, a hint of a smile was heard in his soft voice. "Can you please stop lying to me?"

My mouth dried up, which made my tongue thick and in the way. And the knot in my throat deepened my usually higher-pitched voice, adding a level of scratchiness to my words when I said, "Sure thing."

I immediately disconnected the call and blew out a long, deep exhale. He'd caught me. I'd say I didn't know how, but that would've been laughable. I sucked at lying on the spot, and it seemed he wasn't gullible. At all. But at least he didn't sound mad, and from what I could tell, he had a good sense of humor about it. Plus, he wasn't dismissing me.

So as soon as I had my thoughts and nerves collected, I called him back.

"That was fast," he said in lieu of "hello."

"Yeah. I'd say the rain stopped, but I had agreed to be truthful when I called you back."

An airy snicker flooded my ear. "I appreciate that."

"How did you know I was lying? I don't mean today...that was rather obvious. But what made you even go check out whatever retirement village that was, and without her name, how'd you figure it out?"

"I just know things, Jade. I read people."

"I won't lie...that's a little worrisome."

He laughed again, this time louder. "Truth be told, there aren't any retirement places on the island. I knew as soon as you said it you were lying."

"Then why not just say something then?"

"What fun would that have been? But seriously, I figured you had a reason for it. If it makes you feel any better, had I thought for one second your deception was malicious, you would've never heard from me again."

He reminded me of my dad. Anytime I'd done something wrong, he always had a way of talking me down, opening me up, making me *want* to tell him everything. One time, I'd planned to run away, upset over being in trouble for something stupid, and when he found out—I still wasn't sure how—he'd sat me down and made me feel like he'd be lost if I left. By the end of the conversation, he had my entire getaway plan, which wasn't much, considering I was eight and never left the neighborhood, but it was enough to give him an idea of where to start looking in the event I ever followed through with my threat.

Cash possessed the same trait. It was the gentleness in his baritone voice, the concern that weighed down his words. I felt safe, even though I had no tangible reason to. It was unexplainable, but it was there. And it made me take a deep breath, ready to answer him, lay it all out there for him to possibly twist or use against me. I'd seen both sides of the coin in my lifetime. Where my dad had never betrayed the trust I'd given him, my stepdad had — on multiple occasions. It made it hard to tell the truth, knowing it would come back to bite me in the butt. But this was one of those times when I had to figure it out the hard way.

I regarded Aria playing in the sandbox beneath the pavilion and struggled with how to be honest without giving everything away. "I lied about my aunt because a young woman who isn't tied to family, has no one close to her, no one to check in with her, is a murderer's dream come true."

He laughed, and I couldn't deny the way the sound caused my own lips to curl. "I completely understand. And I don't blame you. It actually makes me happy to know you were using your head. There are too many sick fucks in the world to not react cautiously." His tone changed, deepened, as if he had personal knowledge of what he was saying, but before I could analyze it too much, he continued. "But you have to have *some* family, right? Siblings? What about your dad?"

"He died when I was ten. My mom remarried when I was twelve, and I never had any siblings. My grandmother on my dad's side died when I was a baby, and my grandfather lives in Canada, so I haven't seen him since my dad's funeral. My mom has a brother and a sister, both much older than she is. My aunt does live in a retirement village down south, just outside Miami, but I have no idea where my uncle is. Last I heard, he was entering rehab for the sixth time. My grandparents on my mom's side don't have much to do with us, but I couldn't begin to speculate why. I've been told so many different stories that I have no idea what's the truth and what isn't."

He paused, allowing the silence to linger. When he finally did speak, his voice was hoarse and heavy. "So does that mean you're not interested in following through with this? I'm unsure how to prove I'm not a crazy person."

I hummed to myself and thought of ways he could prove himself to me. "Well, you said earlier that we should talk and get to know each other, so why don't we start there?"

"I can do that. What do you want to know? Ask me anything."

I didn't handle being put on the spot very well, but decided I'd just go with it and hope more questions would come to me as we went. "Your name is Cassius, but you go by Cash?"

Humor rumbled through the line and filled his words when he said, "It's Cassius"—he pronounced it *Cash*-us, not *Cass*-ee-us like how I'd said it—"and yes, I've gone by Cash ever since I was a baby. My dad was a huge Muhammad Ali fan, so when he found out he was having a boy, my mom didn't even get a vote."

"Well, at least it came with a shorthand name."

"Except my last name is Nicholson." When I didn't respond, not following his point, he spelled it out for me. "Back in the day, my friends used to call me Buck, short for Buck and Change. At least, that's what everyone settled on after a range of short-term nicknames didn't pan out. With a first name like Cash, and a last name close to nickel, I didn't stand a chance at anything normal. Luckily, I was able to escape it when I moved away after high school."

"Where did you grow up?"

"I was born in Steamboat Springs, Colorado, then moved to Dallas—Georgia, not Texas—when I was twelve. I didn't leave there until I was eighteen."

"Did you go to college?"

There was a slight pause, not long, but enough to catch my attention and make me wonder if I had finally reached something he wasn't overly comfortable talking about. "No. I joined the army."

"Oh, wow. Are you still in it? Is that why you travel a lot?"

"Not really. I was discharged before I made it through basic. I couldn't pass the physical, so I was faced with letting Uncle Sam foot the bill—basically owning me—or leaving. I chose to leave."

"Why?"

Another pause, but this time, it was longer and accompanied by a long exhale. It made me imagine him reclining on his couch, maybe his feet propped up, his head back, staring at the ceiling while talking to me.

"It's funny…I thought I knew what I was getting into when I signed up. I scored really high on the ASVAB and was led to believe there was an elite program for people with my specific aptitudes. My recruiter detailed the government's need for intellect, and not just brawn—I was naïve and believed the half-truths I was told. But once I got there, this program was a joke. It was impossible to get into straight out of basic. It existed, but only to entice people like me—who weren't interested in being infantry—to sign away our lives. Bootcamp was no joke. It's designed to brainwash new enlistees, to make them stop relying on themselves and start living for the unit—following instructions without rhyme or reason. I can't tell you how many holes I dug, only to have a drill sergeant immediately tell me to fill it back in. And then dig it again."

I could've listened to him talk forever. He was so animated with his words, so full of stories and information. If teachers and college professors spoke like he did, they'd have a higher grade-point average in their classes—at least in regard to the females.

"Anyway, there's a second physical once you're there. And during that exam, the army's doctor found an old shoulder injury that he believed needed surgery. And the second I was given the choice to let them cut me open or take a medical discharge—although, it's not really a discharge because I never completed basic—I elected to get out, because I knew what would be asked of me, what my future would essentially look like. But it wasn't *until* I was given the choice that I realized just how much of myself I would have to sacrifice. Nothing I had been told prior to joining the army would ever come to fruition, at least not in the first couple of years I belonged to Uncle Sam. Chasing bad guys was one thing, but sitting around being someone's bitch for a good chunk of my younger years didn't appeal to me."

I nodded, even though he couldn't see me. Part of me understood where he was coming from. As I watched Aria, I was able to sympathize with him. I had known what it meant as soon as those two pink lines showed up. I was nineteen, a student in college, but the second I'd heard her heartbeat for the very first time, I dismissed everyone's complaints and decided I could do this. But even now, after two years of loving her more than I ever thought I could love another, I still found myself wondering if I'd made the wrong choice. I'd never experience what it's like to go out drinking on my twenty-first birthday, staying out until the bars closed down. Waking up and heading out to the beach with friends on a hot summer day would never be in my future. And every purchase, even gas for my car, came with a laundry list of pros and cons.

Yet there was nothing that would ever make me turn back time and change it. I just had to keep my head up and figure this parenting thing out the best way I could. I had to make the best choices with what was offered.

I hadn't responded to his ad because I had seriously thought about moving in with him. But ever since last night, I'd found myself naturally falling into that mindset, having to continuously reiterate to myself that I would never follow through with it.

"After that," he continued, reminding me that he was still on the phone, "I decided to go to school and took IT classes. I'd always enjoyed computers, but I never thought about making it my profession."

"So you were a computer nerd?" I pictured him with bottle-cap glasses and a shirt buttoned up to the collar, tucked into jeans that didn't cover the tops of his white, New Balance tennis shoes.

"Not even close," he replied with a husky laugh. "I played sports—fit in with the jocks—excelled in math and sciences, and I had an easy understanding of anything technical, so I had friends in every corner of the school."

"Mr. Popularity," I teased.

"Nah, I just got along with everyone. What about you?"

I hated how the conversation had turned back to me, but as long as we were enjoying ourselves, I couldn't complain about who we were talking about. "I was a bit of a loner. Although, I wasn't bullied or anything, basically ignored. The cool kids would speak to me in class if it pertained to the lecture, but I'm sure none of them remembered my name. It didn't bother me because I had my best friend, and she was all I needed. She's a social butterfly and always included me in everything."

"Is that the girl you live with now?"

"Yes, Stevie."

"That's cool you guys are still friends. Do you both go to college together?"

And my heart sank. "No. We did at first, but I dropped out." Not waiting for him to ask why, I offered a reasonable excuse. "School isn't for everyone. I attended for a year and a half, dropping out in the middle of the spring semester, just before I finished my second year."

"You made it that far and called it quits?" He sounded genuinely interested.

"Yeah. My, um...the guy I was seeing made things difficult."

"Your ex?"

I hated referring to him like that, but I didn't have much of a choice. "Yes. Although, he was more of a tyrant than a boyfriend."

Cash's voice dropped impossibly deeper when he asked, "Did he hurt you?"

"Not physically." I shoved down the voices telling me how untrue that was, that what he did to me *was* physical—as well as mental and emotional—but I couldn't explain all that. No matter how safe Cash made me feel, I wasn't ready to shine the light on those skeletons.

"How long were you with him?"

"It started when I was sixteen and lasted for three years."

"Has he bothered you since you left him?"

I'd run out of ways to spin it if he kept prying, so I gave him the simplest answer I could. "Not really. He's made my life a lot harder, that's for sure, but his reign of terror has ended." At least, I hoped it had. "Enough about that…I get that you'd like to keep a level of anonymity between us, but why don't you tell me what you look like?"

With a slow inhale and elongated exhale, I could vividly picture a man struggling to drop the topic at hand. But in the end, he gave in and moved along with the conversation. "Well, I'm tall. I have dark hair and dark eyes."

"You're horrible at this," I joked, covering my mouth to contain my laughter. "Slow down. Tall can mean anything. I'm five two, but compared to a toddler, I'm tall. So spill it—give me the stats."

"Why does this feel like a horrible dating game? Okay, fine. I'm five ten on a good day, and I weigh two-ninety-five first thing in the morning—which by the end of the day could be slightly over three hundred…depending on what I ate. Does that make you happy?"

I had no idea if it was a joke or not, and considering we didn't really know each other, asking could've insulted him. So I chose to keep the questions to myself. Eventually, I'd see what he looked like—*maybe*.

"Yeah, I'm happy. Now, what about your eyes? How dark is dark?"

"Unless I'm outside, or a light is shining on my face, you can't see my pupils."

"Interesting. Now…your hair. Are we talking black, or just really dark brown?"

"I have no idea," he blew out with a hearty chuckle. "It's dark."

"Fine. That'll have to do. How long is it?"

"Short. A little longer on the top, but not enough to cover my forehead when brushed forward. Damn, these questions aren't easy to answer. Guys don't pay attention to these kinds of things."

"In the event I go missing, what distinguishing marks do you have on your body?"

His laughter roared through the line, which brought about my own. "I have a birthmark on my right hipbone that you can only see when I'm out in the sun a lot."

"Any tattoos?" I kept the questions coming.

"One, but you'll have to wait to find out more about it."

"Tan? Freckles? Fair skin? Do you burn easily?"

"Yes, I'm tan. I don't have freckles, nor do I burn. My mom's side of the family has Native American in them, and my dad's side is straight-up Italian. So I'm sure you can imagine the level of tan I am, and what I'd look like after a day in the sun." He didn't break long enough for me to ask anything else before turning the tables once again. "Now it's your turn. Same questions—don't leave anything out."

I hated describing myself, and I suddenly realized what Cash had felt like when I'd put him on the spot. "I've already told you I'm short, but I refuse to tell you how much I weigh because—"

"That's not fair. Men are just as sensitive as women are about their bodies," he teased.

Figuring he wouldn't give up until I gave him something, I decided to go big or go home. Even though I hadn't ever truly dated the way other girls my age had, I still knew a thing or two about the appeal of a woman's body.

"Fine...but if you stop talking to me, it will be obvious why."

"I'm not trying to date you, Jade. So it doesn't matter if you weigh ninety pounds or five hundred. I don't give a shit when it comes to my friends, which means I care even less about the numbers on the scale of a platonic roommate."

I bit the inside of my cheek before blurting out, "Two hundred and twenty-seven." The number just came to me, nearly a hundred pounds over the truth. Even though I hadn't stepped on a scale in a while, I could tell by the way my clothes fit that I wasn't too far from my pre-Aria weight.

"Good, and thank you. Now, you may carry on with the rest."

I rolled my eyes and settled further into the wooden bench, watching my daughter, who could've lived in the sandbox if I'd let her. "I have brown hair and blue eyes. No tattoos. No birthmarks or strange moles." As soon as the words came out, I wanted to smack myself. I'd yet again made myself a prime target for anyone looking to abduct me. Not only didn't I have family who'd report me missing, but I also admitted to having no distinguishing traits to identify when my body was discovered. I grimaced at myself and carried on. "And I'm not really tan or fair-skinned. Just smack-dab in the middle."

"Sounds rather average." Before I could complain, he followed it up with, "And there's absolutely nothing wrong with that. I personally think average people are the easiest to get along with. Less judgment."

"What's your middle name?" I took advantage of the lull in our friendly interrogation.

"Dylan. I think I remember you saying yours is Duran...where'd that come from?"

And again, he found a way to redirect the questions. "Ever heard of Duran Duran? Well, let's just say your parents weren't the only ones who were fans of someone, and then gave that name to their kid. At least yours is cool. There's nothing cool about mine."

"I disagree. I like it."

"Thank you." My cheeks burned, and it had nothing to do with the sun.

He started to say something else, but I had to interrupt him and end our call. I didn't want to take the chance he'd hear my screaming toddler call me Mommy. Luckily, I managed to press the red button just after saying goodbye but before she got close enough, covered in sand, crying for me to scare the bug away. I had no clue what she'd seen or where it had gone, but I did my best to pretend I'd killed it, then I let her play for a little bit longer, all while contemplating what I should do about Cash.

In all honesty, if he turned out to be a nice guy without a criminal background—or a tendency to chop people up and hide their remains in a deep freezer—I wouldn't mind taking him up on the offer of renting his spare room. But it wasn't that easy. First, there was the dilemma regarding my job...or lack thereof. I couldn't exactly pay him money I didn't have, and no one in their right mind would let me live off them for free. Add on top of that, I had a two-year-old who still hadn't been potty trained because I didn't have access to my own bathroom—it was difficult to teach her how to go when all we had at times was a kitchen sink.

So needless to say, it didn't matter how amazing he was or how badly I needed to find a place to live, Cash Nicholson wasn't a viable option, and the sooner I came clean to him, the better off everything would be. When I assumed he was a creep, I didn't mind wasting his time. But now that I knew—*presumed*—he wasn't, it felt wrong to mislead him.

ᵀᴴᴱROOMMATE ᴰⁱˢAGREEMENT

✢

Regardless of the many reasons I told myself why I should admit the truth to Cash, I couldn't find the strength to actually speak the words. And anytime he would call, I'd answer, unable to ignore him. The only explanation I could come up with was that he allowed me to pretend for however long I had him on the phone. He didn't have details about my family, about Aria or her father. He didn't have a clue about my struggles and the hardships I'd endured day in and day out. With him, I was just Jade. I was a young, single, carefree woman looking to pack her bags and move across the state, swapping out one beach for another. And a part of me wasn't ready to give that up, knowing it would end the second my secrets passed my lips.

So for two weeks, we talked either through text or calls—the calls only came at night, unless it was on a weekend, but he traveled a lot for work, so I chalked it up to him simply being busy with his job. A job I still knew nothing about. Anytime I would ask, he'd give me a bunch of garble, using fancy tech terms that went right over my head, until I finally stopped asking. Then, one day, he suggested a video chat, which wouldn't have been a big deal if I didn't have a kid with me all the time who referred to me as Mommy. And taking the risk of calling while she was napping wasn't something I was comfortable with. I never knew how long she'd stay asleep. It left me without many options.

Desperate to get it over with so he wouldn't think I'd lied about everything and was unwilling to show him my face, I'd asked Stevie to sit with her while I ran out to look for a job. I took her computer with me and headed down to a local coffee shop a few miles away. I hated lying to my best friend, but after I asked, she jumped at the chance to spoil her favorite nugget.

I followed the instructions he'd given me, having never used Skype before, and waited while the picture on the screen connected. My heart hammered in my chest, threatening to give out as each second stretched on. I wasn't sure how possible it would be to recognize a serial killer, but I had hoped there'd be some mark to get my attention. A sign or flashing arrow would be too much to ask for, but just a simple stamp on his forehead to alert me of danger would've sufficed.

But that's not at all what I got.

As soon as the picture switched from the call screen to his face, I quit breathing altogether. He hadn't lied when he'd described himself a couple of weeks ago on the phone. His features were exactly what he said they were—onyx eyes, cropped, dark hair. However, what he'd left out was his square, chiseled jaw; the dimple in his chin; a full, arched top lip and plump bottom one to match. Then there was the straight, angular nose; the dark brows that added a hint of mystery to his deep-set eyes lined with inky lashes, making him the epitome of sexy; and a wide, smooth forehead that I believed would tell his secrets in his expressions. He was the spitting image of a younger Johnny Depp without the grunge.

"Hi." He smiled, and I thought I'd die right there in the middle of a coffee shop.

CHAPTER 4

Cash

As much as I loved technology, I hated it, too. The Skype chat with Jade didn't do much, considering her connection was weak, which made her picture blurry, heavily pixelated, and choppy. At times, it even cut out completely, and all I had to stare at was a black screen. The conversation didn't last long before we switched over to the phone.

Apparently, she didn't have any issues with her picture, and she could hear me just fine, but as far as my end was concerned, I couldn't see shit. It only made me more desperate to see her, despite my reasons for the no-picture rule. I hadn't added that rule because I didn't care what my future roommate would look like; it had more to do with not wanting to sexualize the possible relationship. I may have had no interest in dating anyone, but I wasn't blind to the magnetic pull sexual attraction could have. I could fend off women all day long—and had to some days—but my concern was more out of being unable to fight my own needs…something I hadn't contemplated when starting out on this venture.

I loved a woman's body just as much as the next man. The curves and lines, soft skin, dimples, and overall flow of the female form was utter perfection, no matter the body type or the size of the dress she wore. However, and maybe I'm the odd man out, but there were only certain people who could spark the attraction within me. If I didn't feel it, then it didn't matter how little she wore or how much makeup she caked on her face, it wouldn't change the built-in circuit inside me.

I'd managed to get ahold of her driver's license picture and a few photos that were online of her, but they were all at least four to six years old, and the ones online didn't give anything away. So I needed to see her, face to face. I'd told myself that was all I needed before moving forward with Jade. We had good, easy chemistry over the phone—the kind everyone seeks in a worthy friend—so I needed to find out if I was visually attracted to her. But when her computer threw a monkey wrench into that plan, I was left with nothing. Her phone didn't send pictures, and for one reason or another, she couldn't get one taken on the computer and sent via email. I'd started to think she was making shit up until I tried walking her through adding an attachment. Jade seriously had no concept of technology. How she'd managed to make it this far in this day and age was beyond me.

I thought Skype was foolproof. It was not. After less than ten minutes, I suggested we switch to the phone and just talk. The more I tried to get a good picture of her, the more frustrated I became.

"I was married for six years. I'd gone through school, gotten a job, and when I met Colleen, I was ready for the next step in life. Being dedicated to my job meant it took me away from her more than she expected, more than she could apparently tolerate. I made the decision to leave, but only because she'd taken the first step in ending it." I wasn't sure how we'd even gotten onto this topic, but for once, I didn't feel the need to shut it down.

"When she cheated on you?" she asked, already having heard the story. I hadn't given her all the details, only the bits she needed, and I was surprised by how easy it was to open up about it.

"Yeah. At first, I was angry. Pissed at the world. Then, after about six months, I realized I wasn't so much mad as I was lonely. It's a strange realization when most of my job is spent in solitude. I work in almost complete isolation. But it was those three nights a week that I didn't have her next to me that twisted the knife in my back. That's when I thought about finding a roommate."

"Why a female, though?"

I had no idea how the truth would sound to her when I explained. She was already on the fence about this, and the last thing I wanted to do was push her off, make her believe her fears were warranted. I loved how open her eyes were to the world, but even with as trusting as she could be, she was one step away from fleeing. All it would take to flip that switch would be another hint of doubt in regard to my character.

"I have guy friends, and if you don't, let me explain what a day in that life would look like." I cleared my throat to get into the role of the animated narrator. "I'd come home and Joe Blow would be on the couch, a beer in one hand, the remote in the other. Depending on the type of guy Joe is, dinner would either consist of pizza—new or leftover from the night before—or meat and veggies. I'm good with the healthier choices, not so much for early death delivered in a cardboard box. I'd eat, take my shower, and go to bed. If we spent any time talking, it would typically be about sports. Or the weather."

She snickered, but continued to listen intently.

"Not all men are messy, so I can't say I'd have to pick up after him—just like not all women are clean freaks. If Joe is a loner, things around the house would be quiet, but if he's got a group of friends, there'll likely be a few of them coming and going. I don't mind other people at my house, but I have to be able to trust at least one of them. And let's be real, if I'd chosen to live with a guy, I wouldn't have been afforded these last few weeks of getting to know him. No man would talk on the phone to another as much as we have."

"So you chose to live with a female because getting to know her would be easier than getting to know a male?" Her skepticism was evident in the slight lilt of her tone.

"That's one reason, but the main reason is that I simply miss the company of a woman. I miss the conversations, the companionship only a woman can offer. I'm not saying I want someone to sit around with to talk about my feelings. But like I said, I am alone on the job. I go hours without speaking to anyone, and when I do, it's not typically for conversational purposes. I just prefer not to come home on the weekends and be secluded in my room, or sit by myself on the couch. I can do that now. Most men don't care about talking—they're happy with a beer and *Sports Center*. I'm not. I used to be, and then I got married. I guess that's one more thing Colleen fucked me over with."

She was quiet for a moment, then she asked, "Why didn't you two ever have kids?"

I blinked, oddly surprised by her question. "Uh...it just never happened, I guess. Colleen had talked about it a few times, but I didn't feel like the timing was ever right. It's hard to be a dad when I'm not home five days out of the week. In the end, she'd resent me, and I figured things would be better off without adding kids to the mix."

"So you don't ever plan to have any?"

That seemed like a strange question to ask someone you weren't romantically involved with, but we all had things that helped us understand each other better. "No. I don't. I have no desire to ever get married again, so therefore, I don't ever see kids in my future."

"Do you not like them?"

"I have no problem with them. I just don't have any desire to have them. I like my life the way it is, and babies complicate things. If I had another job, maybe I'd feel differently, but I'm good at what I do and don't plan on changing careers before I retire."

"That's a fair answer." And just like that, the conversation was dropped. As if we'd been talking about it this whole time, Jade told me all about some summer camp she and Stevie had gone to when they were teenagers.

✦

The phone calls continued for another two weeks before I decided to arrange a meeting. Originally, I'd asked if she would be willing to drive over here so she could see the place for herself, but she adamantly refused. I couldn't exactly blame her—the woman probably still expected me to Buffalo Bill her. We'd joked about it, but I knew it was a lot to ask of her.

She was playing it smart, and I respected that. I even offered to meet her halfway, but she said with work, that would be difficult, and again, there was no room for argument. I appreciated her level of commitment to the family who paid her. But regardless, this meeting had to take place before any other arrangements were made. I still needed the full background check, and to do that, I had to have sensitive, personal information I would never expect anyone to pass over to a stranger on the phone. I also planned to give her mine, as well. She still seemed skeptical, and if I wanted to ease her mind, I had to offer the same as I had asked of her.

Realizing the meeting would never happen if I didn't make the move first, I suggested I come to her. It took her a few days to agree, and then we settled on the following Saturday. Oddly enough, I was nervous to meet her, and I couldn't explain why. I'd spoken to her on the phone, saw somewhat of an image of her, and had discovered enough preliminary history to determine she wasn't a threat. From everything I could tell, she was who she said she was. My only guess to the anticipation I felt was that she'd back out. Or that her full history would show something I couldn't accept.

Over the last month, she'd become a friend, someone I actually looked forward to talking to when I wasn't bogged down on the job. If I were in the car during a reasonable hour, it was her number I dialed. At night, providing it wasn't too late, she was the one I called, the last voice I heard before sleep. I didn't usually get a ton of free time during the week, depending on the job, but she played along and resorted to text messaging. I'd tried to convince her to get a real phone, but she said there were other expenses she had to cover that were more important than a device that could connect to Facebook. She had me there. Although, I still wasn't so sure what these "other expenses" were, and I didn't feel the need to pry, considering I'd eventually get her entire credit history—even the parts that normally dropped off after so many years.

I couldn't fall asleep to save my life the night before heading over to Fort Pierce to meet her. Too much excitement coursed through me, nerves, and an unfamiliar pang of worry stabbed at my chest. I couldn't figure it out. I hunted people for a living. I tracked them, cornered them, and on some level—depending on how you looked at it—tortured them to get answers. I'd even gotten their blood on my hands.

And I'm not talking about the kind that washes off.

Yes, I have a conscience. I have the ability to differentiate right from wrong. Sometimes, nightmares find me when I least expect them, and they haunt me, reminding me of the things I'd done under the veil of my job. It wasn't easy, but that was clear going in. Although, I never expected to be tasked with the things I had, and that had been a bitter pill to swallow in the beginning—I still found it difficult from time to time.

So I certainly wasn't immune to the weaker emotions, the ones that had the ability to cripple some and drown others—things like regret, remorse, nerves, and compassion. I felt all those emotions, but not often. Not after seeing some of the things I had. There was no way a person could witness the purest form of evil that ever walked the earth and not grow cold inside. I once had a friend who applied to the police academy. He'd finished and had started his training, but one day, he walked onto the scene of a double homicide, and the second he realized he felt nothing, he quit. Some people can handle it, others can't. I just so happened to be one of the few who could close off parts of myself without falling into the category of a sociopath.

Needless to say, other than a year ago when I'd caught Colleen in that parking lot, the only times I'd felt anything other than loneliness was in regard to Jade. The only times I'd laughed had been with Jade. And I couldn't recall when the ache of anxiety had last settled in my chest until I tried to go to sleep the night before meeting her.

And it followed me from the Gulf Coast to the Atlantic, the entire three-hour drive. We'd agreed to meet at a local restaurant for lunch, but I managed to arrive a full half hour early, so I wandered around, wondering if I could get a feel for her life here. Even though Fort Pierce and Geneva Key were both typical Floridian beach towns, they couldn't have been more different—even if a continent separated them rather than just the interior of the state. On this coast, everything moved at a much faster pace, with more congestion on the roads and around the actual buildings; whereas, on the other side, life passed at a more leisurely pace.

Before I knew it, I was five minutes late meeting her. I checked my phone, but I didn't have any missed calls or texts. I hoped that didn't signify her canceling. I raced down the sidewalk to the small restaurant and rushed inside, surprised to see just how compact it was. The center of the room was crammed with tables, booths lining the right and back walls. To my left, a fresh case resembled the likes of fish markets along the beach back home, and a hostess stand waited for me in the front. I tried to glance around, in search of a short brunette with blue eyes, but before I finished scanning the fourth table, the blonde behind the podium grabbed my attention.

"Just one today? Or are you waiting on someone?" She smiled with more enthusiasm than I'd expected from a hostess, but it wasn't foreign to me. Female gazes followed me, no matter what I looked like that day.

I could've gone a week without shaving, been a solid month overdue for a haircut, and donned wrinkled clothes like I'd just crawled off a park bench in New York City, and they'd still giggle while whispering to their friends, giving me the side-eye. I was well aware of what I looked like. I trained religiously, had to for the sake of the job, and even in the loosest-fitting shirts, the sleeves still hugged my biceps like a baby cub clinging to her mom.

I offered an easy grin and continued scanning the tables behind her. "I'm actually meeting someone here, but I'm a little late."

"Oh, then your friend must be late, too. I haven't seated any partial parties today."

I nodded and allowed her to guide me through the room to the last booth on the right. The hostess set the menus down, but other than noticing her hospitable gesture, my radar left her and shifted to the active area of the restaurant. I took the side of the booth facing the front door, and kept my sights glued on the entrance, grateful the entire front wall was made of glass so I could be ready for her and see when she approached.

The tightness in my chest never eased.

Every time I noticed someone open the door, my body grew rigid. Normally, this happened on the job when I had extreme levels of adrenaline pumping through my veins. But this wasn't the same. This was just lunch—I hadn't expected an ambush; I didn't have to pin my timing down to the hair of a second. It should be easy. Plain and simple. Yet it didn't at all feel that way.

Glancing at my phone, I realized she was fifteen minutes late. Still no word from her. But when I pressed on her name to call her, a shadow approaching the table caught my attention. I picked my head up just in time to hear a ringing phone growing closer with each step the blonde took. And as soon as she made it to my side, she stepped out of the way, leaving me with an up-close view of the friend I'd made over the last month.

The hostess forced a smile and retreated. After Jade slipped into the booth in front of me, there was nothing but silence. No greeting, not idle chitchat. Just the murmurs of the crowd seated around us. Despite the nervous energy that hovered over us like a dense rain cloud, the tightness in my chest had vanished, leaving behind a dull ache meant to remind me of its existence.

She was everything I'd expected, yet nothing at all like I'd pictured. Her brown hair—much darker than I'd imagined—was long, probably enough to conceal her breasts if she draped it in front of her shoulders across her chest. And it was curly. Not tiny ringlets, but big spirals even I knew weren't created with a tool. They were natural, and from the looks of it, slightly wet. The rich color that had to have come from a bottle made her blue eyes pop. They were bright, appearing to have some sort of light source behind them.

I'd imagined she'd come wearing makeup and clothes that were typical for a girl her age. But she didn't. Not a drop of color graced her face—other than the wheat tone of her skin and thick, kohl lashes that couldn't have possibly been real. Rather than a skirt or dress that promised passersby the possibility of seeing her goods, she had on a pair of khaki shorts. And even those were longer than what I assumed most her age wore. She paired it with a tank top—in this heat I didn't blame her—yet it still left her relatively covered.

A wave of ease washed over me when I realized there was no sexual attraction. She was beautiful, absolutely stunning, but on a physical level, I didn't feel anything. And that's exactly what I'd hoped for. I'd already convinced myself I was done looking for a roommate, and would've been crushed if she changed her mind, so had there been anything else below the surface, I would've been back at square one.

"Did you lose about a hundred pounds in the last couple of weeks?" I teased while passing her the menu. There still hadn't been a greeting, but I was over it. No sense in making shit even more awkward.

She cocked her head to the side and squinted, her brow furrowing with confusion.

"You told me you weighed over two hundred pounds. Looking at you now, I'd say you're a buck twenty-five, tops." She definitely had curves, which were accentuated by her short stature, but she was nowhere near what I had imagined before seeing her approach the table.

The way she refused to talk, keeping her mouth closed, made me wonder if she had some odd insecurity. A girl I'd dated back in high school had a slight gap—her parents couldn't afford braces—and if she wasn't forced to show them, she never did. It was a shame, because she really did have a beautiful smile.

But the second Jade's lips split, I couldn't take my eyes off the row of perfectly straight, white teeth that about had me speechless. Her lips were average, nothing overly special about them. They weren't big or dark with natural color, but when she smiled, they completed the picture.

"Says the guy who claimed to be...what was it? Three hundred pounds?"

I shrugged, not recalling all the different ways I'd deceived her in regard to my appearance. "Yeah, I hit the gym a few times between then and this morning. Just keep the bread away. I'm not sure how much longer I'll be able to hold my breath to keep my gut from falling out."

When she laughed, she covered her mouth with the tips of her unpolished fingers and dropped her gaze to the table. I'd heard laughter that pulled me in like a toxic melody, the kind that sent me running for the hills, and occasionally, the kind that shot a spark of excitement straight to my cock. But Jade's was different. It held the ability to soothe and calm a raging storm, quiet a riot, heal the weak, and save the defenseless. I'd heard it dozens of times, but there was something uniquely different about living it in the present, feeling it cascade over me, cover me, consume me. Fill me with an ease I'd never experienced before.

Confusion set in with that thought.

I sat there, staring at her, sensing nothing other than a kinship between us, friends lost long ago who finally rediscovered each other in a different life. It made the perfect roommate. But I couldn't stop the uneasy threats I felt when I found myself lost in her.

Rubbing my chin, I dismissed the concerned voice in my head, the one that told me to be careful with this one. But I knew myself. As long as I had no desire to become intimate or fall for her in any way, there was no problem. Not to mention, I'd been hit on by countless women in my life, so I'd be aware if she fit into that category. And considering she didn't look at me like she wanted to rip my clothes off and ride me until the break of dawn, I shut down the paranoia and continued with our lunch.

When the waitress came by, we both went ahead and ordered lunch, as well as drinks.

"Thank you for meeting with me, Jade," I started as soon as we were alone. "I'm sure this whole process has been strange—trust me, it's been new for me, too. I figured if we got together, it might be easier to tell if this is something we are both still interested in, or if we should just walk away with a new friend."

I could read anyone; it didn't matter if it was the first time I saw them or not. The flicker of eye movement, curl of a lip, even nostrils flaring could tell me everything I needed to know. Hand movements, stuttering, blinking. The most casual swipe of a person's tongue over their lip meant something. So I couldn't figure out why in the hell I couldn't get a read on Jade. Her subdued behavior didn't tell me *anything*.

But even though I couldn't figure anything out by her level of calmness, the moment she glanced up and to the left, it became clear she was hiding something. And if anyone could get her to spill, it'd be me. I wasn't arrogant by any means, fully confident in my abilities to read people, to judge them, to find them and smoke them out of hiding. Those were things I was good at—yet comforting a woman who was clearly at odds with her own secrets wasn't my forte.

"We've talked a lot, about a lot of things, but now is the time to get it *all* out on the table. After this, a background check will be run, and that will be my deciding factor—as well as yours. I plan to give you all the information you need to research me, and I advise you to take advantage of it. My goal is to protect myself and my property, and you should do the same."

My no-nonsense tone captured her attention and set her posture rigid, ramrod straight, across from me. At first, I expected her to tell me never mind and to run out of here like a bat out of hell, but instead, she folded her hands on the table and nodded in agreement.

She drew her lip into her mouth, clamped it gently with her teeth, and trailed her gaze along the tabletop. She had something on her mind, but I could tell she warred with whether to speak up or keep quiet. I'd give her a little bit of time to come forward, and if she didn't, I'd have no choice but to pry.

Then, out of nowhere, she asked, "What all will you be looking for on a background check? I've never done one before, so I don't have a clue what to look for on yours. Is it like a credit report? Or more like a criminal search? Will there be medical things on there?"

Settling into the role of confidant, I leaned forward—without touching her—and lowered my head until I caught her attention. Whatever she was hiding, she worried I'd find it in my search. Little did she know, the access I had would tell me how many times a day she flushed the toilet. There wasn't anything I couldn't pull up, including what kind of toothpaste she used. Where most people couldn't tap into sealed records, I could have them flying open with the snap of a finger. Most minor records were redacted, but not the copies I could get.

"There are all kinds of reports that can be run. Why?" When she hesitated, I reached out and placed my hand over hers, forcing her to drop the napkin she'd shredded. "If there's something you think I'll find, go ahead and assume I will. If it's something that you think will change my mind about you moving in, then either way, I'll change my mind—whether it's now or when I get the report back. Keeping quiet won't prevent me from finding out."

"I was actually worried more about yours. I don't know what information I should be looking for. And if you're going to pull up mine, I think I have the right to know what types of things you'll search for, so I know what I should be paying attention to. Do you not agree?"

Speechless. Again. I was convinced she was about to spill whatever it was she didn't want me to know, but as it turned out, it had nothing to do with that at all. Jade Robertson seriously made me question if I was losing my touch.

"I look up criminal records, involvement in any police reports—such as you being a witness to a crime or whatnot. Financial records, but all I'll really see is what shows up on a credit check. Like I said, it's just to protect myself."

She licked her lips and stared at our hands, reminding me that I was still touching her. I backed away, but I wasn't sure if it was more for her benefit or mine.

"Are you looking for an answer today? Is that what this lunch is for?"

My chest tightened at the thought of her changing her mind. Quickly, I grabbed the papers I'd brought with me off the seat and set them on the table. "Before you make a decision about moving forward or not, I thought maybe we should go over this."

"I thought you said you weren't going to make me sign a lease?" She watched me with concerned eyes from across the booth.

"This isn't a lease. It's just some rules and things I felt we needed in writing. Like an agreement of sorts. It helps keep things from getting murky in the event I do something you don't like, or vice versa; no one can say they weren't aware."

"A roommate agreement?" She giggled before adding, "Okay, Sheldon Cooper."

"I'm far cooler than that nerd." I wagged my brows, pulling more laughter from her and causing her to snort. "Anyway, I've laid out my thoughts, expectations, things I'll ask of you while you're staying with me. I figured we'd go over it together, so when you do make a decision, you'll be completely informed. You can add anything you deem necessary, and we can keep it updated as we maneuver around living together. I'm sure more will come up as we learn new things about each other."

"Expectations?" she asked, her voice filled with skepticism and an undertone of trepidation. Out of everything I'd said, that had to be the one word she stopped on.

I ran my hand down my face, fighting my need to smile. I didn't want her thinking I was making fun of her, but...well, I kind of was. It was cute how she constantly reverted back to assuming I was the next Ted Bundy.

"Let's just go through it. You'll see." I placed the printed agreement on the table between us, a pen clipped to the front to hold the papers together. "First are my expectations."

Her posture stiffened, and as I glanced at her profile, I watched her clench and unclench her jaw. For a second, I wondered what had happened to her to cause this kind of reaction, but then quickly dismissed it, figuring she wouldn't tell me anyway. So I turned my attention back to the list in front of us and carried on.

"I have no problem with you inviting people over. All I ask is that they respect my things. I'm trusting you to protect my house while I'm away, which means I have to trust the decisions you make. I obviously haven't met your friends, so I'm leaving it up to you to make the best judgment call. With that being said, I fully understand that accidents happen. If something breaks, and you can't fix it, either shoot me a text or wait until I get home to tell me. Please don't try to cover it up or lie to me about it."

"Are you sure you're not a father? Because you certainly sound like one."

I hung my head in shame. "Oh my God, I'm so sorry, Jade. I don't have a clue what the hell I'm doing here. I just thought if we were both on the same page, it would eliminate unnecessary arguments or hiccups, so I added anything and everything I could think of. Here"—I slid the paper in front of her—"finish reading it, and if you have any questions, just ask. If you need to amend something, you have the pen."

She cleared her throat and took the paper. I observed the way her lips moved as she went through the list and mouthed each word to herself. Her eyes narrowed from time to time, and it made me wonder if she needed glasses.

The only thing that made me stop analyzing her every move was when she pointed to a line on the list, and without glancing up at me, asked, "No sex?"

"Not with each other," I clarified, and showed her where that part was stated.

She flipped her dark curls over her shoulder and flashed expressive eyes my way. "So we can kiss, make out, touch each other, and play show and tell with our baby makers, but we can't have sex? Is that just vaginal penetration with your penis? What about oral? Anal? I mean, what do we categorize as 'sex'?"

My eyebrows rose, leaving behind an ache in my strained forehead. "Um…all of the above?" When she rolled her eyes and went back to the list, I decided to speak up. Screw it if I sounded like a parent going over house rules while they went away for the weekend. "I've said this a hundred times—I'm not interested in anything romantic. I want—"

"I was just giving you a hard time, Cash." She moved her finger up the list and said, "You literally have bullet points for everything on here…except the no-sex policy. Like here, when you mentioned the mail. You have a line about what to do with bills, another line about junk mail, another in regard to the rest of what comes from the post office. Then there's a bullet point for UPS and FedEx. The financial section is broken down, as well as your expectations. Yet down here"—she moved her neatly trimmed nail about three-quarters of the way down—"all you say is no sex with each other."

"If you would feel more comfortable adding in clearer details, feel free. Just make sure you put on there: No anal sex." I watched the crimson creep up her neck and settle into her cheek, adding a natural glow of embarrassment.

"That's okay, just as long as we're both on the same page."

"Don't try to sneak into my room at night, and we'll be okay."

"I don't see anywhere on here that I can't watch you sleep."

I snatched the paper from her hand, grabbed the pen from the table, and scribbled next to the "no sex" line: *No watching me while I sleep*. As soon as I finished, she regained control of the paper, and just below what I had added, she included: *No falling in love*.

"That's for you," she said, tapping the pen over her words. But before I could respond, she turned her glacier-colored gaze my way, and with the straightest face, added, "I'm completely unclear as to your intentions. For all I know, you're looking for a new wife, and I'm not interested in being tied down at my age. This needs to stay strictly platonic."

My mouth opened, ready to ask what she meant by that, but the smirk playing on her lips gave her away. "I guess I've beaten that into the ground, huh? I'm sorry. I'm not accusing you of having ideas, nor do I believe you'll get your hopes up. That's not it. I guess I just needed to say it—*repeatedly*—so it was out there."

"No worries." She turned her attention back to the list. "That's why I included it."

"On the next page"—I flipped it over to a new sheet of paper—"I left you space to fill things in. I got most of this information from the questionnaire you filled out back in the beginning, but I don't have specifics on any of it."

She nodded with her bottom lip tucked between her teeth. I was too busy picking apart her expression that I almost missed all the writing she added to the blanks I'd left for her. When I turned my attention to her neat handwriting, I couldn't do anything other than blink, completely baffled by her answers.

"Um, Jade. You had said your price point for rent was between two and four hundred dollars. I left it blank here because that's a rather large gap, so I thought it made more sense for you to give me a more definitive answer."

"Yeah, and I did," she responded without looking up.

"You wrote zero."

"That's all I can afford."

This had to be a joke. But she wasn't laughing. I wanted to laugh, but I needed her to start so I could join in. And she didn't do anything but sit there and watch me.

"Care to explain?"

Suddenly, the stare I had assumed was meant to mock me transformed into something so tragic. She hadn't been sitting there watching me, fucking with me. No. She was about to break, like a porcelain cup on the edge of a table.

"In the questionnaire…I selected the rent to be more than I can afford."

"But surely you can afford more than nothing, right?"

She dropped her focus to the paper. "I don't have a job."

Something wasn't right. But in order to figure it out, I needed to see her face. I reached across the table to hook my finger beneath her chin and lifted it so I could see her eyes. The blue shone even brighter than before, and it only took me a second to realize why—they were glazed with a sheen of tears.

"What's going on, Jade?" I couldn't keep the concern from reaching my words. We were just laughing and fucking with each other, having a good time like we always did when we talked. So I was lost how we managed to end up here.

"I don't have a job." The lie I thought I'd catch in her facial movement never appeared. Her eyes remained on mine, not even an exaggerated blink. No twitch in her lip, no excessive pronunciation. Nothing. This girl was telling the truth.

"But I don't understand…I thought you had a job lined up on Geneva Key. What happened to the little girl you were going to watch?"

"I'll still have to watch her. But it doesn't pay anything. I get no money for it."

What she said didn't make sense—no one would expect her to care for their child for free. It had to have been deception, but nothing about her expression, her reaction, her demeanor, or her tone told me that was the case. Either her presence had completely thrown me off my game, or there was more to this than she'd given.

"Then can't you find another family who is willing to pay for your services?"

That's when her face crumpled, and as if my finger hadn't been tucked beneath her chin, she dropped her head, her shoulders jumping with each soft, almost silent sob. The pain she shed was real, as real as the air I breathed.

I grabbed her hand, squeezing it like she was about to float away and I needed to hold her here. "Jade…what's going on? Talk to me."

Using the napkin she'd decimated, she wiped away the evidence of her breakdown, though she never met my stare. Instead, she focused on the white paper between her fingers and explained. "On that questionnaire, you asked about pets. I told you I have a small breed, two years old."

I waited her out, blindsided by something I never should've been caught off guard with in the first place. I was trained to predict things before they happened, yet I'd found my wife fucking another man, and not once had I anticipated anything was wrong. And now, I sat in front of someone who had clearly kept something from me, and from what she was saying, it was all in the form I'd sent her weeks ago.

She took a deep breath and gave me her sad, broken attention. "You didn't have a question on there about kids. So I thought I'd put it there and explain later…if we made it that far. I didn't know anything about you, and I was scared to include my daughter. I couldn't risk anything happening to her."

The floor opened up and swallowed me whole, spitting me out in some alternate universe. I knew she'd kept something from me, but not once had I imagined it was a child. Maybe I thought that with her age, it wasn't a possibility, but now that I sat here, I realized it had been a foolish assumption.

"You have a kid?"

CHAPTER 5

Jade

I wanted to flee, slide out of the booth and run as fast as my short legs would carry me. The stunned look on his face said it all. His wide, onyx eyes, his full lips parted in surprise. He didn't have to elaborate. I knew this wouldn't be easy, and in fact, I hadn't planned on telling him at all—I figured we'd get to the end of lunch and one of us would say it wouldn't work out. Call me delusional, but for some reason, I found myself believing it could.

"You have a kid?" he asked, the shock from his rigid posture mirrored in his question.

"Yes, Aria. She's two."

"So you're not a nanny?"

I looked away from him, contemplating the version of truth I would offer. "Not really, no. I joke with my best friend how I'm a nanny who doesn't get paid, so when I had to write in my job, that made the most sense."

He didn't say anything else, just stared unblinkingly at me.

"Listen, I'm sorry about misleading you. I wasn't sure what I was getting into at first, and then I somehow started looking forward to your calls. You allowed me to be someone other than who I am. Stevie now sees me as the houseguest who won't leave, her boyfriend considers me and my daughter a live-in cockblock, and Aria just sees me as her bitch."

Out of nowhere, completely unexpected, a rush of humor tore through Cash. Almost every ounce of shock vanished before my eyes. "I have never heard you cuss. You go out of your way to say heck instead of hell, and you just said your daughter thinks of you as her bitch."

I laughed, although I didn't see the humor the way he had. "What about child support?"

"It's complicated."

"Yeah, you keep saying that."

I let my hand fall flat on the table and tilted my head, teetering on the verge of defeat. "Well, what else should I say, Cash?"

"How about the truth? I'll find out about it anyway."

I shook my head. "No, you won't."

"Don't be so sure of that."

"No one knows who her father is, so good luck finding information that doesn't exist."

He jerked back, probably surprised by hearing me finally take a stand. But I couldn't hold it in. I'd answer any question he had—*except* that. I'd talk about anyone other than him. "Birth certificate?"

"No father listed."

"Do you not know who he is?" This wasn't a question I had never heard before, but it stung just the same.

"Yes, I know who it is. But I don't want him having anything to do with Aria, so I've kept him out of everything. I'd rather struggle alone than take anything from him."

His gaze narrowed, hard and intense.

"I've spent almost two months on my friend's couch— technically on the floor because the couch isn't big enough for Aria and me. I told Stevie four weeks ago that I would find another place to live, and I've spent those days and weeks talking to you. The clock is running out. And it's clear this isn't going to work, so there's no point in going in circles, wasting even more time."

The shadow over his eyes cast by his knitted brow made him appear angry. Although, his words didn't match. They didn't sound happy; rather, the tone resonated with more confusion than anything when he asked, "You don't have a job, so how are you planning on moving out of your friend's house? How do you expect to pay rent?"

"I have savings. My dad had a college fund set aside for me, but I never used it for that. I attended a community college and had a scholarship that covered seventy-five percent of my expenses. I lived at home so I didn't have room and board. I can pay rent, but until I can find a job that will help put some of that money back into the account, I can't afford much."

"So you're living off your savings? How long will that last you?"

"Depends on how much rent is. Aria's still in diapers, so that's an added cost that will drop off once I settle somewhere with an accessible bathroom I can use to train her in."

"Wait…" He held up a hand to halt my explanation. "What do you mean an accessible bathroom?"

"Stevie's place only has one, and it's in her room. So after they go to bed at night, I can't use it."

"If you have to pee, where do you go?"

My cheeks flamed with the heat of a thousand fires, and I tried to look away, but no matter where my eyes went, his followed. "The kitchen."

His mouth fell open, anger on some level highlighting his face. "Why did you move out of your mom's house?"

"I already told you; I don't get along with my stepdad."

"It's so bad you couldn't stay there until you figured something else out?"

"Yeah." No matter what I said, he wouldn't understand.

He nodded and then turned his head to the side, staring at something off in the distance—or nothing at all. "Were you serious about moving to Geneva Key? You were ready to pack you and your daughter up and relocate across the state? Away from your family?"

No, I wasn't. I hated change and disruption.

But by now, I didn't have much of a choice.

"As long as…" I couldn't even say the words, realizing how desperate I sounded. No mother in their right mind, regardless of age, would move her small child in with a stranger—a male, at that. Though, what had started out as something to entertain myself, had turned into something I least expected. I may have been naïve and slightly irrational due to the inconsistency of my life over the last two months, but I truly believed I could trust Cash.

"As long as you know I'm not a bad guy?" He finished my sentence for me.

"Yeah," I whispered with a nod.

"Like I've said before, Jade…I don't have a way to prove that to you. I can give you every piece of information about me to do your own research, but other than that, my hands are tied. If I pull my own report for you, you'll never trust that I didn't tamper with it. If I give you names of people to call for character references, you'll continue to have doubts about the people I didn't give you numbers for. I can't win here. I want to help you, I really do, but there's not much else I can do. We're innocent until proven guilty, but with all the fucking crazy psychos and evil in the world, there's no such thing as innocent anymore, either."

He leaned forward and took my hands in his, locking his gaze on mine. In the depths of his raven eyes, I saw a sincerity I never knew existed. He spoke quietly, directly to me, when he said, "I completely understand where you're coming from. I hope you realize that. Your daughter comes first. Her safety should always be your number-one priority, and I have nothing but respect for you for doing what needs to be done for her. I hate the living situation you're in right now, but if it's better than where you were before, then don't ever doubt that."

Tears filled my eyes. I had learned the hard way that people only let you see what they wanted you to. It didn't matter if you knew someone for an hour, a day, a year, or ten years, you never truly knew who they were in their heart until they were ready to show you. So, at the end of the day, everyone is either a stranger, or you choose to trust them all until they prove themselves unworthy of it.

The problem comes when your trust is broken. When the devil inside shows his face. You're lucky if it's something superficial, something that won't cut you off at the knees. But as I'd learned about evil hiding in plain sight, when the angelic mask comes off, you're already broken into unmeasurable pieces, unable to put yourself back together again.

Even Satan had wings at one point.

Cash reached up and wiped a falling tear from my cheek with his thumb. "It's going to be all right, Jade. You'll figure it out. One way or another, you'll land on your feet."

I didn't believe a word he said, but I wasn't about to argue. "Thank you," I whispered while using the back of my hand to finish clearing away the evidence of my pitiful agony. I hated crying, the weakness it portrayed, but for whatever reason, I couldn't hide that from him. "I'm sorry I've wasted so much of your time. I know you really want to find a roommate, and I monopolized four weeks that you could've used searching for someone else."

He moistened his lips and sat back, just in time for the waitress to bring our food. I was no longer hungry, and by the way he pushed his plate forward, I assumed he felt the same. "You didn't waste my time. In truth, I just needed companionship, and you gave that to me. I'm the one who should be apologizing to you."

"Why? What'd you do?"

"You needed a place to stay, and I needed someone to talk to. I got what I was looking for—you did that for me—but your need hasn't been met yet. And I hate that. It makes me feel selfish."

"Don't blame yourself, seriously. You didn't know I have a kid, so it's not your fault."

"I'm not worried about her, if that's what you're thinking." His jaw clenched and his eyes narrowed as he hunched forward with his elbows on the table. "You think I'm saying no to you because of your daughter?"

"Well...yeah. You don't want kids, so I think it's a safe assumption that means you don't care to have them in your house. I can't afford much in rent, because I can't get a job *and* cover daycare. You said yourself you wish you could help me, but your hands are tied."

A smile formed slowly on his lips, causing his eyes to squint and his shoulders to soften like a brick had been removed. "Jade..." He shook his head and tried again. "I have no problem with you moving in—providing your background comes back clean. You're the one who said you can't take the risk with your daughter unless you trust that I'm not a threat. That's what I meant when I said my hands were tied. I can't prove that to you."

My head was spinning. As I thought back on the entire conversation since my confession about Aria, I only grew more confused. "But...you said you don't want kids."

"Unless you're planning on making me the father of your child, I'm not sure how my lack of desire to procreate has anything to do with your daughter. Just because I don't ever care to have one of my own doesn't mean I don't like to be around them."

"It's more than you bargained for. You realize this, right? You're not getting one roommate; you're essentially getting two. One of which can be very bossy at times—to be clear...I'm not talking about me. And that still doesn't fix the rent situation." I wasn't sure why I chose to argue against my favor, but I couldn't stop. I guess I wanted him to fully grasp what he was getting himself into, so he couldn't come back later and point these things out as if they hadn't been disclosed ahead of time.

"Her father has nothing to do with her? No visitation? I don't have to worry about him coming to the house while I'm not there and starting shit?"

"No. He's aware of her, but he's never claimed her. Never had anything to do with her other than creating her. And I have no intention of telling him where I live, so I don't foresee him stopping by."

"Okay, so listen…" He grabbed the paper from me and began to scribble on the last sheet, keeping his hand over his words to prevent me from reading it. "Let me worry about the rent. And as far as—"

"Whoa." I slapped my hand over the agreement he was writing on and waited until I had his full attention. "No. I can't let you do that. I'm not looking for pity or charity."

A smile curled his lips, slowly. It would've looked sinister had his eyes not twinkled and widened the tiniest bit. "You have got to be the strongest woman I know—or the most stubborn. I haven't decided which one yet. Let me do this for you, Jade."

"Why? Why do you want me to live with you so badly?"

"Would you believe it's because you're my only friend?"

"Not for a second."

"What if I told you I was dying and this was my last wish?"

"Depends…how much longer you got? Six months…I could handle that. Six years…not so sure." There was a pause before his head shook slightly with an almost silent puff of laughter passing his lips. "For real, Cash. Why?"

"The first answer was the honest one. It's not that I don't have friends, just none who are close. I've already told you why I was looking for a roommate to begin with, and why I wanted it to be a female. I need a friend to keep me from…"

I waited and waited, but he never finished that sentence. "Keep you from what?"

With a shrug, he said, "Loneliness. Boredom. Take your pick, because if I continue, I'm afraid I'll just end up making myself look utterly pathetic."

"What makes you think you haven't already done that?" I winked to show him I was only joking. "If you are serious about the rent, then you would obviously want something in return. I want to know what that is before I agree."

"Clearly it's not sex. That's already in the agreement. How about little things around the house? Fluff pillows. Change lightbulbs when they burn out. Take out the trash when it's full and I'm not home."

"You want me to be your maid?"

"No, that's not—"

"For heaven's sake, Cash. Just agree. Being your live-in maid would make me feel like far less of a leech than I do right now."

"Oh...maid. I'm sorry, I must've misunderstood you. I thought you said...never mind. Yes, that's exactly what I was suggesting. You move in to be the cleaning lady while I'm gone, and your payment will be living with me."

I snickered, the grin almost permanent on my face. "You make it sound like living with you is this amazing honor."

"It is. I'm pretty awesome."

"What about Aria? Have you ever lived with a kid before? I don't want to get into this and after a couple weeks you change your mind and kick me out because she's too much."

"I'm gone most of the week, as it is. The way I see it, she'll just add to the entertainment at the house while I'm home. I'm pretty sure she'll make things far less lonely." Everything about him— his eyes, his voice, the subtle smile gracing his lips—screamed sincerity. Honesty.

"You sure?"

He pointed at me and crooked an eyebrow. "As long as the screening checks out."

I didn't have any doubt about that.

We swapped information and left with plans to talk further. I needed to figure out how to research him, but other than a Google search, I wasn't sure of my options.

✣

"You're kidding, right?" Stevie lectured when I told her of my plans to move. She hadn't taken it well, and from the deep-cherry hue of her cheeks, it was a safe bet to say fury was on the top of her emotion list.

Cash had called me after he got home from lunch. We talked like normal, like I hadn't had an emotional breakdown at the table. Most of the conversation was filled with questions about Aria. For a man who had no interest in children, he certainly was fascinated with mine. It was as though he had to learn everything about her before we moved in—which still hadn't been decided by that point.

A week later, to the day, he called to inform me that everything had checked out when he ran my information. That wasn't a shock, considering I had nothing else to hide. Then we made plans for me to drive out there and see the place the following weekend. I asked Stevie to watch Aria for me because I wasn't comfortable bringing her. I knew I wasn't meeting Cash for a date, and there was no chance of anything romantic between us, but I just had personal qualms about introducing her to men. Cash was a man.

A very fine man.

I shook that thought from my head before I allowed it to go any further.

"It's fine, I promise." I tried to calm her down, but nothing worked.

"You don't know this guy!"

"I've been talking to him for over a month now, and I've met him once."

She grabbed my hands and pulled them to her chest. "You met him on the internet. What about this seems okay to you? Didn't your mother ever teach you about stranger danger or the risk of online dating?"

"Stevie, calm down and listen to me. I'm fully aware of what I'm doing. I've looked him up, even had a cop run a check on him. He's clean."

"And Hannibal Lecter was a psychologist before they found human remains in his f-f-fava beans." How she managed to say that with a straight face was beyond me.

"First of all, that's fiction. Secondly, if you think I didn't look at this from all different angles, then you're sadly mistaken. Remember who you're talking to, here. I'm the one with the trust issues, so if I'm telling you it's all right, then you should probably believe me."

"Says the girl who wound up in a three-year relationship with a psychotic, married man and had his baby." The second those words came out, she regretted them. Her mouth opened and closed, as if she were trying to swallow them back down, but it didn't change anything. She'd crossed a line, and she was well aware of it.

I ripped my hands away and retreated a few steps, needing to be away from her but not having anywhere to go in her tiny apartment. Out of everything, I couldn't believe she'd chosen that to throw back in my face.

"I'm sorry, Jade. I have no idea why I even said that."

"Sure you do. You said it because that's how you feel. To hear what you truly think of what I went through, hurts…really badly." I thought about grabbing Aria up and leaving, but I didn't have anywhere to go. And I was pretty sure Cash wasn't prepared for us to move in today.

"I never hid how I felt about that asshole. That's never been a secret. I've spent six years hating a man I didn't know, because you refused to tell me anything about him. Sometimes it takes a second to remember the truth—who he is and what he's done to you. I hated him then, I hate him now…those things will never change. I'm just the horrible bitch who sometimes forgets the whole story."

She meant what she said, and as much as I wanted to be mad over her throwing it all in my face the way she had, she made a valid argument.

"Just...will you please do this for me?"

"Do what, Jade?" She seemed exhausted, defeated. "Watch Aria for you? You know I will. But I'd feel a helluva lot more comfortable if you'd let me go with you."

I shook my head, my mind already made up. "Irrational or not, this is my decision, and I don't want her meeting Cash—or vice versa—until later. If this all works out, I plan on moving in next Monday, when I know he'll be gone for the week."

"If you're so concerned about him, why are you doing this?"

"I'm not concerned about him. I'm worried about Aria."

Her brows pinched together and her gaze darkened. "Worried about what?"

"I don't want her to get attached if this doesn't work out. I don't want her freaking out or being scared and giving him the wrong impression, making him change his mind. I also don't want her to misunderstand anything. She's two, so I don't expect her to know what's going on, but look at it for a minute, Stevie. We lived at my mom's house where she was practically ignored. She had to watch me cry all the time. Then we come here, and this isn't stable. We're living out of a suitcase and sleeping on the couch. I have no idea what to expect from Cash's house, so I want to absorb all this first, and *then* work her into it. It'll be an adjustment, and I just don't know how she'll handle it." When I finally stopped talking, I felt out of breath.

"I just can't figure out what would possess you to move in with a guy you know virtually nothing about, a guy you met *online*. Can you explain that to me so I can wrap my brain around it? You of *all* people should understand the dangers of what you're doing."

"You won't understand."

"Try me." She wasn't arguing, more like pleading for an ounce of insight.

I fell onto the edge of the couch cushion and busied myself with folding our bedding. Aria sat on the floor, her sippy cup in hand, and watched cartoons as if nothing else was happening around her.

"I need to get out of this town. I can't afford to live here, and you don't have room for us. You didn't two months ago when you took us in, and you don't now. Derek is ready to feed us magic Kool-Aid just to get rid of us. But I don't blame him. This place is far too small for three and a half people, and if I'm being honest, it's unfair to ask me to bathe in the kitchen sink. I can't afford to keep buying diapers for a two-year-old who should be potty trained by now, but I can't do that because I don't have a toilet at my disposal." My frustrations began to mount, and I worried if I didn't stop now, I'd end up saying something I couldn't take back.

I owed Stevie—and Derek—so much for taking us in when we had nowhere to go. None of my anger had anything to do with them or their immense generosity. But it was time to leave. I'd overstayed my welcome tenfold, and the longer I waited, the worse it became.

"Have you looked at other options? Or did you just jump at the chance to leave?"

"You're joking, right? Of course I've tried to find alternative solutions, but I have none. What do you want me to do? What is it you think I've ignored or haven't thought of? I even went to the college and called random strangers about their room-for-rent posters. You're all concerned about me moving in with Cash, but how is that any different?"

"At least you'd be in town, closer to me if you need anything."

I sighed and closed my eyes, trying to calm my racing heart and lower my climbing blood pressure. "I appreciate everything you've ever done for me, and all you continue to do, but I can't stay in Fort Pierce any longer. I feel trapped here, and the cost of living is too high."

"And you think Geneva Key is better? Jade...have you seen the houses there? Hell, have you ever been there? I'm fairly certain a bottle of water at the corner store is close to five bucks. It's a tourist trap, run by retired millionaires with nothing better to do with their time than take money from poor, unsuspecting travelers on vacation from up north."

"I'm working it out with Cash."

"So you still have no idea how much he plans to charge you?"

I shook my head, unwilling to fight anymore.

"What if you can't afford it?"

"Then I'm back to square one, aren't I?" I tossed Aria's blanket on the seat next to me and folded my hands in my lap. "Like I said, you won't understand. All I'm asking is for you to help me with Aria tomorrow so I can drive over there and check it out. Nothing is set in stone. I haven't moved. I can still back out, just like he can still change his mind."

Her lips twisted to the side. "I'll agree to watch her while you're gone tomorrow, but it does not, in any way, shape, or form mean I'm on board with this cockamamie idea of yours. Let the record show I think this is a horrible decision."

"Don't worry, it's on record." I stood and crossed the room, where I wrapped my arms around her and pulled her close. "Thank you. Really, I appreciate everything."

"Remember this when you're three hours away and need someone to watch her, and you have no one because you left me behind."

I laughed to myself and let her go, shaking my head at her stubbornness.

Stevie skipped classes, and we spent the rest of the day hanging out. For the first time in weeks, Derek went to bed alone while Stevie stayed up with me. Cash sent me a text, and I replied with a quick, "I'll see you tomorrow, hanging out with the BFF tonight."

The next morning, I woke up early to get a head start on the drive. Six hours in a car in one day—three there and three back. It was the longest I'd ever spent away from Aria, so I knew if I didn't leave when the sun came up, I'd change my mind. Stevie would've loved that, but it wouldn't have helped at all with the stress over my living situation.

I followed the directions and managed to make it across the state faster than expected. Driving down the boulevard with the sand and surf on one side, high-rise condominiums and quaint shops on the other made me believe I was in a different world. Although, Stevie had been right about the ritzy people. I passed cars that made my Jetta look like a Pinto. Granted, mine was ten years old, the paint on the hood, roof, and trunk had faded, and someone had backed into the rear quarter panel in a parking lot and didn't leave a note, but it was still drivable and paid for. I couldn't afford to be embarrassed by it, yet the brand-new luxury cars on the road alongside me made me feel otherwise.

When I pulled up to his house, I just sat there in awe. A small, residential road ran along the front, just wide enough for two cars to pass safely. The Gulf stretched on one side, a row of houses on the other, each appearing to have been built at least fifty years ago. Some seemed to have been updated along the way, while others still stood in what I could only imagine was their original state.

There wasn't much lawn between the front porches and the road. Just as I questioned where everyone parked their cars, as I didn't see a single garage, I took notice of the skinny pathways that ran between the houses, disappearing behind each of them. It was odd, but only because I'd never seen anything like it before. This street was nothing like Stevie had described. Nothing screamed money, and everything had such a comfortable aura about it.

I sent Cash a text to make sure he was awake. The morning was still young, but that hadn't stopped the beachgoers from staking claim on their favorite spots with towels and umbrellas. I watched the waves slowly roll in, like they were lazy, not quite awake for the day. It was so different than what I was used to on the Atlantic side. It seemed much calmer, and I could already tell it was exactly what I needed.

The knock on the passenger-side window made me jump in my seat. I turned my wide eyes from the crashing waves on the shore to the man standing outside my car, and blinked for a second before realizing it was Cash. The last time I saw him, he was wearing jeans and a polo shirt. Now, he had on athletic shorts and a T-shirt, his hair messy and unstyled. It did nothing but prove he was sexy no matter what he wore or how much time he put into his appearance. And once again, I had to shake off those thoughts. Living with a man who could embed himself into my most embarrassing fantasies wasn't such a good idea.

I rolled down the window and a warm, salty breeze rushed in and stirred the air around my cheeks.

"Morning," he greeted as he leaned down and propped his forearms on the open window. "Sorry, I wasn't expecting you so soon. I was hoping to jump in the shower after my workout, before you arrived, but it appears I didn't plan it very well."

"That's okay. I can sit out here while you shower. Or I can take a walk on the beach. There's no need for you to change your plans."

"Don't be silly. Just take the drive around to the back of the house. Park next to my car. I'll meet you at the back door." He pointed to the narrow side driveway that ran between his house and the one next door.

Nodding, I put the car in gear and followed his directions. Rather than finding a garage, I pulled around the back to a slab of concrete that looked big enough for two cars. I found a shiny black

Range Rover, which I assumed was his, and parked beside it. Once again, my little Jetta didn't fit in.

Taking in my surroundings, I admired the tiny back yard that took up the rest of the space behind the house. It looked to be sectioned off by the same white picket fence lining his front porch. In fact, it seemed every house on this street had the same.

I climbed out of my car, closed the door behind me, and turned to find Cash standing in the open doorway, leaning against the frame, a smile on his face. "Did you find the place okay?" he called out to me.

"Yeah. It was an easy drive. Thanks."

I took the three steps that led inside, and he moved aside to make room for me to enter.

Up until this moment, I had no idea what to expect. It reminded me of a cottage, small and comfortable. It was the epitome of a home. The furnishings looked new, as well as the hardwood floors. Everything neat and in its rightful place. I stood in the empty space just inside the door and tried to take it all in. The interior seemed so open and bright. Straight across from me was the living room, which had a large window that faced the street and ocean. A door was to my right, but it wasn't fully open, so I couldn't see inside, although I suspected it was Cash's room.

Cash walked into the kitchen to our left, and I followed. I marveled at the clean space while he grabbed a water from the stainless-steel refrigerator. Granite covered the countertops, and the carved, whitewood cabinets were adorned with decorative, silver handles. The window over the utility-style sink faced the back yard—I would have had to crane my neck to find our cars parked on the other side of the fence. From what I could see, the small patch of hunter-green grass had been kept neatly manicured, and flowers lined the tiny lot in a multitude of color.

I turned to look at Cash, a question on the tip of my tongue, but immediately lost my train of thought as he swallowed the rest of his water and ran his fingers through his short hair.

At the restaurant two weeks ago, we hadn't stood side by side. He was seated when I approached, and he remained there as I left. How I'd missed his height when I came inside was beyond me; the only explanation I could come up with was my nerves had blinded me, and my awe over his home demanded my full attention, preventing me from taking in the sight of him.

"Didn't you say you were like five ten or something?"

He straightened his spine and squared his shoulders, standing tall like a Greek statue. "Yeah, but I hit the gym this morning. I think after my last workout, I'm roughly six four." His eyes sparkled with the same mirth that played at the corners of his mouth. It brought my attention to the five o'clock shadow lining his masculine jaw and hardened cheeks.

"Maybe I need to join your gym. You've lost a lot of weight *and* grown six inches."

He sidled up next to me and pressed his hand on the top of my head, proving just how much taller he was than me—fourteen inches to be exact. "You could use a few inches. Although if you did that, I wouldn't be able to slyly check your scalp for dandruff."

I shoved at him, feigning offense. It didn't take long before we both lost the cloak of nervous energy and fell into an easy fit of hilarity. He tossed the empty water bottle into the trash—which I learned was in a pull-out drawer next to the sink—and led me to a hallway off the kitchen.

"The bedrooms are back here"—he pointed to two closed doors, one at the head of the hall, the other halfway down on the right—"and the bathroom is here." He gestured to another closed room, across the hall from the second bedroom. But rather than stop at any of them, or at the very least, let me see inside, he unlocked the door positioned at the very end. A small window set in the middle, thin plastic blinds blocked the light from the outside, and what appeared to be a handmade curtain had been draped along the top.

"And this is the back yard." He opened the door, which led to two wooden steps ending at the thick, healthy lawn.

I stepped out, not planning on doing anything other than take a look, but the second I noticed the plastic sandbox set in the corner, a child's beach umbrella stuck in the grass beside it, I gasped and clutched my chest.

"Did you...?" I pointed to it and covered my mouth, trying to swallow my emotions before they bubbled out.

"You said she liked the sandbox at the park. I checked out the local ones within walking distance, but there's only two, and both seem to be geared more for older children. I even drove to the one at the end of the island, just before the bridge, and it didn't have a sandbox, either."

"So you bought her one?" I was seconds away from losing the fight against my tears.

He shrugged as if it were no big deal that he'd purchased something for my child to make her happy, even though he'd never met her. I longed to hug him—no one had ever done anything like that before—but I refrained and stepped back inside.

When he opened the door to the bathroom, the first thing I noticed was the size. It wasn't big, but the way the builder had designed the small space left plenty of room to move around. Not to mention, it appeared a woman had decorated it.

"Who picked out the décor?" I teased—there was no way it had been him.

"I had someone come over last week while I was gone to get it all set up for you. I knew you didn't have anything other than clothes, so I wanted to make sure everything was ready when you moved in."

Just before leaving the room, I noticed a child's training potty in the corner next to the toilet. "Did you tell her to get that, too?" I gestured to the pink and white seat on the floor.

"You said she needed to learn. Better here than on my couch." Again, he acted like it wasn't a big deal, like anyone would've done the same. But I knew better. My own mother hadn't so much as bought one box of diapers since the day Aria was born, let alone a training pot and sandbox.

I wasn't sure what I expected, or why it came as such a shock, but I was rendered speechless when he showed me the bedroom across the hall. The walls were divided in half with white wainscot on the bottom and pink paint decorating the top. White decals of cherry blossom trees extended from the far corner of the room. Below it, a toddler bed was made up with a pink-and-white blanket, and a safety rail ran half the length of the tiny mattress. A matching dresser sat against the opposite wall with a ballerina nightlight perched on top that looked to be made of porcelain. The shallow panels of the wainscot were painted black, catching my attention since it didn't go with the rest of the room.

When I leaned down to run my finger along the dark wall, Cash said, "It's chalkboard paint. She can draw on it and it'll come right off. The decorator suggested it. I'd never heard of it before. But kids like that kind of stuff, right?"

I stared at him, my mouth gaping, eyes rapidly blinking.

Worry consumed his features as he took a step back, one foot in the hallway like he was prepared to flee. "We can paint over it. It's no problem. You didn't say anything about her liking to draw, but I thought it might make learning to write fun. I did a lot of research and thought it was a good idea, but I didn't mean to step on your toes. You're her mom. If anything in here is wrong, just tell me, and I'll have it fixed before you move in. And that goes with the rest of the house. If you see a safety hazard, point it out. I have no clue what I'm looking for."

I officially lost the battle with my emotions and scurried to him, where I fell against the hard planes of his chest, my fists gripping the sides of his shirt as if to steady myself. His heart thrummed beneath my ear, and after a moment of me silently appreciating him, he finally enveloped me in his embrace.

"Thank you," I whispered into the damp material of his T-shirt.

"So...it's okay? I didn't fuck up?"

I shook my head, giggling, and pulled away, not at all caring about the sweat that had transferred onto me from his clothes. "No, you didn't mess up at all. It's perfect. So unbelievably amazing, I have no words."

Relief filled his eyes as he pulled in a deep breath and slipped out of the room.

CHAPTER 6

Cash

Jade was so hard to read at times, and it worried me that I'd lost my touch. Seeing the truth in people's eyes and picking up the deception in their reactions were things I'd prided myself on for nine years. Yet somehow, a tiny brunette with eyes that resembled the hottest part of a flame came into my life, and I found myself all sorts of turned around.

She'd cry one second, show affection I wasn't used to the next, and before I knew it, she'd shake her head and laugh, as if the whole thing had been a joke. I had no idea if I'd done something right, wrong, or what. But she didn't have anything other than a suitcase full of clothes and her car, and with her money dwindling from her savings account while she tried to feed, clothe, and diaper her child, the last thing she needed to do was buy furniture for my house.

"I didn't do much to your room. I wanted it to be feminine yet give you a canvas you could make your own." I wasn't sure how she'd react, considering what had happened after the last two rooms I showed her; although, I could tell by the look on her face that she loved the white-washed wood and pastel coloring.

"It's absolutely beautiful just the way it is." She ran her fingertips along the bedspread and peered at me from over her shoulder, the slightest smile gracing her lips. Maybe it was because she'd just used the word "beautiful," but that was all I could think of as I watched her eyes light up.

"If the dresser isn't big enough, just let me know. The store had a bigger one that matched the bed. I only chose this one because I thought you'd rather have the mirror instead."

"You picked out the furniture? I thought you had someone come in and do it for you?"

I tried to play it off by shrugging and moving into the hall. "She did most of it. I only picked out the set for this room because I figured it's something I could keep for guests when you're done with it."

Jade didn't say anything else, only took one last glance into her room and followed me out.

I led her to the kitchen and gestured for her to take a seat at the table. "There's really not much else to show you about the house. You see the living room"—I waved a hand toward the open space—"and my room is over there."

She glanced around, taking it all in.

"I figured you'd want to go over this again." I grabbed the few sheets of paper off the bar and sat next to her at the table. "I retyped it all and printed it so we'd have a clean copy. But I wanted you to go through it so you'd know I added everything we talked about before."

Jade took the papers from my hand and began to skim, more than likely searching for the additions. "I see you've included maid duties." She peered at me out of the corner of her eye and smirked, her brows lifted and arched. "Where's the pen?"

I placed the same pen we'd used at the restaurant in her open palm, and then leaned forward to see what she was writing.

"You have on here that I'm expected to 'pick up' after Aria. This isn't specific enough. Please, Cash, elaborate. What specifically do I need to make sure I pick up?" She tried to act stern and professional, but the way she held her lips tight proved she had to hold back her smile.

"Considering I don't really know what she has or what she could possibly make a mess with, I have no idea how to be more specific. I just know the thought of stepping on Legos when I come home late on a Friday night, or waking up on a Saturday morning to find a naked Barbie doll on the coffee table doesn't sound like fun. Just basically pick up her, you know…kid things."

"I can handle that." Humor danced in her tone as she jotted down notes, such as: *Put away naked dolls* and *No Legos*. "You also have shopping on here. What kind of shopping are you looking for? Clothes? Shoes? Cars?"

I couldn't contain the bubble of laughter that erupted at her last question. "I won't usually be here during the week, so the fridge might be a little bare. I normally go grocery shopping once a month and stock up on chicken. Occasionally, I'll hit up the fish market while I'm home, but I eat what I buy and don't keep leftovers. I like fresh veggies, so I'll grab enough to last me two days. As you can tell, I don't keep things around that'll go to waste. So I just ask that you handle the food shopping. And if it's not too much trouble, if you happen to be at the store on a Friday, I'd greatly appreciate you picking up vegetables from the produce department so they're fresh."

"Wow, you're really making this easy on me. If the secret gets out, you'll have quite a few maids looking for employment." She pulled her lips to one side. "On second thought, it might be best if no one find out about this arrangement."

"Why do you say that?"

"Because I'm sure you could find someone who would do a way better job at cleaning your house than me." She didn't waste any time before going back to the list in her hand. "What about the other bills?"

"Like what? Electric and water?"

"And cable and internet."

"I already told you. Don't worry about them."

"No…you said *rent*. You never said anything about all the other expenses."

"Yeah…because it's all included."

Rather than say anything else, she lowered her head and began to jot down another note under the section for "maid duties." She added a few more things, such as sweeping and dusting, probably to make up for the utilities, but I didn't argue. If this made her feel better taking a room in my house for free, then I wasn't about to say anything.

We finished going over the agreement, making tweaks here and there, more so to add clarity than anything else. She wrote a few more things down and made fun of me for some of what I had added. At the end, she made a joke about how this was more of a roommate *dis*agreement with all the changes and scribbles. Then I agreed to have a new one with all the latest inclusions ready and attached to the fridge by the time she moved in.

I'd suggested that she move in next weekend so I could be there to help, but she made a good point that I hadn't thought about. She needed time to acclimate Aria to a new house, with new rules, as well as being around me. Jade figured it made more sense to tackle one at a time, and to give her a week to adjust before having her so close to a man she hadn't met and wasn't familiar with.

The plan was for Jade to move in next week, putting one more weekend between now and when she settled in, but when I handed her the keys, I told her she was welcome whenever she was ready. I had to leave early Monday morning, so she'd have all week to decide.

About an hour after she got home, I received a text saying she'd be heading over on Monday with Aria. She wouldn't tell me much when I asked if everything was okay, only that she'd had a run-in with her ex. But again, just like every other time I'd asked about him, she told me it was complicated and she didn't want to talk about it.

⚜

It was just after one in the morning when I pulled around to the back of the house. Everything was dark, inside and out, so I assumed Jade had gone to bed. Ever since finding out about Aria,

I'd become more aware of the time at night when we'd talk on the phone. Her early bedtime made more sense when I realized she had to get up every morning with her daughter, and I found myself hesitating before calling, not wanting to wake her. But she'd told me not to worry about it, and if she was asleep, she just wouldn't answer.

Yet every night this week, she answered when I called.

Tonight was late, though. I didn't expect her to still be awake when I got home. Normally, I'd arrive at the house around eleven, but my day hadn't gone as planned. In fact, nothing had gone as planned since I'd left the house early Monday morning. All week long, I'd thought about Jade. About her moving in, about Aria and how she was adjusting, and then getting home to spend the weekend with them, excited to finally have someone to come home to again. Yet my job had a different agenda.

And now I wouldn't be able to see Jade until morning.

I held my side, feeling every step, every move, every fucking breath I took, and unlocked the back door. The soft creak of the hinges as it opened had never bothered me before—I'd never noticed it, never had a reason to pay attention to the natural groans of the house. But now, consciously aware that there were two other people asleep inside, every sound seemed magnified.

The lamp on the corner table in the living room between the couch and loveseat had been left on. This was something else I wasn't familiar with. Walking into a pitch-black house late at night was what I was used to, not having a beacon of light lead the way from the back door to my bedroom.

Peeling off my shirt left me winded. I had to grind my teeth, my jaw clamped shut so tightly I could've broken a molar, just to keep the agony from rushing out of me in an animalistic roar. I could deal with a lot. Not many things threatened to break me, but the pain that started on my right side radiated throughout my entire body. It sent a wave of unbearable heat ripping through my torso, nearly sending me crashing to the floor on my knees.

Slowly, I managed to pull myself from the haze of physical anguish long enough to get a shower and wash off the stress of the week. I wanted nothing more than to close my eyes and start over in the morning, spending the day with the only person who made me feel like less of a monster and more like a human.

Jade had once told me that I allowed her to be someone else— that I didn't see her as an unwelcome houseguest or a mom. I understood that more than anyone. When she looked at me, she saw a network engineer. She didn't see the blood on my hands, the days spent hiding in plain sight, the nights cloaked in darkness, sneaking around, plotting. I'd detonate, implode, if I didn't have some level of normalcy...even if it was only over the phone here and there and in person on the weekends.

As the water swirled around the drain, I thought back on my week. God, it'd only been six days, yet it felt like an eternity. Like I'd lived a hundred lifetimes since I'd last been in the same room as someone with a pure heart beating within their chest.

I'd tailed my mark long enough—three weeks to be exact— and had the ins and outs of his days tracked. There wasn't a minute of his entire existence I hadn't been made aware of since he hit my radar. The weekend warrior—sometimes referred to as the babysitter or part-time shadow—kept detailed logs of his comings and goings, which matched everything I had on him already. This week should've been easy. It should've been a quick grab and go...but it wasn't.

I hated doing the sweep at the end of a week, knowing I would be gone for two days and ran the risk of not seeing it through, but I didn't have much of a choice. The plan was to wait until after a phone call we anticipated he'd get on Wednesday, assured it would give us valuable information. The call never came, so we waited. By Thursday night, I'd notified my boss of my decision to hold off until the following Monday. We were pushing it too close to the weekend.

To my surprise, the phone call had come in early this morning. I'd been alerted to the transcript, and once I confirmed we had what we needed, I was left with no choice but to order an imminent sweep. I knew his schedule, so it was nothing more than waiting for a blind spot and using it to ghost him. Movies show a man standing on a sidewalk all the time while a bus drives by. As soon as the bus passes, the guy is gone. That's what I did. One minute, my mark was there, the next…gone. Like a ghost.

The window of opportunity was small, but I had confidence I could execute it. I'd done it hundreds of times over the years with very little problem. And this time, like the handful of previous sweeps gone wrong, it was out of my control. A memo had come down, but by the time it was supposed to reach me, I had already gone dark. The phone call we'd expected on Wednesday, the same one that came in early this morning, informed us of a visitor who would arrive on Monday, hence the need to move rather than wait. However, intel discovered the visitor was already here, and that was information I hadn't received in time.

I'd gone in for the sweep, oblivious of the danger I'd unknowingly walked into. In the hair of a second between grabbing my mark and making him vanish, his friend attacked from the side, almost taking me down. And he would have if I hadn't been high on the natural adrenaline I got from the task. It wasn't as smooth as I had planned, or as flawless as I'd prided myself on, but at least it wasn't a failure. Rather than one devil incarnate, I brought in two.

I also came home with a slightly broken body.

After my shower, I dried off and slipped into a pair of gym shorts, but I decided to forgo the shirt. I figured if Jade and the kid were asleep, it wouldn't matter, and I hoped by morning, I'd be able to endure the pain long enough to cover my chest. But as of right now, the ache was too fresh, too aggravated, too unbearable to slip on a shirt.

As soon as I walked out of my bedroom, on my way to the kitchen for water, I stopped dead in my tracks, unable to move. It appeared Jade had been sucked into the same time freeze as I had. She stared at me from across the house—which from where we were was only the span of the living room. She was heading my way, tired eyes wide and mouth barely parted.

"I'm sorry. I didn't wake you, did I?" Earlier in the bedroom, I'd tried to muffle the discomfort of undressing, but now I worried I hadn't been as successful as I thought.

"Oh, no. I was awake—waiting up on you, actually."

"Yeah, I got in later than expected. Thanks for keeping the light on."

"I didn't hear you come in, but I heard the water running. I was just coming out here to turn off the lamp. Figured you'd be tired and crawl into bed after your shower."

The entire time we stood apart, nervously talking as if we'd never met, her eyes remained on mine. But I guess curiosity had gotten the best of her, because her gaze trailed down to my chest, her hands fisting at her sides as if she had to physically restrain herself from touching me, despite the length of space between us. It was odd, especially coming from her, since she'd never given me any indication that she even found me attractive, much less...*this*. Although, what was even stranger was how it didn't turn me off like it normally would have coming from anyone else. I ignored it, stopped the thought from lingering, and assumed it had been because I'd felt a level of comfort with her that I didn't normally have with other women.

I took a step toward her—actually, toward the kitchen for water, but she remained in the entryway so I had to pass her to get there—but stopped as soon as the harsh, panicked gasp left her lips. She immediately covered her gaping mouth with her fingertips, her impossibly wide eyes glued to my right side.

"Oh my God, Cash," she whispered beneath her breath while rushing to me. "What happened?" Not once did she look me in the eyes, but rather, kept her focus on my battered ribcage.

The second her finger came in contact with my skin, I winced. Although, it hadn't inflicted any pain. I wasn't sure if my dramatic reaction was premature, knowing how bad it'd hurt if she touched it, or if it was caused by the spark of electricity when her skin met mine. Either way, it had happened, and she immediately took a step back, her worried stare finally meeting mine.

"How did this happen?" she asked again, not accepting my silence.

"Hazard of the job."

"You need ice." And as if she were a trained nurse in the emergency room, she scurried into the kitchen, rummaged around in the freezer, and came back with a wadded-up dishtowel. It was clear in that moment she was a mother. A nurturer. A healer. And because of that, I dismissed my need to be a man, and allowed her to care for me.

CHAPTER 7

Jade

Cash could act like a tough guy all he wanted, but there was no way he wasn't in complete agony. When he'd first come out of his room, I was stopped by the sight of his dark, sculpted body glistening from his shower, and it took everything in me to maintain eye contact. The way he stood with his loose, black athletic shorts hanging low on his hips, he practically begged me to stare, and his bare chest called for my attention. But I held out as long as I could.

Finally, I'd given in and allowed myself a moment to memorize every line of muscle that acted like a roadmap to the treasure I convinced myself he concealed beneath his shorts, needing it to hold me over during the long nights I lay awake, alone in my room. But before I could salivate at the sight of his happy trail, or the deep V that disappeared beneath the elastic waistband, I discovered the fresh bruise on his side, decorating his ribs in a tapestry of deep purples and angry reds.

He tried to fight me off, but after a second, he gave in and allowed me to baby him. It made me question if anyone had ever done this for him before. I didn't have a lot of information about his ex-wife—other than she was a disgusting woman who had cheated on such an amazing man—but I found myself curious if he'd ever needed her to take care of him. Everyone got sick, even macho men. And I couldn't help but wonder if he was the type to work through the fever, suffering alone, or the kind who craved the soft, healing touch of a woman. From the way he relaxed into the couch and closed his eyes while I carefully held the ice pack to his tender side, I was willing to bet he was the latter...he just didn't know it.

At least this gave me plenty of opportunity to stare at his naked chest, the abs I could literally count from across the room, and the dark hair that trailed from below his bellybutton to the waistband of his shorts. His arms were massive, but not riddled with bulging veins like most bodybuilders, which made me believe he didn't bulk up for show. This was the body of a man who took great care of himself and worked out to stay in shape, not to win a trophy.

"Less than one hour into our agreement, and you're already breaking the rules." His deep, rumbly voice grated through the air, heavy with sleep and humor.

I lifted my gaze to his face, only able to see his profile with the way he rested his cheek on his fist, his elbow propped up on the armrest. His eyes were closed, but a smile curled his lips—utter contentment that filled me with comfortable warmth.

"And what rule is that?" I prodded from where I sat curled up on the cushion next to him, holding the ice-filled rag against his side.

"Watching me sleep."

"Technically, you aren't sleeping. So I haven't broken any rules."

He turned his head just enough to peer at me from the corner of his eyes through the tiny slits in his lids. "Then I guess I need to amend the agreement in the morning to include time of rest."

"Well, smarty pants, what is it you suggest I look at while you're *resting*?"

"The walls are a great place to start." He let his head fall back, using the cushion behind him as a pillow, and moved his right hand from the small space between us to my thigh. He didn't flex his fingers or make any uncomfortable advances, just expanded the gap between his arm and his side to give me more room to hold the ice against him.

"How'd this happen, anyway? You said it was hazard of the job, but I'm having a hard time wrapping my brain around any situation a computer technician would be in that would leave him looking like he'd gotten beaten by a lead pipe in a barroom brawl."

"You have no idea what I do, do you?" His lips still held the same teasing grin as before, his eyes remained partially open and set on my face, but his brow gave him away. Just like I knew it would, the wide, smooth space tightened just a fraction, enough to hint at an involuntary reaction to a hidden emotion. I had no idea what it meant, but something about it sent a rolling wave of sorrow through my gut.

"Not really…but you've explained it so many times, I figured it wasn't safe to ask again."

His tongue ran along his lower lip, wetting it and calling my attention. Thankfully, he closed his eyes and faced the ceiling, preventing him from catching me staring at his mouth. "I engineer infrastructures for communications using technology."

"Yeah…you've said that before. But I have no idea what any of that means. In my head, you wear khakis and a red polo shirt while sitting in a cubicle behind a computer, talking on the phone to people who need help rebooting their modems. Oh…and in my head, you also wear black-framed glasses. Don't ask where those came from or why you don't wear them on the weekends."

He started to laugh but quickly stopped when his face scrunched in silent pain, his left hand crossing his chest to cover the offending area. Yet his right hand remained on my thigh, only this time, he gripped it while forcing himself to breathe. I scooted a little bit closer—any closer and I'd be in his lap—and adjusted the ice in an effort to help him through it.

Once he got himself under control, he resumed the conversation as if nothing had happened. He relaxed his expression, yet never opened his eyes. "Well, a network engineer can do many things, but my job deals with towers. That's why I travel all the time. I could be in Texas this week, Maine next, Colorado the week after. Wherever they need me, they send me."

"Oh, I thought you did stuff with computers."

"I basically do. We use computers to tie everything together and make it work as a unit. But at the core of what we do is a network. Printers, scanners, phones, radio towers, cell towers, internet…they're all tied to a network."

I'd always assumed Cash was smart, but his level of brilliance wasn't apparent until this second. Even though he'd finally explained his job in terms I could understand, I still couldn't imagine any of it in my head.

"So…how'd this happen? What were you doing when you got hurt?"

"Fell." And that was it; no more explanation.

It left me picturing him falling off a tower, hitting the poles on the way down, yet as far as I could tell, he'd only been injured in one place. Although, I didn't ask any other questions. It was obvious he was tired, and when I glanced at the clock over the TV, I noticed it was two in the morning. Aria would be awake in four to five hours, and if I had any desire to enjoy his company while he was home, I'd need to go to sleep before too long.

"Where do you keep your pain relievers? I'll grab you some before you go to bed."

He hooked his thumb over his shoulder in the direction of his bedroom, his eyelids remaining closed. "I have some in my nightstand. I just need water. That's actually why I came out here to begin with—before you decided to play nursemaid." His tone was light, full of easy mirth.

"I'll get that for you."

He squeezed my leg once more before pulling away and dropping his hand on the cushion between us. I shifted on the couch, removed the ice from his side, and took a peek at the bruise. It was a deeper red than before, but that was most likely due to the ice. Realizing he was probably minutes away from sleep, I rushed to the kitchen, took the cold, wet cloth to the sink, and grabbed a bottle of water from the fridge.

"Thanks," he muttered when he slid the drink from my outstretched hand.

"Do you need help getting into bed?" Apparently, my maternal instinct knew no bounds, regardless of how mortifying it could be at times.

His dark eyes flashed wide for a split second before a smirk tilted his lips. "No, I got it."

I stood next to the coffee table, waiting for him to pull himself off the couch in case he needed assistance. Of course, he refused, leaving me to watch helplessly while he clenched his jaw, held his breath, and forced himself to a standing position, biting back the rumbles of agony threating to tear through his chest.

While he steadied himself on his feet, taking deep, controlling breaths, I touched his arm to remind him that I was still there if he needed me. Once he settled down, I offered him a smile and turned to leave. I only made it halfway across the room before he called out to me, making me whirl around to face him.

"Thank you..." He waved a hand toward the couch. "For tonight, this...everything."

I had no words, so I simply forced a broad grin and nodded. It must've been enough for him, because he dipped his chin and angled around to his room in the opposite direction. The second his back came into view, my breathing escalated into desperate pants, saliva pooled beneath my tongue, threatening to spill out in endless rivers of drool, and my heartbeat decided to fall to the space between my legs, throbbing with each intensified pulse.

Stretched out along his entire back, a male angel had been inked from shoulder to shoulder, just below his neck down to the two glorious dimples at the base of his spine, and spanning from the left side to the right, where the bruise was more prominent. The wings appeared to be dirty, as if the tips were covered in soot, and a pair of hands held a sword and a book.

I wanted to ask about it, touch it, trace the details with my finger while memorizing every line, every shaded area until I could vividly see it behind closed lids as I fell asleep at night. But instead, I watched Cash barricade himself in his room, leaving me with yet another fantasy to obsess over while alone in my bed…in *his* house.

✦

My eyes slowly opened to the morning sun brightening my room through the cream-colored drapes over the window. At first, I stretched and thought to myself how well rested I felt. Then I jolted upright, realizing how well rested I *really was*. Having a toddler that woke with the sun made that impossible—add in how late I'd stayed up last night, and something had to be wrong.

I glanced at the clock on my nightstand, double-checked to make sure I hadn't been seeing things, and threw the covers off while practically falling out of bed. It was after eight thirty. The only times Aria had ever slept that late…that was a lie; she'd never slept in that late.

My heart climbed its way into my throat, closing off most of my airway. I flung my door open and ran down the hall. The first thing I noticed was her bedroom door left ajar. The only thing that had comforted me having her in her own room was the fact that she couldn't reach the knob, so I didn't have to worry about her wandering around the house while I slept. Every morning this week, she'd alerted me to her being awake by crying behind her door. How I'd slept through that, I didn't have a clue.

But she wasn't in her room, which served to heighten my panic while my bare feet slapped the hardwood floors on my way into the main part of the house. As soon as I cleared the hallway and made it into the kitchen, I stopped dead in my tracks. The sight in front of me both settled my nerves and made me swoon all at once. Aria sat on the couch, spine stick-straight, hands in her lap with her feet dangling off the cushion like a well-poised princess. Next to her, Cash reclined into the corner with his feet propped

96

on the coffee table, crossed at the ankles, a coffee mug in one hand and the other tucked protectively between his side and the armrest, reminding me again of the injury he'd sustained at work. Both had their eyes glued to the TV screen mounted to the wall out of my view—I had no idea what they watched, but both appeared to be incredibly engrossed in it.

"Why didn't you wake me?" My question came out far more accusatory than I had planned, my fear and anxiety not yet fully dissipated. I walked through the kitchen—at a much slower pace—and approached them in the living room.

Aria's attention never left the show playing in front of her, but Cash turned his gaze to me. A slight grin toyed at one corner of his mouth while his dark eyes flashed wider, just the tiniest amount, before returning to the TV.

"You were sleeping," he mumbled, his lips close to the rim of the mug in his hand.

His short answer and lack of attention worried me, but I pushed past it and moved to stand closer to the couch next to Aria. "What time did she get up?"

He shrugged with his good shoulder, hiding a flicker of a wince with a slow blink. "Around six thirty."

I stared at him in disbelief, my tongue and eyes suddenly dry and unmoving. However, it was a wasted show of surprise, because neither audience member offered me so much as a glance. "That was two hours ago!" Shock lifted my voice into a near screech.

Finally, Cash—keeping his head straight forward—turned his sights on me, but only for a fraction of a second. His nonchalance had really started to grate on my last nerve. "Like I said, Jade...you were sleeping."

I balled my hands into fists, trying to contain my displeasure. He only meant to help, and I appreciated that, but I couldn't ignore the frustration over the fact that her whole schedule was now turned upside down. "If she eats breakfast now, she won't be hungry for lunch, which means her nap will be late." I closed my eyes and counted back from ten, hoping I could rewind time to take back my ungrateful words.

"She already ate. I gave her a waffle." His words snapped me out of my mental countdown.

"You made her a waffle?"

"Oh, shit. Was I supposed to heat it up first?" He finally whipped his entire head around to face me, brows quirked high, eyes round yet bright. "I just grabbed one out of the freezer and let her gnaw on it with her tiny little teeth. I wasn't supposed to do that?"

We entered into a stare-off, me against him. I remained silent and frozen, unable to figure out if it was a joke, but he didn't cave, which only made me more nervous of his sincerity. But right before I opened my mouth to question him—hoping my words didn't come off sounding condescending—his lips split into a grin, and he returned his attention to the show.

"I followed the directions on the box." His voice was almost monotone. Only the slightest hint of humor still lingered, even though his expression went blank. Then he peered at Aria out of the corner of his eyes and said, "Although, I think she needs a new diaper. I left that for you."

I didn't blame him for not wanting to change a child's diaper, but I was also grateful he hadn't. Stevie had done it a few times for me while I was running an errand and she watched her, but that was different. The thought of a male—*any* male—handling that made my skin crawl. But I didn't have a clue how to express that without making it sound like I thought of him as a pedophile. So, rather than address it, I simply thanked him and began to pick Aria up.

The second my arm hooked beneath her bottom, the cold wetness caught my attention. I immediately set her on her feet and scrubbed my forearm against my shirt, desperate to rid myself of the feeling.

Cash chuckled beneath his breath, so softly I wouldn't have known had I not glanced at him. It was obvious the action caused him pain, but he couldn't stop the hilarity from rolling through him. "I told you she needed to be changed. Did you not believe me?"

"I guess I didn't imagine it was that bad considering you let her sit on the couch."

He flicked his chin to the now vacant cushion beside him, and once more, his lack of eye contact gnawed at my consciousness. "I put a towel down. She was fine."

"And when would you have decided to wake me up to take care of it?"

"When she soaked through the towel. I figured I still had an hour or so before that happened." His left shoulder lifted a few degrees in the most pathetic one-sided shrug I'd ever seen. "It can be washed. No big deal."

I waited a few seconds to see if he'd look my way, and when he didn't, I was left with no other choice but to leave the room. I grabbed the towel off the couch and took Aria's hand in mine to lead her back to her room for a fresh diaper.

After cleaning her up and giving her a new outfit to change into, I took a moment to compose myself. I still couldn't figure out why Cash refused to make eye contact. Surely, cartoons were not that riveting. I ran my fingers through my hair—well, I tried to. That's when I realized I probably looked like Medusa and had scared him so badly he *couldn't* look at me. Curly hair was nothing to play with first thing in the morning, and considering how fast I'd jumped out of bed and ran into the living room, I hadn't thought twice about the rat's nest on my head.

I took the elastic band off my wrist and tied my unruly locks back, piling it into the best topknot I could without heavy amounts of detangler and a brush. Leaving Aria with the task of dressing herself—she'd recently started to pitch a fit anytime I tried to help—I made my way back to the living room, taking a seat on the other sofa, but close enough to Cash.

He was still in the same position as when I'd left the room, feet on the edge of the table, ankles crossed, mug in hand...and eyes on the television. When I glanced to the side to see what he'd found so fascinating, I couldn't help but laugh.

"I didn't take you for the type to watch *Barbie's Dreamhouse*."

He took a sip of his coffee and said, "It was on, and Aria liked it."

My jaw clenched, my teeth so close to grinding. It was odd because I wasn't angry with him or his interest in the cartoon. Nor was I still jumpy over the situation I'd woken up to. My irritation was more spurred on by self-esteem than anything, which only further confused me. It wasn't like I wanted him to stare at me or tell me I was pretty, but when someone took such effort to avoid looking at you, it stung.

"Did she wake you up this morning?" I tried again, hoping to engage him in conversation.

"Nah, I was up. Heard her crying and figured if you didn't, it meant you still needed sleep."

Well, at least I got more than two words out of him that time. Next step was to get him to take his focus off Barbie and actually participate in a discussion. I didn't care what it was about, just as long as he didn't act like I wasn't in the same room—literally a foot away from him with only an end table and two armrests between us.

Just then, Aria skipped into the room, her shirt on backward, and climbed up next to Cash. Other than a hug in her room after her diaper change, she'd barely acknowledged my existence— seemed to be a theme with these two. I took a moment and observed them. Aria sat ramrod straight, not at all relaxing, which led me to believe she hadn't allowed herself to feel fully comfortable around him yet. And I understood that. But considering she'd chosen to sit by him rather than me told me she wasn't scared.

Cash leaned closer to her just enough to whisper, "She has a lot of clothes." Aria's face lit up with a giggle, but other than that, she didn't say anything. As soon as Cash shifted to sit up straight again, his eyes closed and his lips tightened, and I knew immediately his side had bothered him.

"Are you in pain?" I asked, ready to do whatever he needed to make it better.

Blowing out the full breath he'd been holding, he blinked his eyes open...and set his gaze back on the cartoon. "Nothing I can't handle." Another short answer.

I took note of his thin, zip-up hoodie, and asked, "Are you cold?" The air was on, but not low enough to be considered uncomfortable. Even though his sleeves were pushed up on his forearms, he had to have been hot in it—unless he had a fever.

"No, but I figured this was better than going shirtless since I didn't care too much about fighting a T-shirt so early in the morning." A longer explanation, but still monotone. I had to pick my battles, but it was like no matter what he gave me, nothing was good enough. It was either one- or two-word answers, even and unemotional tone, or a shrug. All while avoiding me at all costs.

"Are you going to see a doctor?" I tried again.

"Already did."

I waited for more, but got nothing. "What'd they say?"

And there went the slight, one-shoulder lift again. "That I'll live."

I stared at the wall across from me, the one with the window leading out to where we parked our cars, and fought back the sting of rejection. This man wasn't my boyfriend, not even a prospective lover—just a friend, and if I were being honest, our friendship didn't really hold too much depth. So it was silly of me to feel dismissed by him.

"Do I have something on my face?" I wiped my palm over my lips.

He glanced briefly at me before turning back. "No."

"Well, there's gotta be some reason you won't look at me. I know my hair can be scary in the mornings, but I've already tied it up."

"Yeah, I noticed you pulled it back. Didn't need to, though. I kind of liked the wild mane you had going on," he said with his mug pulled close to his lips, a grin tugging on the corners.

"Then why won't you look at me?" It was more of a demand than a question, but I'd long since given up on reining in my insecurities. He'd been married before—this couldn't have been a surprise to him.

He peered at me out of the corner of his eyes, his head unmoving, brows arched in what I could only depict as silent humor. "I can see your nips through your shirt."

I glanced down and realized I'd never pulled my T-shirt back on after waking up and was only wearing the thin cami I slept in. Immediately, I slapped my hands over my chest and jumped up from the couch. Before I had the door closed to my bedroom, I heard Aria ask, "What'er nips?" To which Cash answered with, "Nipples," as if a two-year-old would understand.

Even after changing into real clothes, taming my hair, and brushing my teeth, I was still too mortified to head back out to the main part of the house, but since my daughter was out there, I couldn't very well hide forever and expect him to tend to her. So, I tucked my tail between my legs and met them back on the couch, where they sat in the same positions as when I ran off. However, this time, Cash rewarded me with not only his eyes, but a smile, as well. I ignored the mockery in his expression and accepted it as a friendly greeting.

"I'm so sorry, Cash. I didn't think at all about covering up before coming out here."

"It's fine." He turned to glance at the little girl next to him, who now sat slightly hunched in a more relaxed way. "Although, I think you have some explaining to do. I might have confused her a little."

Hesitantly, I asked, "What'd you tell her?"

"Well…" His cheeks darkened and his brows furrowed. "She thinks nips are" — he cupped a hand around one side of his mouth to keep Aria from hearing — "boobies," he whispered. "And I wasn't sure how to handle that, so I told her they weren't *exactly* the same thing, and that boys had them, too. Now, I'm pretty sure she believes boys have…" He repeated the motion with his hand to the side of his mouth, and whispered, "Boobies."

I shouldn't have, but I laughed, uncontrollably. Rolling fits of giggles consumed me until I was left clutching my stomach, unable to breathe. "Oh my God, Cash…have you ever been *around* a kid before?"

"Not really." Rather than joining in on my fit of hilarity, he simply smiled, masking the pain he was in. "I figured I'd learn. It hasn't even been one day…give a man a break. By next weekend, I'll be a pro at this shit."

"Oh, yeah? You might try to watch the curse words."

He blinked exaggeratedly at me. "I can't cuss?"

"It's your house, you can say whatever you want."

His expression softened and all humor vanished between us. "No, really…the way you raise her beats out the fact this is my house. I hadn't thought about the words I use, but I'll be more conscious of them."

"Should I add that to the agreement?"

"Only if you don't punish me if I happen to slip and break the rule from time to time until I get used to censoring my language."

"Deal." I got up and headed to the fridge to add the amendment. I grabbed the pen from the drawer, but before I could write anything down, the laughter came back at the sight of the unexpected addition.

Just below the rule about not watching him sleep, he'd added: **Or during any time of rest**. At the bottom of the page, I wrote as neatly as I could: **No cursing in front of baby ears**.

CHAPTER 8

Cash

I had to admit, I wasn't sure what I was getting into when I agreed to letting Jade and her daughter move in, but after a single day with them, I was pleasantly surprised. Aria was entertaining to say the least, with her contagious giggles and tiny-human voice. Although, the little girl didn't talk much. She'd spent a few hours with me on the couch this morning watching cartoons, never speaking one word other than to ask me things no man should ever be asked by a child. But once Jade became part of the equation, I could see Aria's demeanor change, as if watching her mother interact with me made her less cautious and more trusting toward me.

And dinnertime proved me right in my decision to move them in.

Rather than my typical weekend meals of grilled chicken and steamed broccoli, Jade made a feast without forcing me to sacrifice my healthy eating habits. Granted, had she made a plate full of carbs, I would've eaten it with a smile, just so she didn't feel her gesture was unappreciated, but thankfully, that wasn't the case. Baked chicken with a blend of seasonings that melted in my mouth, accompanied by a mixture of broiled vegetables, all of which tasted like she'd spent hours in the kitchen, but considering I'd been home while she cooked, I knew she'd pulled it off with little to no effort.

I'd asked her how she learned to cook, but with sad eyes, she simply said she didn't have a choice after Aria was born, and the topic was dropped. After dinner, she bathed Aria and got her ready for bed while I flipped through the channels, finding nothing worth watching. It seemed having people here didn't suddenly make my weekends any more exciting, just less lonely. With a couple of fractured ribs, I had to lay off the gym—and basically, any physical activity—but if I had to sit on the couch much longer, I would go stir-crazy.

By the time Jade came back from putting Aria down, I already had my shoes on. "Where are you going?" she asked with a hint of intrigue.

"I've been inside all day, and if I don't at least get some real air into my lungs before I go to bed, I might not wake up in the morning."

"Oh my gosh, Cash. Why didn't you say anything earlier? We could've gone somewhere or done something."

I waved her off, not wanting her to blame herself or think she was the reason I hadn't gone anywhere. "Aria took her nap, and then you started on dinner. Plus, I didn't begin to feel trapped until a few minutes ago. I'm used to being outside, but these bum ribs are fucking with my lifestyle."

"Oh, okay." Her gaze dropped to the sandals on my feet, then to the back door. "I guess I'll just take my shower while you're gone. That way, when you come back, if you're up for company, we can watch a movie. Or just hang out or talk. Whatever you're up for."

I couldn't keep the smile from taking over my face. "I figured it'd be nice to walk across the street to the beach before the sun completely sets. There's still a sliver of light in the sky, so it won't be as hot…plus, there's a breeze."

She swung her gaze from the back of the house to the front window, the one that faced the wide-open stretch of sand and surf, barely visible at this time of day. "That does sound nice. Very peaceful." With a quick nod, she added, "Then I'll make my shower quick."

"Well, I was kind of hoping you'd join me."

"I'm not sure…Aria just went to sleep. If she—"

"She can't get that door open—we both know that—but if it'd make you feel better, we can use our phones to listen out for her. Just call me from your phone, put it in her room, and then we'll mute the call on my end. I'll even get earbuds so you can hear if she gets up."

The way her head tilted just so to the side and one corner of her mouth twitched with the fight against a soft, easy grin, I could tell the thought of joining me appealed to her. But then she gently curled her lower lip between her teeth and glanced away—that was enough to prove her hesitation. I couldn't begin to imagine the kind of sacrifices she'd had to make over the last two years, but this didn't need to be one of them.

"We'll lock the house up, and you'll be able to listen to her without her hearing you. We don't even have to walk down the beach, just straight out front to the surf."

"Yeah…but what if she wakes up, realizes I'm not here, and gets scared? It'll take me too long to get back to her."

I crossed the room and took her phone off the kitchen table. Flipping it open, I handed it to Jade, and then tugged mine out of my pocket.

"I'm not a parent, and this is your child, so I won't push you on your decision. But if it helps, she won't have a clue that you're not here if she wakes up. By the time we get back, she'll very likely think you were in the other room, or possibly the shower. Again, this is your call, but I would really like it if you'd join me on the beach. Just for ten, fifteen minutes."

Without a verbal response, she pressed a few keys on her outdated phone, answering me with a call and a twinkle in her eyes. It didn't take long to get the phones situated—hers in Aria's room, and mine in her pocket with one bud tucked into her ear—before we were out the door.

"It really is peaceful out here," she said once we made it to the sand.

"Have you come here at all this week?"

She glanced up and down the nearly deserted beach, the breeze blowing through her dark, curly hair. "No, there's been too much going on with getting Aria settled and whatnot. It took me an hour to find the grocery store the other day. That was fun."

"Why in the world did it take you that long? I don't think it'd take me an hour to run from one side of the island to the other…on foot. Where all did you go?" I wasn't making fun of her, and by the soft purr of laughter, I could tell she knew it.

"Well, I don't have GPS in my car—I don't think navigation systems were around when it was made—and it seems I've officially discovered a solid reason why a smartphone would come in handy. I stopped and asked someone for directions…twice. Then I figured I'd find it on my own. After making about twenty right turns, only to wind up in the same spot, I caved and called Stevie."

"She's familiar with Geneva Key?"

"No," she said with a breathy giggle and a light shove to my good side. "But I told her where I was, so she was able to pull up a map on her phone and walk me through the directions. Thank God I'd had the wits to give her your address before I moved; otherwise, you would've come home to an empty house because I wouldn't have been able to find my way back."

I turned around and squinted at my house, taking in the dark-purple sky behind it. Unfortunately, it also made Jade whip around, probably out of fear that I'd seen or heard something, and her first thought was Aria. So to ease her worry without calling attention to it, I pointed off to the side and said, "There's a mom-and-pop market two streets over that way. It's easily missed since it looks like a house. I grab my dry goods from them when I don't need to load up on anything else."

She followed my finger's trek from the left of my house to the right.

"And over there, probably less than two miles, just after where my street ends at the main road, there's a meat market. The prices are a little higher, but it's all fresh. Mostly seafood, but they do get in a daily supply of chicken and red meats. You just have to get there early, because they don't keep much on hand. But the fish is locally caught and cleaned. You can't miss it—smells like a boat."

"Well, considering you had almost nothing in your house, I needed to stock up. And for that, I had to get off the island to find a real grocer. You know…the kind with a produce department, freezer section, dairy coolers?"

"I'm sorry I didn't give you all this information before you moved in. There's a Publix on the island." I pointed in the opposite direction, down the beach to the left. "If you take this road all the way around the curve at the end, you'll hit a traffic light. Turn north, like you're leaving the island, and you'll see a side road, easily missed because it's not well marked. It's back there, butts almost right up to the north end of the beach."

The dying sunlight hinted at the scowl on her face.

"What's wrong?"

"That's where I was headed. I'm starting to think everyone on this island can tell I don't belong here—because, you know, my Jetta is a rather sure sign of that—and they find great entertainment in making me drive in circles. If I had Facebook, I'm sure I'd see an entire thread dedicated to the poor woman in the midnight-blue hooptie who drove up and down the island looking for milk."

I started to laugh, and had even opened my mouth to offer reassurance, but rather than words coming out, my amusement turned into an airy "oomph" just before being sucked back into my lungs in a whistling inhale through clenched teeth and tight lips. The back of her hand had barely connected with me, and had mostly come in contact with my pec and upper arm, but the way my body coiled tight and flinched against her innocent assault left my ribs screaming in agony.

"Oh my God!" she cried after realizing what she'd done.

Her teasing attacks were fine when we faced the water, but when we both turned around, it put her on my right side. Couple that with our height difference, and the range of motion when swinging her arm lined up perfectly with my injury.

"I'm so sorry, Cash. I didn't mean to do that. I wasn't thinking." She spoke so fast it was like one, long word broken up by hyphens, but she wouldn't stop. Even if I could breathe enough to speak without sounding like my balls were lodged in my throat, she wouldn't have given me enough room between her profuse apologies and repentant excuses.

I grabbed her by the back of the neck with my left hand and tucked my right arm across my abdomen, pulling her closer for a couple of reasons. One: to shut her the fuck up. And two: I needed something to steady me while I fought to regain normal function. It took a lot to knock the wind out of me and keep me down this long. But with her forehead to my chest, I clung to the physical support she offered while I composed myself.

One time, in my first year on the job, I'd been so zoned in on my mark that I missed the car heading down the road in front of me. Well, that was a lie…I hadn't missed it. In fact, I realized it was there when I stepped out into the street only to be thrown against the windshield before rolling off the hood. In my defense, it was a smart car, and couldn't have been going faster than fifteen miles per hour—basically, no different than a child on a bicycle. But still, even after that, I'd gotten up and brushed myself off. Yet this little spitfire tapped me with nothing more than the back of her hand in jest, and I was ready to crawl into the fetal position and head toward the white light.

After I could finally take in enough air without feeling every molecule of oxygen in my ribcage, I slowly released her, but she didn't back away. Instead, she remained in front of me, glistening eyes set on mine, her hands gently holding my hips.

"Seriously, Cash…what did the doctor say?"

"It's nothing, Jade. Just a few minor fractures. Nothing they can do about it. I just have to let them heal on their own, but right now, the worst pain is coming from the bruising and swelling. Doc said I'll be able to move again in about a week or so." Actually, he said I was lucky it wasn't worse, and not to expect to resume normal activity for six weeks. I heard one week.

"Fractured ribs? Did they give you pain meds?" Panic swept across her face.

I shook my head and ran the pad of my thumb down her soft cheek. "Yeah, but I refuse to take them. I'll stick with ibuprofen."

"But if you're in pain…"

This time, I placed my thumb over her warm, moist lips and set my eyes on hers. "I don't like to not have control over myself. Drugs—of any kind, prescribed or not—fuck with your head. As does alcohol."

"So you don't drink?"

"I'll have one or two from time to time, but not enough to feel the effects."

The waves crashed behind us, rolling onto the shore before being sucked back out. The breeze blew all around, winding between us like strips of cool satin. Nothing else could've been heard for miles other than nature's rhythmic melody.

After a moment of nothing but staring into each other's eyes, she quickly dropped her gaze to my chest, and in a controlled, steady voice, she said, "Let me take a look."

When her fingers found the zipper pull to my hoodie, I clasped my hand over them. "Jade, it's dark out here; you won't be able to see anything."

She glanced around, as if just now realizing the fading colors of the sunset had vanished into the night sky, leaving little to offer her for a visual inspection of my chest. But that didn't stop her plight—probably still consumed with guilt over hurting me in the first place, and needing to make sure I didn't have a bone protruding from my side. "It'll just take a second."

Giving up, I allowed her to unzip my jacket and slide it over my shoulders, down my arms, until she had it pulled completely off my body. I was unable to lift my arm without feeling faint, so she nestled herself into the small amount of space I provided and drew her attention close to the almost black cloud covering my ribs.

Her fingertips barely grazed my side, tracing the lines of discoloration. It wasn't enough to inflict pain, but it was the kind of touch that healed the broken. I mimicked every breath she took, feeling her soft exhales dance along my skin like warm, whispered prayers willing me back to health. I grew dizzy at her attention, but not from pain or lack of oxygen. I wasn't sure what had my head all wrapped up and ready to float away, and I wasn't sure I liked it, but I didn't have the wherewithal to make her stop.

Finally, she took a step back, her hand falling down my arm until our fingers were linked in the lightest hold—so light it felt like I was holding the hand of an angel. "Let's go put ice on it. I haven't seen you do it all day." And then she led me through the sand, across the road, and up the three wooden steps to the front door.

I'd been to the beach countless times since moving here, but none had ever been like that. Even without getting my feet wet once, or even venturing off enough to say I'd walked along the shore, it fulfilled something no other visit had.

⚓

The next day during Aria's nap, Jade had just fallen asleep on the couch. Her soft snores filled the otherwise quiet room, when Aria decided she was done with her nap. I'd just sat down on the loveseat when I heard her tiny knocks on her door, followed by, "Mommy? I awake, Mommy."

I glanced over at Jade, the sun filtering through the window behind her, making her brown hair shine with hints of gold. We'd stayed up late last night—as well as the one before—but this morning, she'd gotten up with Aria rather than sleeping in. My being home had thrown her off her schedule, even though her little tyke never veered from hers, so I decided to let her sleep a while longer.

After rummaging through the dresser in Aria's room, I managed to find a bathing suit and hoped it fit her. I told her to put it on while I changed in my room, and then I'd be back to get her so we could go see the waves. That made her baby blues shine like the rarest sapphire, which acted like a defibrillator to my chest, accelerating the natural beat of my heart. Then I wrote a note for Jade, informing her where we'd be in case she woke up before we came back, and stuck it to the fridge, right next to our roommate agreement that seemed to be growing by the day. I couldn't help but smile at what she'd added after lunch today: **Hotdogs must be cut into slices, then quartered, NOT put on a bun whole with condiments.** In my defense, she was the one who'd bought the buns, so I hadn't thought anything of it.

Once I'd gotten myself ready, I went back down the hall to check on the princess. True to her promise, she sat on the edge of her bed, dressed in her ruffled suit. "Are you supposed to wear a diaper with this thing?" I asked gently, having no idea what the protocol was for this. She simply nodded with expressive eyes, so I didn't argue. "I guess that'll keep you from shitting in the ocean."

She giggled, the kind that made her squeeze her eyes closed, cover her mouth with her tiny fingers, curl her shoulders in, and hunch forward, like she'd just heard the funniest thing in her very young life.

Then I realized what I'd said. "Don't tell your mommy I said shit. Okay?"

She laughed again, this time harder, and it made me glance over my shoulder to make sure it hadn't woken Jade. Thankfully, the house was still quiet, so I figured it was safe. I took Aria by the hand, making her arm stretch out so far I worried I'd pull it out of socket—poor girl, she'd probably end up getting her mother's height. I then silently led her through the house and out the front door, leaving Jade and her purr-like snores on the couch.

Before heading out to the beach, I grabbed the sunblock and floatation device from the bench seat on the front porch, hoping I'd picked out the right thing. While getting the house ready for Jade and her daughter a few weeks ago, I'd anticipated they would want to go swimming, but I wasn't sure if Aria had water wings, so I'd added that to the list for Marcia to do while I was gone. I'd looked up every option available to mankind in regard to this, and after poring over all the safety stats and reviews, I'd settled on this one.

I had to say, she was one very well-behaved kid. Rather than run toward the surf, she waited for me to spray her down with sunblock, and then stood still while I slid her arms into the holes and fastened the harness around her chest. It was awkward and bulky looking, her arms sticking out to the side, but as long as it kept her afloat, I couldn't complain. At least she wasn't griping about it.

Turned out, women had a thing for a man with a kid. I thought I'd gotten enough attention just being by myself, but take my shirt off, splash some water on my chest, and give me a kid, and I turned into the bachelor from that show with twenty-something women fawning over him. It didn't matter that my ribcage was black and blue and made me look like a piece of evidence from a back-alley fight. I wouldn't be surprised if that added to the appeal. And no matter how many times I tried to tell them she wasn't mine, it was like I was ignored.

Granted, most of the women who stopped were older. With their floppy hats and long, cotton sundresses, they paused to tell me what a good father I was. And more than likely, they hadn't ignored my arguments about her not being mine; they just probably couldn't hear me without their hearing aids. Others simply liked to coo at Aria and gush about how cute her suit was.

So, in reality, they weren't really hitting on me...but that didn't mean they didn't flock to me like a bird to bread.

After half an hour of chasing the waves, digging in the surf, and briefly swimming in the water, we were ready to head back. I figured Jade would be waking up soon, and if not, she'd be pissed at me for letting her sleep so late. Not to mention, Aria would need to be rinsed off from the sunscreen and salt water, and that was out of my jurisdiction.

By the time we made it back to the porch and had her life preserver hung over the railing to dry, my entire right side throbbed, making it difficult to pull in a deep breath without feeling the effects radiate throughout my body. But as soon as we opened the door, everything changed.

"Stevie, I have to let you go. They just walked in. I'll call you back." Jade flipped her phone closed, ran to us, and knelt on the floor in front of Aria. Panic consumed her from her constricted pupils to the tremble in her lips, down to the way her hands shook as she inspected her daughter from head to toe.

I figured coming inside, soaking wet, both in bathing suits with sand stuck to our feet would've indicated where we'd been, but I guess it didn't register to a mother overtaken by worry and fright. She'd listened to Aria chatter away about jumping waves and something else I couldn't understand, before shooing her off to the bathroom down the hall.

Then she turned her heated stare on me.

She was the epitome of a momma bear protecting her cub. Her top lip curled, almost in disgust, but I could tell it was a reaction rooted deep in maternal instincts. I held my breath and waited for the fangs to come out, or the razor-sharp claws ready to slice me open.

"You can't just take off with her without telling me," she lectured me in what only could've been described as a growl. "And to the beach? Are you kidding me? She's two, Cash. She can't swim. I don't even want to think about what could've happened out there while I slept, oblivious to it all. Not to mention, you didn't even put on her sun hat. She's too little to be in the sun that long. She'll burn without protection of some sort."

I was tempted to point out the note I'd left, explaining where we'd be. Or that I'd coated her plenty with sunblock and used water wings. I thought about telling her it had only been thirty minutes. But there was no use. She was right, and I was wrong. I had no authority to take her to the water—or even out of the house without her permission. Note or not. Sunscreen and floatation device or not. Aria wasn't my kid, and I'd crossed a line.

"I'm sorry," I said while looking her straight in the eyes, hoping she could see my sincerity.

The pain in my side had subsided at the sight of Jade's frantic disposition when we'd walked in. In that moment, it wasn't as important as her fear. But now, after clenching my hands into fists at my sides, angry at myself for not taking a step back to see the bigger picture, the ache intensified. It settled deep into my bones, creating a heat within me that threatened to steal my breath away. Not able to put it off any longer, I apologized once more and moved around her frozen body.

I'd only tried to help, but that wasn't a good enough excuse. While I stood in the shower, letting the water fall over me, I tried to imagine what it had been like for her when she first woke up, not having an inkling where her child was. But no matter what I did, I couldn't put myself in her shoes, and that only made things worse. My only saving grace was knowing I'd be gone first thing in the morning, and I wouldn't be back until late Friday night. I had hoped by next weekend, she would be able to find it within her to accept my heartfelt apology and move forward.

A knock came from my closed bedroom door, and there was no doubt it had been Jade. Aria's sounded more like a tap with zero oomph behind it. Yet even this one wasn't harsh—loud enough to be heard, but not driven by the force of anger.

I'd fallen onto my bed after my shower in nothing but a clean pair of athletic shorts. I was about to call out and tell her to hold on a minute while I put on a shirt, but the thought of climbing out of bed made the lingering pain in my ribs spur to life. After another round of ibuprofen and however long I'd been in bed, the ache had started to settle. Just the thought of moving made it throb. So instead, I called out, "Come in," and waited for her to open the door.

At first, she stood in the doorway with her arms crossed over her chest, her shoulder leaning against the frame. Her entire stance screamed anger, as if she were ready for a fight. But the second I regarded her expression, I realized how misleading her posture was. Sadness lined her lower lids, fear ticced in her jaw, and apprehension lingered in her downcast eyes. She wasn't standing there, holding back or readying herself for an attack. No…she was protecting herself. Although, I couldn't figure out what from.

"Come here." I curled my finger, calling her toward me. "What's going on?"

When she made it to the bed to stand next to me, I held my breath and used my good arm to raise myself up, then swiveled my legs to dangle off the side. Her need to protect herself became apparent once more as she put distance between us. If I'd reached out, I could've touched her, but I knew better than to push.

"I owe you an apology." Remorse filled her whispered words.

I swallowed harshly and narrowed my eyes on her. "For what? You don't owe me anything. I'm the one who left while you were asleep, *and* took your child with me. There's nothing for you to be sorry for."

"Yes, there is." She was adamant, and all I could do was sit and wait for her to get it out so I could ease her mind and assure her that she had done nothing wrong. "When I bathed Aria, I noticed she had on sunblock. I'd accused you of not protecting her in the sun, and I was wrong. And when I took her bathing suit to the porch to dry, I found the floaties. I wasn't aware you had them, so I thought you'd just taken her to the beach with nothing."

"Jade—"

"I also found the note." She wouldn't let me speak until she was done—she made that clear with her sharp interruption—so I sat and waited my turn. "You have to understand something...I've never woken up and found her gone. That's never happened to me before. So it scared me, and I guess that fear made me irrational and kept me from calmly figuring it out. And because of that, I didn't handle myself properly when you came home and I realized she was fine and safe."

I waited until she paused long enough to give me space to talk. "Jade...you have nothing to be sorry for. You were right. I shouldn't have taken her out of the house without your permission. You'd just fallen asleep when she woke up, and I thought she'd have fun playing in the waves, and you'd be able to get some rest since I'd kept you up late two nights in a row. But that was never my call to make. You don't know me well enough to trust that I'd take care of her and keep her safe. Hell, *she* barely knows me. You had every right in the world to be pissed—you still do."

She lowered her head and covered her face with her hands, her elbows tucked close to her body. I wasn't sure if she was crying, but I could assume by the way her shoulders remained still, not jumping, and her breathing appeared labored but not erratic, that she wasn't sobbing—she only needed a moment to collect herself.

When her hands dropped to her sides, her bright eyes met my dark ones. "I'm just not used to this. Yesterday morning and now today..." She shook her head and glanced to the cracked door before rewarding me with her attention again. "This is all so new. Everything is."

"That's fine. It is for me, too. But we'll figure it out. It's been one weekend, and in time, we'll be so used to this arrangement, we won't know anything different. I understand she's your kid, not mine, and I have no say over anything that involves Aria…but if you'd let me, I have no issue helping you out. If you're tired or sick and I'm here, let me be an extra set of hands."

"That's just it, Cash…I'm lost with an extra set of hands. All weekend I've felt like I've been living with an octopus when the last two years I've been a T-Rex trying to clap."

I didn't need her to act it out in order to imagine it, but she did anyway. With her elbows tucked close to her body, she flapped her hands together, resembling more of a seal than a dinosaur. Unable to stop laughing, no matter how badly it hurt to do so, I reached out and pulled her close, settling her between my parted legs. I dropped my forehead to her shoulder and held onto her hips. I hadn't thought twice about it, only needing a little support while I tried to stop the rumbles from ripping through me long enough for the agony in my side to diminish.

Once I was calm enough to speak, I hooked my fingers into the belt loops on her side, and held her face with my good hand. "In all seriousness, Jade, she's not a problem. She's a kid. A smart and funny and extremely well-mannered little girl. I don't ever want you to feel like you can't lean on me when it comes to her. Or hell, when it comes to anything. If I'm here, let me help."

"My mind is all over the place right now. I think it's going to take me longer than a week to figure it all out. We hadn't even gotten comfortable here before you came home"—her eyes widened—"I didn't mean it like that. It's your house; I'd never suggest—"

"Jade…" I shook my head and breathed out an airy wave of laughter. "It was clear what you meant. And trust me, this is a learning curve for me, too. I may have been married, but I've never had a little kid running around the house, especially one I have no rights to. I should've thought about it before I took her to the beach today, but I couldn't see past letting you sleep in order to understand the ramifications. It won't happen again."

As if suddenly realizing how close we were, her gaze fell about four inches to my lips. That one move was enough to relinquish my hold on her and allow her to step back, both of us panting wildly as though we'd just been caught making out by our parents.

"So...we're good?" She awkwardly stuck her thumbs into the front pockets of her shorts.

"Not until you clap for me again."

Her eyes closed, head tilted back, and a wave of the best song in the world flooded my room when her laughter filled the space around me. "Well, then...I actually came in here to tell you dinner's ready." Her lips turned up at the corners into a demure grin. "So I guess that means you don't get to eat."

"Oh, come on. Just once. Let me see it one more time."

"In your dreams." She winked and left the room.

Yeah...in my dreams.

CHAPTER 9

Jade

As strange as it was to adapt to Cash being in the house, it was even harder to get used to him being gone. It made me wonder if that was how his wife had felt. It seemed like as soon as I had become comfortable around him, he was packing a bag to leave. And the worst part was trying to explain it all to Aria. She didn't understand any of it, and the more I tried to spell it out for her, the more confused she got.

After an entire day of answering her questions about Cash and where he was, I gave in and called my best friend. I'm sure she'd expected me to cry and tell her how horrible it was here, or confess to Cash doing something awful—especially after my frantic call to her on Sunday. But that's not what she got. Instead, I filled her in on everything that had happened, half of which she'd already heard from previous calls last week, but she was more interested in what went on while Cash was home. Before we hung up, I suggested she come for a visit and spend the day with us. Not expecting her to say yes, I was floored when she made plans to drive over on Wednesday. I immediately called Cash to make sure it was okay with him if I had someone over. It wasn't until Tuesday afternoon that I finally received his response, letting me know he trusted me, and that any friend of mine was welcome.

Wednesday arrived, and so did Stevie. And it was so good to see her.

"So you guys talk all the time?" Stevie asked from her spot in the surf.

Another wave ambushed us, eliciting the wailing cackles of my two-year-old, who had perfected the art of jumping them—

thanks to Cash. "Kind of…I guess. I mean, we used to. Before I moved in, back when I was living with you, we spoke almost every night, and even more on the weekends. Last week, I think it was every night for at least a few minutes, but maybe that's because he wanted to make sure we'd settled in okay. Then everything happened on Sunday with him taking Aria to the beach and me freaking out, and now…it's just weird."

"How so?" She seemed far too interested in my life.

"Well, when he came home Friday night, we stayed up talking. On Saturday night, we talked for a bit, and then he put on a movie. We ended up not going to bed until after two. But Sunday night, he went back to his room shortly after Aria went down. Then he left early the next morning. I didn't hear from him at all that day, barely heard from him yesterday—which was just a quick text saying he didn't care if you visited—and nothing from him today. I think I messed everything up."

She touched my arm, then wiped off the sand with a smirk. "Let it go, Jade. He's probably busy with work, and all you're going to do by obsessing over it is make things even more awkward when he comes home again."

She was right, but I couldn't drop it. I'd gotten over the whole incident, but his silence was what ate at me. I stopped myself so many times over the past few days from sending him a text and asking if everything was okay, because I refused to be *that* girl. He'd made it abundantly clear that he had no interest in any romantic relationship, sexual or otherwise, and even though we'd shared a few intense moments over the weekend, I didn't want him to assume I'd thought more about it than what it was. So instead, I'd stuffed it down and tried to pretend the worry didn't exist.

Leave it to Stevie to sniff out.

"So this guy's hot?"

I whipped my head to the side, analyzing my best friend with my finest scrutinizing gaze, even though she couldn't see it behind my dark sunglasses. "What made you ask that?"

"No need to explain. That was all the answer I needed."

"Seriously, Stevie. Why'd you ask?"

"You're all twisted up in knots over him. It's written all over your face. I've never seen you smitten with anyone, and that includes Jordan DeCanter from summer camp." She dropped her head back and hummed toward the sky. "I don't think there was a dry pair of panties anywhere in that camp. Damn, he was fine."

"We were sixteen. That's gross. I'm pretty sure the image of him you're conjuring up right now might be on the wrong side of pedophiliac."

"I hate you. Way to pop my fantasy." She dug her heels into the wet sand and let the rolling surf wash over her feet. "Have you talked to your mom since you moved?"

I debated between shoving her face into the ocean until she caught a fish in her mouth, and telling her to mind her own business. But she was my best friend, after all, and she only asked because she cared. And because of that, I decided to answer. "No." However, that was all she'd get about it.

"Liar. She called me looking for you."

I resigned to my fate of telling her the ugly truth. "Fine. She called last week, all concerned because I didn't tell her I'd moved, and then she gave me a guilt trip for refusing to give her my new address. She really wasn't happy when I wouldn't tell her what city I'd moved to. Let's just say it wasn't a good conversation."

She snickered next to me, calling my attention back to her. "Do you two ever have good talks?"

I scrunched my nose and faced the water in front of me. "We'd have to actually talk in order for that to be possible."

That was the saddest part. We used to be close, we used to talk all the time, but that was before I'd pulled away. I had only wanted her to notice me—for her to see me and recognize something was wrong. But she'd chalked it up to repressed anger over losing my father and brushed it all under the rug. Eventually, I'd stopped trying to get her to pay attention and closed myself off from everyone. Then when I'd found out I was pregnant, my mom threw her hands into the air and gave up. And that was pretty much the end of any kind of a relationship between us.

"How's Derek? Everything still *blissfully* amazing?" I needed the topic away from my own personal problems.

"It's good. He got a promotion at work, so next week, we're going to look at bigger apartments." And there was her reason for jumping in the car and driving across the state, as well as her interest in Cash. "We have a few three-bedrooms on the list that are in our budget, but they're all older buildings. Although, we did find some really nice two-bedrooms to check out. If you're free, you should drive over and look with us."

I didn't even bother to face her. "Why would I do that?"

"Just in case living here isn't what you thought it'd be, and you decide to come back."

Waving toward the surf literally in front of us, I asked, "What's not to love?"

"Yeah...so there's this big body of water called the Atlantic Ocean, you might've heard of it. It's on the other coast. You know...where I live. Where you used to live." She turned her head to the left, then to the right, before leaning in close and whispering, "Plus, the water is prettier over there, too."

I shoved her with my shoulder and shook my head, trying to hide the humor tugging at the corners of my lips—not from her words, but her actions. "Did you miss how it took us like ten steps to get here from the house? I've lived my whole life on the other coast, always within fifteen minutes of a beach. Ask me how many times I actually went. Not to mention..." I leaned closer and whispered, "The sand is nicer over here."

Stevie's soft giggles quieted, and the silence worried me. That always meant she had something serious to say—most of the time, something I wasn't interested in hearing. "Doesn't it worry you that he's always gone? Like really, what kind of computer geek works out of the area, sometimes late into the night, five days a week? Not to mention…who just takes a kid out of the house without telling its mother? And then offers to help her with said kid after only being around the child for a day? Admit it, Jade. It's a little odd. How much do you really know about him—*aside* from things he's told you?"

I refused to tell her she was right about a lot of it, or that a few of those questions had crossed my mind, as well. That would only fuel her fire, and I didn't need that right now. "First of all, he's not some computer geek. He works on towers, so he travels. He could work late into the night—or heck, he might be avoiding me. Or maybe he's on the other side of the country so he's three hours behind, and by the time he gets back to the hotel and takes a shower, I'm already asleep."

"It'd be nice if you stopped making excuses for him. The bottom line is this: you don't know him. You're assuming things to justify the actions. I can do the same. He's married and spends the week with his real family, where he has a real job."

"And he spends his weekends with me? Why?"

"Haven't figured that part out yet. But I'm sure I can speculate on the spot if you'd like."

I blew her off and went back to watching Aria play in the waves. "So far, he's been nothing but nice and helpful. He's letting me and my daughter live in his house, free of charge."

"That's another thing. Why would he do that? What's his motive? What does he get out of it?" The thought of drowning her held a certain appeal right about now.

"I don't know, Stevie. Maybe he's a nice guy. He lives in a house with no mortgage, so maybe he saw an opportunity to help a single mother and took it. You gave me a place to stay when I left my mom's and didn't charge me a penny. You helped me with

Aria when I needed it. What was your motivation? Huh? What did you get out of it?"

Her shoulders dropped with her long exhale, and if her eyes weren't hidden behind the dark shades of her sunglasses, I would've seen them soften with pity. "Jade, babe." Her voice lowered to a comforting hum, the same as she always did when trying to talk me off a ledge. "I'm not trying to upset you. I just want you to be aware of what's going on around you. The last thing you need is to fall for this guy, only to find out he's not who you thought he was."

I had to look away from her, unable to handle the emotion in her tone.

"I love you and only want what's best for you. I'm not saying everyone who offers their help has an ulterior motive. Derek and I only tried to get you out of a bad situation so you could stand on your own two feet. And…maybe that's Cash's MO, too. But we don't know that. What we *do* know is next to nothing about him—other than he's gone a lot and apparently has no family."

I didn't want to doubt Cash or think he had some sinister reason behind offering me his spare room. So far, he'd been good to me *and* Aria. He'd had several instances when he could've done something, yet he never did. Sure, we'd shared an alluring touch here and there, although they were probably innocent on his part—my desires not so much—and at least twice he'd been with Aria while I was asleep, yet he cared for her the way I'd dreamed a man would ever since the day she was born.

But then my mind started to drift into the endless pit of doubt, the place I always had a hard time pulling myself from. He'd come home Friday night with fractured ribs, looking like he'd been attacked. His explanation of falling on the job seemed plausible when he explained he worked on towers, but even then, the questions continued to plague me. Now, allowing myself to dissect it all, the uncertainty I naturally planted in *every* situation began to thrive. The more I fed it, the bigger and angrier it got. It grew louder until I'd made up an entire story in my head, one about Cash being a criminal who'd been nice to me so I would trust him, and once I did that, he'd show me his darkness.

"I don't want to talk about this anymore," I mumbled, half to myself and half to Stevie. I needed to face it head-on; my daughter lived in his house for crying out loud. I needed to figure him out before it was too late. But not here, not on the beach or in front of Stevie, because she wouldn't stop until I had my bags packed and loaded in my trunk, following her back across the state.

We soaked up the sun, playing in the ocean a little while longer, then headed inside to wash off the sand and salt. Stevie agreed to stay for dinner, as long as I didn't spend all afternoon cooking, and by six o'clock, she had her arms around me, saying goodbye.

"I'm always here for you, Jade."

My heart melted at her sorrowful tone. "I know."

"I have the best intentions when it comes to you. I miss you like crazy and love you like a sister. There's nothing in this world I wouldn't do for you and your little minion. Please promise me you'll do more research. Not just a criminal background check. He'd only show up in that database if he's been caught doing something. I don't think I need to remind you of how easy it is for someone to get away with doing horrible things."

I took a deep breath and nodded. "I promise."

Aria and I walked her out and waved as she drove off.

The entire time I ran through my nightly routine, my brain wouldn't shut off. While bathing Aria, I thought about why a guy who worked with computers didn't have one in his house. He'd told me he worked with networks, getting them set up and linked together, yet his house was void of one—aside from the internet that only his phone and the TVs were connected to.

While putting her to bed, I dissected his words about his family. He hadn't told me much, so there weren't many things to pick apart, but what he had told me didn't make sense. His grandfather had passed away, but as far as I knew, his parents were still alive. So it baffled me why this house wouldn't have gone to one of them, or even an aunt or uncle. It was paid for, free and clear, in his name for ten or so years, yet he'd only recently moved in. I didn't understand why he hadn't lived here with his wife.

With my head on my pillow, the lights turned off, nothing but the moon highlighting my room, I began to question it all. Everything about it from the very beginning up until this moment, disbelieving every second. And by the time I woke up the next day, I had myself convinced that it was all a scam, that I'd put my daughter in a situation that would scar her for life.

I needed to keep her safe.

I had to leave.

CHAPTER 10

Cash

From the moment I'd touched down on Monday, nothing went the way I'd planned. I was informed during a briefing in the car from the landing strip to the steel box that my job had been completed. Apparently, early Sunday morning, my mark had squealed, sang like a motherfucking canary. I didn't believe it. There was no way he'd given everything up in less than forty-eight hours. Not before I'd gotten to him. Rarely did we get information that soon. So, hearing this one folded while in the presence of the babysitters didn't sit well with me.

"I'm telling you, Cash, we didn't do anything more than we always do on our shifts. He sat in the hotbox"—Kryder had hitched his thumb over his shoulder to the room made of one-way mirrored glass—"with nothing but a saline drip. Same as always."

"Why didn't anyone wait for me to get here? Twenty-four hours…that's all it was."

Kryder just shook his head with his hands propped on his hips while I'd stood there, feeling slighted by my own team. "Listen, man, I don't know what to tell ya. He was ready to talk, and we were there to listen."

"You're not a damn psychologist."

"Quit being a baby, Nicholson." He'd smirked and slapped my arm. "You can take the next one."

"Gee, thanks, fucker. Maybe if you'd quit being an ass-kisser, trying to butter Daddy up to make him love you as much as he loves me, I'd be able to do my job *all* the time." It'd been a joke between us for years, although this time, I'd meant it a little more than usual.

"We all know who his favorite is…and it's not you." Then he'd patted me on the shoulder and headed out, his time in the field done until Friday.

They'd given me the transcripts, as well as the video footage that would be buried once this was over, and let me hide out in one of the control rooms to pore over it all. I'd spent all my time behind that desk, flipping through file after file, reading line by line, every single word of the entire interrogation.

By Tuesday afternoon, Rhett Toll, my direct supervisor, had sent me back to the safe house and ordered me to take a shower and log some sleep before coming back. It wasn't until then that I realized I hadn't spoken to Jade since Sunday night. I'd sent her a text before crashing, only to see her in my dreams. I'd shrugged it off as lack of sleep, undue stress at work, and simply not talking to her like I had since the beginning. And when I'd stepped back into the steel box late Tuesday night, I made it my mission to get the answers I sought so I could go home and let Jade turn me back into a human.

Hearing his confession made me sick, physically. I'd seen blood, more blood than it would take to paint a town red. I'd witnessed death—both innocent and deserved. Not much got to me after nine years on the job. Except him.

But then I'd think of Jade and Aria.

One minute, those images would blend with the ones we had on the vegetable strapped to the chair in the hotbox, and it'd send me straight to the edge of insanity. But in the next minute, I'd close my eyes and picture Jade and Aria, and it calmed the beast within. It saved my soul for one more hour. One more day. The way Jade's blue eyes shone in the sun like a beacon of light brought me peace. The way Aria would giggle so hard she couldn't catch her breath, her hands slapping her knees with her tiny body hunched forward, afforded me comfort. Those were the things that kept me going, that slowed the need for revenge.

THE ROOMMATE disAGREEMENT

I wasn't God. I never even claimed to be working for Him. I wasn't part of some cult who believed they heard His voice call upon them to murder people. I was well aware of where my directives came from, and who had sent down the orders. I knew who hired me and who I answered to. None of which were God or Jesus. They weren't Allah or Buddha, or any other god, for that matter. They were people, like me, who sacrificed their souls to save the innocent. And when it became my time to answer for my sins, I'd tell the guard at the pearly gates the same thing—I did what I felt I had to do in the war on evil.

If I were wrong, then I'd have to answer for it.

But if I were right…then I'd burn in hell with a clear conscience.

I wore the image of the archangel Michael across my back as a reminder that even good had to sometimes wield a sword.

"Everything check out?" Rhett leaned against the doorframe into the control room.

"Yeah." I wiped my eyes, suddenly feeling the exhaustion setting in. I picked up my phone—which was nothing more than a paperweight that kept the time while inside the steel box—and noticed it was nine o'clock on Wednesday night. I'd been at it for close to twenty hours since my last nap and shower.

"I told ya they handled it. You coulda been home most of this week takin' it easy. But *no*." He dragged out the word, shaking his head. "You had to be a stubborn ox and hold up my cleanup crew."

"I just can't wrap my head around him breaking like a twig in a summer breeze. How can we be sure he didn't play us and give us a bunch of shit, feed us nothing but fabricated lies that would lead us away from the scent trail? That's what gets to me the most."

He shrugged and stalked into the room, taking a stance across from me at the desk, his shoulders squared and spine straight. At sixty-five, he was still one scary motherfucker. He'd had two hip replacements, a knee replacement, a shattered elbow he claimed to have healed by rubbing dirt on it, yet he could still kick someone's ass half his age.

"That's somethin' you'll never know. If these men choose to weave tales to end the torment, they'll do it regardless of how long they've been sittin' in the box. Day one, day five...whenever they decide they can't take any more. But that's not your job to worry 'bout. These reports"—he pointed to the stacks in front of me on the desk—"are sent to yet another team who dissects ev'ry word, and then they compare that to the information they have."

He was right. Rhett had been doing this since the beginning of time. We had a standing joke that he had been one of the ones allowed on Moses's ark during the flood. If there was one person in this business to trust, it was him.

I released a sigh of defeat and leaned back in the chair, ignoring the ache that had long since turned the right side of my torso numb. "I just hate it. These jobs consume so much of my time; it's frustrating not to see it to the bitter end."

Rhett scrubbed his bear-like palm down his face. "I get it. Trust me, I do. But if there's any advice I can offer, it's this: Don't let this job define you. Live your life outside this place, love fiercely, and never, *ever*, worry 'bout things that don't concern you. You're given a target, and you get 'im. If he needs a push to confess, handle it. But anything that takes place one minute b'fore your task begins or one minute after you're dismissed is not your problem. Got it?"

I nodded, knowing better than to argue or question him.

"Listen, son. You've done your job, and we all appreciate it. Now go home. Enjoy two extra days off, and for cryin' out loud, take it easy. You'll need the use of that arm come next week." He gestured to the dead weight hanging limply by my side—the wasted limb that was once my arm.

I glanced at it, trying not to notice the loss of muscle mass, and then once again, nodded my response. I still had to make it back to the safe house to take a shower and change my clothes before heading to the landing strip. Then I had about a three-hour flight to Florida. I'd been up since two o'clock Monday morning with roughly six hours of sleep since. I was lucky I wasn't drooling on myself and wondered if it made more sense to sleep off my exhaustion and just head home in the morning. But then Jade crossed my mind, and I decided I needed the simple human connection she offered and wasn't interested in waiting.

Just after two in the morning, I pulled my SUV around the back of the house. Jade didn't expect me home for another two days, so I worried I'd frighten her by going inside. I quickly typed out a text and hit send, giving her a heads-up that I was on my way in. That way, if the alert on her phone woke her, she wouldn't be scared when I opened the door. And if she slept through it, she'd see in the morning that I was there.

The entire way up the back steps, I hoped she'd heard her phone.

Carefully opening and closing the door, I hoped she'd woken up.

Even after my shower, I hoped she'd be awake.

But she wasn't. She'd slept through it all. And even though I'd barely gotten any sleep and had to almost drag my feet with every step, I couldn't manage to succumb to the night. I did nothing but stare at my ceiling, wondering how I'd gotten so dependent on one person in such a short amount of time, but it made sense when I realized she was the only person actively in my life who wasn't privy to the things I'd done.

✤

A screaming child was not the best thing to wake up to. I flung the covers off and threw myself out of bed all too fast. By the time I made it to my bedroom door, I felt like I'd snapped all the ribs on my right side in half. But that didn't stop me. The high-pitched wail lit a fire under my ass, and no amount of pain would keep me from getting to her.

Then I made it to the living room and found Aria on the ground, her little fists pounding against the floor. Jade stood over her, desperately trying to get her to stop. That's when I realized she wasn't in trouble, and the world began to spin again—bringing on the throbbing agony I'd pushed down.

"I'm so sorry, Cash. I was trying to get her out of the house before she woke you."

I took one glance at Jade and offered the most reassuring smile I could, while trying to regain my composure and strength. When I made it to Aria, I waved her mother off and took a seat next to her on the floor, practically falling to my knees at her side. She stopped long enough to turn her head, find me there, and then launched herself into my unsuspecting arms.

The world quieted, and there was no such thing as pain. Darkness didn't exist and evil was an urban legend. I had no idea what I'd done to deserve this, but I wished I did…so I could do it over and over again.

"I'm so sorry. I made the mistake of telling her to be quiet because you were asleep. I guess all she heard was that you were home, and she made it her personal mission to get to you. So I thought if I could get her out of the house, you would be able to sleep in, and that's when she decided to throw a tantrum." Jade knelt down behind Aria, facing me, and attempted to pull her daughter out of my arms.

I shook my head, showing her it was okay. She made a face, one I could've probably read had I not been so lost in the tiny arms of the angel in my lap. But rather than analyze her furrowed brows and constricting pupils, I held onto the trembling child until she calmed.

"Where were you going to go?" I took note of her purse on the floor next to the door.

"Oh, um…we need groceries." She shifted her gaze toward the door, not looking at me when she answered. She didn't need to admit it was a lie, because her reaction did it for her.

However, I also wasn't going to call her out on it. I figured if she wasn't comfortable enough to tell me the truth, I'd make it incredibly hard for her to keep up the charade. Fully aware she wouldn't agree to leaving Aria at home with me when she went to the store, I gave her the only option I had left. "Give me a couple of minutes to clean up and change, and I'll go with you."

"No, you don't have to. You got in late. I'm sure the last thing you want to do is walk up and down aisles looking at food with us. Not to mention, Aria can be a handful in the store. Really, it's fine. I can handle it." Something was off, and if I had to compare nutrition labels all morning to discover what it was, then so be it.

"I don't mind at all. It's clear my sidekick missed me, so it'll just be easier if I go, too."

The corner of Jade's mouth curled ever so slightly. Her eyes brightened and dropped to her child, who still had her arms wound around my neck. "Your sidekick?"

"Yeah, but don't get jealous. She still loves you."

"Okay, fine. But hurry. I'd like to be back before lunch." She grabbed Aria's arm and said, "Sweetheart, you're going to have to let him go so he can get dressed if you want him to come with us." That was all it took to get Aria off me, her face so expressive with excitement.

I'd never understand how going shopping with her translated into such enthusiasm.

Fifteen minutes later, I was dressed with my hair combed and teeth brushed. Jade tried to put up a fight when I suggested moving Aria's car seat to the Range Rover, but when I pointed out how much easier it would be to haul groceries in the trunk of my car versus hers, she caved.

"Why are you back so early?" Jade casually asked, while comparing prices of two different kinds of sandwich meats. She'd kept her distance all morning. No matter how many times I'd tried to engage her in conversation, she seemed too lost in her own thoughts to offer much more than distracted answers. Even now, she appeared more interested in the boxes and cans of food on the shelves than she did talking to me.

I leaned against the handrail of the cart with my elbows, bending down to Aria's level, who sat in the kid seat. If Jade didn't have any interest in asking more than a random question here and there—usually about a brand or price—at least I could count on the little tyke to entertain me. I wasn't positive, but I believed my taking her to the beach had solidified our bond.

"There wasn't much I could do with fractured ribs, so I went over paperwork for three days until they told me to go home." I grabbed the package of string cheese off the hook that Aria had pointed out and tossed it into the cart when Jade wasn't looking, earning me a toothy grin from the little girl.

Jade shopped and I pushed the cart behind her, entertaining Aria by grabbing junk off the shelves and adding it to the pile we had going behind her. All the while, Jade was none the wiser. Maybe if she'd paid us as much attention as she did the slices of American cheese, she'd realize we had far more in the buggy than she had on her last-minute list.

"And you couldn't get home before two in the morning?" Again, she spoke while focusing on a label.

"I'm not a pilot, Jade. Nor do I have my own, personal jet. I can't control when the flights leave and take off, and I don't have any say in layovers." My tone was clipped, sounding like I was annoyed with her interrogation. In truth, I was lying out of my ass, but she didn't know any different.

"So who did your job when you were sitting at your desk?"

"The rest of the crew."

"I thought you said you work in isolation."

I made a face at Aria and made her giggle, not bothering to rush into an explanation when it felt as though she would question me if I told her the sky was blue. "That doesn't mean I'm the only employee, Jade," I deadpanned. "How'd your visit with Stevie go?"

"It was nice. We spent the afternoon on the beach." That translated into Jade wearing a bathing suit, and I couldn't help but conjure an image of what that would look like. Oddly enough, my imagination wasn't centered around her breasts or ass. Instead, I wondered if she'd worn a one- or two-piece suit, which then led to a mental debate over what her stomach looked like.

I blamed it on staring at Aria. Normally, a woman's stomach wasn't even close to the top of the list as far as a female's body was concerned. I was more of an ass man, but of course, I appreciated every curve of the female form. But knowing she'd carried life inside her, it made me ponder if there'd been any evidence left behind. And what was even stranger, was that I found it fascinating—the child whose eyes lit up when I grabbed a bag of cookies and tossed it into the cart had been created inside someone. Not just *someone*, but Jade. And that there was a possibility of seeing proof of that on her skin.

"She's looking at bigger apartments next week." That grabbed my attention. "She asked me to go looking at them with her."

"Oh, yeah?" I wasn't sure what to say.

My heart began to beat inside my throat at the idea of Jade leaving—and taking Aria with her. I had no claim over either of them. Jade and I weren't romantically involved, and I liked it that way. Not to mention, Aria wasn't my child. They'd lived in my house for less than two weeks, and I'd spent a total of two days with them there, but with the way I felt last night when Rhett had told me to leave and take a couple of extra days off, I couldn't imagine leaving the job with no one to come home to. Without their presence, nothing would make me feel human and balance out the scale of good and evil.

"So…are you going to?" I could barely breathe while waiting for her answer.

She shrugged, grabbed a loaf of bread, and placed it gently on top of the stack of food. Clearly, she was distracted; otherwise, she would've noticed the box of Ding Dongs and container of yogurt—as well as the plethora of other crap I'd added along the way. "I don't see why not. I just sit at the house all by myself anyway, so what's the harm in driving over and spending the day with my best friend?"

I couldn't object to her point, but I knew there was more to it, which was what I had the issue with. "Is this your way of opening the door to a discussion about you leaving? Stevie gets a bigger place, so now there's room for you and Aria to stay without sleeping on the couch?"

Even with her back to me, I could read her. I didn't need to see her expression. The way her feet faltered just enough to take an uneven step, coupled with the slight jerking motion in her shoulders, told me I was right. And no matter what she said, her fluctuating tone shined a light on the truth in her words. "I don't know. We haven't discussed it."

"You mean you and I haven't…or you and Stevie haven't?"

"I'd say we're discussing it now. But other than Stevie saying I'm always welcome, nothing else has been mentioned. No plans or even a conversation about *making* plans." Again, her voice swung throughout her words, dipping low before lilting high like a roller coaster of deceit.

"Well, I disagree. I wouldn't consider this a conversation about it at all. I'd call this you laying your cards out on the table so that when I come home and you're gone, your shit absent from your rooms, you can say you told me about it."

Jade stopped in the middle of the baby aisle. She turned on her heel so fast her dark curls whipped around like the wind had blown through the store and whirled around her. "If this is going to be an argument, can we hold off until we're back at the house? That way, I can put Aria in the sandbox out back so she's not subjected to your language."

So, the only way to get Jade to show her balls was when it came to protecting her child. I couldn't complain. That definitely should've been the time to grow a pair—for any parent—but it'd be a lie if I said I didn't wish she'd learn how to defend herself, as well.

Rather than respond, I glanced to the side at the wall of diapers. I assumed Jade had turned down this aisle because she needed a box, but before she could grab one, I'd halted her purpose. I tipped my chin toward a package of training pants and asked, "How's the potty training going?"

With a roll of her eyes, she turned her back to me again, pulled the cheapest box of regular diapers off the shelf, and slid it onto the rack on the bottom of the cart. "Not good. I didn't start it last week because there was so much going on, so I figured I'd wait until this week. But she spent all day Monday throwing temper tantrums, and then Stevie was here yesterday. Needless to say, it hasn't worked in my favor quite yet."

I tilted my head and made a goofy face at Aria until she giggled. "You don't wanna go pee-pee in the big-girl potty?"

"I not sit in ocean." This kid had impeccable timing. "I sit in diaper."

I couldn't help but laugh at her inability to pronounce certain letters.

"No, sweetheart," Jade piped in. "You sit on the potty chair."

Aria shook her head, her baby curls brushing along her cheeks with every movement. "Cash say I wear diaper so I not sit in ocean."

"Oh, look…Goldfish." I pushed the cart before Jade figured out what her kid was saying, and ultimately, where she'd picked it up from. I grabbed six—or ten—bags of the fish-shaped cheese snacks and filled the cart, basically using my arm to sweep them into the almost overfilled basket. "I think that's it. Time to go."

"If you think this won't be added to our discussion when we get home, you're sadly mistaken," was all she said as she followed behind me to the checkout stands.

When there was enough room to start unloading everything onto the belt, I handed Jade the keys to the car and asked her to start the engine so the interior could begin cooling down. At first, she tried to fight me, using our agreement against me by pointing out the groceries were her responsibility. But I didn't back down—if she saw the amount of shit I'd added, she'd put it all back, and that would not make the pint-sized princess happy. Giving me a wary, side-eyed look, she snatched the keys and headed outside.

The ride back to the house was spent in complete silence, Jade staring out the passenger-side window while I drove less than three miles home. It was awkward to say the least, but more because of the reasons why we lacked conversation. Jade had something on her mind, but until she was ready to open up about it, there was nothing I could do. Sure, I could spend the time around her trying to read her body language, yet that wouldn't prove anything more than I'd already learned. I'd been trained to detect when someone was lying, telling the truth, keeping something, scared, anxious—every emotion known to man. The one thing I couldn't do: read minds.

"Did you seriously buy all this crap?" Jade's voice stopped me when I came back into the kitchen after taking Aria to the back yard to play in the sand. She was angry, that much was apparent by her harsh tone, then it was reiterated with her waving hand in the direction of the counter where bags of food lined almost every available inch.

"Aria wanted it," I answered, adding a nonchalant shrug for good measure.

"Seriously? She asks for everything. One time, she begged for an entire gumball machine. Do you plan to buy her one of those, too?"

It was obvious her anger wasn't about the groceries or my reasons for buying what I did. It was directed at me, meant for me, but about something else entirely. "Aside from a few things, most of what she asked for was decently healthy. I didn't see the problem."

"That's your go-to excuse when it comes to *my* child."

"Is that what this is really about?" I leaned against the counter with my hand, my arm extended in an effort to trap her. I refused to let her leave or distract herself with putting the food away. "If you're pissed off over my decision to buy snacks and shit for Aria without running it past you first, then fine. I'd be happy to talk about that. I'd love to hear the boundaries I'm allowed to stay inside in regard to *your* kid. Lord knows I've fucked that up enough in the last week. If you have some special diet of hotdogs and French fries for her, please tell me. If you have a problem with me making *any* decisions when it comes to her, such as feeding her lunch or giving her a goddamn napkin to use to clean her hands, then tell me. I'm fully aware you're the parent, and I won't argue about your rules or go behind your back. I won't push your limits or pressure you into things you aren't comfortable with where it concerns Aria and me. But I don't think this has anything to do with a container of strawberries or a pack of pudding."

She kept her mouth clamped so tightly, the muscles in her jaw ticced. Her pupils shrunk to the size of pinpricks—and she might as well have "pricked" me with them, given the amount of sheer rage that shot from her electric-blue eyes.

"Then what's this about, Cash?"

"I don't know," I said, almost whispering, bringing my head closer to hers. "Why don't *you* tell *me*. You're the one who's been either looking for a fight all morning or trying to get away from me. I don't have a clue what happened between the time I woke up Monday and now, but I'd really love to find out."

Jade pulled her lower lip into her mouth and scraped her top teeth along it until it popped back out. With a dramatic exhale, she blinked up at me and said, "Nothing happened."

"Then tell me why you're okay with me pushing the cart at the store while your kid sits up front, but you suddenly got your panties in a wad over a few extra things I picked up for her. I'm trying to understand here, Jade. I really am. The last thing I want is to cross the line with you. I've already told you that I understand the roles and respect any decision you make about Aria. You're the mom. But I'm having a hard time figuring out what I can and can't do, because *everything* I do is wrong."

"Then maybe it's a good thing that Stevie is getting a bigger place."

"Why? So you can move back? Because I'm so hard to deal with two days a week?" I didn't care to fight with her. I would've much rather had this conversation on the couch using normal voices without the heated frustration between us. But it didn't seem to be an option at the moment.

"It's just hard living with someone who doesn't know anything about kids. You've been around her for two days, and she's already repeating what you say. And it's not about *what* you bought, it's the principle. You can't give her everything she asks for, unless you're trying to spoil her and prevent her from understanding the word no. Do you have any idea the predicament you just put me in with her? You're the good guy. I'm the bad one. I have no income, so I can't afford pudding and Jell-O. I'll tell you what you did...next time we go to the store, she's going to ask for something, and I'm going to have to tell her she can't have it. Then she'll cry for you for days because she knows Cash will get it for her. She'll eventually spend all week begging for you instead of me."

In an instant, I shifted away from my position against the counter and stepped into her personal space, taking her face in my hands and forcing her to look at me. God, the hint of tears in her eyes gutted me. "She'll always love you because you're her mom. When she's hurt, she'll cry for you. When she's scared, it'll be you she seeks for comfort. No one's going to replace you. Not me, not Stevie, not the next guy or roommate. No one. Got it?"

She nodded as best as she could with the way I held onto her.

I swiped away the stray tear from her cheek with my thumb, grazing her soft skin. "But if you prefer I not buy her things, then I won't. Just please, give me rules, lay out the guidelines so I can navigate this better. Show me the boundaries before calling it quits and leaving."

Her eyelids fell closed with a slight tremble in her lips. "I don't care if you buy things for her. It's your money—I can't tell you how to spend it. I'm just worried, okay?" She blinked up at me and locked her gaze onto mine. "I want to protect her, but I can't. I don't have the means to do what's best for her, and that scares me."

"What do you mean, Jade? Protect her from what?" My stomach dipped at the possibility of it being a "who," not a "what," and then it twisted into tight knots at the thought of her saying me.

She wrapped her thin fingers around my wrists, pulled out of my touch, and stepped away until her back hit the counter behind her. "I can't talk about this right now."

I tightened my hands into fists, desperately holding onto what I feared was slipping through my fingers. My only saving grace was the fact I'd been sent home early, which had given me more time with her—to either convince her to stay, or to cherish what I had in the hopes it would get me through a little while longer. I had no idea what I'd do after the memories expired, but I refused to think about that, because I wasn't ready to give up just yet.

Living with someone else always came with an adjustment period. Hell, moving in with Colleen had felt like the worst idea ever at first. But once you start figuring each other out, it could be the best thing in the world. Having someone there, even in a cocoon of silence, was something most took for granted. I never did, because I knew the darkness that existed without the presence of another person. We weren't made for isolation. We weren't designed to live alone and spend our lives without constant companionship. There was a reason for emotions such as happiness and love and serenity, and it wasn't a coincidence that those came wrapped in a package of flesh and a beating heart. It was a gift. And only the truest form of such emotions was given to us by others, not things. Not money. Not houses or cars or jewels. Be it a pet, a friend, a lover, a child, or a stranger...it was always another living thing that offered them.

And I wouldn't survive if she took that away.

CHAPTER 11

Jade

Cash had left while I unpacked the sacks from the grocery store. I hadn't meant to make him run off—I only needed a little space to think—but he didn't hesitate before grabbing his keys off the counter and driving away. Had I thought about it, I would've grabbed Aria's seat from his car, but that had been the last thing on my mind.

Until I tried to leave.

I didn't have anywhere in particular to go, considering I hadn't spent much time exploring the island. I just needed to get out of the house. Being there without Cash while he was away at work was one thing, but the stagnant silence that lingered in his abrupt absence after an emotional dispute was something else entirely. Sitting around and waiting for him to come back was torturous.

I'd contemplated shooting him a text, asking where he was and when he planned to return, but I figured that'd only make things worse. I'd prepared myself to use the car seat as an excuse, yet after his reaction to the possibility that I might move back home, there was no doubt that would solidify my decision in his mind—even though I hadn't made one yet. I still had a lot to think about. One of those things was how simply being around him in person lessened the doubt I had about him.

So after I fed Aria lunch, I decided to head across the street to the beach. She needed a nap, and by pushing it back, I ran the risk of having a very cranky toddler on my hands, but I refused to sit around while she slept. I had picked my battle.

Even though Aria was sleepy, it didn't stop her from hitting the waves hard. And by the time we made it back to the house, she was completely depleted of energy. It was all I could do to rinse her off and change her clothes before laying her down. Other than asking about Cash once or twice, she hadn't brought him up or pitched a fit about him not being there, which was a slight miracle. I should've worried about her attachment to him, especially since it happened so quickly, but I couldn't find it in me to feel anything less than blessed that she'd found someone to love. And at least from what I could tell, he was just as fond of her as she was of him.

Thinking back to this morning when she threw herself into his arms, and the way he cradled her to his chest like she was the most precious thing in the world, my heart warmed and grew. It took extreme mental effort to remember where my head was at less than twenty-four hours ago. I had to remind myself of the doubts and questions I'd pondered while going to sleep last night. Part of me thought to make a list so I wouldn't be able to forget and fall victim to his deception. Yet, another part of me turned that doubt onto myself, wondering if maybe I'd simply painted my own picture of Cash and his intentions just to see what I wanted to. Because if I used my eyes, I saw a decent man with the purest of intentions. If I used my heart, he was kind and giving, asking nothing of me but my company and very little time. Although, if I used my head, things became a jumbled mess until I had no idea what I was looking at.

While Aria napped, I ran a load of laundry, prepared dinner, and exchanged texts with Stevie. I'd told her about this morning, about Cash coming home early, fully aware she wouldn't play devil's advocate. But that was the problem with not having many friends in your life—your options of people to turn to when you needed unbiased advice were limited. It was always good to hear arguments from both sides, so only getting one opinion made things more difficult. Yet I trusted Stevie—she didn't have an ulterior motive when discussing Cash—so I felt confident she'd given me the most solid advice she could.

THE ROOMMATE disAGREEMENT

I had a stack of clean clothes on the couch with my phone flipped open on the coffee table when the back door opened and Cash came in. He carried one brown bag by the handle, certainly not enough to have kept him out most of the day. Rather than offering a greeting, he took one look at me, set the bag down by the door, and headed into his room. And that's where he stayed for close to ten minutes.

After taking my folded clothes to my room and putting them away, I came back to a text, asking me if Aria was awake and if I had time to talk. I quickly typed out my reply, my eyes dancing between the screen and his bedroom to keep an eye on his whereabouts, and then I pressed send.

> **Me**: He's in his room, but the door is open, so he might hear me. I have no idea what he's doing in there. He came home and has been in there ever since.

While I sat on the couch, I kept my eyes glued to his open door until another text came through. It was odd, not making sense. I read it again before noticing the name of the sender.

> **Cash**: If you're talking about him, maybe he has a right to hear what you're saying.

I felt sick to my stomach after going back to the last text, asking if I had time to talk, and realized it hadn't been from Stevie. Had I taken one second or paid just a bit more attention, I would've seen his name, and could have kept myself from sticking my foot in my mouth.

Rather than wait for him to come to me, I pulled myself off the couch and slowly approached his room, where I found him sitting on the side of the bed, hunched forward with his head in his hands. I carefully made my way to him and took a seat on the mattress by his side. Not once did he look up or drop his hands.

"Did you think you were texting Stevie?" His voice was so low it resembled gravel being raked across pavement.

"Yeah. We were texting, so I didn't pay attention to the name."

"When I asked you earlier about moving back, you said you hadn't discussed it with her. Was that a lie?" He turned his head to the side to regard me. "Tell me the truth, Jade. I think I deserve that at this point. If you're planning on leaving, I have a right to know."

And he did. He'd spent so much time and money turning the back bedrooms into what they were for Aria and me. The detail that had gone into her room alone was enough to make me feel like a horrible person for even contemplating going back.

"You're right, and I'm sorry. You paid a lot of money for furniture and a decorator—"

"Stop." He finally dropped his hands and pressed them into the mattress on either side of his hips, straightening his spine and squaring his shoulders. The muscles in his arms bulged and strained against the sleeves of his shirt. "This isn't about the money. Forget about that. Just tell me what I've done to push you away. *Something* happened, Jade. We were fine Sunday night, but for some reason, when I woke up this morning, it was like you already had your bags packed. I'm willing to bet that had I not come back early, I would've walked into an empty house."

This had been easier when I planned it in my head. When you avoid confrontation, it makes dealing with things so much harder. But I'd managed to get myself here, and he was right—he deserved an explanation. "I haven't made up my mind yet. So it wasn't a complete lie. I've just been thinking about a lot of things and how some of what you've told me just doesn't add up."

He grabbed my hand and held it on the bed between us, the heat from his palm soaking into my skin. When my gaze found his pleading eyes, I couldn't look away. It made everything hit me harder when he said, "Then talk to me about it. I have no idea what you've discussed with Stevie or anyone else, so I don't have a clue what they've told you. But something has you ready to run for the hills, and all I'm asking for is a chance to possibly offer you some clarification. Maybe I can help you add it up so you stop looking at me like I'm going to hurt you."

I had to turn away, unable to hold his gaze and confess the ridiculous reasons that led me to question him. "Yes, I've talked to Stevie about it. When she came over yesterday, she asked me what your motivation was to let me live here rent free. I couldn't answer her because I don't know. When she suggested I look online to make sure what you've told me hasn't been a bunch of lies, I started to think about my inability to do so. Then I began to question why a network engineer wouldn't have a computer in his home. It gave me some doubts."

He withdrew his hand and leaned toward his nightstand without saying a word. After opening the doors on the bottom, he pulled out a laptop with a hard, black case covering the top and bottom. And I immediately felt like a moron.

"You've never asked or made any comments about needing to use one, so I never thought to tell you about it. But here you go." He held it out for me and waited until I took it, until I cradled it in my lap while staring at the image of an apple on the center of the lid. "I keep it right there, but you're more than welcome to use it. The power cord is in there, too."

"I'm sorry," I whispered, not sure what else to say.

"No need to apologize. But there's no way you got yourself this worked up over a computer. There's got to be more. Don't stop now; keep going. Anything you've questioned or Stevie has brought up, ask. If I can, I'd love nothing more than to clear the air now, rather than drag this out and chance you packing up and leaving."

He was right. And the more I held back, the longer the doubt would linger. "You've told me what you do, but I have no idea what company you work for. When you're gone, I call you on your cell because you work in the field, but is there a main number to the office? *Is* there even an office?"

"It's called WireComm—wireless communications. And yes, there's an office with people who answer phones." He stood, walked to his closet, and disappeared inside for a moment before returning with a business card. "That's the number. If you call, they'll either dispatch it to my cell or take a message, to which they just send me a text. That's why I never give out the main number, because it's no different than calling me directly."

I pinched the card between my fingers and held it in front of me, pretending to read the words printed on the front. Really, I didn't care what it said. I'd convinced myself he'd lied about his job, and this just proved me wrong.

"Go ahead, call the number and ask for me."

"I don't need to, Cash."

"Jade…" He angled his body toward me and dipped his chin, bringing his eyes level with mine. "You've already told me you question if what I've said is the truth or not. And you and I both know there's no way to truly prove I'm not lying unless you do more than just believe the words I say. So please, call the number and ask for me."

I set the computer down behind me on the mattress and flipped open my phone. The call rang in my ear twice before a woman answered. "WireComm, how may I direct your call?"

Peering into the midnight eyes next to me, I said, "Cash Nicholson, please."

The sound of her typing on a keyboard filled the line. "I'm sorry, he's off duty right now. If you'd like, I could take a message."

"Oh, it's more of a personal call. He, uh…he owes me money." I sucked at lying on the spot.

Overhearing the conversation, Cash closed his eyes and shook his head with a smirk tugging at his lips.

"I can send you through to his voicemail if you'd like?"

"Please. That'd be great." I made sure to stop talking before doing any more damage.

A few beeps resounded seconds before his screen lit up in his hand. It rang in my ear as well as in the room. I disconnected the call, satisfied at the uncertainty of his job being cleared up. While I sat there with my phone in my hand, he waited me out patiently, sensing there was more I needed to say or ask.

I bit my lip, steadied my focus on the corner of the baseboard leading into his bathroom, and took a breath. "Do you talk to your parents? Like…are you close with them?"

"Of course. I mean, I'm as close to them as I can be with them living in another state and me being gone so much. We talk, though. And I see them every Christmas. What would you like to know about them?"

This just seemed silly and made me look paranoid. And unless I planned to call all his relatives to verify what he told me, there was no use in bringing it up. "Nothing. It doesn't matter." I didn't even get my rear end to the edge of the mattress when he carefully halted my movement with a gentle hand around my upper arm.

"It *does* matter, Jade. Whatever you're thinking, it means something to you. I have no problem answering any questions you have about my job or my family or how I grew up. Don't be embarrassed or worried about how it'll sound." He must've noticed the burning in my cheeks, and I wished I could've blamed it on the sun.

Realizing I needed to get this over with, my posture slumped with a rushed sigh, and I closed my eyes, bracing myself to just lay it all out there for him. "I just never hear you talk about them other than in stories about when you were younger, and it caused me to question things." It suddenly dawned on me that I was a hypocrite, considering I never talked about mine, either. "Plus, you said you're lonely, so I guess that made me think you were estranged from your family, which led me to wonder why."

"That makes sense, and I can see why you felt that way. But my parents still live in Georgia, and I'm all the way down here. It's not like I can just stop over at their house for dinner. They call when they have something to tell me, and I do the same, but my dad's not the kind of guy who likes to talk on the phone, and my mom stays busy in her community."

"Then I guess my question would be…when you left your wife, why didn't you move closer to them? Why here where you don't have anyone, instead of with your family who could help you through the divorce?"

"Because I had this house already, so there was no point in getting another one. And I wasn't about to move in *with* my parents at my age. I love them and all, but I've been on my own for the last twelve years. It'd be one thing if I *needed* their help, but I didn't."

God, I both loved and hated how all his answers made sense.

"That brings me to this house." I glanced around his room, avoiding him completely. "Why'd your grandfather give it to you, and why didn't you ever live here when you were married?"

"Well, I used to spend summers with him here when I was a kid, so I assume that's why he chose me. But honestly, I have no idea why he had his will the way he did. I was informed about it by my dad, who was the executor of the estate. No one had any gripes about me taking it, so I did. As for why I didn't live here when I was married…I was twenty-one when I was given the deed to this house. I'd just started my job and traveled a lot. The house is old, and it hadn't been taken care of very well in Granddad's later years, so it needed a lot of work. I didn't have the time to put into it, nor did I have the money. The property taxes were about all I could afford that first year.

"I'd met Colleen when I was twenty-two, and married her a year later. She already owned a home, and when I mentioned this place, she said she had no desire to relocate. She had friends in town, and if we came here, she wouldn't have anyone—plus, she'd have to spend a lot of time updating the place. She wasn't interested in it, and we never spoke about it again. So I moved in with her and continued to let this house sit empty."

"When did you fix it up?"

He drew my attention when he shifted on the bed, turning his entire body to face me with his leg pulled up between us, his foot hanging off the edge of the mattress. "Over the years, I'd do things here and there, but nothing major since no one ever stayed here. It started after someone had vandalized the outside. They used spray paint on the walls and smashed the front window. Obviously, I had to get that taken care of, and then after repainting the outside and replacing all the doors and windows, I just kept it up—one thing at a time. There was a leak in the ceiling in the back bedroom, so I had to get a new roof. The carpets smelled because the electricity had been off for so long that the moisture in the house from the humidity soaked into them, so I ripped it up and put down wood. After that, I couldn't leave it empty without running the air conditioner, so I replaced that."

"And your wife had no clue where all this money was going?"

It was his turn to drop his gaze, but I wasn't sure if it was because of embarrassment or a need to contemplate his answer. But while he studied the fabric of his comforter, he said, "Before we got married, but after I'd proposed, I learned of her spending habits. She'd accumulated quite a bit of debt and had several maxed-out credit cards. She lived well above her means. I spoke to my parents about it, because they'd raised me to be financially conscious, and they suggested I protect my assets. It wasn't that I believed we'd get divorced and sought to keep her from gaining anything. My worry was that she'd blow through my savings, and I'd be left scrambling to pick up the pieces. At that time, I was making decent money, but not enough to last too long if she had unlimited access to it. And as far as this house, my dad was concerned a bank could put a lien on it because of marital property."

"So what'd you do?" I found myself enthralled with his every word.

"My mom opened a bank account in her name and gave me access to it. Colleen never pushed the issue to open a joint checking or savings account, just asked that I made sure the bills were paid. So I paid her mortgage, car loan, and all the other household bills, which let her keep every paycheck she earned to do with as she pleased. I put this house in my dad's name after having a lawyer draw up a contract that would protect us both."

"That's a lot of hoops to jump through to keep things from the woman you planned to marry and spend the rest of your life with." Out of everything he'd told me, that was the one thing that left a sour taste in my mouth. If he was willing to be so deceitful to the person he claimed to love, I couldn't imagine the lengths he'd go to so he could lie to me, someone he barely knew.

"I have really good instincts about people, but back then, I think I was just learning how to listen to them. Now, I can look back and see the writing on the wall, but at the time, I was young and in love. I refused to believe she would hurt me. It'd been my parents' persuasion that made me do all those things in the first place. Trust me...I fought them. In my mind, I was only worried about the money I'd been saving for years, not caring to have that wasted on shoes Colleen didn't need, or her purse collection that she kept in the corner of her closet. They convinced me to do it, saying we could reverse it at any time, but that they felt it was needed for at least the first two years. That's the only reason I agreed."

"But you never changed it?"

He shook his head and sucked in a full inhalation before relaxing his shoulders again. "Nah. I'd gotten used to the way things were and never really thought about it again. It wasn't like I needed to have my name on all those things, and Colleen had no idea they even existed."

"So this house is still in your dad's name?" When he nodded, something hit me that I hadn't thought about before. "You said he's full Italian. So where did Nicholson come from? That doesn't sound like a very Italian name."

A slow smile stretched across his chiseled face, bringing my attention to the shadow of scruff he'd yet to shave. "My dad was adopted." His answer almost made me roll my eyes, but I refrained in lieu of hearing him out. "His biological parents were both really young—I don't remember how old they were, though. Anyway, they had to go back to Italy to deal with a family emergency, but they couldn't take their baby with them. I was told their families didn't know they had a baby, and for whatever reason, they couldn't tell them. So they decided to leave my dad, who was only a few months old, with an older couple who lived next door until they came back. But they never returned, so the neighbors ended up adopting him."

As much as I wished I could pick apart the story and find holes, reassuring me it was a lie, that was hard to do. So I just sat there and nodded slowly, letting it all sink in. He must've sensed my hesitation, because he pushed himself off the mattress, walked around me to the dresser against the wall across from the bed, and grabbed a framed photo from the corner. When he handed it to me, I realized I could try to pick his words apart until the end of time, but I wouldn't find any holes.

Behind the glass sat a picture of an older man with green eyes so bright they reminded me of grass in the spring, just coming back to life after a dry winter. His skin was light and his hair a copper color. To the side, slightly in front of him, stood another man, younger than the first. His short, black hair was combed to the side with an off-center part, reminding me very much of Cash's, just worn in a different style. His eyes squinted with his infectious grin, making it appear that the image had been snapped mid-laugh. So much about this man, from his olive skin color to his muscular build resembled Cash, who I assumed was the child in the photo, standing in front of both men. They all looked happy, and I could tell they were a family, even though it was obvious the eldest didn't share the same blood.

I handed it back to him with a smile.

After returning the frame to its original place, he ran his finger along the edge and came back to sit next to me, facing me. "What other concerns or doubts do you have?"

I was amazed at how much of an open book he was, considering he'd always come across so closed off—guarded. He'd given me opportunities to ask questions before, and even though I had, I'd never expected him to be so willing to offer such personal information. Then again, that wasn't his fault. It was mine for assuming.

With only one question left weighing on my mind, I opened my mouth and asked, "Why did you offer to let me live here?" I held out my hand to stop him from responding before I could clarify my question. "I understand you were looking for a roommate and the rent check wasn't important to you, but why *me*? You were aware I didn't have a job, no income, and I'd be bringing along a two-year-old. Good deeds aside, you had to have some motivation behind your decision. Anyone else would've walked out of that restaurant, but you didn't, and for the life of me, I can't figure out a reasonable explanation that doesn't make you look either pathetic or criminal."

Cash dropped his chin close to his chest. At first, I thought it was to shield me from seeing the truth in his eyes, but when his shoulders began to bounce and he lifted his head to reward me with the same squinty eyes as the man in the photo, I recognized the humor he'd found in my question.

"I must be pathetic because I'm not a criminal." His laughter slowed when I couldn't bring myself to join him.

"I'm being serious, Cash."

"So am I, Jade." He swallowed so harshly his Adam's apple bobbed in his throat, his gaze now set to the open doorway leading out to the empty living room. I wasn't sure if he was looking at something or staring off into the distance, but I could tell by the way his eyes softened, whatever ran through his mind wasn't a joke. "In all honesty, I enjoyed our conversations and found you incredibly easy to talk to, which was exactly what I was looking for in a roommate. I thought you were funny and you made me laugh."

"So you're saying you only offered me a room because I made you laugh?"

"That...*and* I found myself looking forward to your calls and texts. That's when I realized, lies or not, I was interested in seeing it through. And somehow, during that month we talked on the phone, I guess I started seeing you as a friend. You were literally the perfect roommate. But before I moved forward, I had to see your face."

"Why? To make sure I wasn't an ogre?"

He shook his head, lips pulled wide in a contagious smile. "No. Honestly, I was hoping you were." He must've sensed the question burning the tip of my tongue, because he continued to explain. "Considering I was only looking for a friend, someone to talk to and spend the weekends with, it would've been a deal-breaker if I found that person sexually attractive."

"Oh..." I whispered, the wind in my sails falling flat.

He placed his warm palm over my hand and met my stare. "That came out wrong. To me, personally, there's a big difference between a beautiful woman and someone I'm *physically* attracted to. With that being said, I find lots of women good looking, ones I would even testify in court as being drop-dead gorgeous, yet I don't have any desire to be with them romantically—or physically. That's all I was trying to say."

Which translated into "I don't ever think about you naked."

"No, I totally get it. You went looking for a roommate, not a bed buddy. Sex complicates everything, so it makes complete sense." I tried my best to shove down the insecurities and ignore the bruise to my self-esteem. He hadn't said I was ugly, just that he'd never have sex with me—because he had no desire to. "Trust me, I'm the one who had a baby at twenty and now has to care for her all alone. So you don't have to explain anything to me."

His eyes shifted between mine as though he tried to read my mind. He did say he was good at reading people, so I only hoped I had been convincing enough. The last thing I wanted to do was make him think I felt rejected, because that would mean I'd thought about sleeping with him.

"Okay...so you met me and realized there was nothing to worry about on that front. But then I told you about Aria and how I didn't have a job. And still, you offered me a place to stay. Why? Why open your home to a woman who admittedly lied about several things? Someone you had no ties to, no obligations to help? A single mother with no income. I don't understand your motivation."

"You needed a place to stay, Jade," he said quietly, holding my stare as if his answer was the most obvious and I was blind to have not seen it. "You and your baby were sleeping on a couch. You had to pee in a sink—and not just any sink, but in the kitchen, where I'm sure you had no privacy. You needed a room, and I needed a roommate."

I licked my lips and hesitated, needing the answer to one final question. "Then why are you so against me moving back? If Stevie got a bigger place, I wouldn't be in the same situation. So really, you shouldn't have any reason to want me to stay...but you do. What is it?"

His gaze swung once again to the open doorway, but rather than stare off into the distance, he blinked and allowed his posture to practically melt. His smooth forehead relaxed until not one muscle in his entire face strained, betraying the sorrow that danced in his eyes.

"I can't imagine being here every weekend without Aria."

CHAPTER 12

Cash

She gasped and pulled her hand away to cover her mouth with her fingertips.

I hadn't meant to say it. I'd tried to make it about her, to say I couldn't imagine being home on the weekends without *her* here. But as I allowed myself to picture what it would be like if she left and took Aria with her, my mouth opened and the truth came tumbling out.

"I don't understand." Jade's voice was so soft it was almost inaudible, and when I looked at her to get a better understanding of where she was emotionally, confusion and worry marred her expression.

"She's like this living, breathing example of all that's good in life. She's not ruined by reality yet. To her, there's no such thing as evil, and I can feel that when she's around. It makes me wish I could live in her world, the magical place she sees when she opens her eyes. A world where a box of sand is exciting. Where everyone you pass smiles at you, or goes out of their way to make you laugh. What I wouldn't give to live through her eyes and fall in love every ten seconds with something new."

"That's a nice fantasy, but that's not the reality."

I couldn't respond without laying it all out there. Jade had no idea of the world I lived in, the things I had to do to protect kids like Aria. Having her around reminded me that I had a purpose, and at the end of the day, people like me needed angels like her around. We needed to know who we were fighting for. Seeing photos of strangers didn't prove anything while I sat alone, engulfed in silence. But hearing her voice and watching her smile, seeing her eyes light up in awe, that made it mean something. It was hard to believe you were still one of the good guys if you never saw the face of the people you were protecting.

Luckily, I didn't have to say anything. Aria chose that moment to inform us that she was done with her nap and ready to join us. Jade slid off the bed, not another word out of her mouth, and left the room. I followed but stopped just outside the door to grab the bag I'd set down when coming home.

Aria ran into the living room while Jade followed behind her at a much slower pace, a new diaper hanging by her side between her fingers. "Come on, Aria. You're wet. Let's put on a dry diaper."

I sat on the couch and called the little tyke over. "I got you a present, but you can only have it if your mommy says it's okay."

"Way to put me on the spot." Jade crossed her arms and stood in the middle of the room, looking like she was ready to take my head off no matter what I grabbed out of the bag.

But Aria jumped up and down, squealing in delight, completely oblivious to her mother's irritation. I reached into the bag and pulled out a package of toddler underwear, to which she grabbed and held to her chest. I was sure she had no idea what it was, but regardless, she was happy.

"She hasn't even started potty training yet," Jade argued.

"I know, but hear me out. While I was gone, I did some research, and from what I found, children do better when they realize what happens if they don't use a toilet. Right now, she's used to pissing in that thing." I pointed to the absorbent pad in Jade's hand. "Since underwear won't hold it, it'll make her start to correlate the sensation of having to go with *actually* going."

"Oh, yeah?" She raised her eyebrows in mock question, a smirk toying on her lips. "And what kind of research did you do? Where did you learn all this information, oh wise one?"

I reached into the bag again and held up a magazine.

She apparently found it more humorous than I had. "You bought a parenting magazine?"

"Why not? I seem to fuck up all the time; might as well learn everything I can so you can stop getting mad at me."

"Is there an article in there about dropping the F-bomb in front of two-year-olds?"

I glanced at the cover before flipping it open, avoiding my fumble with the curse word. "Not sure. But I wouldn't doubt it. This thing has it all. Breastfeeding, baby shampoo comparisons…oh, and there's even a page in here that talks about the benefits of organic foods."

"Yeah…sounds like it has everything."

I couldn't tell if she was teasing or if I'd done something yet again to piss her off. But rather than question her, I took the remaining item from the bag and tossed it at her. "Don't worry, I got you something, too."

She caught the oversized T-shirt and held it up to read the front. As soon as her eyes met mine again, I couldn't help but enjoy the crimson that had taken over her neck and cheeks.

"What? What's wrong? Don't you like it?"

It was a nightshirt that said *Just enough to cover my cash and prizes* as a play on words. I thought it was fitting.

"What's there not to love about it?" Her sarcasm was thick, but she couldn't resist laughing along with me, finally giving in and finding the humor in it. "But seriously, Cash. As much as I appreciate you buying my child panties, it was just a waste of money. She'll end up peeing all over your house."

I shrugged, because honestly, I didn't care. "I have a mop. Give it a try and see how it goes. If it doesn't work and she's not learning, then go back to the diapers, and then use the underwear as incentive. Oh, and, Jade?"

She cocked her head to the side and waited for me to continue.

"Two things. One: please don't ever refer to her underwear as panties again. That's just disturbing on all levels. In fact, let's just put that word in the box with the F-bomb and bury it. Okay? And two: I don't mind mopping up a little piss, but if she shits in her drawers, that's all on you."

She rolled her eyes and turned to grab Aria by the arm, mumbling under her breath, "I have a feeling I'm going to regret this." A few minutes later, the tiny dancer came back out in nothing but a long shirt—which was pointless because she kept holding it up so we could all see Barbie on the front of her new undies.

I made a mental note to never buy another pack with cartoons on them again.

Jade headed straight for the kitchen to start making dinner, so I followed her. Our conversation had been interrupted, and then sidetracked, and I needed to know where we stood before going on another minute. After she pulled a bag of vegetables out of the fridge and put them on the counter, I cornered her, just like I had after returning home from the store. I had one hand on the granite beside her, arm stretched out as a barrier to keep her from leaving, and my body naturally leaned toward her, eating up most of our height difference.

"Where's your head at, Jade?" My low, gravelly tone surprised even me, and it seemed to make Jade's breathing stop altogether.

"Um...right now it's on making supper."

I grabbed her hip, turned her around, and moved to stand in front of her. My free hand fell away from the countertop and held her steady with her back pressed against the rounded edge of the granite. Now, rather than lean toward her, I towered above her, carefully gripping her hips while her warm palms pressed flat against my chest.

Staring into her eyes as if to plead with her to tell me the truth, I tried again. "No, with moving, staying...me. Where's your head at? What are you thinking? What are you planning to do, or at least leaning toward?"

"Do you need an answer now?" Her question lacked the air it needed to carry the words to my ears.

So I lowered my head and brought my lips to the side of her face and said, "I need something. Anything. It doesn't have to be a promise. I just need to know what you're thinking so I can start to prepare myself."

Her hands fisted the material of my shirt as if to hold me closer. "I'm not going anywhere, Cash. I'll stay." Those were the two best words I'd ever heard, powerful enough to almost bring me to my knees.

I let out a sigh of relief and melted into her, but it didn't last long. Aria's cries pulled us apart and had us both running around the corner to find two tiny feet spread wide, a puddle on the wood between them.

Not wasting a second, I crouched down in front of her and began to wipe the tears from her bright-red, scrunched face. "It's okay, Aria. It was just an accident. The next time you feel like you have to pee, tell Mommy and she'll take you to sit on your potty. That way Barbie won't get wet."

Jade came over with the mop, but before she could start to clean it up, I traded Aria for it. The apology written in her stare was enough to make me stop her retreat. She needed to get her daughter changed, but I refused to let her walk away thinking I was bothered by this.

"This is why I told you pant—*underwear* was a bad idea," she said under her breath.

I lowered my voice to keep Aria from overhearing. "Stop, Jade. It's not a bad idea. The more upset you are, the worse she'll feel. Please don't make her think I'm mad about this. It's called an accident for a reason. You're the mom, so if you choose to put her in a diaper, I'll back you up. But whatever you do, don't make that decision because you think I care about a little mess. I don't give two shits about it."

She nodded and then led Aria down the hall by her hand while I dried the floor.

To my surprise, Aria came out in another pair of underwear, more subdued than last time, but still showing signs of being happy rather than in tears. Jade joined me in the kitchen and resumed her place in front of the cutting board with a bag of carrots on the counter. We moved in sync around the small space, getting everything ready for her to put in the oven.

⚜

I knew the second she noticed our agreement. She'd just put Aria down for the night and came into the kitchen to grab a water. I had no sooner closed the dishwasher when I heard her snicker to herself from behind me. When I turned around, I caught her reading the paper attached to the fridge door.

After dinner, I'd added: **No saying the word "panties"** beneath her earlier addition of no cursing, and at the bottom, I wrote: **Must give Cash proper notice before moving out**.

She pointed to the last one and asked, "What's considered a proper notice? Thirty days? Sixty? I can't imagine you'd need that much time, but I think that's the legal eviction period." She cut her wide eyes to me. "Or so I've heard. I've never been evicted."

"Obviously, Jade. That would've shown up on your screening." I leaned against the counter and folded my arms over my chest, my feet crossed at the ankles. "I was going to say three hundred and sixty-five days, but I'll settle on sixty."

"A *year*? You need me to give you a *year's* notice before moving out?"

I couldn't help but laugh at her outrage. "You asked what I thought was fair for a proper notice, and in my opinion, that's fair. But I'm prepared to negotiate here. If you think less makes more sense, then I'm willing to be flexible. I'm a rather understanding guy."

Without saying anything else, she pulled the pen from the drawer and started marking up the paper. I moved to stand

164

behind her and read from over her shoulder. Just beneath my bullet point about moving out, she added: **Twenty-four hours**.

"Hey, now. That's not fair."

"Fine," she huffed, and brought the tip of the pen back to the agreement.

She scratched out the word "hours" and changed it to "days." I didn't argue, because I had full intention of coming back when she wasn't looking to change "days" to "years," just to see how long it'd take her to notice.

"I guess I should print a new one since you went and marked this one up," I joked. "Keep adding things and we'll have to put it in a binder instead of stuck to the fridge. I doubt a magnet would hold that much paper."

"That's why I call it the *dis*agreement, but you refuse to add the 'dis' to it."

She elbowed me, and like every other time she'd hit me in jest, she chose the right side. I couldn't figure it out. Anytime I'd touch her, it was nice and gentle, yet she seemed to aim for the one bruise I had on my entire body.

"Oh my God, I did it again." She turned to face me and immediately started to pat my chest and arm, as if that would make the ache in my ribs go away. But I could tell she had no clue what to do, and this was her way of comforting me—treating me like a dog.

"It's fine. I'll eventually learn to keep three feet between us at all times."

"Here, let me get some ice."

I grabbed her arm to stop her from pulling the freezer drawer open. "Really, I'm fine. I need to take a shower anyway, so I'll ice it when I get out."

She nodded but remained silent while I held my side and headed back to my room.

After the day I'd had, the hot water felt amazing. I wasn't sure if it was that or knowing Jade had no intention of moving out anytime soon, but it was as though the tension I'd carried with me since last weekend swirled down the drain, leaving me feeling refreshed when I stepped out. I'd contemplated putting on a shirt, but after Jade jabbed me in the ribs with her elbow, I didn't care to deal with one. I would just take it off before I went to bed, so I didn't see the point in making the pain worse, just to do it all over again in a few hours when it was time to take it off.

To my surprise, Jade had taken her shower, too. When I stepped out of my room, I found her in the kitchen with her wet hair twisted into a tight bun and wearing the shirt I'd bought for her earlier today. She wrapped ice in a towel, just like our first night in the house together, and joined me on the couch.

"Nice shirt." I wagged my brows, pulling a soft giggle and eye roll from her.

"I put on sleep shorts beneath it for double protection. Wouldn't want you to see my panties this time."

"*Fuck*," I blurted out, catching her by surprise.

She froze and panic colored her expression. "What?"

"You said panties, so I said fuck."

Realizing what I meant, she relaxed into the cushion again and shook her head. "That's not how that works. Saying one doesn't give you permission to shout the other."

I rested my right arm over her shoulder to give her room to hold the ice pack to my ribs. I wasn't sure if she intended to do that or if she'd brought it over so I could hold it there myself, but I didn't give her an option. "I figured if you broke a rule, it's only right to break the same one so you don't feel like such a criminal."

"How gracious of you."

"I do what I can." Our gazes met, and for some reason, I couldn't look away. Finally, she glanced down at the ice pack in her hand, and it was enough to break the spell. "Speaking of underwear, how'd Aria do? She didn't make a mess out here."

"As much as it pains me to admit this, she did well. After dinner, when I took her to take a bath, she was dry. She took off her clothes and sat on the chair and went...all by herself. I didn't even prod her to do it."

"See? Parenting magazines have all the answers."

"I love how you just jump in and play the part with complete modesty."

"Thank you. I try." With the TV off, I almost felt pressured to talk, to keep the conversation going, even though I wasn't sure what to say. "I can't imagine what it's been like for you, having to do it all alone. Her father never helped at all?"

Jade grew tense, but I didn't push. I simply waited her out, observing her reaction. She blinked a few times, swallowed harshly, and fought to control her breathing while never pulling her attention away from the towel in her hand. To anyone else, it was a simple yes-or-no question. But to Jade, that answer came with memories and heartache, the kind of pain I wished for nothing more than to take away.

"No. He, um...he didn't do anything. He's never even held her, which I'm okay with. I'm actually happy about it. I didn't want him anywhere near her—still don't."

I was about to ask another question, curious as to how he'd managed to have nothing to do with his own daughter. But I stopped short when I noticed the tears streaming down her cheeks. Rather than make things worse, I used the arm I had draped over her shoulder to tug her against me. It was an awkward embrace with the way she sat on the cushion facing me and the ice pack between us, but she adjusted just enough to tuck herself into my side.

"Why are you crying? He sounds like a loser, anyway. You're free of him, so there's no need to cry. Aria is better off without him. She has you, and that's all she needs." I tried to comfort her the best way I knew how, but this was foreign to me. Even during my marriage, there weren't many times I had to console Colleen— probably because I wasn't home enough to do so.

She sniffled and pulled back just enough to sit comfortably and hold a conversation. "When I was younger, I had this picture in my mind of what my future would look like," she said quietly, wiping her face with the back of her hand. "There was me, my husband, and our kids. I mean, the faces of them were blurry because I obviously didn't know who they'd turn out to be. Sometimes my husband was a boy I liked in class, and other times he was a celebrity. But no matter who he was in my fantasies, he loved me and our kids. He was the kind of father mine was before he died."

Up until this very second, I'd always believed you could find out more about a person from a thorough background check than you could from conversations with them. But listening to Jade open up about her childhood dreams of love and family, I no longer believed that to be true. She held more information in a single tear than any report I could've pulled on her.

"And now, looking at how my life turned out, I can't help but be mad that my daughter doesn't have that. I'm sad over the realization that those dreams were nothing but naïve illusions—a child who had no idea how disappointing reality could be. I want to give Aria the world, and it pisses me off that I can't even give her a loving father. I can't even give her a stable home."

I took a moment to rehearse the words in my head before offering them aloud. "I may be biased, but I think this home is rather stable. And in my opinion, she—like every child—just needs to be loved. It shouldn't matter who it comes from or what roles those who love her have in her life. You love her, and if that's all she ever gets, that's enough. And even though I've never met Stevie, I'm pretty sure she loves Aria. Not to mention, that little tyke already has me wrapped around her pinky. And she's only two. There's plenty of time for you to find someone to share your life with, someone who'll love your daughter like she was their own. Hell, when I was your age, I wasn't even married yet."

"That's not very comforting advice coming from someone who's divorced." She hadn't meant it as an insult, and I didn't take it as one. I could tell by her bright eyes as she looked up at me that she only meant to lighten the mood. "It just sucks that the only man who's ever shown her any kind of love, whether he feels that way or not, is you."

I hesitated for a moment, trying to keep from reading too much into it. "Why's that a bad thing?"

She went back to studying her hand, taking a deep breath before speaking. "It's not. You're right...I shouldn't be picky when it comes to people caring about her. But that won't stop my hopes and dreams for her to have an amazing dad, one who buys a cartful of junk just because she asked for it and smiled at him."

My chest constricted and breathing became almost impossible. It was a reaction I wasn't familiar with. Not anxiety or fear. I didn't have adrenaline pumping through my veins or endorphins spreading throughout my nervous system. This wasn't stress. An intense rush of heat filled my chest, confusing me even more. It felt good, but I wasn't sure why. For someone so in tune with other's physical reactions toward emotion, I was clueless when it came to my own.

"And that's the reason why it sucks, Cash." Her exhale seeped past her moistened lips and bathed me in its warmth, wrapped me in its comfort. "Because you're not her dad, and you never will be. You're the guy who lets us live here. And at some point, this arrangement will end."

I tugged her to me once more and rested my cheek on the top of her head, unwilling to let her see me while I worked through the onslaught of emotions her words left me with. I hated the thought of pulling away from Aria, but I understood the consequences of growing the bond we'd already started. I also wasn't interested in letting Jade leave, even though I was aware of how much harder it'd be the longer she stayed. I'd already grown attached to them both, for two different reasons, in two different capacities. The only thing I could do was prepare for the worst and hope for the best.

I had to believe that the friendship we nurtured would survive after she was gone.

And that the relationship I'd fallen into with Aria would last a lifetime.

CHAPTER 13

Jade

By the third week of living in Cash's house, things were finally settled.

After that one accident in her new underwear, Aria was basically potty trained. I still wasn't sure what Cash had done to perform that miracle, but I couldn't complain. He claimed it was the magazine, and ever since then, he'd grabbed a new one every weekend when he was home. However, she still couldn't get through the night without the need of a diaper, but Cash said he'd figure it out.

I wondered how long it'd take him to realize those magazines weren't how-to guides.

In the meantime, we'd installed a baby gate at the entrance to the hallway to keep her from wandering around the house and possibly going outside while I slept. I could no longer close her door at night in the event she woke up and had to use the bathroom. This also created the problem of getting her to go to sleep. As soon as she realized she could get out of her room, she'd make no less than four attempts each night at coming into the living room after bedtime.

On the weekends, Cash took it upon himself to assert his authoritative role. That was laughable. When making her clean up her messes, he'd sit on the floor with her and help. During dinner, he'd back me up when I told her she needed to eat her vegetables, but when I wasn't looking, he'd eat them for her. He thought he was slick, but I wasn't blind to what he was doing; I just decided not to call him out on it. And at night, when she'd climb out of bed and try to join us on the couch, he'd take her back to her room and read "one" more story. I didn't complain because he clearly didn't mind. In fact, I started to believe he enjoyed his newfound role in our lives.

And then I spent a lot of time denying the emotions those thoughts elicited.

But by the fourth week, I started to go stir-crazy. I loved the freedom I had, but I wasn't sure I could take one more day of the loneliness that came with living with Cash. I talked to him about it one night on the phone, telling him how I could relate to his feelings of isolation. Even though I had Aria to take care of, I could only do the same things so many times before my daily existence became torturous. He suggested I use the computer to search for jobs on the island. I didn't care to argue with him, considering he was only trying to help, so I told him I would and dropped it.

The next day, after a particularly horrible tantrum, I used the quiet time during Aria's nap to browse the local employment opportunities. To my surprise, there were several that would allow me to bring Aria along. As much as I needed something more full time for financial reasons, I was willing to take anything if it meant I didn't have to continue drawing from my savings. The only thing that helped keep me from spending as much was the couple of times Cash had done the shopping, which ensured we'd have enough food to last a nuclear holocaust—as long as we were happy living off a random hodgepodge of raw vegetables and chocolate pudding.

"So, tell me about your job," Stevie prodded with excitement ringing in her tone.

I closed the front door behind me and made myself comfortable on the bench seat while watching the waves roll in across the street. Aria was down for her nap, and with her bedroom door left open, I worried she'd hear me talking on the phone and wake up.

"The library on the island has a children's section, so I will go in twice a week to stock it. I clean and organize the shelves, put the returned books back where they belong, keep the toy section in order. Tuesdays and Thursdays for six hours each day."

"And you can bring Aria? Wow, Jade. That sounds perfect. How's the pay?"

"It's not a lot, but it covers my expenses."

"So when do you start?"

It'd taken us a while, but we'd finally gotten to a place where I could talk about my life here without her voicing her concerns. It didn't matter that Cash had an answer for every last one of them, she didn't know him, so therefore, that meant he couldn't be trusted. That all changed a couple of weeks ago when I'd invited her over while Cash was in town. They'd spent one day together, and suddenly, she no longer had a problem with him. Granted, she put him through the ringer, making me believe an interview for the CIA would've been easier than what she'd put him through. Now, she was more concerned about my heart getting broken for a different reason. She claimed he looked at me with hearts in his eyes, and made a big deal about the way he'd touch me—which I'd grown used to and no longer gave much thought. He'd expressed his lack of sexual attraction toward me, and even though it had hurt to hear, I'd accepted that it was best.

"Next week. My first official day is Tuesday." I practically had a countdown on my calendar. Just the thought of getting out of the house and having a place to go twice a week that didn't involve a grocery store made me giddy.

We talked for a little bit longer about Aria, Derek, Cash, her new apartment, and a few wasted minutes on my mother, before her lunch break ended and she had to head back. As much as I loved our phone calls, I hated the physical distance between us. She'd tried several times to get me to drive over and spend a few days on the other coast, but I politely declined each time. I had no interest in returning—other than to see Stevie—but at least she made the effort to come to me. She claimed to understand my need to stay away, but I suspected she'd likely stop making the trip once the newness of my move wore off.

And that's what bothered me the most.

Long after our call had ended, I remained on the porch, lost in thought as the waves moved in and out. A few older women walked along the shore, a dog darting back and forth a few times, and several boats going so fast they looked like they floated across the surface of the ocean in the distance. But mostly, I watched a woman, maybe a little older than me, building a sandcastle with a young boy. It made me realize that even though everything appeared to be falling into place—Aria, getting a job, finding an easy and effortless routine with Cash—I was still missing one thing.

And it happened to be the one thing that pushed Cash to find a roommate.

Aside from the weekends, my life lacked companionship. I'd hoped that hole would be filled with a job—coworkers and the people who'd come in and out during my shifts—but that still left the days in between and the hours before and after void of the kind of human interaction I craved. I yearned for a more steady, reliable support system than a few strangers bringing their children into the library to read a book. And while I regarded the woman and the boy on the beach in front of the house, I found myself daydreaming of having friends on the island. Of getting together with a few other moms and relaxing in the sand while our kids played together on the beach. By the time I shook out of the fantasy, the woman was gone.

"One thing at a time," I told myself as I headed back inside. "Job first, then friends."

✤

I could've gone down the line, starting with Monday and ending with Friday, and given a laundry list of reasons to prove how each day was the worst of the week. Monday because Cash went back to work. Aside from it being lonely, it was also the time

Aria threw the biggest fit. She missed Cash and didn't understand why he was gone, which broke my heart, but it also left my every last nerve sizzling and burnt to a crisp—no, Monday's tantrum *surpassed* fried nerves. I had looked forward to Tuesday, yet by two in the afternoon, it'd earned the title of being the worst day of the week. As much as I enjoyed the freedom of bringing Aria to the library with me, she'd apparently lost interest after two hours, and missing her regularly scheduled nap only made things worse, causing me to be sent home an hour early.

Wednesday wasn't too bad where Aria was concerned, but I became convinced that hump day would never end. This week, I was exhausted after running around the library for five hours yesterday—even though it felt like ten—which only intensified the normal feelings of loneliness I experienced since moving to Geneva Key. Thursday had been much of the same as Tuesday, yet I didn't get to leave early. I worked the entire six-hour shift, of which the last two hours Aria curled up with a giant stuffed bear in the sorting room where she cried herself to sleep. Needless to say, dreamland didn't elude me that night.

And then Friday came. Even before I started my job, I'd wake up convinced it was the worst day of the week. Just the thought of Cash being home when I woke up the next morning made every second stretch on. Even though we spoke on the phone almost every night, it wasn't the same as having him here. His presence offered me a sense of safety—not that I'd ever felt *un*safe without him, yet the comfort of his close proximity set my mind at ease. But more than that, he gave me the company I'd lacked when he was gone.

And today was no different. Once I made it to dinnertime, the rest of the evening was a breeze. It was the one night I didn't have to fight Aria to go to sleep. All I had to do was tell her Cash wouldn't come home if she didn't stay in bed and close her eyes, and she'd be passed out within minutes. Come December, she'd wonder why both Cash and Santa wouldn't show up if she were awake, but I figured I'd cross that bridge when we got there. We still had a few more months before I had to have an explanation.

Normally, waiting up for Cash wasn't an issue. I would be so excited to have another adult in the house that I literally couldn't fall asleep. But after the change in my schedule due to starting my job, I wasn't sure I'd make it. So, rather than lie in bed and listen for the door, I sat on the couch and watched TV. By midnight, I'd gone from sitting to curled up on the armrest. It must not have been much later that I'd fallen asleep, only to be woken when Cash draped a blanket over me.

I rubbed my eyes to focus on him, instantly feeling better as soon as I realized he was home. "Hey," I whispered and tried to sit up.

Seeing his smile before I was fully awake made me melt. When I wasn't half asleep, it was easy to remind myself that he didn't have romantic feelings for me. But while my brain was still under a dense fog of slumber, I didn't have the wherewithal to keep myself from falling for him, allowing myself to believe those smiles were reserved for me.

"Hey," he repeated in the sexiest voice I'd ever heard. "You're tired; maybe you should go to bed."

I shook my head, trying to break free from the white-knuckled grip of exhaustion. "No. I'd rather stay up and talk to a real person."

He chuckled beneath his breath but didn't take a seat on the couch. "Are things so bad you've been talking to imaginary people?"

"You know what I mean—an adult. Someone who says more than 'I hungee,' and 'I go potty.' A real person who doesn't require me to wipe their nose or butt, and who can follow a conversation for longer than fifteen seconds before running off to chase some magical unicorn." The longer I talked, the whinier I sounded.

But Cash didn't seem to mind. He finally fell onto the cushion next to me, laughing at our inside joke about Aria's train of thought. She had run up to him on the beach one day, excited to tell him some story about the waves. Her hands moved a million miles a minute as she animatedly told him things neither of us could comprehend. As soon as she was done, he'd gotten maybe five words out before she turned around and ran back into the water, oblivious to the fact that Cash had been in the middle of a sentence. He'd turned to me, his expression utterly serious, and said, "Oh, look…a magical unicorn."

"You'll make friends. Give it time. Then you won't need me here anymore." He'd meant it as a joke, but for whatever reason, be it hormonal or lack of sleep—or quite possibly, the mental effects caused by unmitigated loneliness—it made me sad.

I automatically curled into his side and draped my arm across his stomach. And without a moment's hesitation, Cash wrapped his arm around my shoulders, holding me close. Even though we didn't sit like this often, there had been times over the last month and a half when I just needed the human contact. At first, he'd been the one who'd pull me into him, probably sensing my need for affection. Now, when I craved the comfort only his embrace could offer—usually when I was tired or sad—I was the one who'd initiate it. And every time, he'd put his arm around me, release a sigh, and relax, as if holding me close consoled him, too.

"How was work?" I asked, breathing in his scent.

"Boring."

I leaned my head back, nestling my neck in the crook of his elbow, and grew lost in those endless pools of rich chocolate. I'd done this thousands of times before, yet this time felt different. The way he looked at me was different. His brows furrowed the slightest bit, as if I had something strange on my face. But it all changed when I reached up to graze the pad of my thumb over one eyebrow to clear away the tension. It appeared my touch had spurred him into action.

He lowered his face, bringing our lips so close I could feel his every breath. Yet he hesitated with the tip of his nose grazing mine. I cupped his cheek, and in the blink of an eye, he went for it. His mouth covered mine, and the realization caused me to freeze momentarily. I just sat there and stared at his eyelids until his lips parted, opening my mouth. His tongue on mine was all I needed to fall into this with him.

I closed my eyes and allowed myself to take everything in—his hand on my thigh, his mouth on mine, our tongues dancing together at the perfect pace. It did something to me, sparked something inside I'd never felt before. It gave me the courage to pull myself over him and straddle his hips, our chests pressed together. This was all new to me—not the action, but the sensation and my willingness. It was like experiencing the sand beneath my toes for the first time. Warm and inviting. Calming. Serene.

Until it wasn't.

Cash grazed the side of my body with his hand before threading my hair through his fingers. His open palm cradled the back of my head, and just as I began to melt into him, he fisted his hand and gently pulled my hair tight against my scalp.

It was enough to remind me...of *everything*.

I gasped and pushed away, frantically climbing off his lap, but it wasn't Cash in front of me. It wasn't Cash's face I saw. Anyone could've been sitting on the couch, and I wouldn't have seen them. I wouldn't have recognized anything other than the face of my nightmare.

Of *his* brown hair and green eyes, trimmed beard, pointy nose and chin.

As I retreated, the coffee table hit the backs of my legs, almost causing me to tumble to the ground. But I caught myself and scurried to the middle of the room. Cash started to say something behind me, but I couldn't hear him, too lost in the dark and damp tunnel of my despair.

"Don't you see what you do to me, Jade?" The way he said my name twisted my stomach.

"You make me weak, Jade." It suffocated me.

"The things you make me do… You're the worst kind of temptress, Jade." Blinded me.

"Jade?" My name was louder, closer, fear woven between the letters and weighing heavily in the one syllable. Nothing like the voice in my head. "Jade? Talk to me. Please." When I turned around, dark-brown eyes narrowed on me. His forehead, normally so relaxed and smooth, was now deeply creased with panic, brows knitted tightly together. "What happened? What'd I do?"

"I'm so sorry, Cash." I took a step back. "I didn't mean to do that. I think I was still half asleep. It'll never happen again, I swear."

"What are you talking about?"

I held up my hands to stave him off, ignoring the way my entire body shook. I hated how I couldn't find my way back to the armor I naturally wore—the one set in place with smiles and jokes and confidence. I'd long since shed the weakness that had painted me like a canvas, but at this moment, it came back—like Carrie at prom, I was soaked in a bucket of pig's blood. I wanted nothing more than to wash it off, disgusted by the way it clung to my skin. But with Cash in the room, the moisture of his mouth lingering on my lips, I couldn't concentrate enough to eliminate the unyielding thoughts of my past.

"You've made it clear you don't find me attractive. I shouldn't have—"

"I *never* said that." His anger had started to hover at the surface.

I needed to run, to close myself off in my room for just a few minutes to shove these emotions down, back to the place I'd kept them all these years. I needed control. But I couldn't do that in front of him.

"Fine...you don't think of me *that* way. You don't want me like that. I get it. I never should've touched your face or curled into your side. I'm sorry."

"Would you fucking stop talking for one goddamn minute?"

The harshness in his tone froze me in place. My lungs quit working, my heart stalled, and my feet were suddenly weighted with cement blocks, preventing me from moving. But my hands...they remained in the air, trembling like I stood on a glacier in the coldest part of the world, soaking wet with nothing on.

When he realized I had stopped, his posture deflated. All anger drained from his face when he said, "You didn't do anything. *I* kissed *you*, Jade. Me. Why would you blame yourself or think this is somehow your fault?"

"Because I started it. I came onto you."

Confusion filled the void that anger had left behind in his eyes. "That's what you think?"

Finally able to regain control of my body, I dropped my hands and prepared to leave the room. But first, I explained, "You don't think I'm sexually attractive. You can't deny that, because you've told me so yourself. So clearly, you didn't make the first move—you wouldn't have. I cuddled up next to you, put my arm around you. I'm the one who touched your face. I'm the one who pulled myself into your lap. That's all me."

"Jade..." He tried to keep me from leaving the room, but I didn't give him the chance.

I turned and hurried through the kitchen, not bothering to close the baby gate behind me on my way to my room. The door didn't close all the way, my fingertips barely connecting with the edge of it while I swung it shut behind me with far less strength than needed to make it latch. But I didn't care. I needed a moment to collect myself, my thoughts. I sat on the bed, feet crossed beneath me, facing the headboard with my back to the door, and covered my face.

A faint knock alerted me to Cash's presence, but I didn't have the strength to say anything. So I kept my back to him and hoped he'd leave. Yet he didn't. From the doorway, he sighed and then whispered, "I really need you to talk to me, Jade."

"For the love of God, Cash. There's nothing to talk about. I'm embarrassed enough as it is, so can we please not do this?" I didn't mean to sound angry, but it didn't stop the harsh words from spewing out.

"What the hell…?" It was barely audible, full of pain twisted with confusion.

His feet must've glided across the floor, because in less than a second, the mattress dipped behind me. Although, he kept his hands to himself—maybe out of fear, could've been due to repulsion. I couldn't tell.

"Jade, please look at me."

I turned to face him, realizing in that moment how badly I needed him with me. I had run away from him, tried to shut myself in my room. When he came to my door, I wanted him gone. I was embarrassed for him to see me like this, but I needed him. I needed the comfort only he could offer. And once I had my body twisted around, I finally calmed down, the tremors subsided.

"I have so much to say, but I don't know where to start." His eyes held the same trepidation that weighted his tone.

"How about nowhere? There's nothing to talk about, Cash."

"You jumped away from me like I was hurting you."

"Yeah, thanks for the reminder." As if it wasn't embarrassing enough the first time, he had to go and bring it up, press me to talk about it. Well, I never talked about it, so little did he know, he didn't stand a chance.

"Can you at least tell me why?"

I covered my face, hoping to conceal the emotions I knew he'd read in my expression. But he refused to let me hide. He carefully wrapped his thick fingers around my wrists and lowered my hands, and then he waited with the patience of Job until I met his apologetic stare.

"Why what, Cash?"

"Why you ran away from me."

"I don't know…I guess I realized what was going on and tried to stop it. But then I almost tripped over the coffee table. It was rather humiliating. I just wanted to get away so I could stop feeling so stupid."

I'd spent years trying to get my mom to pay attention and ask questions. Yet she never did. Some people had assumed I'd acted out due to repressed anger after losing my dad. Others thought I was just a wayward teen who needed harsher punishments or more supervision. No one saw the signs, no matter how many I'd given. And now, someone recognized it. Cash saw what no one else did.

My prayer had been answered.

Even if it was too late.

His tongue ran along his bottom lip, and his gaze briefly fell to my hands before holding my stare. "Can we discuss the misunderstanding about whether or not I find you attractive?"

"Can we not and say we did?" My cheeks burned as if I were standing in the sun on the hottest day of summer. "I mean…there doesn't seem to be much of a misunderstanding."

"But there is, Jade." His need to explain himself was desperate.

"You don't have to tell me I'm pretty to make me feel better. That's not what I'm looking for. You've already explained it, and honestly, I'm okay with it. You've made it clear from the very beginning that you were only looking for a friend, someone to spend time with on your days off, and that you have no interest in anything romantic. So I've never expected anything else."

Grit filled his voice when he said, "I actually find you very attractive, and that's not a lie. I'm not saying that to make you feel better, either. You're beautiful, and to top it off, you're kind and funny and thoughtful."

I shook my head, disinterested in hearing his compliments. They would only serve to give me false hope, to make me believe in the impossible. Been there. Done that. The T-shirt was hideous. "You don't have to explain, Cash. I get it. I already told you that."

"You do? So you understand the difference between finding you beautiful and wanting to fuck you?" The vulgar question made my head snap up until I met his stare. "I didn't think so. That's what I was trying to tell you by saying I wasn't looking for someone I find *sexually* attractive."

"I know." I nodded, almost too eagerly.

He didn't seem to believe me, but at least he moved on, ending my embarrassment...for now. "Why do you feel it was your fault that I kissed you? Why did you freak out?"

I waved my hand in the air, gesturing to physical evidence— him, me, the open door that represented what had happened in the living room—that would help prove my next point. "How can you sit here and look me in the eyes while telling me you don't find me sexually attractive, and then in the next breath, say that kiss was your idea?"

"You kissed me back, and then climbed into my lap...does that mean you want to have sex with me?"

I couldn't tell him the truth without making our living situation even more awkward than I already had. There was no way I would've been able to explain how the sight of his bare chest made my body react in ways I'd never experienced before him. If I did that, it would be a safe assumption to say he'd never walk around without a shirt on again. And if he found out I'd taken notice of—on far more than one occasion—the way his basketball shorts accentuated his dick when he moved, proving he didn't wear anything beneath them, he'd start changing into jeans after his shower, too.

I wasn't ready to give up my favorite parts of every weekend. So...I lied.

"No. I already told you I was half-asleep. I've had a long and tiring week, and the exhaustion must've left me in a fog when you came home. I didn't mean it. I shouldn't have—" The second his fingers gently wrapped around my wrist, my words died on my tongue. That's when I realized I'd been staring at my hands in my lap while lying to him, and the moment I locked my surprised gaze with his, it was clear he'd figured it out.

But rather than call me out on it, he said, "Stop blaming yourself. Stop saying it was your fault. I kissed you. Got it? You didn't do anything to make me do it. Maybe I've had a long week, as well. Maybe I was just as tired, and when I looked at you, I did something I shouldn't have. We both played a part in what happened out there, yet *I'm* the one who kissed *you*. Trust me…I'm a big boy. No one can *make* me do anything against my will. Okay?"

I nodded, even though I disagreed. He may have been a big guy with muscles in places I wasn't aware they existed, but I was all too familiar with how easily the female body could manipulate men.

"What happened to you, Jade?" he asked so quietly I wasn't sure what the question was, but I didn't need to ask him to repeat it because I could read it in his eyes. If they had the power to droop like those ceramic figurines of children, they would have. And even had I not seen that, I would've understood it in the way his chest steadily rose and fell with precise timing, as if he had to assert physical control over every breath he took.

"What do you mean?" I chose to play dumb rather than answer him.

"You were into the kiss at first, and then all of a sudden, it was like someone yanked you off my lap. Like you'd experienced PTSD or something. Couple that with the way you assumed the blame, and I'm convinced something happened to you in the past."

ᵀᴴᴱROOMMATE 𝒹𝒾𝓈AGREEMENT

"Umm…" I tried to start, but I had no idea where to begin. "It's complicated."

He blew out a wave of air that seemed to be laden with frustration. That was proven when he raked his hands through his hair and then blinked at me…as if batting his dark lashes would get me to open up and share all my deepest secrets. Granted, it probably would. But not this time.

"So that means it has something to do with your ex."

"Why do you say that?"

"Because every time I ask about him, that's your answer. Then you immediately change the subject. All I know is you dated him when you were a teenager and have been broken up for three years. I'm assuming he's also Aria's father, but you've yet to confirm that. And if I'm right, then I also know he's not a good person, because you don't want him to have anything to do with her. So tell me…does this have to do with him?"

I shrugged, unable to speak. I couldn't lie, no matter how badly I wanted to, because I knew he'd never believe it. With my luck, I'd try to make something up and end up telling him how Aria's father was Justin Timberlake, but no one could ever find out because Jessica Biel would murder me. So…a shrug was all I could offer.

"Can you tell me anything else? What makes him so bad?"

"He's older and manipulative. He's just not a good person, okay?"

Cash nodded, and for a second, I thought he was about to drop it. But he didn't. "How much older?"

"A lot."

"And when did this start?"

"When I was sixteen." Short answers were all I could give.

"Are we talking like he was in college? Or older than that?"

I fidgeted with my hands, and while I tried to form a response, I couldn't stop the nervous habit of swallowing and licking my lips. He must've recognized it, because he shifted on the bed and placed his hands on my knees. Then he leaned toward me, moving directly into my line of sight. His eyes were all I needed to give me the strength to proceed.

"Older than that."

He clenched his teeth together until his jaw ticced, and his grip on my knees tightened a fraction, just enough to show the slightest hint of a reaction. However, to me, it was a negative response, and I immediately wished I hadn't said anything.

"I provoked it," I justified quickly, needing to calm him down.

"How? How can you say that? I'm an adult, and there's *nothing* about a sixteen-year-old I find even remotely attractive. It's sick. It's fucking disgusting…but that's on him. Not you."

"You don't understand."

"Then help me understand, Jade."

I shook my head and tried to glance away, but his grip on my knee tightened and brought me back to his devastating eyes.

"Is he the reason you believe it's somehow your fault if a guy touches you?"

"Isn't it? If I'm the one who provoked it, how is it not my fault?"

"What the fuck did he do to you?" His question wasn't meant for me. It was soft and full of air, spoken to some ominous being rather than me.

It was like he could see straight into me, straight to the truth I'd kept buried.

The last three and a half months had been a lie.

A façade.

An illusion masking the reality.

And with one kiss, Cash managed to clear away the smokescreen.

CHAPTER 14

Cash

It took everything in me not to flip the fuck out. As if finding out a grown-ass man had touched her when she was only sixteen wasn't bad enough, hearing that he had convinced her it was her fault left me seeing red.

The worst part was I couldn't touch her. I couldn't hold her hand or wipe away her tears. Every part of me itched to comfort her, hold her, assure her I was there. But there was no way I could do any of that without complicating our situation even more. Not to mention, the last thing I wanted to do was prove her ex right. She'd see my affection as something she'd provoked. And I hated that.

My mouth grew dry right before I asked, "Did he physically force himself on you?"

"No." Her answer should've been enough to lessen the anger...but when she spoke, she looked up and to the left. That one simple glance brought the rage back like a black storm cloud on the heels of heavy winds.

"So let me get this straight...you said he's manipulative, a lot older, someone you don't want anywhere near Aria. He somehow convinced you that if a guy comes onto you, it was because of something you did. Yet he *didn't* force himself on you?" I barely got the words out.

It was obvious she was trying to hold her own, keep up the façade of everything being okay. But she couldn't fool me. I was a man on a mission to figure out what had happened to her and why I hadn't seen the signs until now.

"It started with innocent touches—brushing my hair over my shoulder, tapping me on the nose...things like that. Then he started saying things. He'd compliment how well my chest filled out a shirt, or how my butt looked in certain jeans. I developed early, so by this point, I had more curves than most girls my age."

"You were sixteen?" I wasn't sure why I felt the need to clarify that.

"When he started saying things, yes. But the touching and flirting started when I was fifteen."

I didn't know Jade when she was that young, but it didn't matter. The size of her breasts or thickness of her thighs at that age should've never been admired by a grown man. It sickened me.

"After that, he started touching me more inappropriately. If we sat next to each other, he'd put his hand on my leg—not too high, but well above my knee. There were a few times his hand would brush over my chest, but he always played it off as an accident."

"How long did this go on for?"

She shrugged, but ended up giving me an answer anyway. "Maybe six months. Eight. I don't remember for sure. It was before my seventeenth birthday when it progressed into something more." She rolled her eyes. "I'll never forget it. I was wearing a tank top—the kind with the thin straps and built-in bra—but I had a light sweater over it because the room was chilly. He asked if I was cold, and when I told him I was all right, he made a comment about my...my nipples being hard."

Hearing that made me grimace—not only because it was repulsive of him to have said, but because it reminded me of the morning I'd made a comment about being able to see through her shirt. And now that I thought about it, she'd been wearing the same type of tank top she just described from that day. There was no way I could've known, but that didn't do anything to stop my need to turn back time and handle that situation differently. Other than embarrassment, she hadn't acted freaked out. She'd even come back into the room and had fallen into easy chatter with me. However, it didn't change the regret I felt over it.

"There was another time when he took my hand under the table and put it over his groin. It was hard. I'd never done that before, so I froze. I didn't pull my hand away or tell him to stop. I just sat there while he made me touch him over his pants and listened while he told me I had done that to him."

"Were you dating him at this point?" I wished I could've swallowed my question. The last thing I wanted her to believe was that I felt his actions were justified if they were in a relationship—because that wasn't at all what I thought or meant.

But it didn't seem to faze her. "He wasn't really my boyfriend. I mean, we didn't date or do 'couple' things. He told me I was his, and that meant I wasn't allowed see anyone else. I only called him my boyfriend so no one would think I was single—not that I had a line of guys trying to date me. Most of the boys at school referred to me as 'Stevie's best friend.' I doubt they even knew my name."

"And this possessive behavior started when you were sixteen?"

"Yeah...I mean, he made his intentions pretty clear before then, but that's when it stopped being glances and started to become more."

"How much more?"

"He'd touch me between my legs if we were sitting at a table where no one could see."

"Were you okay with that?"

"The first time he did it, I'd asked him to stop. I told him it made me uncomfortable. But he just said it was because I was inexperienced and that I'd learn to like it. He said all girls liked to be touched, and if I didn't, then there was something wrong with me."

The need to find this motherfucker and slaughter him burned hot within me.

"The day after my seventeenth birthday is when we had sex for the first time."

I didn't want to ask, but I felt the need to. "It was…consensual, right?"

"I didn't want to, and I told him that." Her voice lowered, yet she refused to drop the bravado. She was either incredibly strong, or I was making a bigger deal of this than she was. I couldn't tell. "But he promised me it would feel good. He said he would stop if I didn't like it. I told him it hurt, and he said that was normal, that I just had to give it a minute. Then I cried, and he said I was too tense, that if I just relaxed, it would get better. After a few minutes, he was done, but then he got mad."

"What the fuck was he mad about?" I couldn't contain my anger and immediately regretted it when she flinched. All I could do was reassure her with a gentle squeeze on her knee, which I prayed didn't make things worse.

She blew out a stream of air and straightened her posture as if preparing herself to testify. "He was mad because I'd made him do that."

"Do what? I don't understand. He said you *made* him have sex with you?"

"I don't want to say it, Cash. You'll hate me."

"Why would I hate you?" The longer she dragged this out, the tighter my chest became.

"Because your wife cheated on you."

"He was married…" It was more of a realization spoken aloud.

"Yes, and I guess he hadn't given it any thought until that moment. I remember thinking everything he'd done prior to that day had been considered cheating—making me touch him, him touching me, his comments…all of it. But I guess in his eyes, none of that counted."

"I could never hate you, Jade," I whispered, but she refused to meet my gaze.

ᵀᴴᴱROOMMATE ᵈⁱˢAGREEMENT

I tucked my finger beneath her chin and tilted it, needing her to look at me. When her eyes met mine, I was almost silenced by the vibrancy in them. I still wasn't sure what all her ex had done to her, but I could see a strength within her most wouldn't possess in her shoes.

Jade was a fighter.

"So he blamed you for his infidelity...but it didn't make him stop, did it?"

She shook her head, and I could tell this was starting to wear her down. Yet she didn't shut down. "It took a month, but it happened again...and then again...and again. Each time became more frequent. After a while, he stopped getting angry when it was over. He continued to blame me, saying it was my fault he couldn't keep his hands to himself, but rather than use his anger to intimidate me, he resorted to guilt and manipulation. To be honest, I'm not sure which one was worse."

I didn't know who this asshole was.

And unfortunately for him...

Jade had unknowingly chosen a killer to confide in.

My question burned the tip of my tongue until I asked, "Why don't you do anything about it now? That's statutory rape at the minimum. Can't you go to the authorities and let them do something about it?"

"No," she whispered with a slow shake of her head. "The statute of limitations ran out the day I turned twenty-two."

Hearing that made me so angry my hands shook. "There's nothing that can be done?"

"No. There's nothing I can legally do. Even if I decide to say something, having Aria as proof, I have no evidence to back up any claim of it happening before I was an adult—no one knew, because he'd made sure of that. And now, he could say it only happened that one time and make me out to be the bad guy."

"What about when you left him? Why couldn't you do anything about it then?"

"Same thing, Cash," she said with a deflated shrug. "I was nineteen—a legal adult. I don't have anything to show that it had happened before I turned eighteen. The *only* proof I have of *any* kind of relationship with him is Aria. But that doesn't mean anything because she was conceived when I was nineteen."

"I'm not blaming you at all...I just want to understand. Why didn't you say anything when you were a minor? When it was happening?"

"Fear." Her answer was spoken with so much truth, as if it were the only plausible answer and made all the sense in the world. "He had me convinced that if I told anyone, I would be the villain. People would look at me and believe I had seduced the happily married man. That was his MO, Cash. That's how he kept me under his thumb. Guilt, fear...of what people would think of me, of what would happen to me if anyone knew."

"How did you finally get rid of him?"

"I got pregnant." She rolled her eyes, her strength showing more and more. "He wanted me to get an abortion, and to be honest, I'd contemplated it. But as soon as I heard her heartbeat for the first time, I made the decision to keep her. I refused to let him take anything else from me. If I couldn't be strong for myself, I'd be strong for my child."

"And he let you go? Just like that? He wasn't worried you'd say anything?"

Her shrug told me she didn't know, but also, that she didn't care. "He'd make snide comments from time to time about how fat I was, or how loose my vagina would be after pushing out a baby. How no man would ever want me, that everyone would see me as a used-up piece of trash. I guess he thought I'd change my mind or something—that his hateful words would affect me enough to give up my baby. But they didn't. I just ignored him."

"But I thought...I thought you had left him. Were you still with him at this point?"

"Oh, no. I had nothing to do with him by then. I'd still see him around, but that wasn't by choice. I think he found entertainment in messing with me or trying to hurt me. I don't know what his reasons were for anything that he did."

"When was the last time you saw or spoke to him?"

"Whatever day that was that I called you and told you I was moving in a week earlier than we planned."

"That's it? You haven't heard from him since?"

"Not a word. He has my number since I've had the same one for years, but he hasn't called."

I guess there's a silver lining in everything.

Taking in the dark circles beneath her eyes, I reached up to run my finger along her cheek. "You're tired, and it's late."

She covered her mouth to stifle a yawn. "Yeah…I bet you're beat, too."

Her ability to bounce back amazed me. "You good?"

"Yeah. Just as long as you don't try to kiss me again."

Just the thought of it brought my attention to her lips. A shadow of a smirk played at the corner of her mouth. "Deal."

"Night, Cash."

My thumb lingered on her cheek for a second longer before I dropped my hand and pushed off her bed. I made it to the doorway before glancing back, needing to see her one last time before I walked away. "Goodnight, Jade."

I went to my room, but sleep didn't come easily.

I tossed and turned, thinking about *everything* she'd said tonight. She had brought up what I'd told her weeks ago about how I hadn't found her sexually attractive. She could deny it until she was blue in the face, but that had hurt her. I could see that it had. When I had originally told her that, the words had been true. Jade was beautiful, and although I'd recognized how appealing she was that first day we'd met for lunch, the desire to touch her hadn't been there. And I'd allowed myself to believe my own lies when I assumed that desire would never exist.

Truth be told, this realization was a long time coming. Watching her with her daughter, seeing the kind of mother she was, had shone a new light on her. After the misunderstanding that almost led to her packing up and leaving, I was afforded the chance to see her in a more relaxed element. Once we'd found that niche of comfort with each other, it was like she'd let her guard down, and I was able to see the real Jade.

That added a new dimension to her, one I couldn't ignore.

The way she laughed with her head tilted back, just like Aria did so often, ignited something within me that I pretended wasn't there. How she'd come into the house and taken over with the kitchen and dinners, the laundry—including mine—even though I'd never asked or expected her to, never went unnoticed. She'd filled a void I wasn't aware had existed, one that had apparently been there both before and after Colleen.

I'd ignored it for weeks, but while she sat curled into my side after I'd gotten home tonight, all those pieces of her started to come together and form a different picture than the one I'd had from that day in the restaurant. And when she pulled her head back and looked up at me, I couldn't deny my attraction any longer. I might've told her that she didn't *make* me kiss her, and although that was technically true, the moment she touched my face, it was like I'd opened my eyes for the first time.

I'd realized then that the reason I hadn't found her sexually enticing in the booth that day was because she was sitting in the dark. I couldn't see all of her. But over the past six weeks, each time I'd learn something new, or notice another desirable quality about her, it was as if she'd slowly come out of the shadows, shining brighter and more vibrantly. And tonight, I'd finally taken a real look at her, finding her completely illuminated, and there was no denying my need for her. It surpassed the hunger to touch her physically.

I had an ache within me only she could soothe.

™ROOMMATE ⸴⸴AGREEMENT

I was skilled at observing things around me, yet it appeared I lacked that proficiency when it came to discerning things within myself. I wasn't sure when it'd happened, or even what it was that tipped the scale, but somewhere in the last month and a half of living with her—or hell, even the last two and a half months of knowing her—I'd started to fall for her.

And by the time I'd recognized it, it was too late.

I spent the entire weekend with Jade and Aria. In the evenings, after Aria was asleep, Jade and I would hang out on the couch either talking or watching TV. It was like Friday night had never happened—other than my hesitation to touch her, which she must've picked up on. During our regular Sunday walk for shells, she grabbed my hand. It surprised me—not because we'd never done it before, but because I hadn't expected her to be so affectionate after our talk. Honestly, I'd expected our kiss to cause uncertainty between us, but she didn't let that stop her from carrying on the way we had before it happened.

When I woke up Monday morning, I didn't want to leave. It had been the first time in nine years that I didn't want to get on a plane and go to work. I would've given anything to spend more time with Jade—and Aria. And as much as that realization confused me, I knew the reason for it.

I just wasn't sure what I could do about it.

The plane touched ground, waking me from my endless daydreams of Jade. I knew I had to snap out of it before my briefing with Rhett. He didn't care what we did on our days off, but when we were on his time, we had to be focused. In this line of work, there was no room for error—especially the ones caused by lack of attention and concentration.

I was escorted to the hub, which was nothing more than an inconspicuous building or house for all team members to meet at while in the field. It changed depending on location, unlike the steel box and subsequent safe house. The hubs were basically hideouts, like any stakeout scene from a typical detective movie — except they were nothing like Hollywood tried to make them out to be. No one sat in front of a window with binoculars, and we weren't left in the dark. It was far enough away from a target to go unnoticed, and pretty much made to look like a frat house full of bodybuilders.

Rhett met me at the back door and led me inside. At the end of a hallway, we entered what would've been a bedroom had it actually held any furniture. Now, it was crammed with desks that were lined with computers, wires plugged into monitors that were connected to surveillance cameras. Boxes of files and reports filled the closet, and the overflow was stacked in the bathroom. Only the toilet was accessible, as well as a bottle of hand sanitizer on the back and a roll of Charmin on the wall dispenser next to it.

And for the next two hours, he ran through every piece of information we had on my new target. There were files upon files filled with everything I needed to know about him, everything I needed to trail him. However, I barely heard a word of it.

"You should also know he's into some sick shit."

"Oh, yeah?" I flipped through a few more sheets of paper, keeping my head down without ever looking at him.

"Yeah. He likes it when big, beefy men shove their feet up his ass. He takes fistin' to a whole new level." There was not a trace of humor in his tone, and when I finally registered what he'd said, I glanced up, finding none on his face, either. "What's wrong, son? Not get enough sleep last night?"

I shook it off and tried to play dumb. "I don't know what you're talking about."

"I just told ya this guy likes feet in his asshole. And ya just sat there like there's nothin' wrong with it. Either you're distracted, or you think it's normal because you're into the same shit. For my own peace of mind, I'm gonna go with you bein' distracted. So…what is it?"

"It's nothing. Really. I'm listening."

"Are ya? Are ya really, Cash? If you're listening, what pharmacy does he go to on Tuesdays?" He knew he had me, his raised brows proved that much.

"Walgreens." It was the safest choice. Hell, I didn't even know where I was. I'd been so absentminded on the entire plane ride and during the escort to the hub, I wasn't even sure what time zone we were in.

"No, you asshat. He doesn't go to a pharmacy. Ever. On Tuesdays, he never leaves his house." Rhett groaned and pinched the bridge of his nose. "I've known you longer than most of the others here. I've never seen you so far in left field before. Even after you caught whats-her-face with a cock shoved down 'er throat, you came to work with a full deck o' cards."

I was going to correct him about what I'd caught Colleen doing, but I figured that was neither here nor there. Rhett was right. But I had no idea what to do about it. "I'm just tired. Didn't get much sleep this weekend."

"Ain't my problem, son."

I'd never understand why he bothered to ask us what was wrong if nothing was ever his problem. Though, I didn't exactly have a right to argue with him.

"I'll tell ya what…" He leaned forward with his elbows on his thighs and clasped his hands in front of him. "How's about a week at the desk?"

"Seriously?" My anger peaked. "You're going to punish me for being tired?"

"Nah. Don't think of this as a punishment, Cash. Think of it as a vacation. If I were gonna punish you for anything, it'd be lyin' to me. We both know you ain't tired. There's somethin' else goin' on inside that pretty little head of yours. Now, you don't gotta tell me if you don't want to…I just wanna know if it falls under the category of mental health."

"No." I shook my head. "I swear."

He tossed a file on the table and leaned back, locking his fingers behind his head. "Ah, hell. Just go ahead and tell me what it is. I gotta wait for someone else to get here to fill in for you, so I might as well do a little Dr. Phil on your ass."

I couldn't hold in the unsuspecting laughter. "You do resemble him."

"The fuck you just say, boy?" He dropped his arms and narrowed his gaze—it would've been alarming had I not already known it was a joke. "I'd beat his ass. Compared to me, he looks like he got eaten by a wolf and shit over a cliff."

Unable to stifle my laugh, I said, "I don't even know what that means."

"It means he's ugly." His incredulous stare only made me laugh harder. "Stop gettin' off track. What the hell happened to you?"

I didn't want to tell him, knowing I'd only make myself look like a little bitch crying over a girl. But Rhett had a way of pulling things out of me. And by the end—after telling him the entire conversation I'd had with Jade on Friday night—he appeared engrossed in it.

"So you don't know who this guy is?" He scratched his chin, as if this were life's biggest mystery.

"No, sir. She won't tell me, and as far as I know, she's never told anyone."

"Hmmm…interesting." And that was all he said before he jumped out of his seat. In the doorway, he turned to face me and said, "I'll call ahead so the pilot knows to take you to the box. This ain't a punishment, Nicholson. I know how your brain works. Just use this week to sort through your shit and come back next week ready to hunt."

Sitting at the desk should've bothered me, but considering how I felt when I'd woken up this morning, I didn't have much to complain about. So I nodded and watched him leave, resigned to my fate for the next five days.

CHAPTER 15

Jade

"Anyway...the cell reception sucks here, so if you don't hear from me much, that's why. But I'll call you at night from my room." Cash's smooth voice lingered through the line and plastered a smile on my face.

A wave washed over my feet, and when it drew back into the ocean, I watched the tiny bubbles pop up beneath the sand around my toes. "That's okay. I'm hoping to wear Aria out today at the beach so she'll go to bed on time tonight. She's been in one of her moods." Like every Monday.

"I still think you're making this shit up. She never acts like that when I'm home."

"Yeah, yeah." I giggled and watched my daughter run up to me, the floaties around her arms and chest making her waddle. "Speaking of the devil, I think she wants to talk to you." I passed Aria the phone and listened while she blabbered on about jumping and waves and crashing. At least, I assumed she'd said "crash." It could've very well been "Cash."

"She's cute," a voice came from just over my shoulder. When I glanced behind me, I noticed a woman, couldn't have been much older than me. Standing near her, watching Aria walk in circles while holding the phone to her ear, was a little boy. And it dawned on me that this was the woman and child I'd seen a couple of weeks ago after my phone call with Stevie.

She was striking. Her long, dark hair was the color of a midnight sky, and her creamy complexion set off the most alluring green eyes I'd ever seen. Women paid thousands to have a nose that perfect, and when I took in the rest of her, there didn't seem to be a flaw anywhere. But what caught my attention even more than her tiny frame and petite build was the ginger who accompanied her. Her son's fiery-red mop was in desperate need of a cut, but the way the sun reflected off it made him appear angelic. I couldn't help but notice his large, brown irises and the smattering of freckles that dotted his face and arms. But where she was rather short, he was exceptionally tall. The only thing hinting at his younger age was the innocence in his sad eyes.

"Thank you." I beamed at her and then held out my hand. "I'm Jade, and that's my daughter, Aria."

Her soft hand held mine before she gave it a slight squeeze, which kept me from feeling like I'd held a limp noodle. She had a good shake, which immediately earned my respect. "I'm Cora, and this is Legend. He's five. How old's your little girl?"

"Oh, she's two and a half." Just then, Aria came back, holding the phone in my direction. I pressed it to my ear long enough to hear Cash say he had to go and that he'd call me later. After saying goodbye, I flipped it closed and tossed it into the beach bag sitting in the sand next to Aria's toy shovel and pail.

Legend and Aria played in the surf while Cora and I regarded them and fell into easy conversation. "He's having a hard time adjusting…" Her gaze cut to mine before shifting back onto her son. "He's used to being home, and now that he's in school, I've been in a battle with him almost every day of the week."

"That sounds familiar—except the school part," I added with a laugh. "We actually just moved here a couple of months ago…" I pointed behind us to the house across the street. "And I just recently got a part-time job at the library, so Aria hasn't adjusted to that yet."

"Oh, that sounds like fun."

"Once a month they host a kids' theater. They have games and activities…you should bring Legend one night and check it out. I'll grab more information for you tomorrow when I get there. I'm sure he'll love it."

"That sounds amazing. Thanks." Her smile was gentle and sincere, and I knew right then and there I'd found a friend.

We talked a little more while the kids played together, then she announced that she had to leave. Her husband would be coming home so they had to get back and clean off. It was getting late, and Aria would need to be fed and bathed, but I wasn't ready to go home. The silence in the house was stifling on Mondays. So I relaxed in the sand on a towel and fell in love with my child all over again while watching her scoop water up in a green pail, only to dump it out and repeat the process all over again.

Just after five, I called her over to head back across the street.

After Aria was cleaned off and fed, I went into the laundry room to wash her suit and towel. The sight of the tote sitting on top of the washer—riddled with sand both inside and out—reminded me of the phone I'd tossed inside after Aria's conversation with Cash earlier. I dug around the sunscreen and lotion, random hair ties, and a few sippy cups half-filled with water before taking everything out. Once I had every last item placed on top of the dryer, I realized my phone wasn't there. I'd interrogated Aria, accusing her of removing it, but she never copped to it. Then, like a slap in the face, I remembered the pail she'd played with. After she'd handed the phone back and I said goodbye to Cash, I'd tossed it in, not paying attention to where it had landed. And if it had managed to get inside the bucket...

All I could think about was Aria filling it with water and dumping it out.

And my phone—as cheap as it was, the only thing I could afford for myself—washed away at sea. I groaned, praying I was wrong, hoping I'd stuffed it into my pocket and it'd fallen out somewhere in the house. But that was a pipe dream.

I'd been looking forward to my paycheck ever since the moment I'd gotten the job. Just the thought of putting money back into my account gave me a sense of peace. The thought of spending it on a phone left me frustrated beyond belief. I'd gone back and forth about what to do. My savings was depleting on a weekly basis, and I only got paid twice a month—and the amount wasn't much—so I'd decided to forgo the phone. I figured I'd wait until I had gotten the bank account into a place where I no longer stressed about how much milk Aria drank.

In the end, I didn't have much of a social life, so there was really no point in having a cell. The only two people I spoke to were Cash and Stevie, both of whom had email addresses I could use to correspond with in the meantime. Aside from them, I didn't care if I missed a call from my mother, and it wasn't like I couldn't inform the library of my situation and request they reach me by email if necessary. I had Cash's computer, so at least I'd be able to keep in touch that way until I could afford the luxury of replacing the phone.

After putting Aria to bed, I snuck into Cash's room—it never stopped feeling strange to go in there when he wasn't home—and grabbed the laptop. Even though it had a way to send and receive messages, I had no clue how to use it, nor did I have Cash's number memorized, so I couldn't send him a text that way. Instead, I resorted to the old-fashioned method of messaging and typed out an email, explaining what had happened with the phone, and asked him to help me figure out how to use iMessage on the account he'd set up for me.

By the next morning, I still hadn't received a reply. Before heading off to work, I tried again, informing him that I'd be at the library until four, but I'd check my email when I got home. However, the only response I had waiting for me when I returned was from Stevie, who'd asked for my Apple username—she was smart enough to give me instructions on how to find it—and said she'd send me a message.

I actually had somewhat of a life prior to Aria, filled with advanced technology such as smartphones and computers, though none of which were made by Apple. Cash had laughed at me at first, saying I was a visitor from the past, which was exactly how I felt when using his laptop. But I'd gotten the last laugh when I'd introduced him to Netflix.

Before going to bed Tuesday night, I tried again. I assumed he must've been busy or the cell reception was even worse at the hotel, but I figured as long as I sent him emails, he'd at least get them at some point.

Cora found me on the beach Wednesday and sat with me while the waves wore Aria out. She asked for my number, and I sheepishly explained how I was currently without a phone. The pity in her stare nearly killed me, especially since I'd just gotten through spilling most of my life to her—leaving out the heavy parts only Stevie had been privy to—but I could tell she hadn't meant it to come across that way. Instead, she told me where her house was, just down the street, and we made plans to meet up next week. I couldn't hide my elation over having a new friend.

I wasn't tired, but by ten, I forced myself to go to sleep. I anticipated the next day would be long, despite my shifts only being six hours. Trying to parent and work was no easy feat, but thankfully, Aria had been elected the princess of Geneva Key Public Library. The other women fawned all over her, helping me when I needed it. She now also had her very own makeshift sleeping quarters in the storage room, too. But even with all that, it still took mental preparation before a workday.

A loud crash had me jolting upright in bed, the covers tossed to the side in an instinctual move to flee at the awakening sound. It was still dark outside, not enough light from the moon casting in to see more than a shadow when my bedroom door flung wide open and bounced off the wall. I never shut it all the way in case Aria needed me in the mornings, which had left me vulnerable to the man entering my room. The natural reaction for most was to scream, but I couldn't. Pushed up on one hand, my arm extended and elbow locked behind me, not even covered by the sheets that now sat piled in the middle of the bed, I was frozen in fear. My mouth hung open, but not a sound came out. Time seemed to pass in slow motion, although it couldn't have all happened in more than two or three seconds.

The shadow of a large man with wide, broad shoulders moved from the doorway into my personal space. He stalked toward me, practically crossing the room in only a few strides of his long legs until he was on top of me. I closed my eyes tightly and pressed my hands to his chest in a lame attempt to push him away while he sat half on the bed, straddling my legs with one foot still planted on the floor. But the moment his hand came to cradle my face, my skin basking in the warmth of his panicked words, I lost every ounce of will to fight.

"Are you okay? Fuck, Jade...tell me you're all right," he begged while quickly running his hands over me—my face, my shoulders, arms and legs. It was as if he'd found me in a ditch, thrown from a car, taking my last breath, and he had to inspect me from head to toe.

I wasn't sure where the fear had come from, but as soon as I turned to the side and noticed the red digits on the clock next to the bed telling me it was after four in the morning, my first thought was Aria...and my own panic ensued. I must've said her name aloud, because in an instant, Cash was off the bed, storming back through the doorway into the hall. I followed him, stopping just outside her room, and with bated breath, watched Cash in the glow of her nightlight lean over the tiny bed. When he stood, his posture deflated, his shoulders no longer holding the same rigidness as before. And in his audible sigh, I felt his relief. She was safe.

He moved into the hallway, and I took a step back, giving him space to pull the door enough to leave her a crack for the morning. As soon as he stood in front of me, he tugged me against him, his arms around my shoulders, his hands woven in my hair as he held me to his hard chest. His whispered words settled over me like a comforting blanket when he said, "I was so worried, Jade."

I pushed against him just enough to peer into his eyes, made darker by the shadows cast in the unlit hallway. "I don't understand? Why were you worried? What happened?" Then it dawned on me. Being startled from sleep didn't leave me with much cognizant thought about what day it was. "You're home early...why? Is everything okay?"

Rather than answer me, he took my hand, laced our fingers together, and led me to my room, past the dilapidated baby gate that now lay in a crumpled mess on the floor. In his haste to get to me, he must not have remembered its presence.

I headed for the bed, flipped on the lamp on the side table, and climbed onto the mattress with my knees bent, feet tucked beneath me. He followed behind me, but rather than sit like he had the other night, he dropped himself onto the edge of the bed, less than a foot in front of me, his feet still set on the floor, and threw himself onto his back with his arm hooked over his eyes.

"Are you going to tell me what's going on?" Sleep still hung in my voice.

After a long sigh, he finally dropped his arm, but instead of looking at me, he kept his focus on the ceiling. "I haven't talked to you since Monday afternoon. When I didn't hear from you that night, I assumed you'd gone to bed early since you spent so long at the beach. But then you didn't answer or return my calls on Tuesday. I started to get worried then, but I told myself you had work and had probably gotten busy when you got back home, so I tried to ignore it. I figured I was being paranoid. Until I couldn't get ahold of you today. Your phone just kept going to voicemail, and I assumed something was wrong. I thought maybe your ex had found you or something."

I slipped my hand into his, pressing our palms together, and earned his attention for the first time since we came back to my room. "I emailed you...several times. You didn't get them?"

His brow furrowed while he stared at me. "No." Before I could offer him the same reassurance he'd gifted me when I'd needed it, his voice lowered and he added, "Are you leaving? Is that why you haven't answered my calls and only sent me emails? To tell me that what happened this weekend was too much and you've decided to leave?"

It was evident in not only his downtrodden tone, but also in his sorrowful gaze, that his question hadn't been meant as an accusation, but rather, it came from a place of utter fear. I couldn't explain it, but his deep concern over the possibility that I'd leave him did something to me. It gave me an inside glimpse into his feelings, and more than any touch he'd ever offered me, it let me believe he truly cared. There was no false hope on my part. It was as if he'd just given me his heart.

"Cash...I think Aria gave my phone to the fish."

He blinked several times, probably trying to translate my words. In his defense, not only had I been in a deep sleep less than ten minutes ago, but I'd also been lost in the abstraction of his soft-spoken words, the sentiment hidden in his worry.

"After we spoke on Monday, I tossed my phone into my bag — well, it might've landed in the bucket *next* to the bag — and then later, Aria used the bucket to play in the water. I couldn't find my phone after I got back, so I'm thinking she might've accidentally lost it at sea."

Immense ease lightened his features until he lay completely relaxed across my bed.

"I sent you emails explaining what happened. Stevie helped me figure out the whole texting thing on the computer, but I haven't memorized your number, so I couldn't reach out that way, and when you never responded, I just assumed the cell service was bad everywhere."

Irritation marred his brow, but I could tell it was directed at himself, not at me. "The email address you have is the one I use for family. I don't have it set up for alerts, so I never got them. And I never thought to check it. My parents know to call if they need to get ahold of me and can't wait until I go through my email."

"I'm sorry. I didn't even consider how you might've reacted to my silence. Now I feel bad for making you leave work early. You didn't get in trouble, did you?"

"Nah. I was just doing desk work—research and shit. Nothing exciting."

"Do you have to go back?"

"I called my supervisor on my way out this morning, and he said just to keep him updated with what's going on. But by the time I get back out there, I'll just have to turn around and head home for the weekend. Kind of seems like a wasted trip to me. I'll see what he says when I call him tomorrow."

I glanced at the clock, watching the numbers creep toward five. "You mean today?"

Cash groaned and ran his hand down his face. Exhaustion plagued his eyes, but he didn't appear to care. "So why haven't you gotten a new phone yet?"

"I figured I don't really need one, so there's no point in rushing out and spending money I don't have. Now that I'm driving more than I used to, I'm having to get gas more frequently, and even though Aria is basically potty trained, she's still in pull-ups at night—and those aren't cheap. I decided to wait until I can get a few paychecks deposited so I'm not feeling like I'm working for free while still draining the account."

"You need a phone, Jade." He narrowed his gaze on me. "What's your plan if something happens and you have to call for help?"

I shrugged, not having given that any thought when debating the phone situation earlier in the week. "I guess run next door and ask them to call?"

"So if Aria starts choking…your plan is to go door to door until you find someone to call nine-one-one?" It meant a lot that he cared this deeply for the safety of my child, although I couldn't help feeling like he somehow looked down on me or my parenting for not having thought about it. But he didn't give me a chance to speak before squeezing my hand and softening his tone, adding, "We'll go tomorrow to get you a new one."

"There's got to be another alternative, Cash. Your question was legitimate, but so is the fact I don't always have a phone on me. I don't handle fear well—as proven by my lack of fight *or* flight instincts when you came barging in here tonight. I freeze up. So it's not very likely I'd even remember where my cell is in a situation like that."

"We'll figure something out."

I had no idea what options I had, but this wasn't the time to think about them—not at nearly five in the morning when I had Cash lying on my bed. I was ready to curl up and sleep, but I'd missed him and his company, and I wasn't willing to give that up just yet.

"I'm sorry for worrying you," I whispered.

He blinked at me for a moment, and then released my hand to prop himself up. His face was so close to mine, yet it didn't feel close enough. With his free hand, he carefully ran his knuckles down my cheek, stilling at my chin where he held it between his thumb and forefinger. "I'm sorry for barging in here and scaring you."

I tried to brush it off, but I couldn't even manage enough strength to lift one shoulder. "It's fine. I mean, that's what roommates do, right? They don't hear from the other in..." I paused to make the lamest attempt at mental calculation before adding, "Roughly thirty-six hours, and then race home in the middle of the night to check on them. At least, that's how it *should* be."

It was meant to be funny, but he didn't laugh. He didn't even show a glimmer of a smile. In fact, there was not a hint of humor to be found in his entire expression. His eyes remained on mine, holding the intense stare for longer than what was considered comfortable. It was obvious he had something to say—or he'd fallen asleep sitting up with his eyes open. That was a definite possibility. But then his gaze dropped to my mouth, and his breathing sped up.

"I have to tell you something, Jade." His voice was heavy, full of grit, and it made my chest constrict painfully, feeling as though I was being crushed by a wrecking ball. "I broke a rule...one of yours."

"Which one?" My fear increased with each second that ticked by.

His eyes never left my lips when he uttered, "I fell in love."

The weight on my chest crushed my ribs, collapsed my lungs, and freed my heart. None of the common-sense questions mattered—his lack of sexual attraction toward me being on the top of that list. I'd heard the words I never thought would come out of his mouth, and nothing else existed. I wanted him to kiss me. He was right there, eyes on the prize, but he didn't. And that was the one thing that halted my excitement.

He either regretted this, or he was just as scared.

My money was on fear. This had likely come as a surprise to him, and I wouldn't doubt he was in the midst of trying to sort through the confusion. I didn't care to make matters worse by moving too fast or pushing too hard. I'd be devastated if I awoke in the morning and learned he'd changed his mind—or worse, had confused his worry over my safety as something more.

So I decided to play it by ear, test him, have some fun to see if the moment passed. "Oh, yeah? Does this mean we'll have another roommate? I won't have to give up my bed, will I? Because as much as I love Aria's room, I don't think we'll both fit on her mattress."

Finally, his lips curled at the corners, and I rejoiced in the sight. "No, you won't have to share a room with Aria."

Still not satisfied—and also enjoying his smile, wanting it to last a little longer—I kept up the charade. "So I guess you'll be moving her into your room, then? I mean, I'll share my bed if I have to, just as long as she doesn't hog the covers."

Humor danced in his eyes. He was enjoying this as much as I was. "Where she sleeps is entirely up to her. I'd love to fall asleep next to her, but I plan to follow her lead."

I soaked up his words, realizing he had turned this game into an easy, uncomplicated conversation full of answers without the insecurities brought on by making it personal. As long as we spoke about the woman he'd confessed to falling in love with as if she were someone else, we'd be able to better navigate this situation.

"And when did you realize you had feelings for her?"

"Well, I guess you could say it was Friday night." When my body tensed—a natural reaction to assuming he'd confused love with whatever he felt after hearing about Aria's father—he dropped his hand from my chin and placed it on my knee. "But that's not when it all started, Jade. You asked when I *realized* it."

"So you're saying you felt something for her prior to that night?"

"Absolutely. And I hope that doesn't come as a surprise to her."

"Why would you think it wouldn't?"

"Because it was obvious. When I finally opened my eyes and recognized it for myself, I was shocked at how blatant I was about my feelings for her. I honestly have no idea why it took me so long to see it for myself."

I hesitated, only because I worried my next words would blur the line we'd created and leave me vulnerable to his response. But I needed all the facts, so I took a deep breath and went for it. "Knowing you, I'm sure you told her you didn't find her sexually appealing—beautiful, but not in the way that excites you. So maybe you're giving yourself too much credit by assuming it was obvious."

He sat up straighter, this conversation taking a sharp turn toward the land of seriousness. "True, but I'd hope my actions had spoken louder than my asinine words. The ugly truth is this...I've been around women who I thought were very good looking. But rather than salivate at their assets or physical features, I'd simply take note of their beauty. Then there were women who just did it for me. I didn't need to learn their names before picturing all the ways I could fuck them. That's what I meant when I said sexually attractive."

"*Yeah...*" I dragged the word out, quirking an eyebrow at him. "I'm not sure how to take that. Neither sounds all that flattering."

At least it got him grinning again. He dropped his chin and shook his head, a breathy chuckle escaping through his teeth. "No, it doesn't. But I guess that just goes to show you men aren't all that complicated where sex is concerned."

"Okay, so you could admire her, but she didn't leave you with the need to rip her clothes off. Got it. Now how did you get from there to falling in love with her? I think that's what's most important here."

"I'm not sure if there's an answer for that. Part of it might be maturity. I hadn't allowed myself to look at anyone in that way since I was twenty-two. During my marriage, I never entertained those thoughts about other women—I wasn't really around any, other than Colleen's friends. If I wasn't at work, I was home with her."

I rolled my eyes in disbelief. "You can't be serious, Cash. Married people still have eyes."

"Yes, that's true. If I were at a store or out with Colleen and an attractive woman was there, I'd notice. But that's all it was. Nothing more than a simple thought about another human being. I wouldn't think about her beyond that or entertain any explicit fantasies with her in it. Who knows...maybe I hadn't been single long enough to entertain the thought of having sex with someone else, so when I saw...*her* for the first time, sex wasn't even on my mind. Or there's always the possibility that I'd already connected with her on a different level, so my focus wasn't on the physical aspects."

"All great answers, Cash. But I'm willing to bet she won't believe any of them…no matter how true they might be. It doesn't change the fact you saw her as a friend, nothing more, and then all of a sudden, out of the clear blue, you change your mind."

"It wasn't like that."

"Then how was it? Because to me—and I'm not her, so I can't speculate how she'd take it—it sounds like she might've opened up to you about something personal, something I'm assuming you might've had a reaction to…maybe anger on her behalf…and your wires got crossed. Sympathy isn't love, Cash."

"I'm well aware of that. But in order for me to have confused the two, my realization would've had to come *after* her 'possible' admission. And considering I saw the writing on the wall before that conversion may or may not have happened, I can absolutely, without a doubt, say I didn't get my wires crossed."

"Before?" I wasn't sure I'd be able to get the word out. I couldn't get enough oxygen into my lungs, and my heart had picked that moment to finally believe him, tapping out a beat that rivaled the tempo of a techno song.

"Yeah." He nodded, so sure of himself. "Before. We were on the couch, and when I looked at her, it was like my heart stopped trying to deny it. It was always there, I just never saw it for what it was. But that was the moment I couldn't lie to myself any longer. I couldn't make up an excuse for the feelings I had while staring into her eyes. Before that, when I found myself thinking of what she looked like beneath her clothes, I chalked it up to curiosity, wondering if I'd be able to see the evidence of the life she created. When I caught myself thinking about her at night while trying to fall asleep, I told myself it was because I hadn't seen her or spoken to her in a while. But that night, with her in my arms, I had no excuse for what I felt inside."

I cleared my throat, hoping to hide the way his words affected me. But as soon as I spoke, there was no doubt I'd failed. "Well, I'm pretty sure she might believe that. If you're lucky. I mean, it could go either way."

"Any idea what she'd say?"

"It depends."

"On what?"

"Whether or not you kiss her after you tell her all that."

His gaze fell to my mouth again, and I took that moment to trace my bottom lip with my tongue. Something akin to hunger flashed in his eyes, but it wasn't sinister like I was used to seeing. And it bathed me in a fiery desire I'd never experienced.

"Should I kiss her?"

I nodded, eagerly. "Yes, you sh—" And before I could finish my sentence, his mouth was on mine.

CHAPTER 16

Cash

I couldn't get enough of her. The second I'd silenced her with a kiss, everything around us vanished. Her past, my marriage, her troubles, my job. Nothing mattered while I had my mouth on hers. But as much as I yearned to submerge myself in her touch, I had to tap on the brakes before we found ourselves in another situation like last week.

We broke apart, both needing air, but I never dropped my hand from her face. I craved the contact with her, never wanting it to end, yet I couldn't rush this. I had to tread lightly, and there wasn't a single part of me that cared. I'd go as slow as I had to, just as long as she gave me the chance to make her fall in love with me, too.

"There's still so much we need to talk about." I blew the words across her swollen lips. "But I'm pretty sure I can't think properly right now."

When she shifted closer to me, her face still cradled in my hand, it caused her erect nipples to brush along my forearm. "Then stop thinking…" she whispered hoarsely.

I could feel her hesitation and the inconspicuous, nervous tremors that ran through her and riddled her entire body. Had I not been so close to her, touching her, kissing her…I probably would have never noticed. But I did. And I couldn't ignore the contradiction between her actions and reactions.

The way she silenced me with her mouth was brazen and bold. Yet the way she trembled left me hesitant to continue; her response indicated uncertainty. I refused to do anything she wasn't completely comfortable with, so I ended it once more.

"There's no need to rush this, Jade."

She kept her chin tilted and lids lowered, preventing me from reading her expression. "I'm not trying to rush anything. I've just never felt like this before."

"Like what?"

Her gaze slowly drifted up to meet mine. "Good. I can't explain it any other way."

"And I promise it won't ever stop."

My words appeared to settle her, yet the tremors remained. I could only assume they were brought on by adrenaline, because there wasn't an ounce of fear in her eyes when she held my stare and asked, "Will you do something for me?"

Had I not been lost in all that was Jade, I would've given her question more thought. But apparently, nothing was strong enough to break the spell she'd cast upon me, leaving me too weak to do anything other than agree. "Absolutely."

"Will you take off your shirt?" Excitement filled her eyes, and hope danced in her voice.

"Seriously?" I was baffled, not at all expecting that to be her request. But when she did nothing but stare at me, one eyebrow quirked in expectation, I gave in. If Jade wanted me shirtless, then that was what she'd get.

I barely had it off before she was on her feet, making her way to the bedroom door. Her blue eyes sparkled mischievously on her way back to me, and that's when I realized she not only closed the door, but she also locked it. I'd told myself we would take this slow, yet she was making it very difficult to keep that promise.

I stood to meet her, although she stopped my pursuit before I'd taken the first step. Standing in front of me, she closed her eyes, and on an exhale, she brought her lips to the center of my chest. My heart exploded and my knees weakened, forcing me back onto the edge of the mattress.

She situated herself between my legs, now almost eye level, and closed her mouth over mine. The entire time, I let her take the lead, not once stripping her of control, and the longer our kiss lasted, the more lost in her I became. So lost, in fact, that when her hands slid down my stomach, I didn't stop her. When her fingers began to unfasten the button on my jeans, I didn't give it any thought. And when she slowly dragged the zipper down, even the grinding of the metal teeth didn't make me question where this was going.

But as soon as she tried to gain access, unable to get far while I remained seated, I was finally brought back to reality. In an instant, I broke away from her lips. "Jade…this can wait. It's late, and you have work tomorrow. We don't have to do this now."

"I know, Cash. But I want to." She peppered my jaw with kisses, bringing her mouth to my ear to whisper, "I want to touch you…*all* of you." I was aware that her actions were driven by endorphins, causing her to be more forward, but as soon as she hooked her thumbs into the waistband of my jeans, I lost my will to fight against her.

I lifted my hips enough to help her drag my jeans down my legs, my boxers with them. When she stepped out of the way, I toed off my shoes and kicked my pants the rest of the way off, leaving me completely naked in front of her.

Jade took her time exploring my body while I refrained from touching her. But the moment she took my dick in her hand, I nearly lost all self-control. Her palm slid carefully over my shaft, so lightly it only served to tease me. I had to force my ass to stay on the mattress rather than pump myself in her grip, because I needed more friction. The longer it went on, the worse it became. Finally, after I groaned in what probably sounded like pain, she stilled, which forced me to look into her anxiety-filled eyes.

"Am I doing it wrong?" Gone was the vixen, and in her place stood a terrified goddess.

I was aware of her past, of that asshole taking her hand and making her do things she wasn't comfortable with, so I refused to do anything remotely similar. But telling someone how to jack you off was a sure way to go soft.

Keeping my eyes on hers, I carefully held her wrist, silently asking permission. She never gave me a nod or verbally answered me, because her expression told me everything. It wasn't simply consent, but almost a plea to help her through this. She wasn't ready to give up—she only sought to please me, yet she needed to understand how.

I placed my hand over hers, gripping myself but feeling only her touch. I tightened my fingers to show her how hard to squeeze, and then began to slide our hold up and down, slowing toward the head with slightly more pressure than before. After several pumps, I released my grip and let her take over. While she adjusted to working my dick solo, I held her by the back of the neck and took her mouth with mine.

I needed air and broke the kiss. "Fuck, Jade. That feels so good," I rasped against her lips. She didn't say anything, but I didn't expect her to, either. The more I praised her with words and reactions, the more confident she became. And the more confident she was, the closer I got to the peak. "Jade, Jade, Jade…stop," I rushed out, pulling her hand off me.

"What'd I do?" Panic filled every part of her from her eyes to her voice.

"God…nothing. But if you didn't stop, I was about to come all over you."

Her posture visibly eased. "Isn't that the point?"

A huffed chuckle rolled through me. "Ultimately, I guess. But I don't want to come in your hand."

Something shifted in her expression, confusion maybe. "Then where?"

Not wasting another second, I lifted her shirt and tossed it onto the floor with my discarded clothes. Her bare breasts called to me, begging me to taste them. So before I moved to her shorts, I lavished her chest with attention. I flicked one nipple with my tongue, and when it was hard enough to cut glass, I switched to the other, pulling it into my mouth and sucking on it.

Nothing beat the moans coming from Jade. There wasn't a sweeter sound in the world. And I wanted to do everything I could so they'd never end.

I took my time removing her shorts, sliding them over her hips and down her thighs at a snail's pace. And when I had her in nothing but panties, I couldn't even remember the promise I'd made of going slow. It didn't exist. I swept her into my arms as I stood, and then spun her around until I had her flat on her back, my body covering hers.

"Tell me if you want me to stop." I made sure she held my stare while I carefully dragged her panties down her legs. But other than offer a nod of agreement, she just lay there and watched me completely undress her. I crawled back up her body and brought my mouth to her ear. "To answer your question, the only place I want to come is inside you…preferably at the same time you come on my cock."

Her nails dug into my back, which fueled my fire. But then she spoke, and it halted everything. In a raspy, heavy voice, she uttered, "I wouldn't get my hopes up if I were you."

I picked my head up and looked at her. "What's that supposed to mean?"

"Nothing…just that you shouldn't take it personal if I can't…you know."

I couldn't believe what I was hearing. It was late, and I was tired, but it was a travesty to think she hadn't ever had an orgasm. "So you've never gotten off?" Had I planned my words better, I would have softened the question a bit.

She shrugged slightly beneath me. "I have, but only if it's not about me."

"What do you mean?"

The moment she started to speak, the hesitation and uncertainty in her tone was obvious. "I can fantasize about a man, but I can't put myself *into* the fantasy. As soon as I become part of the scene in my mind, it stops immediately."

I could only assume she was referring to playing her own fiddle, but I wasn't going to embarrass her by asking. Instead, I lowered my mouth to hers and said, "I'm pretty certain I can change that. There's no doubt in my mind that I can get the job done." It came off playful and teasing, and she smiled against my lips.

"You sound very sure of yourself." Her whispered words bathed my skin in a song of seduction.

I couldn't help but run my hand along her side and over her bare hip to her thigh. Goose bumps rose on her flesh and tickled my palm, which only served to spur me on. She was playing with fire, but it was one I hoped would ignite her soul and not burn her. "That's because I am, Jade."

Her face tilted up and her mouth found mine, her lips as soft as silk just before she opened. I responded in kind, and our tongues danced together. With each swirl, my dick became impossibly harder. She reached her hand between us and wrapped her fingers around my shaft. Applying the perfect amount of pressure, she stroked the length, once, twice.

"Fuck…" I couldn't help the groan of need, and I loved the murmur of a giggle she gave me in return.

I shifted to the side, just enough to slide my hand from her leg to her inner thigh, and then up to her core. The moment my fingers grazed her slick center, I was done for. I teased the area, waiting for her to halt my actions, but instead, she opened wider, inviting me in.

"Cash…" Had she said my name without a hedonistic undertone, I would have retreated immediately, but it came out like a plea, encouraging me to prove to her I could take her places she'd never been.

One syllable was all it took for me to dip my finger into her warmth and rub her clit with my thumb. I expected her to release her hold on my cock, yet she kept stroking while I added another finger. But when I brought my mouth to her neck, she gave up on the hand job in favor of receiving the pleasure I offered. And I loved every aching minute of it.

She had my undivided attention as I fingered her. She let me know when I hit the spot that drove her wild by arching her back and thrusting her chest toward me. A trail of kisses led me to her breasts, and I took her nipple in my mouth, sucking it while my fingers fucked her. I loved the way her nails dug into my skin, proving she was not only enjoying the fantasy, but she was lost in it.

"Please," she begged, but for what, I wasn't sure.

"Tell me what you need, Jade."

"You." She gasped when I curled my fingers in a come-hither motion. "*All* of you."

There was nothing I craved more than to sink into her, to release the pressure that consumed me, but if she wanted it, she would have to take it.

As if she read my mind, she eased her arm under my shoulder and wrapped me in a hug. My fingers kept working, and she rewarded me with moan after gratifying moan. Then she hooked her leg behind mine and shifted me over her once more, forcing my hand away so I could settle between her legs.

"Jade…"

She silenced me with her mouth, and before I could react, her heels dug into my ass. In an instant, I sank balls deep into a heaven I never believed existed until that moment. With my lips firmly pressed to hers, she gasped for air, rounding her spine, pushing her hips up, and I waited while she adjusted to my size.

It didn't take long before she cupped my ass, trying to coerce me to move. I gave her what she asked for, rocking my pelvis like the waves rolling in before retreating. Undulating in desire, a lust driven by love. Jade was clearly lost in the moment, and I desperately worked to bring her to nirvana.

I locked my eyes on hers and begged, "Tell me…who's here?"

Confusion clouded the blue. "You."

"And…?" I needed her to be here, right here, in this moment.

"Me," she panted, realizing what I'd meant.

The intensity of the heat surrounding my dick grew, and her muscles tightened with each breath she held a little longer than the last. She was close, and I wanted her orgasm more than she did. I shifted slightly, and her nails nearly broke my skin. Knowing I had her within reach, I pushed inside her with each flex and drew my length back out as I relaxed. I gathered her body in my arms, tucked my head into the crook of her neck, and I brought her to the first of what I was sure would be many climaxes, just before I reached my own.

Slowly catching her breath, her soft, whispered question grazed my cheek when she asked, "Will you stay with me? Please?"

The pleading in her tone broke me. I'd move heaven and Earth to give her anything she asked for, and this was a simple request.

I held her face in my hand, our exhales mixing between us. "Of course."

She rewarded me with the brightest smile I'd ever seen. I gently pulled away from her, slowly dragging my dick out of her warmth, and then moved to help her climb beneath the covers. Once she settled next to me, I slid to the edge of the bed to turn off the lamp.

Before I could pull the chain and cloak the room in darkness, a single, cool fingertip outlined the wings and the sword of my tattoo—the archangel Michael. Goose bumps covered my skin at her gentle touch and probing exploration. Other than asking what it was, she'd never mentioned it. But as soon as she sucked in a breath, I knew she wouldn't be able to hold in her curiosity any longer.

"What's the reason you chose this angel?" Her question was so soft I actually felt it against my skin more than I heard it. "Does it represent you, a protector, or was it because you needed his protection?"

Turning my head to the side so she could hear me better, I said, "Maybe a little bit of both." I was powerless against her soft caress. It was like each graze of her nails brought me one step closer to telling her everything. "I think it was more for the comfort of what he stands for, if I'm being honest."

"What does he stand for?"

I was beyond thankful that she remained behind me, because I worried she'd see the truth written on my face while I tried to navigate around actual lies. "Taking any means necessary for the greater good."

"What does that even mean?"

"The Bible makes it very clear that there is no justification for killing someone." As soon as those words left my lips, her hand stilled in its exploration of the ink lining my back. But I didn't let that stop me. "No matter the reason, the cause, how it happens...we are not allowed to cast judgment upon anyone, regardless of their crimes. But I have a hard time accepting that."

"Are you saying you can justify killing someone?" Fear was embedded in her tone.

I had no idea why I'd taken her question this far, but it was too late to back out now. "If a cop arrives at a scene where a man shot and killed someone else, and then turned the gun on the officer...does the officer not have a right to defend himself by any means necessary? Is he supposed to stand there and let the guy shoot him, too? If you're being attacked, and to get the person off you, you hit him in the head with a rock or a lamp...should you be punished if he dies?"

"Well...no."

"According to religion, killing is killing. But here, we have the right to defend ourselves. We have the right to defend others. We may not be prosecuted or ever see the inside of a jail cell for doing what needs to be done, but what happens when we leave here? If the rules for taking a life are black and white on the other side, then does that mean we spend eternity in hell for protecting someone?"

"So this angel"—her fingertip lightly followed the black lines—"is to make you feel better about ending someone's life as long as you have a good reason?"

It wasn't so much her question as it was her tone that told me she'd never be okay with what I did for a living. I'd been married for six years, and not once did I ever contemplate being honest with Colleen about my job, but while I sat here, her hands on my skin, I had to fight against the need to explain it all to her. Now, I had a decision to make: Continue to lie to her while building a relationship and possible life together, or get a new job.

The latter wasn't so easy.

"It's not just that…it's everything. Take every sin, and most of the time, you'll find an exception. Thou shall not lie. What if a lie is the only thing keeping someone you love safe? Thou shall not steal. If you walk in on someone about to swallow a bottle of pills, are you not supposed to steal it away from them?"

When her touch left my skin, I turned to find out why. But then I saw her bright eyes, full of curiosity, not blame. She didn't regard me with hate or disgust. And even though she hadn't said the words, love flowed freely from her gaze, matched by the soft curve of her lips.

I gently tugged on the lamp's chain, and when the light went out, I slid beneath the covers beside her. I lifted my arm the way I'd done countless times before to invite her into my embrace, and she willingly rested her head on my shoulder, forming her body along my side. Somehow, it felt different lying with her in bed than it ever had on the couch, but in the best possible way.

With her palm pressed against my chest, she quietly asked, "Why are his wings dirty?" A yawn hovered at the edges of her words.

"Because not every soiled soul makes for a bad person."

Silence settled around me, and I thought she'd gone to sleep. But as soon as I closed my eyes, she mumbled, "You should've left the light on."

"Why's that?"

"You broke a rule…so it's only fair if I get to watch you sleep."

Amusement rolled through me as I held her closer and gave in to slumber.

✦

Morning came too early…or late, however I decided to look at it. Jade stretched and hummed, the sheet falling away from her breasts and calling my attention to her nipples. It was enough to wake me up and pull her into me. My morning wood made her blush, so she tucked her face into the crook of my neck to hide from me.

"Keep breathing on me like that, and I won't let you go to work," I groaned out.

Quickly, she pulled away and turned her bright, stunned gaze toward the alarm clock on the nightstand. "Oh, crap!" She jumped out of bed and couldn't put her clothes on fast enough. "I have to be at work in an hour, and Aria…"

We stared at each other for an elongated second, both understanding the rest of her sentence. I tossed the covers off and grabbed my discarded clothes from last night while she resumed covering herself.

"I'll go check on her, see where she's at. And then I'll take her back to her room to get her changed, and on my way, I'll knock on the door to let you know it's safe to—" Her words came to an abrupt halt when she finally turned to face me. "Oh, you're already dressed. Okay then…I guess we don't really need a strategy, huh?"

My shoulders bounced with laughter and I shook my head while I stalked toward her. I set my hands on her hips and pulled her against me long enough to press a kiss to her forehead. Then

I grabbed the door handle and twisted it, ready to check on Aria, although I stalled when Jade glanced up.

Panic glittered in her eyes. "What if she asks why you were in here?"

"Why are you so worried about that?" I pinched her chin and smiled. "Just bypass the question and ask her where the remote is. She'll forget all about it."

"Is that seriously what you do?"

With a shrug, I asked, "Hey, Jade...do you know where my phone is?"

She turned and scanned the floor around the bed where my clothes had landed last night. After a moment, she peered at me from over her shoulder with a grin so wide it made her squint. We shared a laugh and then left the room.

To our amazement, Aria was on the couch, remote in hand, eyes glued to the TV. As soon as she saw us, her gaze fell upon me, and she was on her feet in less than a second. She latched herself onto my leg, full of excitement that hadn't been there when we'd walked out.

I met Jade's stare and said, "See? All that worrying for nothing."

She blew me off with a huff before grabbing Aria by the arm. "Come on, sweetheart, we have to get dressed—Mommy's running late."

Aria screamed, refusing to release my leg, and it visibly irritated Jade.

"I don't have time for this. We need to hurry."

"Just leave her here," I offered, surprising even myself. I enjoyed spending time with Aria, but I'd never entertained the idea of taking care of her alone. Anytime it was just her and me, Jade was, at the most, across the street.

"I appreciate the offer, but I can't accept it. She's my child, my responsibility."

"I'll respect your decision, but I honestly don't mind. You're already running late, and I'll be here anyway, so I don't see the point in rushing to get you both ready while I sit around the house all day."

She glanced down at the princess who pleaded while bouncing on her feet, arms still latched around my leg. "I would...it's just the whole bathroom thing."

I understood what she meant without any further explanation. Even though she'd never said it out loud, I was well aware she wasn't comfortable having me change her daughter or help her use the bathroom—and honestly, neither was I. "That won't be an issue, I promise. She's capable of doing her thing on her own, right?"

"Yeah, but she still needs help wiping."

"What better way to make her learn how to do it by herself?"

It didn't appear she liked that answer much.

"Okay...so you'd just have a pair of underwear with skid marks to clean when you get home."

Or that one, either.

"I'm just trying to help, Jade. You don't have to take it. I won't push it on you, nor will I get upset. You're the parent, and like I've always told you, you make the call, and I'll back it up." I held her hand, needing her to *feel* my truth.

"Fine. Okay, yeah." She nodded. "But you better call me if you need anything—and I mean *anything*. Got it, Cash?"

"I think I've got this handled." No one could say I didn't have confidence. Even when fear trickled into my head, I remained steadfast in my decision. I could do this. It was only for a few hours—or six—and Aria was an angel.

Jade raced against the clock to shower and dress in order to make it to the library on time. After a quick goodbye, she dashed out the door...only to run back in a minute later, defeat painting her face red. "My car won't start. Seriously...why today? I don't have time for this."

I stood from the couch, where Aria and I watched *Barbie's Dreamhouse* while she ate her breakfast. I dug my keys out of my pocket and tossed them to her. "Take mine."

They landed at her feet. She didn't make one move to catch them, just stared at them flying through the air and watched as they crashed to the floor in front of her. Her large eyes, completely filled with fear, met mine. "I can't drive that thing!"

Confused, I asked, "Why not? It's a car...not a tank."

"Yeah, a car that's worth more than...more than..." She glanced around as if searching for something to use as a comparison. Not satisfied with anything, she waved her arms by her sides in irritation and said, "*Everything* I own put together."

"I'm not following what the cost of the car has to do with you driving it."

"Uh...because I can't pay to have it fixed or replaced if something happens."

"Then it's a good thing I have insurance." I pointed to the keys at her feet. "Take it."

Reluctantly, she did, and with a sheepish grin, she waved and left once more.

"Looks like it's just you and me, Tyke." I settled back into the couch and soaked up her infectious giggles at her nickname.

CHAPTER 17

Jade

I pulled around to the back of the house, anxious to get inside to check on Aria. It wasn't that I didn't trust Cash with her, but I'd never left her alone with anyone other than Stevie. This was all new to me, and other than wanting to hold my daughter and shower her with kisses, I had a growing list of questions for Cash. I eagerly climbed out of the SUV and set the alarm.

The second I opened the door, I was hit with a wave of something delicious. It felt like a lifetime since I'd last come home to the smell of dinner cooking in the oven, and it made my heart skip a few beats. The living room was empty, and when I went around the corner toward the hallway, I'd noticed no one was in the kitchen, either. The timer on the stove was set, and all the preparation items were put away, so I assumed Cash had started supper and took Aria across the street while the timer counted down. But after I slipped off my shoes and set my purse on the bed, I heard the familiar baritone coming from down the hall, followed by an ear-piercing squeal and Aria shouting, "No!"

I ran out of my room, making it to Aria's in only a few steps, frightened at what I'd walk into. I'd done my best to keep her safe, and all I could think of was how I'd failed at the one and only task I had as her mother. A desperate demand to leave her alone stopped short of coming out when my gaze landed on Cash—on his knees, cleaning a black square on the lower half of the wall—and then on Aria, a fat piece of pink chalk clutched in her tiny hand. While he calmly explained to her that he had to make room for more art, I stood still and regarded their interactions, neither noticing my presence with their backs to me.

"Okay, Tyke...let's try this again." He sat back on his haunches and lifted Aria off the ground to set her in front of him, closer to the now-clean space. "Draw me a picture of Mommy."

My heart melted, completely and utterly turned to mush. I watched in awe as Aria scribbled her version of a picture, which took up the entire area, none of it resembling any actual shape or form.

"I think this one's even better than the last."

Aria pointed to her masterpiece and explained what everything was. "Dat's Mommy. Dat's me. And dat's you!"

"Oh, yeah? Where are we?"

She turned to the side, giving him the "are you for real right now" face with her hands on her hips and head cocked to the side. But before she could effectively ream him out for what she clearly deemed a stupid question, she caught sight of me. Her face lit up, no longer showing any traces of the attitude she'd just worn, and she ran to me.

Her excited chatter filled the small room as she took my hand and led me to her artwork. Cash stood, wiped his hands on his cargo shorts, and leaned down to press a chaste kiss to my cheek. It was sweet and almost made me swoon...the only reason I didn't was because Aria started explaining her drawing, catching me by surprise when she said, "And dat's Daddy!"

Cash and I both swung our heads toward the bouncing child between us.

"No, Aria...I'm *Cash*," he corrected her, and it tugged at something inside me. He wasn't her father, and we'd only just taken the first step toward a relationship about twelve hours ago. Yet hearing him correct her felt wrong.

I shook it off, reminding myself that this wasn't something I even needed to contemplate right now, and effectively changed the subject before any more was said. "I hadn't expected to come home to supper. It smells amazing."

"Yeah, Tyke and I have been busy today." His eyes widened and he held up one finger, as if remembering something important. "Oh, and I got you something while you were gone."

"How? You didn't have a car."

He headed out of the room, talking over his shoulder, yet I struggled to follow and pay attention to what he said. "It was only the battery, so I called a mechanic, and the guy brought a new one out."

I stopped next to the kitchen table where he grabbed a bag from the floor and set it in one of the chairs. From inside, he pulled out two white boxes, one much longer than the other. "Hear me out first." Which meant there was a good chance I would argue with him about his purchase.

Before agreeing to anything, I took a closer look at the boxes on the table and noticed the apple on both. "No, Cash. Whatever those are, I don't want them. You're delusional if you think I'm going to accept anything with that logo on the box from you."

"You haven't even heard me out yet." Covering the packages with his hands, he continued, obviously refusing my objection. "You need a phone in case of emergencies." He slid the smaller box toward me.

"First of all, an iPhone isn't an in-case-of-emergency device. That's what cheap flip phones are for…you know, the ones you get with prepaid minutes. I'm well aware of what it costs for a data package every month. It's out of my budget—like *way* out. Secondly, did you not hear me last night when I explained I suck in traumatic situations? This fancy piece of technology won't do crap if I can't find it—or worse, can't figure out how to use it."

"And that's what this is for." He slid the longer box toward me. When I expressed my confusion with narrowed eyes, he began to explain. "It's a watch that pairs to your phone, and it has this neat function on it that allows you to make an emergency call."

Well, I didn't really have much of an argument about that, other than…

"Are you out of your mind?"

"No…actually, I'm not. It's a completely rational purchase and answers all your concerns."

"Except the financial part."

He held up a hand and smirked with his head cocked to the side. "I added a line to my account. I had to get you a new number, though. I couldn't transfer yours over, but it's only ten dollars a month extra."

"I highly doubt that. The data alone is more than that."

"I switched to a family plan so now we share a data and text package. I figured since you're home most of the time, you'll be connected to the internet, so you won't use much." He continued to explain how many gigabytes we had to share each month, but my brain had heard "family" and stopped processing anything else.

It shouldn't have affected me the way it did. It was a stupid mobile account. You could share one with anybody, and it wouldn't mean anything. But for some reason, my head told me something else.

"Why did you add me to your plan?" My question barely came out, stopping him in the middle of whatever he was saying. "That seems so permanent."

Apparently, he found humor in my concerns. "Jade…it saves you money, and it makes me feel better when you're here alone. I don't like the idea of not being able to reach you, or you not having a way to call for help if you need it. And it was a one-year contract, which is not even close to being permanent. If you aren't comfortable with this, I can cancel it and return everything. But I'll still need you to get a phone."

"I can give in about the bill and even being on your account…but how am I supposed to pay for these?" I held up both boxes, one in each hand. "I'm sure these are well over a thousand dollars. My guess is closer to fifteen hundred."

"You don't need to worry about how much they cost or paying me back." He moved around the table, came to stand in front of me, and settled his hands on my hips while I continued to hold out the boxes in my hands. "I kinda earned the right to get them for you."

"Excuse me? *Earned* the right? How?"

"I won the bet."

Batting my eyes, fully confused, I asked, "What bet?"

"You said I wouldn't be able to make you come. And I did."

Instinctively, I glanced around, searching for Aria to make sure she didn't hear him, as if she'd understand what he meant. "That wasn't a bet."

"Fine...then call this my reward for doing the impossible."

"I'm the one getting expensive gifts—plus the *other thing*. How is that *your* reward?"

"If it means I get to speak to you while I'm gone, then I don't care what you call it. And better yet...now we can FaceTime each other, so I can see you when we talk. Damn, the perks just keep piling up."

I huffed in resignation and dropped my forehead to his chest. His laughter rumbled through him and filled my entire body with the vibrations. I didn't want to concede, but I had a feeling he would continue to argue with me no matter what I said, so I gave in and accepted the fancy devices he was so excited to give me.

Cash set up the new phone and watch while I prepared the table for dinner and quizzed him about how Aria did today. Other than having me use my fingerprints on the device's home key, I didn't have to do anything. But right as I was about to tell him to put it away, the alerts started going off.

"What'd you do? Break it already?" I teased, but my smile vanished at the sight of the concern embedded in his brow. "Cash? What is it?"

"You got a few messages."

"From who? I thought you said I have a new number."

"You do, but I signed on with your Apple ID, so any messages you haven't read yet just came through." His penetrating gaze captured mine and held me prisoner. "You need to call Stevie."

I didn't like his deep and haunting tone, but I refused to believe it held any merit. "I will after supper. The oven is going to beep in..." I glanced behind me, needing the reprieve more for myself than to verify the time. "Fifty seconds. So put it away and we'll pick it back up later."

"Your mom's in the hospital." He'd blurted it out like it was some random fact. *The weather forecast shows rain tomorrow.* And even though it was so cut and dry, I was able to pick up on the warning. The hint of alarm that took it from informing me of late afternoon showers to telling me about a brewing storm off the coast that could wipe everything away.

"W-what'd she say?"

He held out the phone, but I couldn't do anything other than stare at it like it was infected with some flesh-eating disease. "She said you need to call her. Go...take the phone back to the room. I'll get Aria fed. Don't worry about this—I've got it handled."

Finally, I took the cell from his hand and headed back to my room, my heart lodged in my throat. But before I called, I needed to read her messages so I could attempt to prepare myself. No, my mother and I hadn't gotten along for years. She'd pushed me away instead of pulling me closer. She'd cut me off when I needed her the most. But that didn't mean a sob wasn't ripped from my chest when I read Stevie's text about my mom being hurt.

I barely let her answer the phone before I asked, "What's going on?"

"I don't have much information—the hospital won't tell me anything."

"Just tell me what happened!" I snapped.

Stevie hesitated for a moment and then released a long sigh into the receiver. "Do you remember Alissa Townsend from high school? Well, I ran into her today, and she started asking about you, like when you would be coming back. It threw me for a loop because I wasn't aware she even knew you had moved away."

"I haven't seen her since graduation… I have no idea how she would've found out."

"Well, she was asking because she works at the stables Jessica Hamilton's dad used to own. I don't remember what it's called now. But anyway, your mom was there yesterday, and there was an accident. All Alissa could tell me is she was bucked from a horse and then trampled over. She was transported to the emergency room. That's why Alissa had asked if you were coming."

"*Yesterday?*" Tears flooded my eyes and I lifted a hand to cover my mouth, hoping to hold back the sobs. "W-why hasn't anyone told me? Why am I just finding out?"

"Jade, how would anyone be able to reach you? You don't have a phone."

I bypassed the phone issue for what was most important. "So what's going on? She's still there?"

Silence drifted through the line, gutting me. "I went up there today to see what I could find out. Alissa said it was bad, and even though I'm not family, I was hoping they'd tell me *something*. I told the woman at the front desk that you didn't live around here and didn't get along with your mom's husband, and I guess she felt bad for you because she told me she's in ICU." She took a deep breath while I processed it all, and then she added, "I think you need to call the hospital yourself and see what you can find out."

"What about Aria? I can't leave her here with Cash that long. And I'm *not* taking her to a hospital. What am I supposed to do?" My voice cracked, allowing the pain and heartache to pour through and flood my words with tears.

"Just call the hospital first. If you decide to come, I'll help you with her. You don't have to do everything alone, Jade." Her soft tone covered me like the heat of a campfire, soothing me when I needed it the most.

I managed to find the courage to dial the hospital where Stevie told me my mom had been admitted. My heart slammed against my sternum repeatedly with each ring of the call. My hands and voice shook when the operator answered and I asked her to connect me to the ICU. Then my lungs burned and my face grew hot when she told me she couldn't do that. Somewhere, in that moment, I found an inner strength I wasn't aware I had. After fighting a losing battle for years, I thought I'd lost the spark within me, but as the lady argued and told me ICU wasn't allowed calls, that spark reignited into a roaring inferno.

Then the operator went silent and the line began to ring.

And again, my heart attempted to break free.

When a woman answered, my lips quivered.

When she told me she couldn't give me answers over the phone, my lungs deflated.

Then she said, "But…if she were my mom, I'd get here as fast as I could," and my muscles gave up. I crumpled to the floor and bawled. As I tried to piece it all together, unforgiving sobs surged through me.

"Talk to me, babe." Out of nowhere, Cash was by my side, his arms clutching me to him. I never heard him come in or sit next to me.

But his words…those got to me.

His voice calmed me.

His touch almost healed me.

Almost.

Through tears, stuttering, and gasping for breath, I managed to get it all out. My mother had been trampled on by a horse and was in ICU, and there was a chance she wouldn't make it. Guilt assuaged me over not speaking to her since I'd left—and for a while before that, as well. And because of that, a divide had kept us apart for far too long. And now there was a chance I'd never be able to make it right.

"Come on...let's go." He grabbed my hand and gently tried to tug me off the floor.

"Where are we going?"

"Fort Pierce. You need to see her, so we're going."

"You don't have to come with me. It's *my* mom...I can go."

Still holding my hand, he lowered himself back to his knees, pinched my chin with his free fingers, and urged me to look at him. "You don't have to do this alone. I understand she's your mom. I also understand how upset you are right now. Even if I would let you go alone, there's no way in hell I'd let you get behind the wheel and drive across the state like this with Aria in the back."

"Even if you *let* me? You think just because we slept together that means you own me and can make decisions on my behalf? If I choose to take my child and leave right now, you couldn't stop me." It wasn't that I was mad at him, it was just the entire situation. I was angry over the hospital's refusal to give me information, and furious at myself for allowing such distance to spread like the plague between my mom and me. I ended up lashing out over the whole thing, and unfortunately for Cash, he got the brunt of my misplaced rage. I immediately regretted it, but I was too weak to admit it.

However, his gentle approach never wavered. "The only decision I'm making right now is to drive you to see your mom...*because* I hate the idea of you being on the roads late while you're like this. If you walked out that door with Aria, and something were to happen...everything I care about would be gone. So no, Jade...this isn't about me owning you. This is about my unwillingness to lose either of you when I can do something to prevent that."

"I—"

His lips covered mine and stopped my confession, halting me from telling him how I felt. Before he stood again, he said, "Pack a bag. We don't know how long we'll be gone, and you will probably want a few pairs of clean clothes."

Then he pressed a careful kiss to my forehead, stood, and exited the room…leaving me on the floor, watching him retreat. It could've been a few seconds or a few minutes, but eventually, I got up and did as he'd suggested. After haphazardly tossing clean clothes and panties into a plastic grocery bag, I headed down the hall to do the same with Aria's things. But as soon as I made it out to the kitchen, Cash took one look at the sack and shook his head.

He came back from his room with a duffel bag and backpack. My clothes joined his in one bag, and then he repacked Aria's clothes and overnight diapers into the other, as well as a couple of her sippy cups from the cabinet. The entire time he moved around me, my head swam. I couldn't think straight, proving him right about being unable to drive alone. Cash had taken charge, and I once again regretted the way I'd spoken to him in the other room. He hadn't deserved that.

I'd make it right at some point.

Providing I didn't wait too long like I worried I'd done with my mom.

I continued to live in the haze of fear while Cash drove. He'd packed up the dinner we hadn't eaten and brought it with us, but I wasn't hungry. The thought of eating made me sick to my stomach. Aria yammered away from the back seat, and thankfully, Cash was there to keep her entertained. The entire time, I did nothing but stare out the window at the signs and trees whipping by, hoping and praying my mom would make it through.

It was almost nine by the time we pulled up to the hospital. Stevie had stayed in touch so she could meet us there, but when I sent her a text informing her we had arrived, she said she was still a few minutes away.

"I'm not taking her in there." I pointed to the bright-red emergency sign.

"Go…I'll stand out here with Aria and wait for Stevie. You head inside and find out what's going on. It shouldn't be too long. I'll try to get up to the ICU waiting room, but if they won't let me in, I'll just shoot you a text to let you know where I'll be."

The thought of going in there alone, without Cash, terrified me. But standing out here with my mother lying in a hospital bed was even worse. It came down to the lesser of two evils, so I gave my daughter a kiss and then squeezed Cash's hand before walking through the sliding doors.

I'd expected chaos, lots of people running around, coughing, maybe some kids crying in chairs, holding a broken arm. But there was none of that. The doors opened up to a large atrium with a fountain, glass elevators along one side. An open hallway stood to the left, and through it, I could see what I assumed was the food court. A wooden desk loomed straight ahead, past the fountain, with another hall to the right.

My feet carried me forward until I stood in front of the receptionist. She looked friendly, older with glasses that appeared to have no rims. A beaded chain dangled from the thin, gold stems to her shoulders, wrapping around the back of her neck.

"I'm here to see my mom." I immediately lowered my voice, worried it would carry in the quiet, open space. "I believe she's in ICU. Her name is Lindsey Pierce. She was in—"

"Do you have a photo ID?" Apparently, this woman wasn't as sweet as I'd initially thought—either that, or she assumed I was upset and decided to cut me off before I continued to waste her time with my rambling.

I dug my license out of my wallet and passed it over the top of the desk. She typed a few things into her keyboard, the clicking sounds slowing time even more. I was impatient, and it didn't appear this woman was in any hurry.

"I'm sorry…" She glanced at my ID again before handing it back. "Ms. Robertson, but there's a note on here that she's not allowed any visitors."

"I know. She's in the ICU, but I was told family could see her. I'm her family."

"Well, according to my screen, she only has one family member permitted to see her."

Tears danced behind my eyes, a lump formed in my throat, and my heart raced at being *this close* yet so far away. I paused for a moment to collect myself, and then I tried again. "I can follow those rules. I don't have any problem with that. I just need to get up there so I can talk to someone about her, so I can find out what's going on."

"I'm so sorry, but I think you've misunderstood. I'm not saying only one person in the room with her at a time. Her information in the computer has it as she only *has* one relative. Her husband is here if you'd like to speak with him."

I gritted my teeth, repulsed at the thought of having to deal with him. But I wasn't left with much of a choice. If I had any desire at all to see my mother, I had to grin and bear it. I had to suck up the hatred for the man and get through it.

Just then, his voice carried down the hall to the right. No one had needed to call him. It was like he'd sensed I was here and had come running just to taunt me, to prove one more time how my mom would always choose him over me. I wouldn't have put it past him to have altered her familial information when she'd arrived. If she were unconscious, he would've been the one to fill out her paperwork…and he would've kept my name off just to spite me.

"I didn't think you'd show up." He came to a stop and leaned against the desk.

I fisted my hands at my sides, desperately holding back the fiery anger that boiled inside toward him for so many things, but most importantly, for keeping my mom from me for so long. I knew that he had swayed most of her decisions—and he never bothered to hide that fact from me. I squared my shoulders, lifted my chin, and made sure he understood I wasn't going to back down.

"My mom is in the hospital, in the ICU...why wouldn't I come? Just because you filled out paperwork to exclude me from her list of *approved* visitors doesn't mean I'll give up. It won't stop me. I'll have the director of this hospital on the phone, and I bet he'll let me up there to see her."

"Now, Jade..." He rested his hand on my shoulder and tilted his head, adding to the condescending way he said my name. "There's no need to revert to the problem child just to get your way. I'm sure there's a compromise somewhere."

My skin crawled where he touched me. Utter disgust ran rampant through me until I shrugged him off and took a step back, my hands still clenched.

Just then, the woman behind the desk cleared her throat, reminding me of her presence. "Do I need to call security?" She glanced between the two of us, probably unsure as to which one would cause an issue. And at this point, I more than likely appeared as hostile as I felt.

"I don't know..." I stared at him, narrowing my gaze with heavy tension in my brow. "Does she? Or are you going to let me see my own mother?"

The way the corners of his mouth practically curled with his smile reminded me of the Guy Fawkes mask from *V for Vendetta*. It was sinister and caused bile to rise and settle in the back of my throat. Instinctively, I wrapped my arms around my waist, as if attempting to protect myself.

When he held my shoulder again, giving it a tight squeeze, something snapped inside me. It was as if fear and anger formed an alliance and created an emotion unlike any other. It burned hot with rage, and desperation added a level of impulsivity that made it as dangerous as an uncontrollable fire. But it was restrained by maturity—although that was nothing more than an illusion of safety. Like the hydrogen nestled inside the confines of the Hindenburg, waiting to dock before igniting in a blaze of untamable fury.

Without slinking away like a coward the way he probably expected me to do, I swung my forearm up and collided it with his to remove his hand from my shoulder. All the while, I shot daggers at him with my eyes. However, it didn't seem to faze him. Instead of reacting, he simply smirked and said, "I'm on my way to get some coffee. Why don't you take my spot upstairs for now?"

I hated the way he made it sound like he was doing me a favor. As if this was a choice he'd made out of the kindness of his own heart. Then again, this was nothing new. This was exactly how I remembered him.

"Go ahead and print her a badge if you would, please, Darla." He may have been speaking to the elderly woman, but he never took his eyes off me. "She's been estranged from her mother for some time now, and I think the right thing to do would be to let her have a few moments to make peace with her, considering the severity of the situation."

Finally breaking eye contact, I retreated one step and turned my attention to the woman with silver, wispy hair, who managed to avoid us while tapping on the keyboard. Within a few seconds, she had a printed visitor badge for me to stick on my shirt.

It took mental effort to lose the attitude when thanking her. After all, she wasn't the villain here. She was simply an employee following the rules—who may or may not have become friendly with the heartless man in front of me.

When I moved to step around him, he held out his hand and caught me around the waist. Instinctively, I shoved against his chest, freed myself, and picked up the pace as I walked away. And once I reached the elevator banks, I took a deep breath and allowed the anxiety to dissipate.

Giving the tiniest space in my chest for pride to swell.

I didn't back down. I didn't cower in a corner or concede to his manipulation. It may not have been much, but it was enough to make me believe I could win.

I waited for the elevator with a smile on my face…and dread in my heart.

CHAPTER 18

Cash

"You're going back in there, right?" Stevie's voice was full of concern as she strapped the car seat in the back of her Camry. "Like...you're not leaving her in there all alone, are you?"

I glanced over my shoulder at the bright lights on the tall building while holding an almost-asleep two-year-old in my arms. "No, I just had to wait out here until you came. I sent her in to find out what she can and told her I'd find her after you leave. Why? What's going on?"

Aria squeezed my neck as tight as her sleepy arms could, which only slightly distracted me from the panic emanating from Stevie. I held her close for a moment before I buckled her in the car. Once the door was shut, I leaned forward, nearly trapping Stevie between the vehicle and myself. I needed to get a good read on her expression, as well as make it clear that I expected answers.

"What's going on, Stevie? Don't bullshit me. Jade was apprehensive about going in alone, and now you're acting like I have a reason to be concerned. Is there something you need to tell me?"

Her gaze shifted over my shoulder and then right back to me. She shook her head and dropped her attention to my chest. "No. She doesn't deal well with hospitals. I think it has something to do with her dad dying. He was in a motorcycle accident and spent three days in the ICU before passing away, so this is probably bringing back those memories. I don't think she should be alone, that's all."

Jade told me about her dad dying, how a driver had cut him off without paying attention and caused him to crash, but I'd never heard the part about his hospitalization until just now. I wanted to believe that was the reason for Jade's hesitation, but something told me differently. However, the more time I spent out here, pushing Stevie for answers, the longer Jade was inside by herself.

I couldn't risk getting in there late and missing Jade. The thought of having to wait for her to find me when she was done didn't sit well with me. It was clear she needed me—or at least, *someone*—and I wanted nothing more than to be there for her.

"Thanks again for watching Aria. You're a really good friend, Stevie." I offered a half-smile and then opened the back door, finding an angel on the verge of sleep. "Night, Tyke. I'll see you soon, okay?"

"Night, Daddy." I swear, right or wrong, my heart grew impossibly larger.

I didn't bother to look at Stevie as I closed the door and turned around. Whatever her feelings were in regard to hearing Aria call me "Daddy" were none of my concern. Instead, I allowed the euphoria to fill me as I made my way inside.

The sight of Jade's long, curly, cocoa-colored hair from the entrance pulled me from the cloud I rode in on. I had her name on the tip of my tongue, ready to call it out to gain her attention, but before I could utter the first sound, I was stopped dead in my tracks. She was with a man, and it was clear to anyone watching that she was uncomfortable. When she tried to walk around him, the man reached out and *touched* her. My blood boiled at the sight, followed by a rush of blinding rage so hot it left my body ice cold. But before I could do anything, she pushed him away.

I couldn't take my eyes off her as she ran around the corner, making sure she got away safely. Once she was out of sight, I pulled my attention back to the guy at the front desk. He leaned over the counter, saying something to the woman in front of the computer, but all I could see were his lips moving. I couldn't hear his words, although whatever they were made her smile. After a quick laugh, he slapped the counter and turned to leave, heading straight for me.

My pulse strengthened, something I was used to in the field when on high alert, and I quickly ducked into the hallway before he could see me. As he approached, I studied him, really taking note of his features, almost memorizing every pore on his face, as if my instincts told me I needed this information. I recognized him from somewhere, but I couldn't place it. His sharp, angular nose brought my attention to his thin lips. His chin came to a point, his jawline forming a V. There was something *off* about him. It was written in his sneer, resounded in every heavy step, and was reiterated by his rigid posture as he made his way to the exit.

"Oh, Mr. Pierce?" the woman from the desk hollered.

He turned around, but I didn't hear anything else. I *had* seen him before, in the file I'd created during Jade's background check. It had information on every person in Jade's family, including her stepfather. Aside from having basic details on him, I didn't know much else. But his face...I recognized that face.

And once I realized who he was, I couldn't stop replaying their interaction from a few moments ago. The way he tried to grab her, *touch* her, how she pushed him away. I was aware they didn't get along, so it wouldn't have come as a surprise to most to witness her avoidance of him. But for me...I saw so much more.

My jaw ached from grinding my teeth while I thought about her clenched hands as she pushed him away, the way her shoulders curled up and in, as if protecting herself from danger. My chest constricted as I recalled how her head almost bowed— not cowardly, but as if she couldn't stand the sight of him. And when I thought about how she couldn't walk away from him fast enough, my throat closed, blocking my airway.

In order to be good at my job, I had to understand that everyone handled situations differently. Some may cry in the face of tragedy while others needed time to process it before it became real. And when confronted by someone you loathed, some lashed out, yet others shut down. We all fight for different reasons. We all laugh at different things. But there was one thing I knew for sure, no matter how unique each person could be…fear isn't easy to hide.

Jade didn't just dislike her stepdad.

She was *terrified* of him.

And there was only one man she had reason to be scared of.

I'd just gone from trained and skilled to blind with vengeance.

I followed him outside, but rather than stay behind him, I veered off to the left in the direction of where I'd parked. A quick peek around the light poles offered insight about what areas were being recorded and which ones weren't. Once I was certain my parking space was in a blind pocket, I picked up the pace.

"Hey!" I called out to him and waved my arms in the air to gain his attention. When he turned toward me, maybe thirty feet away, I called him over. "I need your help! Please!"

He glanced to the left, then to the right. When he realized there was no one else in this well-lit lot, he came over, but his apprehension was clear. I didn't give him the chance to question me, just spun on my heel and kept moving toward the Range Rover, checking every few seconds to make sure he was still behind me. And when I got there, I stood by the back door, slapping the window frantically.

"You have to help…there's a baby locked inside. I can't tell if he's breathing." It didn't take much effort to play up the hysterics for his benefit—I'd lost the usually controlled mindset I had on a job when this became more than an assigned task. I assumed if he were the type of person to touch a child the way he had Jade, rescuing a baby wouldn't be his driving force, but I hoped it would call to some primitive need to play the hero.

His borderline disgust was evident enough that he had no interest in helping anyone. "Call the cops. What do you need me for?" And it took everything in me not to throttle him right here, right now.

As he stuffed his hand into his pocket for what I assumed was his phone, I reached out and grabbed him by the front of his shirt. "There's no time! *Please*…help me break the window. Help me get him out." With my hold on him, I directed him closer to the back door and released him.

Before he could notice the lack of a baby in the car, I took him by the back of the neck and knocked his forehead into the glass to disorient him. Anger rolled through me, drowning the adrenaline that had gotten me to this point. After nine years on the job, so much of it was autopilot for me. If I didn't need to analyze a reaction or learn certain habits or schedules, most of what I did could've been performed with my eyes closed.

But not this time.

Emotion compelled me.

Drove me.

Consumed me until I'd lost sight of my training.

His knees weakened and he began to slip from my hold, his dead weight catching me off guard. Suddenly aware of the situation, I whipped my head around, reassuring myself that we were still alone. We were. But I couldn't guarantee for how long. So I yanked the door open, folded him inside, and then climbed into the driver's seat.

Turning my head to see him, I realized exactly how unprepared I was. Blood rushed through my ears like a roaring river, deafening me to the consequences of my actions.

I thought I understood what hate was.

But it wasn't even close to the real thing.

We couldn't stay here, so I was left with no other option but to drive—without having anywhere to go that wouldn't put me in jeopardy. Thinking on my feet, I leaned behind me, stretching between the front seats, and grabbed his wallet from his back pocket. After removing his license, I shoved the worn-leather billfold into the console and pressed the button to start the engine.

✥

This part of the job was foreign to me. I took care of the sweep, and another part of the team handled the transportation. Not only did I lack experience, but I didn't have help. Just because I could toss him over my shoulder and carry him inside didn't mean it was a good idea. I had no clue what his neighbors were like—if they sat by a window and kept watch, or if they would have their eyes glued to a TV screen. I didn't care to take that chance.

I couldn't risk anyone seeing me or taking note of a strange vehicle in the driveway, so I hurried inside to open the garage door. Luckily, he didn't have an alarm. As soon as I had the Range Rover concealed in the garage, I wasted no time dragging the bastard inside. Although, he became more alert of the situation and refused to make things easy. At least I had been able to restrain his hands behind his back before his real fight kicked in.

I'd gotten him to the kitchen and had planned to put him in a chair, but the second his teeth broke my skin, I dropped him on the hard tile.

"What the fuck do you want from me?" he asked through labored breathing.

I no longer had rational thoughts in my head, only rage-filled desires. I squatted down with my knee pressed into his chest and grabbed his throat, his windpipe trapped within my grasp. Then I lowered my face to his to ensure he heard every word I said while I denied his brain oxygen. "I want…to make…you cry."

His eyes watered, but not the way I needed them to.

"No…" I tsked. "Cry like Jade used to. When she'd beg you to stop, when she'd tell you she didn't want you touching her…like that."

Realization shone bright in his wide eyes. After a moment, he fought against my hold and squirmed on the floor beneath my knee. When I released his throat, he took in as much air as he could with my weight still pressed against him, awkwardly pinning him down with his arms trapped beneath him. Then I backed away, offering him the false belief that he could survive.

Mind games were my favorite form of torture. Fucking with someone's head could prove to be more beneficial than inflicting physical pain. Either way, the person would reach a point and give up, beg you to end it, unable to handle what you were doing to them any longer. They'd give you any answer you wanted to hear, as long as it meant the torment would stop.

But I didn't need answers from him.

Only retribution.

After allowing him to catch his breath, I applied pressure to his windpipe again. While he twisted his body in an attempt to free himself, I stared into his eyes, hoping he could see the hatred he filled me with.

His face turned red. I'd done this enough times to calculate exactly how long I had before I lost him. That was the key...take them right to the edge, and then give them a reprieve. Once they regained awareness, you pushed them right back to the breaking point, only to pull away at the last second. Over and over again. It was basically an endless cycle of giving and taking, all done by one person.

When I let go, he rolled to his side and curled into himself as best as he could, coughing and gasping for air. "Who are you?" he choked out.

"It doesn't matter who I am. But if it'll make you feel better, then I'll tell you." Once again, I shoved him onto his back and pinned him to the floor with my knee—this time, holding most of my weight off his chest. "I'm the blade of a sword, the brass tip in the chamber of a forty-five, the noose around your neck. I'm the judge...the jury..." I wrapped my fingers around his throat again. "And the motherfucking executioner."

I had to pull away before I completely lost control—I was only hanging on by a weak and tattered thread. My hands shook and my neck flamed with intense heat. An ache settled into my jaw and set about a ringing in my ears. I'd never experienced anger like this. I was familiar with the desire to hit something or someone. But never, in all my life, had it brought me to the breaking point. The moment when I thought of nothing more than reaching inside a person's chest and ripping out their heart with my bare hand.

His chest heaved beneath my knee as he fought to catch his breath. He lifted his head to lean forward, and against all logic, I let him. "I never forced her to do anything."

Blinded by hate, I choked him again. "Did you come onto her when she was sixteen?" Realizing he couldn't answer with my grip suppressing his airway, I added, "Blink once for yes, twice for no. The faster you answer my questions, the sooner you can breathe again."

This time, before I'd stolen his oxygen, he'd taken a full inhalation. He thought he was smart, but all he did was completely expand his lungs without any way to relieve the pressure. Realizing this, he blinked his large, panicked eyes—once.

"Did you take her hand and make her touch you?" Blink. "Did you take her virginity?"

He rapidly opened and closed his eyes multiple times, as if repeating his answer. When I pulled away, he appeared to be on the verge of tears, desperately trying to ease the pain in his chest. But even that didn't stop him from fighting back. "*She never said no…*" More coughs, more strangled gasps. "I swear."

"*That doesn't make it right!*"

Needing physical distance, I stood and stumbled a few steps away, my hands pressed against my temples in frustration. If I didn't pull myself together, this kitchen would be a crime scene with evidence of my presence all over the place. And there would be no coming back from that.

"I'm not a pedophile. I know that's what you're thinking, but I'm not," he argued in a borderline pleading tone. "I've never so much as looked at another girl her age."

"Then why *her*?" I felt like I had lost my mind. This asshole didn't deserve the right to explain his actions. I didn't need to hear his response, but I couldn't stop myself from asking. My chest burned beneath the tightness, and I swear my heart cracked behind my breastbone.

He stared at the ceiling, only one shoulder resting against the tile. With his hands trapped beneath him, his chest heaved with the labored exertion of breathing. "I married Lindsey when Jade was twelve."

"I don't give a *shit* about memory lane. I asked a fucking question." The words slipped through my gritted teeth while I held my hands in fists at my sides. The muscles in my arms strained against the sleeves of my shirt.

His head rolled to the side, and his green eyes found mine. "And I'm trying to answer you." When I didn't interrupt, he returned his stare to the ceiling and continued. "She was shy, so to get her out of her shell, I'd joke around with her. After a while, she started playing along."

My jaw clenched impossibly tighter.

"When she was fourteen, her laugh changed. It was no longer sweet and childlike, but more flirtatious. Then she started touching me."

I couldn't listen to any more.

But I couldn't do anything to make him stop.

I was frozen—a reaction so foreign to me I was helpless to stop it.

"She'd shove me with her shoulder or playfully slap my arm. Her clothes got tighter, and the neckline on her shirts got lower. Her body was changing, and it was like she *wanted* me to notice. She may have been a teenager, but she was shaped like a woman." He turned his attention to me again and added, "I'm not a pedophile. *Girls* don't do it for me. But she was built like a grown woman."

In two long strides, I stood over him with my feet on either side of his contorted body. I squatted down far enough to grab him by the front of his shirt, yanked him up so his shoulders came off the floor, and brought him closer. "You're a sick son of a bitch. I don't care what size bra she wore, she was a fucking *kid*. One you manipulated and took advantage of. You used the control you had over her as her parent, and you abused the trust she should've had in you. Then you knocked her up and left her to fend for herself."

"Is that what she told you?"

I didn't just let him go—I pushed him back to the tile and then swung at him. My fist connected with his jaw. I wanted to hit him again, but he curled his shoulder and pressed his cheek against the floor.

"I told her to have an abortion, to get rid of the baby, but she didn't listen. If she had to fend for herself, it's her own fault. She knew I wouldn't be able to help her with a baby, but she chose to keep it anyway." Then he cut his eyes to the side to look at me, and my world turned red. "If Lindsey doesn't pull through, you better believe I'll go after Jade and get custody of that kid."

I was standing over him one minute, and kicking him in the ribs the next, screaming, *"She's mine, you motherfucker! You can't have her! Aria's mine!"* The only reason I stopped was because I was physically dragged away. My arm was twisted behind me, a hand pressed against my heaving chest, restraining me.

Then I saw a pair of black boots, and it was enough to break the spell hatred had over me. I realized the position I was in, my arm locked behind me, a hand over my furiously beating heart, and my red world turned black.

"W-what are you doing here?" I stammered, unaware of how breathless I was until I tried to speak.

"Here? You mean in this house? Or in town?" Rhett didn't play games. He never asked a question he didn't already have the answer to, but sometimes, he'd ask something without actually seeking a response. This was one of the times I wasn't sure which kind of question it was.

He took a step toward me, ignoring the wheezing man behind him.

"I came to town to do a li'l investigatin' on her ma's ol' man. I'm here, in his house, because I found one of my men in it—unauthorized."

I shook my head, as if I could convince him that this was all in his imagination.

"I find it interesting that you're here an' all, when ya told me you'd be home…on the other coast of Florida."

There was no point in arguing…but I couldn't let it rest. "Jade's mom was in an accident and is currently in the hospital. We came here for that."

"Well, butter my butt and call me a biscuit. I didn't know this was a hospital? How 'bout you, Kryder?" Rhett's eyes shifted to my right, answering the question I'd yet to ask—who was behind me. "Did you have any idea this was a place of healin'?"

Damn Rhett and his sarcastic intimidation. "Would you let me explain?"

"Explain what, darlin'…how ya managed to end up at the house of the man who'd taken advantage of your girl? Not sure how you'll do that, but sure. Go head. That oughta be good."

"I didn't know it was him until I saw him with Jade at the hospital."

"Hmmm…likely story. But anywho, that's neither here nor there. I don't give a flyin' fuck when or how you figured it out. Because I don't recall givin' you instructions to take this guy out. Last I checked, you work for me. Or did ya get your panties in a wad over bein' sent to the desk and decide to start your own business?"

I struggled against Kryder's hold, but he didn't release me until Rhett gave him the nod of approval. My shoulder ached and my bicep burned, but I refused to admit it and appear weak. Not to these men. "What made you think it was him?"

"Because I know what the hell I'm doin'."

"So do I!" I roared, not caring that it was my boss taking the brunt of my rage.

"Oh, ya do? Well, you bypassed the stop sign 'cause you were lookin' for a traffic light. You weren't usin' your fuckin' brain. The very *first* place you always look is at the family. But if I'm bein' honest…I didn't *know* it was him. I only came here to check it out. And considerin' I found you in his kitchen, I'd say it was a lucky guess."

I stared at the piece of shit on the floor, snarling at the sound of his moans. I hated him for what he did. He'd hurt the woman I loved, and all I wanted to do was make him pay.

I turned to Rhett for guidance. "So now what do we do?"

CHAPTER 19

Jade

I thanked the Uber driver and closed the door behind me, unable to get out of his car fast enough. He didn't creep me out, and he wasn't rude, but he smelled like peanut butter, and I found that odd. Not odd that he reminded me of a sandwich, but when I'd asked him what he'd eaten for dinner—for small talk—he went into a whole story about some family meal. A family meal that had *nothing* to do with peanut butter.

Then again, I hadn't used Uber since I was in college. I'd forgotten all about how odd some of those drivers could be. I hadn't gotten one often, but on occasion, I had no choice but to let the woman with the really deep voice drive me home. Those nights had been fun.

When I turned around and took in the sight of my old home, a mixture of dread and nostalgia wrapped me in a cocoon of conflicting emotions. I had so many memories, good and bad, but I couldn't separate them while staring at the front door that held so many secrets. I'd loved and been loved behind those walls. I'd also suffered so much, both grief when I'd lost my dad and depression from *his* abuse. Now, after having been away for nearly a year, there were parts of me that almost didn't recognize the house.

I'd sworn to myself I'd never come back here, but after the ICU nurse told me about some study where coma patients did better when they had someone talk or read to them regularly, I knew I had no choice but to return. When I was younger, my mom would lie in bed next to me and read, always from the same book with the binding so worn the title was no longer recognizable. I had to find it so I could sit beside her and read from those same yellowed pages. I didn't think it would be possible when I couldn't locate Cash's car in the parking lot.

The Range Rover hadn't been in the spot he'd parked it in, and while glancing around to see if he'd moved it, I'd spotted the distinguishable two-door, 1980 Mercedes Benz Roadster. Cash may not have been there, but *he* was, and that meant he wouldn't be at the house. I had to take the opportunity given. I'd quickly sent Cash a text, letting him know where I would be in case he was still around the hospital, and downloaded the Uber app. If anything, I'd be gone for less than an hour, so I hadn't thought anything of it.

Until I stood in front of the house that had haunted me for years.

As I slowly began to put one foot in front of the other, the grass melting beneath each step, I took in all the differences ranging from the most subtle to the obvious. My old bedroom window faced the front, and for the last five years I'd lived here, the curtains remained closed. But now, they were open. It was dark out, so I couldn't see in, but I closed my eyes and tried to imagine what the room would look like in the daytime with the warmth of the sun's rays flooding the space.

When I approached the corner of the house, I couldn't help but stop and touch the bright-pink flowers, and run my fingertip along the soft petals. Those were new, and I wondered if my mom had planted them—she had given up gardening after my dad passed away. The hedges that ran along the sides and back yard were much bigger than I remembered, taller, and they offered far more privacy than they had before. But I stopped studying them the moment I remembered when they had been planted—just after my seventeenth birthday. Mom had refused to put up a fence, saying they were tacky, so *he* built a wall of shrubbery.

Once I made it to the back of the house, I took a deep breath and held it. The burn in my chest as air filled my lungs helped quiet my thundering heart.

"He's not here," I reminded myself quietly, needing the pep talk before heading inside. I'd sworn to myself I would never come back, but here I was, and no matter what happened, I'd never regret it. My mom needed me, and the only thing I wanted to do was read to her from *our* book. I closed my eyes and felt around on the brick wall, right at shoulder level, and as soon as the tips of my fingers hit the right spot in the mortar, I released a sigh of relief.

When I was younger, during my rebellious years, I'd sneak out late at night or come home well past curfew. In order to get inside without coming through the front—that had gotten me caught many times—I'd hidden a key in the wall next to the door that led to my bathroom. It was technically the pool bath, meant to be used as a quick entry inside from the lanai, but it was across the hall from my bedroom, so it was mine. And I'd taken advantage of its access many times.

I carefully slipped the broken piece of mortar out using the divots I'd created so long ago for my fingers to grip each side. As it gritted along the bricks, I held my breath, praying the key hadn't been discovered or removed. But once I had it all the way out and snuck my fingertips into the narrow space, cold metal brushed my skin, and nothing had ever felt better.

I only had one more obstacle in my way.

The key slipped effortlessly into the lock, but I took a second before trying it out. It'd dawned on me that I'd come all this way, made it this far, and this could be the giant red stop sign that turned me away. If they'd changed the locks after I left, I would have no way to get inside, which meant I'd have no way of getting that book. I couldn't even remember what the title was—Mom and I had always just called it "our book"—so it wasn't like I'd be able to buy it at a store in the morning. I came here for one thing, and if this door didn't open, I wasn't sure what I'd do.

I silently dropped my forehead to the metal, said a prayer to myself, and turned the key. To my surprise, it worked. The cold, brass knob sent a chill up my arm—a warning I passed off as residual dread caused by the memories that hid within these walls. But I pushed past it and pulled on the handle, rejoicing in the absence of squeaky hinges. The memory of when I'd coated and waxed them to silence my late-night departures and arrivals put a smile on my face and washed away the unease. But that high didn't last long.

I closed the door behind me, careful of my movements in the dark room, and began to slowly shuffle my feet toward the hallway. The kitchen light appeared to be on, the glow radiating down the hall and shining through the crack in the door, and it guided me across the bathroom. It may have been almost a year since I'd been here, and there was a good chance Mom had redecorated it with new mats and possibly a fancier shower curtain, but I could navigate the space with my eyes closed. After sneaking back in so many nights, the house pitch black, I could almost tell you the exact distance between the toilet and sink, down to the inches. And even though that would still be the case, it didn't mean I wasn't cautious.

My breathing stopped at the sound of a male voice. No one was here, I was all alone—I knew this because Mom was lying in a hospital bed across town, and when the Uber driver picked me up, the pale-yellow Mercedes with the light-brown convertible top was still parked in the same spot. I closed my eyes and tried to calm down so I could hear over the sound of my frantically beating heart. And once I had regained control of my breathing, I was able to hone in on the words coming from down the hall.

"So what do we do?" His throaty voice called to me, as if I'd recognize it anywhere. But I had too many thoughts and fears and questions bombarding me that I couldn't place it. It was so familiar, even though I had no idea who it was. I wondered if it was someone I'd gone to school with, and he'd taken the opportunity to break into the house and rob the place.

"I don't know…why don't ya tell me? You're the one who came here first." The more I listened, the more I convinced myself the TV had been left on. The words didn't make sense, and aside from the first voice, this one wasn't familiar at all.

"Rhett…" A third man spoke in warning, deep and unforgiving, and it once again made me believe this was nothing more than a movie playing in the living room. "I don't mean to be disrespectful, sir, but could you possibly save the lecture for later? We have a man tied up on his own kitchen floor. I'm pretty sure that takes precedence over your irritation at his stupidity."

I held my breath and covered my mouth with my fingers, trying to tell myself it was the TV, yet I no longer believed it. A man was tied up in the kitchen, and there were at least three others in the house. I needed to flee, run away, get out of here as fast as I could…but I was frozen. Once again, my fight or flight instinct had failed me and left me in a solid state of unmoving panic.

That was…until more was said.

"Fine, I can wait to tear 'im a new asshole. But tell me this, Nicholson…what was your plan?" *Nicholson…Nicholson…* I gasped as tears filled my eyes, blurring the already dark room. "Kill him in his own house? Leave him hogtied for dead? Any thoughts as to how you'd explain to the cops why your fingerprints were all over the place, or why someone could match the description of your car and report seein' it here? I have a feeling that wouldn't go over too well with your girl."

It couldn't be true. It couldn't possibly be real.

This had to be an oddly coincidental movie.

"I wasn't thinking about—"

"Of course you weren't, Cash." This *wasn't* a movie. There was no coincidence. Any doubt or prayer I'd had vanished at the sound of his name. Such intense anger had filled the man's voice that it had given me a mental image of a red face, possibly a bulging vein in his forehead. "That's the problem...you *weren't* thinkin'. Which is exactly why taking matters into your own hands is dangerous—especially when you're a trained killer."

"*What'd you want me to do?*" Cash screamed, and it was so loud it made me take a step back. "He said he's going to come after Jade and take Aria." His voice cracked, which was the only thing that kept me quiet.

Fear pinned me, rooted me to the floor, covered my body like a weighted net. I couldn't move. Couldn't breathe. Couldn't think past Cash's words—*he* planned to take my baby away. He could come after me all he wanted—I'd survived it before and would do it again—but I'd be damned if I'd let that monster anywhere near my child. He sought the control, fed off it like it was his last meal. He didn't care about me or Aria...only the control.

Whimpering moans were followed by an interrupted grunt when the third man spoke again. "What are we going to do with him, boss? We can't leave him here. The first thing he'll do is call the cops. And I'm willing to bet someone notices if he goes missing."

I couldn't tell who was the boss, whether it was Cash or the other guy. And I assumed one of the other two men's names was Rhett. But I couldn't figure out if that meant there were four guys or just three, and the fear of who they were kept me from moving.

"Nah, he won't say anything." The gruff voice of what I assumed was the second guy gave me chills. They ran up my arms and down my back at the way he spoke, almost tauntingly with a threatening undertone. "Because I happen to own a fancy tool, somewhat like a pair of meat tongs, that comes in handy when removin' a tongue. And if that's not incentive enough for ya, how 'bout this..." I wasn't sure who he was talking to, but his voice lowered when he said, "I could kill you without a single person findin' out, and leave without a trace like a breeze through the night."

I took a step back, then another, my hand still covering my face and my eyesight glued to the light flooding in through the crack in the door. A sob had lodged itself in my chest, expanding and taking over, making my heart fight harder for space. My sternum ached like it would shatter at any minute.

I needed to get out of there.

Finally, my flight instinct kicked in, but it wasn't smooth. Trembles overtook my entire body while I spun on my heel and rushed for the door to the lanai—only, I was off balance and working with two weak knees. I ran into the ledge of the counter with my hip, and searing pain radiated through my pelvis. When I tried to grab ahold of the vanity to catch myself, my arm knocked into whatever had been sitting on top of it, and what sounded like glass bottles and aerosol cans went crashing to the floor.

In the split second of silence while I stood still, entrenched in fear, I heard one of the men say, "Kryder, go check that out." Then, his voice came out higher, full of concerned questions when he asked, "Is someone in the house? Did you happen to check the perimeter before turnin' this place into a fuckin' crime scene?"

I bolted toward the door, taking the knob in my grip. But before I could turn it and flee, light poured into the room, and thick, angry fingers wrapped completely around my bicep. Whoever it was pulled my back against his hard chest, nearly knocking the wind out of me, and locked me in place with his strong, masculine hold across the front of my shoulders. I couldn't manage to retain anything in that moment. Not the light-colored, curly hairs on his forearm or the tropical scent wafting from his shirt. I didn't take note of how the back of my head came to his collarbone or the way his chin grazed the top of my ear while we stood. Anything that would've helped identify this man vanished from my thought process when he dragged me from the bathroom, down the hall, to the kitchen.

"*Let her go!*" The vicious, almost feral demand hit me hard in the chest, and immediately, I was released.

My eyes flew open, not realizing I'd shut them, and my sight fell on a very angry Cash. His stare pierced the man behind me.

Seeking safety, I ran toward Cash. In less than four strides, I was wrapped in his strained, unyielding arms. He held me to him. I pressed my face against the solid planes of his chest and breathed him in, his familiar scent engulfing me in effortless security. The comfort only his embrace could offer immediately calmed my breathing and slowed my heart rate.

"Any other witnesses you'd like to invite to the party?" The voice came from behind Cash, startling me. The way he snarled his question was enough to bring me out of the moment and remind me of the situation at hand.

I pulled away, but Cash's unforgiving hold wouldn't let me go far. An older man, built like a two-ton truck, stood next to the kitchen table, his heavy, black boot pressed into a man's chest. From where I was, I couldn't get a good look at the victim's face to recognize him, but I was able to see his arms tucked behind his back, pinned beneath him, and his legs, twisted oddly, hooked beneath his bottom. The way he lay on the floor, contorted with his limbs trapped under his body, anchored to the tile with a large boot confining his already constricted movements, seemed excessive.

But then he turned his head.

And those haunting green eyes made my blood run cold.

I fisted the sides of Cash's shirt, desperate for his gravity to keep me from falling away. His words from only moments ago—yet it felt like ages had passed since hearing them—ran through me. *He said he's going to come after Jade and take Aria.* Both unbridled fury and deeply rooted fear bred within me, charging me with the electrifying combination. Heat rolled through my chest like an unfurled fire, burning fast and furious up my neck and scorching my face.

Simultaneously, I released my grip on Cash and pushed away from him, frantically fighting to get to the bastard who'd ruined my life. The hatred and terror he'd groomed within me aroused the normally dormant wrath inside me. The animosity, resentment, and suppressed bitterness rushed forward in a torrent of unrestrained condemnation. *"You won't get her! You can't touch her! She'll never be yours!"*

Cash's grip around my waist kept me from him. I kicked my feet out from beneath me while Cash held me in the air, disregarding my flailing arms and wild legs. I'd probably even scratched him with my nails when I dug them into his arms, trying to break free.

"Get ahold of her, Nicholson," the older man with silver hair commanded.

The room tilted when Cash swung me around, only coming to a screeching halt once he had my back against the counter with his arms on either side of me, trapping me in place. The way he towered over me left me arching my back, and his chest rising and falling in exertion close to mine.

I lifted my chin to find his stormy gaze.

But he didn't say anything.

And neither did I.

The chaos continued around us while we stared into each other's eyes. But the longer it went on, the more in tune I became to the conversation happening behind Cash. I could now clearly separate the two men without having to see them. And by the slightly higher-pitched voice and lack of subtle Southern drawl, I identified it was the younger one who said, "He looks like a shitshow, man. There's no way he won't say anything. The first person who sees him will know he's had his ass handed to him."

"He may only got one oar in the water, but he ain't stupid enough to talk...are ya, you ol' buzzard?" A few soft slaps filled the air, and I assumed he'd smacked his face to punctuate his oddly worded insult. "He knows what'll happen to him if he opens his gator."

Cash closed his eyes, a rush of air leaving his lips as his head fell forward. And then his shoulders began to shake with the roll of unexpected humor that rumbled in his chest. He glanced over his shoulder, an easy grin on his face, and said, "Any other references to animals you'd like to make? I've got a few if you need them."

The entire situation caught me off guard and made my body tense at the possibility he'd gone crazy. Once I started questioning the reasons behind such a theory, it brought my focus to the here and now. The words and confessions I'd overheard from the bathroom filled my head, and the fact there were three men in my mom's house, my stepdad beaten on the floor, intensified the paranoia and persuaded me that the man in front of me was a stranger, someone I didn't know at all. *You're a trained killer* echoed in my mind.

When I'd come into the kitchen and saw the green eyes of that monster, I'd blocked out everything around me.

But I couldn't do that anymore.

Reality smacked me in the face.

I'd been living with a liar, a horrible person.

"*Oh, God.*" The words slipped past my lips. I was unable to cover my mouth fast enough before I drew Cash's attention to my revelation. I'd had Aria in his home, alone with him, in his care. In the presence of a killer. He'd been in my bed—inside *me*—but nothing was as bad as his role in my daughter's life. "No, no, no, no…"

I tried to skirt around him, but he was too fast. His arm wound around my waist, his giant paw gripping my hip. There was no escape, no freedom. No way out of this. The panic increased with each second that ticked by. The longer he touched me, the hotter my skin burned, until I felt like I was melting from the inside out.

"We gotta get her outta here, son." The older man's voice had calmed, lost most of its menacing tone. It was almost filled with concern, maybe compassion.

But I refused to go anywhere with him, so I continued to fight against the hold Cash had on me. "No! I need to get a book. I came for a book to read to my mom, and I can't leave without it."

The burly arms that acted as chains loosened some, but not enough for me to wrangle free. "Come on...let's go get it. Where is it?" The same deep, buttery tone I'd heard many times before flooded my ears and tricked my brain. It called to my heart and promised me safety. It told me of all the things his touch always conveyed—that he would protect me, love me, wield his sword in my defense.

Nothing more than lies decorated with velvet.

"Living room," I choked out in the hopes he wouldn't pick up on my trepidation.

Although, it'd been foolish to think he'd missed the hitch in my voice. He grabbed my hand and led me around the corner, past the staircase, toward the front of the house. His stumble and uncertainty of the layout proved he hadn't ventured far from the kitchen, and it made me wonder what exactly had taken place before I'd shown up.

While I scanned the bookshelves in search of the broken spine and illegible title, he remained behind me, as if watching my every move in case I tried to flee. I'd spotted it almost immediately, but rather than grab it so we could leave, I hesitated, hoping it'd offer a moment to escape. However, yet again, Cash was able to read me like a bold headline.

His arm stretched out over my shoulder and hovered in front of the line of books. It reminded me of the indicator on a metal detector, swaying slowly from side to side. The more I reacted, the closer he came to the one I had my eyes set on. And the moment he touched that particular spine, I lost the game.

There was no point in fighting him—I wouldn't win.

And honestly, I wasn't sure I wanted to.

Even now, I had a hard time separating the man I knew from the one I found in the kitchen.

I turned to face him, yet not look at his face, and grabbed the book from his hands. I held it close to my chest and hoped it would hide my accelerated breathing. It did not. Instead, it called his attention until he had his hands on my shoulders, keeping me directly in front of him.

"He won't hurt you," he assured me.

One glance into his eyes, and the dam threatened to break. "It's not him I'm worried about right now."

It was like my words were knives shoved straight into his heart. Every ounce of the tough guy inches away from me seemed in pain, physical agony caused by my truth. "You think I'll hurt you?"

"I-I don't even know what to think anymore."

He cradled my face in his hands and held my stare. "I love you, Jade. Know that. *Trust* that."

"I have to go. I have to get back to my mom," was all I could whisper.

Without another word, he took my hand and led me away. He must've sensed my fight had depleted, because his grip wasn't as tight as before, although it wasn't loose enough to slip free.

When we made it back to the kitchen, I glanced down at the person who once controlled so much of my life, who had embedded so much fear in me, yet I couldn't even muster the strength to hate him the way I should. I detested him, yes…but not with the ferocity I'd had earlier. Not with the need to attack him and prove that I had won.

Because I hadn't won.

I'd lost…so much.

And I wasn't sure how I'd ever get it back.

If I'd ever get it back.

THE ROOMMATE DISAGREEMENT

My fight instinct had taken flight, and all I was left with was hopelessness.

CHAPTER 20

Cash

Rhett didn't trust me to leave with Jade. Either that, or he didn't trust Jade to leave at all. He left the cleanup for Kryder to handle, met us in the garage, and demanded he drive my car. I had no idea how they'd gotten here—and if they drove, where they had parked—but I was in no position to ask. Not to mention, he'd never answer, anyway.

I climbed into the back with Jade while Rhett ran inside. She was so distant, but I couldn't exactly blame her. She'd walked in on me at my worst, and there was no explanation I could offer. Not sure what all she'd heard or even how long she'd been in the house, I had no idea where to begin. But the bottom line was…she'd lost all trust in me. I saw it vanish from her eyes when I had her against the kitchen counter. The admiration and conviction in her stare was there one minute, and then empty the next. I had no clue what had happened in those few seconds, but whatever it was left a divide a mile wide between us, and it only seemed to get bigger.

"Talk to me, Jade. Please," I begged quietly, afraid of coming off too strong.

She curled into the door and leaned against the window. We were still parked in the garage, and the only thing she had to look at was the wall lined with shelves. I doubted she could focus on anything, and she more than likely just used it as an excuse to ignore me.

But I wouldn't let her. I inched closer to the middle and angled my body to face hers. With one hand on the passenger seat and the other on the headrest behind her, I closed the distance even more. "I don't care what words you use, just *please* say something."

"I'm not sure what else there is to say, Cash." Her fingers covered her lips, which muffled her soft-spoken argument.

"Yell. Scream. *Anything.*"

She tilted her head, something in the garage catching her attention. And when I glanced away from her, I noticed Rhett heading back out, stalking toward the driver's side door. He yanked it open in a blatant show of his irritation and settled behind the wheel. Kryder appeared in the entryway, half in, half out, his hand hovering over the button on the wall to raise the garage door. When Rhett gave him a quick nod, he tapped it. Then the engine purred to life.

I sat back in my seat and settled in for an incredibly uncomfortable ride.

"Where are we takin' your friend, son?" He raised his eyes and locked his gaze on mine in the rearview mirror. We never had to speak to communicate. Silent words passed between us, then he returned his gaze to the road and carefully drove away. Rhett didn't have to glance around like a paranoid addict looking for possible witnesses. He could spot them in his sleep.

I turned my head and observed Jade. She still hadn't moved away from the door; her head still rested against the glass with her thumbnail between her teeth. We'd come here so she could be with her mom, yet everything had imploded. Although, I couldn't say I minded all of it. I didn't want to give her up, but if it were between that and going after the man who'd taken advantage of her…I'd do it again in a heartbeat. Just knowing he'd never be able to touch her again would lessen the sting of not being with her.

"I guess the hospital," I mumbled with my heart in my throat.

"I don't mean to scare ya, darlin', but I'm gonna need you to keep quiet about what you saw tonight. Am I clear?" He hadn't come across as intimidating, just direct and upfront regarding his expectations. However, it still caused her to flinch and tense in her seat.

"Yeah, she understands, Rhett. She won't say anything."

Jade whipped her head to the side and peered at me in the dark cab. I would've given anything to look her in the eyes and learn what she was thinking, but I couldn't see anything past the shadows veiling her face. Her harsh swallow resounded between us seconds before she returned to her position away from me.

Silence played on repeat until we pulled up to the hospital entrance. Jade couldn't get out fast enough—she barely waited until the vehicle had come to a complete stop. I hopped out and chased after her, catching her within ten feet of the idling car, and interrupted her hasty exit by grabbing her hand. The expression on her face when she turned around was enough to slice me open from tip to toe.

Her jaw tensed and flexed with her teeth clenching, and her lips were flat and pressed together. Instead of the clear skies that normally shined on me, drawing me in with the allure of sparkling, shallow waters on a sunny day, they deepened into an angry sea in the midst of a storm. Her brow was hard and pulled tight, casting a shadow over her heated eyes. I wanted to make it all go away. I needed the softness to return so I could make things right again. But something in my gut told me I wouldn't get that chance if I let her walk away from me.

I lifted my hand to her face, ignoring the way she flinched, and grazed my knuckles across the smooth skin on her cheek. And when I ran the pad of my thumb along her bottom lip, some of the doubt fell away from her expression. It wasn't much, but I was willing to take what I could get.

"I'll be back to get you. Call me if you need anything."

"No, Cash." Those were the first words she'd spoken since we left her mom's house, and they were the ones I feared the most. "I'll have Stevie pick me up in the morning. I can sleep here for tonight. You should probably go home."

Not once did she meet my eyes or lift her chin to look at me. I refused to believe what it meant, even though the truth was right in front of me. "You're going to come home, right?" I sounded desperate—then again, that's exactly what I was.

"I'm going to stay here until my mom gets better. After that…I'm not sure what I'll do." She held her hand up between us as if to keep me away, even though I hadn't moved toward her. "I just need time to think."

"What about the library? Your job?"

"I'll call them in the morning and explain about my mom. I'm sure they won't hold my position for me, and I can't really ask them to. I have no idea if I'll be back, so it's unfair to ask them to hold my job when I can't guarantee I'll fill it anytime soon."

"We need to talk. And honestly, I don't feel comfortable with you being here alone."

"I'll be fine. I have Stevie, and I'll be here at the hospital." Then her gaze slowly trailed up my chest to my face before cautiously holding my stare. "You and your friends—or dad, or whoever they are—don't have to worry about cutting my tongue out. I won't say anything. And I'm pretty sure he won't be a problem, either. He may act tough around me while he's got me under his control, but I don't think even he would enjoy getting another visit from a group of *trained killers*."

Any ounce of hope I'd clung to until that moment deflated. My shoulders dropped and all the air in my lungs fled my body. "We really need to talk about that, Jade." I glanced around, lowered my voice, and added, "But this isn't the right time or place. Just promise me you'll give me the chance to explain."

Her throat dipped with her hard swallow before she nodded. Her gaze fell to the ground, and in a last-ditch effort, I curled my fingers around the back of her neck, pulled her head to my lips, and pressed a desperate kiss to her hairline. It didn't last long, though. Rather than linger and watch her walk away from me, I dropped my hand and turned to climb into the passenger seat.

The second the door shut, Rhett shifted the car into drive and rolled away. I didn't want to see her, but that didn't stop my eyes from drifting to the side mirror. I found her standing exactly where I'd left her. The farther away we drove, the smaller her image became, yet throughout the entire time she appeared in the reflective glass just outside my window, she didn't move.

"So now are ya gonna to tell me what the fuck happened tonight?"

I wasn't stupid enough to think Rhett would let it go. I had no idea where he was taking me, but it didn't matter because it wasn't like I had a choice either way. My only option was to sit back and take it, give him what he asked for, and hope I still had a job.

Sighing, I rolled my head on the back of the seat and closed my eyes. "I already told you, Rhett. We came here because her mom's in the ICU, and when I saw them together and heard someone call his name…I snapped."

"There's a reason I have rules set in place for shit like this. I tell all my men to come to me with personal vendettas—and I know I've told you the same. I don't care what it's about; I need to know."

"I did tell you about it."

"Yeah, well, ya didn't call me."

I huffed, not in the mood to argue, but also yearning to have my point heard. "I didn't have time, Rhett. It's not like I went looking for the guy. I walked into the hospital to find Jade, because she'd gone in ahead of me, and that's when I saw them together. I had no idea who he was at first. But I couldn't ignore her reaction to him, and within seconds, I realized who he was."

"So you sayin' it all happened in the blink of an eye?" A slight smirk played on his lips.

"Yes."

His abrupt, roaring laughter startled me. "I thought you said ya saw him in the hospital? Yet I found ya in his kitchen. Unless I heard ya wrong—which ain't possible since I got the hearin' of a greater wax moth—ya told me you saw him with your girl...so why'd she seemed so su'prised when she walked in?"

"A wax moth?" I already knew the point he was trying to make, so I figured I'd attempt to change the subject.

"A *greater* wax moth, get it right. Damn thing developed the keenest sense o' hearin' in order'ta keep from getting' eaten by them bats." He shook his head in exaggerated, mock disappointment in me. I thought I'd won, but then he said, "Now, back to your claim that ya didn't have time to call me."

I closed my eyes and groaned inwardly.

"To me, it seems like ya had time to debilitate 'im, to get 'im in your car, to drive to his house, to get 'im inside, and somewhere along the way, ya had time to have a conversation with 'im. Yet ya didn't have time to call me?"

"You know what I mean, Rhett."

"You're right. I do. It's got nothin' to do with time, b'cause ya clearly had enough of that. You was blinded by madness, deafened by vengeance. I get it. And that's exactly why I don't let my men handle that shit on their own. It's not that I don't trust y'all to handle a job, b'cause I do. You're one of the best men I have—when you're usin' your brain. But you can't use your brain when chasin' after a personal vendetta. No one can—myself included. Too many lines blur until you're makin' stupid mistakes, like grabbin' a grown-ass man from a well-lit parkin' lot in front of a fuckin' hospital, for Christ's sake."

"I checked for cameras," I argued. "There was no one out there. No one saw me."

"You're so smart, son. Maybe you could teach me a few things." It would've been better had it been a real, sincere compliment instead of sarcasm smothered in mockery. "I think I can retire now knowin' I got someone to take the reins."

"Fine." I raised my voice, tired of the passive-aggressive verbal attacks. "I fucked up."

"Yeah ya did. And as if that ain't bad enough…you took 'im to his house. Without gloves. Without protection or even a damn plan. You can't sit here and tell me any of that was done with a clear head."

He was right. From the moment I'd pieced it all together, common sense had evaded me. Not just that, but my training and experience, as well. Everything I'd ever been taught about staying in the shadows and not crossing the lines between my professional and personal life went out the window. I had one thing on my mind, and that was to take him out. Blinding emotion led me to kidnap him in a place anyone could've walked by and seen. One witness, one phone call to the cops, would've ended me on the spot. But I didn't let that stop me—hell, I had barely given it any thought. Desperation and a thirst for revenge drove me to his house. Again, putting everything I'd ever worked for in jeopardy.

I was smarter than that.

Apparently, weakness didn't discriminate.

"You went against everything I ever taught ya." The anger that had been in his voice was no longer present, and instead, all I could pick up on was disappointment.

"I apologize. It wasn't intentional."

"You're human, son." He peered at me briefly from the corner of his eyes. "You guys are lethally trained, just as potentially dangerous as a loaded gun. In the right hands, everyone's safe, but if it found itself in the wrong situation, it could prove to be deadly. You're not a monster. I don't have to worry about anyone who works for me turnin' their skills into a public hazard. But we're human, Cash. We *all* have a trigger, and when it's squeezed at the wrong time—generally speakin'—the wrong person can get hurt."

He didn't have to explain it to me. I understood what he meant. Following orders and taking out targets was one thing, but when we strayed down the dark path of our own vengeful desires, we took the chance of getting caught, of our families finding out what we really did at WireComm. And not only could it have negative repercussions on our own lives, but the lives of our entire team, as well.

He pulled up to a motel and parked in front of a building decorated with matching red doors, each with a brass number hanging on the front. The clock on the dashboard read ten till eleven, and I wondered where the time went. It hadn't felt like two hours had passed since I'd driven into town, but with all the chaos of the evening, it wasn't like I'd kept track of the night. I grabbed my phone from the cup holder, where it'd been since the hospital, and remembered the wallet in my console. Rhett would want it, but for a split second, I questioned keeping it for whatever information it held. I'd already put myself in the line of fire tonight, and I didn't need more, so I reached inside the compartment between the seats, took the wallet out, and handed it over to my very surprised boss.

"You must really wanna keep your job," he joked, and then turned off the ignition.

We each climbed out, and Rhett made his way to a door marked with the number nine. He slipped a card into the reader to open the door. I followed his lead, but as soon as we stepped inside, I came to a screeching halt.

"I know you're all about being a team and whatnot, but how the hell are three grown-ass men supposed to fit in two double-sized beds?"

He slapped my shoulder with a resounding thud and laughed as he moved around me. "What? Don't like to cuddle? I promise not to spoon ya if you swear ya won't fork me." Fucker thought he was a comedian. "Nah...Kryder will be busy all night. You're stayin' here with me 'til he comes back, then you can head home in the mornin'."

"That's it? Just like that? You come in, tell me what a piece of shit I am, and then let me go after a full night's sleep?" Rhett had made it incredibly clear how much he didn't tolerate his men going rogue, and even though I hadn't intentionally done so, I still expected more of a backlash than a night in a motel.

He fell into one of the two chairs at the tiny, round table in front of the beds. I didn't care to be too close to him in case this was his old age kicking in. There was always a chance that in a few minutes, he'd remember who he was and what he'd caught me doing. Being within arm's reach for that was a little too close for comfort. So I settled on top of one of the mattresses and propped myself up with all the pillows it came with.

"Nah, don't be foolish, Cash. I had to reorganize multiple teams just to move ya to the desk for a week. Now I'm gonna have to put my best man on suspension, which means more interruption for the entire crew." A lot of the guys called him Sam Walton, saying he had more departments than a Walmart Supercenter. None of us fully understood the entire organization or what most of the other teams did, but we were all aware of Rhett's operations. "If I didn't think so highly of ya, you'd be gone."

I nodded, accepting my fate.

When he spoke again, his voice was low and growly. "Was it worth it?"

I stared at him, not needing a second to contemplate the answer, and unequivocally said, "Yes."

"Even if you lose her?"

Now, *that* I needed to think about. "I don't want to, but at the end of the day, if she's safe, I'd say it was worth it. He's not just someone who lives in this town, who she may or may not see when she's here—he's part of her family. She would never be able to get away from him, not with him married to her mom. So if she leaves me after this, at least he won't hurt her again...or ever touch Aria." My throat closed, making it hard to say her name. The idea of her not being in my life was too much to bear, and I refused to think about it until I learned more of where Jade's head was at.

"What do you plan on tellin' her? I mean, you're gonna talk to her...right?"

I nodded and swallowed the lump blocking most of my airway. "Does your wife know? Have you ever told her who you are and what you do?"

"I've told her what she needs to hear. I've never lied to her, and she understands enough not to ask questions. The less she asks, the easier our lives are, and she gets that. I tell 'er things I feel she needs to know. When I kiss her goodbye or tell her I love 'er before endin' our nightly calls, she's fully aware it could be the last."

I had so much to think about. The only people in my life who were privy to the truth about me were in the same position I was—working for Rhett in one capacity or another. They had to accept me, because they were the same. But Jade wasn't, and there was no reason for her to stick around if what I had to say was too much for her to handle.

"This fucking blows..." I stared at the popcorn ceiling, blowing a long breath past barely parted lips. "Maybe it's for the best if she leaves me. She makes me stupid, man."

"Don't all women?" he asked with a short laugh.

"No...not like this. Hell, I've been married before, and aside from Colleen fucking that dude, there wasn't a time I was ever off my game while I was with her. I picked up on every lie she ever told, and I'm pretty sure I subconsciously ignored the signs of her cheating to protect myself. I refused to believe my wife, the woman I'd promised to spend the rest of my life with, would be the unfaithful type, because that would mean I hadn't profiled her correctly to begin with."

"You can't blame yourself for your wife steppin' out on ya, son. This business is hard, and we're gone all the time. We need the kinda woman who we can trust with our secrets, someone to go home to after a shitty fuckin' week who'll just *be* with us any way we need it. Judy is the only woman who's ever seen me weak, but ya know what? Even when I'm breakin' down, she still looks at me like I'm the strongest motherfucker alive. *That's* the kind of woman guys like us need. But you can't fault them for not being that person if ya don't show them who you really are. Ya don't need t'give specifics or blow the entire operation, but ya can't expect her to try to heal you after a shitty week when she thinks you've done nothin' but climb cell towers."

Once again…he was right.

And if I didn't admire him so much, it'd piss me off.

"So what's the plan for Jade's stepdad?"

He ran his palm over his mouth and paused. "He won't be a problem."

That was all I needed to hear.

We spoke for a little while longer—basically, him giving me advice and telling me the story of how he'd first met his wife. At least it made me laugh to listen to him admit that he had thought she was into him when she really thought he was an arrogant asshole and wanted nothing to do with him. Then I settled in and tried to sleep, but it wouldn't come. I had too much on my mind. I needed to talk to Jade, and it kept me tossing and turning all night.

The next morning, Kryder showed up around eight. After a quick shower, I headed out in search of Jade, but that proved to be one roadblock after another. I wasn't allowed in the ICU because I wasn't family—they wouldn't even tell me if she was there. Her phone kept going to voicemail, and I didn't have Stevie's number, let alone where she lived, and I had no way to get that information without my computer. By the afternoon, I had no choice but to return to Geneva Key and wait to hear from her.

With my suspension, I was left with endless days filled with worry, aggravation, heartache, and the most intense longing I'd ever experienced. I took up walks on the beach just to pass the time. The air had started to cool, which in Florida meant it was slightly better than the pits of hell, so I found myself strolling along the shore for hours each day.

On Thursday, I returned home from the gym just as the sky started to turn colors, alluding to the pending sunset. I would've stayed out all night if I could've, but after a certain point, it became loitering. You'd think after living alone for so long, the quietness wouldn't be so difficult, but it was. Although, not near as hard as parking my car next to Jade's behind my house, only to walk inside and she not be there.

Just like I did every time I came home from somewhere, I took one last look over my shoulder at the blue Jetta with faded paint and dented fender, and then went inside. It took two steps for my world to come to a screeching halt. A total of six seconds from the front door to the kitchen to make my heart stop.

It had taken three and a half breaths before my lungs ceased to inflate.

CHAPTER 21

Jade

"What are you doing here?" My voice got stuck in my chest, making the words sound like they were croaked out. I took one step back, but the bed stopped me, and I realized I had nowhere else to go. I wasn't afraid, yet my hands trembled and my breathing shuddered. Heat consumed me without any explanation, the emotions inside not making sense. "I-I thought you'd be gone."

Over the last week, I'd had a lot of time to think. Even after Mom had come out of the coma, I'd spent many hours in silence, watching her sleep, which afforded me the opportunity to sort through what had happened with Cash. The fear I'd felt toward him had long since subsided, the anger had diminished, and what I was left with was hurt—unfathomable betrayal.

And confusion. Lots and lots of confusion.

He slowly put one foot in front of the other until only a couple of feet separated us. It wasn't predatory, but almost as if he couldn't believe I was here. His eyes searched mine while his shoulders rolled like a slow tide with each controlled breath.

"You came back..." He glanced behind him, through the open bedroom door, and then back at me. "I saw your purse on the kitchen table, and I thought my eyes were playing tricks on me, but they weren't. You're here. You came back. Where's Aria?"

The elation that exuded from him tore me apart. I hated being the bad guy, hated to hurt anyone, which was why I'd chosen to make the trip when he wouldn't be home. I couldn't face him. It was no secret he wanted to talk, but I had nothing to say to him.

Eventually, we'd have to have a conversation about it, but not while I was still caring for my mother.

"She's in Fort Pierce with Stevie. Derek had to go to Tampa, so he dropped me off on his way, because my car's here. I'm not staying. I just had to get a few things. You took everything with you, and all I had were a few outfits and pull-ups for Aria. You weren't supposed to be home. You were supposed to be at…at *work*. Or whatever it is you do during the week. I'm pretty sure it has nothing to do with networks or towers."

"I was suspended for three weeks." Disbelief dripped from his tone, yet it wasn't caused by his suspension. "Why haven't you answered my calls or texts? I couldn't get ahold of you, and it's had me worried. I even tried Stevie. At least she answered, but you were never there; she promised she'd take a message. The ICU doesn't accept calls, and no one there would tell me anything about your mom. I've been here…alone…worried sick."

"I was busy. I've had a lot going on."

"How is she?"

"My mom? She's good. Alive…and that's all that matters." I meant to stop there, give him the answer to his question and be done with it, but I couldn't. I'd needed someone to talk to, and while Stevie was such an amazing friend to help me out, it just didn't feel the same. Even though she'd always been my best friend, talking to her made me realize things had changed—not between us, but with that particular role in my life. Someone else had filled those shoes, someone who wasn't there to listen because I'd pushed him away. "She woke up on Sunday, and all the tests and scans have come back clear. Now it's just waiting for her body to heal. She has a fractured hip and some bruises, but those aren't permanent, so I can't complain."

The scruff on his face made him appear darker, his skin more sun kissed. And his eyes weren't as black as I was used to; now they almost shined like polished coal. There was a sadness to him, but as he stood in front of me, it was like the weight of the world had fallen off his back and he could breathe again.

"I take it things are going well for you two?"

"Yeah." I couldn't fight the smile, so I didn't even try. However, I did drop my gaze while I offered more. "She was really happy to see me. I found out she's been in therapy, has been since I moved out. I had no idea. That's actually what she was doing at the stables—equine therapy. This entire time I thought she didn't want me around, like she was embarrassed by me, but that wasn't it at all."

I'd always known that everything—even down to the decision to cut me off financially once I had Aria—had all been *his* ideas. He'd told her she needed to be strict with me and not coddle me, that I needed "tough love." But my biggest problem had always been that she'd listened to him instead of doing what was right.

"Apparently, she used to fight with my stepdad a lot over how to handle me. She didn't think his method was working, but as soon as I got pregnant and stopped acting out, he used that as proof that she was wrong. He said it was more important that I behaved than her and I having a close relationship. She didn't get along with her mom, so he told her she shouldn't be concerned about whether or not we did."

"He won't ever hurt you again." His voice was so soft it coated me like cotton. He came closer and gently lifted my chin so he could see my eyes.

This man had meant so much to me, and now I had no idea where I stood. The need for a little entertainment in my life had sent me to him, which had provided a friend, then someone I found comfort in before he'd turned into more. My feelings for him had changed, morphed into something bone-deep, and even though I was lost in a constant state of confusion over who he truly was, that feeling seemed to remain embedded in me.

"I know." And I did. I fully trusted that he wouldn't touch me after Cash and his friends had their way with him. I hadn't seen him since that night, but I also hadn't gone to the house. If I wasn't at the hospital with my mom, I was at Stevie's. And anytime Mom had asked about him, I told her the truth—I didn't know where he was. The reason I didn't know was because I refused to ask. Honestly, I wouldn't have cared if he'd been hauled out into international waters and tossed overboard with cement blocks around his ankles, but that didn't mean I wanted the confirmation. There was no way I would've been able to bring myself to admit that I'd moved my daughter out of a child molester's house and into the home of a murderer.

"And Aria? Is she okay?" That was all it took to completely shatter my heart.

I refused to tell him that she'd spent all week asking for him. And he'd never find out how much it had killed me to hear it. He didn't deserve it, not after Friday night. "She's good. Happy. If Stevie's home, she stays with her, and if not, she comes to the hospital with me. My mom has been desperately trying to make up for lost time with her and has spent most nights crying and apologizing for the way everything happened…for not being there for us."

"Did you tell her?"

He didn't have to clarify what he meant. "No. And I never will."

"You *never* plan to explain it to her?"

I shook my head and inhaled deeply, needing a moment before giving him my reasons. I was confident in my decision, but I didn't care to listen to him disagree. "She blames herself for so much. She convinced herself that after my dad died, she'd spent too long grieving and didn't give me the proper attention I needed. I was a child—her child—who'd lost a parent, and for a while, I'd lost both. So in her mind, my rebellious actions as a teen were caused by her brief absence during a time I needed her. And she feels I left because she wouldn't help me."

"That should give you *more* reason to tell her the truth—to keep her from believing everything was her fault."

"If I tell her what really happened, the reason behind the crap I pulled in high school and leaving, all it'll do is move the blame from her to him. But then she'll feel guilty for marrying him, saying it's her fault I was abused. I would rather her believe I acted out when I was younger because she was too busy dealing with the death of my father, and believe I'm so selfish that I moved out because she wouldn't give me money, than to dump the responsibility of my abuse in her lap."

He nodded, and for the first time since stepping into the room, his attention moved away from me. He glanced over my shoulder to the bed, and the moment he spotted the small suitcase, his forehead creased. The softness of his brow had grown taut, and it cast a shadow over his eyes.

"You can't leave yet. We *need* to talk, Jade."

I was conflicted, torn between what I wanted to do, and what I had to do. My heart ached to give him a chance, to hear him tell me I had misunderstood everything I'd heard Friday night. It fought for him, and I knew this feeling wasn't wrong. This was real. Every beat was meant for him. But my head told me something different. It told me I didn't need to hear him explain anything, that whatever he had to say would be a lie, anyway. This was his chance to rope me back in, and not only did I have my safety to think about, but I had a daughter, and I would never allow her to be put in danger again.

"There's nothing to talk about, Cash. You can't use your pretty words or empty promises to make me forget what I heard…what I saw. There's nothing you can do that can convince me it was a misunderstanding." The walls had started to close in, and if I didn't get out of here, he would witness my total destruction.

But then Cash did something I hadn't expected. He closed the door, trapping me inside the bedroom with him, keeping me from leaving. Forcing me to hear him out. The knot in the pit of my stomach grew and tightened. This wasn't panic — I'd lived with that for years — and he didn't fill me with fear. I truly believed he wouldn't hurt me the second he turned around and his easy, warm gaze fell upon me. But that didn't calm my anxiety. I *was* apprehensive, though not over what he would do to me. If I gave him the chance to explain, I worried I'd fall for his every word — hook, line, and sinker. And I had no desire to do that.

"You overheard three very pissed-off men in an extremely intense moment. I can assure you that whatever you think you know, you don't have a clue. I can't even begin to guess what you heard that night before you came into the kitchen, so I'm not going to offer excuses for any of that. And as far as what you witnessed…it was no different than what any other boyfriend would've done to defend the woman he loves."

"I heard someone say you're a trained killer, Cash. I don't care about anything else. You could've killed him right there in front of me, and I more than likely would've turned a blind eye. Nothing that happened that night matters — *except* hearing what that man said about you." I threaded my fingers into my hair and held my head. Nothing made sense, and I needed to be farther away from him than I was, so I moved around the bed and leaned against the wall. "A *trained* killer, Cash. I can't even wrap my head around what that means."

There we were, two people standing on opposite ends of a room, backs against a wall. I had no idea how I was looking at him, but he stared at me like a little boy who'd just been scolded for wetting his bed. I couldn't look at him or I'd cave, so I hung my head and closed my eyes.

"I don't work on cell towers. When I'm away for work, I…" He huffed and I held my breath. "I'm given specific people to target. I follow them, track them, and then I basically kidnap and interrogate them until we have the information we need."

I covered my face and slid down the wall until my feet gave out beneath me and my bottom hit the hard floor. His confession was nothing more than a jumbled mess of words I couldn't even begin to sort through.

"Rhett, the older man who drove us to the hospital that night, is my boss. Kryder, the other guy in your mom's kitchen, works on my team. I didn't call them over, nor was I aware they'd be there. After you told me what had happened to you, I had a hard time focusing and Rhett noticed. He asked me what was going on, so I told him. He ordered me to a week behind a desk doing paperwork, but then I rushed home, and honestly, didn't think too much more about it. Not after spending the night with you. But then I saw you with him at the hospital and put two and two together. That's when I took matters into my own hands. Rhett and Kryder came after the fact. They had no idea I'd be there."

"Then why did they come?"

"Rhett wanted to tail him for a few days, just to check him out. He thought there was a chance he was the older man who'd abused you and figured it was worth looking into."

I dropped my hands and gawked at him. "I didn't need you or anyone else coming to my defense. He no longer had any control over me, so there was no reason to do what you did. I'm not a victim, Cash. I survived. I got out of there. I got Aria out of there."

Defeat lingered in his eyes, and the sight cut me wide open. "I couldn't let him get away with what he did. It doesn't matter how strong you are or how far away from him you moved. I couldn't let him live after knowing what he did to you."

"I don't get it...are you a criminal? A cop? You said you interrogate people, but you don't sound like law enforcement. Not to mention, you guys seemed pretty concerned about the police getting called."

"I'm not a cop." With that confession, my throat closed. "And whether or not I'm a criminal would depend on who you ask." And with that, my head spun.

"Have you ever killed anyone?" I wanted the truth, but that didn't stop me from praying for the answer that would help me sleep better at night.

"Yes. Sometimes, in my profession, it happens."

"Your *profession*?" I balked. "And what's that? Are you a hitman? A thug? You work for the Italian Mafia?" I remembered what he'd told me about his dad's biological parents. "Oh my God. That's it, isn't it?"

"I'm not in the Mafia, Jade."

"Then what is it?"

His feet slid out in front of him until he mimicked my position on the floor. "The company I work for is contracted out by the government to track down potential terrorists who are in the country. Information on the target is collected, then given to Rhett, who then passes it on to me. I'm sent wherever I'm needed, and aside from coming home on the weekends, I remain there until I have what I need. When the time is right, I grab him, and then he's carried off to our main headquarters for interrogation. Whatever we get from him is then used to help understand their plots and plans, and hopefully, prevent other terrorist attacks."

"So you work for the government?" Hope blossomed, and I prayed he'd say yes.

"No." The hope wilted. "I work for Rhett. We are essentially hired by the CIA and State Department, but not directly. The orders come from them, but it has to go through countless departments before it gets to us, so if anyone ever finds out or if we're ever discovered, their hands are clean."

"I don't understand. Why would they need to keep their hands clean?"

"Because we use enhanced interrogation methods that are illegal. And if anyone found out that our government had hired people to carry out the kinds of torture we demonstrate, then we'd possibly face another war...potentially within our own country."

I stared at the floor but couldn't focus on anything. As soon as something started to make sense, it stopped, and I ended up more confused the longer I tried to understand it all. "So…if it's illegal, and the CIA and whoever else could get in a lot of trouble for it, why do it? If they aren't from here, why can't you just let them go? Send them back where they came from? I mean, if they have enough information on them to send you in, why can't they use that as an excuse to kick them out of the country?"

"If we did that, how would we be able to find out what they're planning?"

"Well, can't you figure that out other ways and still send them back?"

"So they can capture one of our soldiers and behead him—or her—on camera? So they can plot something else and end up doing more harm? No. You may not agree with what I do…hell, not many people do, but what's the alternative? Stand there and do nothing? Watch while innocent people die? It's not just planes in buildings anymore. We're looking at bombs at dinner parties and movie theaters full of kids. Or concerts and clubs."

The archangel Michael.

The ink decorating his entire back.

It all made sense.

But I was torn. Cash killed people, except they were bad people. That couldn't possibly make him a monster. However, no matter which way I looked at it, he was responsible for taking countless lives.

"I don't know, Cash. I'm confused as to what this all means or how it affects me and Aria."

"I'll tell you how… What I do is messy, and it's dark, and it eats away at me when I'm alone. But it keeps you safe. You can take Aria to the library or the park and not worry about some guy with a bomb strapped to his chest."

"Are you kidding me?" My fight came alive. "That stuff happens all the time. You can't stop them all. And not everyone who commits a crime is a terrorist. You can't prevent it from happening. With or without you playing the role of the angel on your back, it will continue to go on."

"So you're saying we should stop arresting criminals because crime will never end?"

My stomach rolled and a knot formed in my chest. Once again, I was at odds with how to feel or react. He made sense, but I couldn't let go of the resistance. This wasn't black or white. There were pros and cons to both sides, yet my brain wouldn't function enough to compare the lists. I had no idea which was the lesser of the two evils.

Numb to almost everything, I decided to be brave and ask the question I hadn't been ready to hear the answer to until just now. "What happened after we left my mom's house? He hasn't been around, and you told me he'd never hurt me again. Did you…?"

"No. There was a report made to the police department about a man who sexually assaulted a city council member, and your stepdad's name was given. He was picked up early Saturday morning for questioning and is currently behind bars."

I thought I was about to throw up. "Is it true? Did he really do that?"

"Well, he denies it, but the DA has evidence that says otherwise." Nothing about his expression told me anything useful. I already knew what a good liar he was, which made it impossible to discover the truth.

"And it just so happens that this all took place that night?"

He shrugged, as if it didn't matter.

"Listen, I'm all for him going away. He deserves to be in there whether this incident was fabricated or not. What he did to me wasn't. I just need to hear the truth." My lips trembled and my voice began to shake. "I *have* to know if he really did that."

"No, Jade. I can't tell you if he's ever hurt anyone else, but this time, no. A few calls were made, lab reports were run, and he's where he belongs."

As relieved as I was to hear that, a little voice in my head wouldn't quiet down. "So you're a trained killer, who targets and interrogates terrorists, and prevents them from killing innocent people." I'd phrased it as a statement, but I waited for him to nod in agreement before continuing. "And these orders are sent from DC, which is then handed down through a long line of government departments, and then out to non-government factions, before it's given to your boss." Again, he nodded. "And then you get this proof that this person is evil, so you go after him and torture him until you get information."

"Yes," he agreed with another nod, his stare holding mine.

"And you don't see anything wrong with that?"

His gaze narrowed while his lip hitched just slightly, showing his genuine confusion.

"Cash...despite whether he deserved it or not, a man is sitting in jail for a crime he didn't technically commit—with actual evidence against him. I'm not saying I disagree with that, but the same people who had set that up are the ones who give you orders to chase after others for crimes you're told they've committed, with evidence against *them*."

"They're terrorists, Jade." He was thoroughly convinced of this.

"So you're told. And they may or may not be. But how can you believe someone who you know is capable of using the system for their own gain? How do you not question that? Because I'll tell you this: you kept this major part of your life from me. You've looked me straight in the eye and lied. It's hard not to question every word out of your mouth, so I don't understand how after seeing what these men are capable of, you don't think twice about it. They tell you so-and-so has done this and that, and you go after him. And then *torture* him. No questions asked."

He blinked a few times, his sight falling to the middle of the floor. I could tell my words had gotten to him, but to what extent,

I wasn't sure. He was a good man. That much was understood by his reaction, the way he trusted the men he worked with and for.

"I'm just giving you food for thought. What you do with it is up to you. This doesn't even concern me; I just wondered if you'd ever questioned it before. You know?"

"What do you mean it doesn't concern you?" He glanced around the room, panic filling his dark eyes. When he stood, his movements were quick and desperate, causing me to pull myself to my feet, as well. "You said you were only getting clothes because you were helping your mom."

He frantically checked the drawers and closet. I wanted to go to him, to settle his nerves, but there was nothing I could say to calm him down aside from reassuring him that I'd be back. That I wasn't moving out, only packing a few things to hold me over for a couple of weeks. And I couldn't tell him that. Because I wasn't sure how truthful that would be. It wasn't until he noticed I hadn't packed everything that his demeanor calmed and he faced me once more.

I moved closer to the bed and grabbed the small suitcase by the handle. "I don't know when I'll be back. It all depends on how long Mom will be at the hospital. I've been staying with Stevie in her spare room, and she's offered it to me for as long as I need it."

"What about your job? What about me?"

My eyes burned with the threat of tears. "I had to quit my job."

"What about *me*?" His desperation wrapped around my throat like a noose.

I couldn't speak—even if I knew how to answer him, the words wouldn't come out. So I offered him a shrug, without looking at him, and dragged the suitcase off the bed.

"You can't leave, Jade." The pain in his voice stroked deep within my chest, ran through my veins, and coiled around my lungs. "Please, don't leave me. Don't take Aria from me."

A tear slipped from my eye and slid down my cheek. "I have to go, Cash." And without waiting, I moved past him and out the door. Stopping for my purse, I noticed the watch on the kitchen table. "I can't accept this gift from you, and as soon as I can replace the phone, I'll give that back, as well. Unless you need it now."

"I don't fucking need anything from you…just you, Jade." He stood behind me, but I couldn't turn to see him. I couldn't look at him. His words were hard enough to hear, and if I saw his eyes, nothing would be able to stop me from breaking down. "Don't leave. *Please*, don't fucking leave."

The second his fingers wrapped around my upper arm, the bag fell from my hand and my body turned into him as if on instinct. I dropped my forehead to his chest and fisted the sides of his T-shirt, letting the material soak up my tears. And then he wrapped me up in the only comfort I'd ever truly known.

"God, I love you so much, Jade. So fucking much. I can't be here without you. I'm so sorry I lied, and I'll do anything it takes to make it right. Tell me what to do. I'll do it in a heartbeat." His pleading words blew through my hair with his lips close to my ear.

"I can't tell you what to do," I mumbled into his chest.

"Then at least give me the chance to make it right. Let me prove to you that you can trust me."

That was just it, though—I already trusted him. I may have started to question everything he'd ever told me, but as a person, I trusted him completely. I knew he'd never hurt me. I believed him when he said he loved me. And there was no doubt in my mind that if he could claim Aria as his own, he would.

"We'll talk, okay?" I pulled away from him but refused to let go. When I tipped my head back to see his eyes, he stroked my cheeks with his thumbs, clearing away the pain that ran down my face. "I need to be there for my mom, so I have to go, but at some point, I'll come back—to either pack my things or stay. But I can't make that decision right now. I have far too much on my mind to add this to it."

"So if I call, you'll answer?"

"If I can, yes."

"And if you can't?"

For such a large, strong man, he appeared so weak in this moment. "Then I'll call you back."

With his hands on my face, he leaned down and pressed his lips to mine. It was soft and quick, but that's all it needed to be for his point to come across. He loved me, and he didn't need more than a chaste kiss to prove it.

✤

My phone had gone off several times during my drive to the east coast, but I didn't look at it. I needed to pay attention to the roads, and I knew if any of the texts were from Cash, I'd have to pull over to compose myself. I didn't have the time to do that. I'd already wasted more than I had by staying behind and talking to him.

When I made it back to Stevie's apartment, Aria woke up. She'd missed me and refused to go back to sleep. As soon as she found out I'd gone back home, she had even more questions about Cash—mostly, where was he. Stevie could tell something was wrong, but she didn't ask. I hadn't told her about what had happened last week, and I'd excused Cash's absence as work related. But I knew she could see right through me. Luckily, she decided not to pry.

It wasn't until midnight before I lay in bed and finally had a chance to check my phone. There were two texts from Cash. The first was a document that took far too long to figure out due to my inexperience with this phone, but once I had it opened, I couldn't stop the tears.

Honesty Agreement

-I will never lie to you again.

I exited that and went back to the messages. His second text made me laugh.

Cash: Feel free to make any amendments you wish. This agreement will hold up in court.

Smiling with tears clinging to my lip, I responded.

Me: You're missing a few bullet points.

His reply was immediate, as if he'd been staring at his phone for hours, waiting for me.

Cash: I didn't think it needed any. It's fairly cut and dry. I wouldn't want to leave any room for interpretation.

Me: What if I ask you if I look fat in a bathing suit?

Cash: You think I'd lie?

Me: You'd tell me yes, I look fat?!

Cash: HELL NO! And it wouldn't be a lie.

My heart swelled while I tried to push back the fear that we were rushing things.

Me: OK...what if I'm sick and I ask you if I sound like a dude?

Me: And I really do, so it wouldn't be a matter of opinion.

The bubbles popped up, and then his reply.

Cash: Then I'd tell you that you sound sexy

Me: Would that be a lie?

Cash: Nope

Me: So you think dudes sound sexy??

Cash: I walked right into that one, didn't I? How about, it doesn't matter what your voice sounds like or what you say, because I'll always think you sound sexy.

I stared at his words on the screen and thought about other situations.

Me: What if I made dinner and forgot an ingredient and it tasted bad?

Cash: You'd be eating it with me, so I don't think I'd have to say anything

My smile stretched wider.

Cash: Babe, there are no exceptions. I won't ever lie to you again.

Me: I do need one thing added.

Cash: ???

Me: Omission of the truth is still a lie.

Cash: So if you color your hair puke green and I don't tell you I hate it, that's still a lie?

Me: Yup.

Cash: Fine. Making the changes now. Will send when I'm done.

Two minutes later, another document came through.

Honesty Agreement

-I will never lie to you again.

***An omission of the truth is still a lie.**

***Please don't ever color your hair puke green.**

I had to cover my mouth to keep from waking the house with my laughter.

Me: Deal. No green hair.

Cash: Thank God!

Me: Night, Cash.

Cash: Night babe. I love you.

I love you, too.

CHAPTER 22

Cash

The dark room, coupled with her soft, melodic voice in my ear could've almost convinced me that she was with me while I lay in bed. But the heat of the phone against my face and the cool sheets next to me were enough to disprove the illusions I tried telling myself. In the four days since she'd come to the house, we'd spent two of those nights on the phone, and the other two texting. I would've taken any form of communication, including carrier pigeons, but nothing—aside from having her here—beat the sound of her voice.

"So how'd she take it?" I closed my eyes and pictured her—her long, curly hair, hypnotic blue eyes, and the lips I couldn't stop dreaming about. I tried to imagine what she was doing while she talked to me on the phone, if she were in bed or sitting on the couch. But as soon as I realized how far away she was, I had to push the picture out of my head.

"I'm not really sure. I wasn't with her when they talked about it. Bryn thought it would be best if I wasn't in the room, and since she's the professional therapist and all, I agreed. Mom's been so wrapped up in making up for lost time and reconnecting that having me there when she learned about her husband might distract her from dealing with the situation at hand."

Her mom had been released from the hospital this morning and moved to a rehabilitation center for her hip. She had been awake for a week, and with each passing day, her concern for her husband's whereabouts grew exponentially. Finally, realizing she couldn't avoid it once the discharge papers were signed, Jade contacted the psychologist her mom had used in conjunction with equine therapy and brought her up to speed on the arrest.

"I'm going to visit her tomorrow, but I have no clue what to say. Do I bring it up? Wait for her to say something? She has so much going on right now, and I worry this will just make everything worse. Her number-one priority should be getting better, but it hasn't been. I think she's put too much focus on having Aria and me around that her healing has taken a back seat, and I hate that. Now with this going on, it's just one more thing to pile on her plate."

I tried to bite my tongue, fully aware of her stance on the matter, but I loved her too much to hold back. I only had the best intentions for her, and she had the same for her mom. "Now that she knows about his arrest and what it was for, it should be easier to tell her about what he did to you."

She huffed, and I worried I'd pushed too hard. I couldn't risk her hanging up, but her mental health was more important to me than how often I got to talk to her. "It doesn't change anything, Cash. There could be a hundred girls coming forward saying he'd done the same to them, and it still wouldn't lessen the guilt she'd have about me. You're not a parent, so you wouldn't understand, but if anything ever happened to Aria and I hadn't protected her, I'd hate myself. And even worse, if she'd been hurt because of someone I'd introduced into her life…" She didn't even need to finish her statement; I understood it all too well.

"I may not have conceived a child, but that doesn't mean I can't comprehend that kind of pain. It doesn't mean I can't put myself in her shoes. And I'm not disagreeing with you, babe. I get that you have the best intentions for your mom, but you're not looking at the entire picture. This relationship you're building with her has been founded on a lie. You're aware of it, yet you're not doing anything to correct it. Not to mention, you deserve to heal just as much as she does. Keeping this secret won't make anything better for you. You're trying to protect her, fine, but someone needs to look out for *you*. That's all I'm doing."

"She can't change the past, so what's the point in telling her? If she had just done something that hurt me, I can see the value of being honest—to make her aware of her actions and hope she learns from it and doesn't repeat it again. But she can't do that with this. What good would come from it? So she doesn't marry another pervert who'd take advantage of me? It's a little late for that."

"It's not too late for Aria."

"What's that supposed to mean?"

"He's behind bars for sexual assault. But those charges won't keep him there forever. Doesn't Aria have a right to be protected from him when she gets older? Your mom may not have been able to stop him from doing those things to you, but now she has a chance to keep him from doing the same to your daughter—her granddaughter. Plus, doesn't she have a right to know she's married to a pedophile? Shouldn't she get to make the decision if she wants to stay with him or not after he gets out?"

Jade was silent, nothing but wisps of her exhales filtering through the line, and I knew I'd gotten to her.

"You really need to stop looking at this as what it'll do to your mom. You need to see it as the effects it has on you. Keeping the secret versus confronting it, and then moving on as a family, healing together. Maybe you should talk to that Bryn woman about it, see what she thinks."

"One thing at a time, Cash." This was the beginning of the end to our conversation, I could tell. "And right now, I'm more concerned about her getting better and working through her feelings about the arrest."

"Can you just do me a favor? Think about how you felt when you found out I had lied to you about what I do for a living. And keep in mind I couldn't just come out with the truth. Doing so would've potentially put my team and the entire organization—not to mention, the country—at risk."

She was quiet for a moment, and I could almost hear the wheels turning in her head. I only hoped she had truly heard what I said. "Did your ex-wife know?"

"No, I never told her. To be honest, I never considered it."

"Did you ever think about telling me?"

I didn't need the time to contemplate my answer, but I took it anyway. "There were times when I did. When I'd come back from a particularly bad week and felt like if I held it all in for one more second, I'd implode. But then I wouldn't say anything because the thought of you leaving was worse than what my secret would do to me, so I kept it to myself and just learned to settle for the comfort of your presence."

"Ever wonder what life would be like if you had told your wife the truth?"

"I think it worked out the way it was meant to…it brought me to you. But I will admit that lying to you has come with far more emotional damage than I expected, and I don't wish the same for you. This is the time to open up and let her in, to offer her the opportunity to be there for you. I know that hurts you a lot—that you tried to get her attention and it didn't work. You wanted her to hold you then, and you deserve that now… Hell, she deserves the chance to do that now. Your time of healing has come. Don't make the same mistake I did and let it pass you by."

"I just can't, Cash," she said with a long sigh. "I see your point, but the two aren't the same. Your reasons for not telling me the truth aren't comparable to mine. But I do understand what you're trying to say."

"You really should talk it over with Bryn. Hopefully, she can help facilitate the closure."

"Thanks, Cash." My name was followed by a yawn, and I knew I didn't have much longer with her tonight.

"Hey, babe?" I waited for her sleepy hum before I said, "I need you to make me laugh."

Anytime we talked on the phone, I wouldn't let her go without turning our conversation around. It didn't matter how deep our discussions were, I needed to hear something light before hanging up. It wouldn't have surprised me if she wrote a few down, anticipating this part of our calls.

Her smile filled her words when she asked, "What's orange and sounds like a parrot?"

"A carrot." Even though I knew the punchline, it didn't stop the smile from forming. "That was easy. Give me another one."

"Fine. What's clear and smells like red paint?"

I thought about it for a moment before giving up. "I don't know."

"Chloroform. Shhhh."

Laughter hit me so hard it boomed in the dark room around me.

"Goodnight, Cash. I'll talk to you tomorrow."

"Sounds good. Night, babe."

I didn't even bother to put the cell away, just dropped it onto the mattress next to me and rolled over. But sleep didn't come easily. I tossed and turned, replaying her words in my head—*all* of them. They were still on repeat when I finally woke up, after only what felt like a couple of hours of sleep, and the replay continued until mid-afternoon.

Me: Are you busy?"

I worried about texting her, about bothering her, but I needed my own closure. Without answers, I'd forever be plagued with questions and what-ifs. So, I sucked it up and sent her a message, and then stared at the screen in anticipation of the bubbles indicating her typing.

Colleen: No. Is everything ok???

™ROOMMATE *dis*AGREEMENT

Ever since the night I'd packed a bag and left, I hadn't spoken to her. She'd tried for a while once she realized I was truly gone, but by that point, I was over it—not over what she did, but rather the idea of being with anyone. I didn't need her excuses or to listen to all the ways it was my fault. When it came time to serve her with papers, I'd let my attorney handle everything. He'd been the one to deal with Colleen, and luckily, the divorce was smooth. She didn't ask for anything, and I didn't care for more than what I had.

So I didn't blame her for worrying if everything was okay when she finally heard from me.

> **Me**: Yeah. I just have a question, and I really hope you'll answer. I never gave you the chance to talk before, but I hope you understand I was just too angry and hurt to hear it. But now I need to know…why'd you do it? Why cheat on me?

The bubbles bounced on the screen, and the longer it went on, the more impatient I became.

> **Colleen**: I feel like anything I say will be wrong in your eyes

> **Me**: Cheating was wrong. Your reasons are just that…your reasons.

While waiting for her response, the phone began to vibrate in my hand, Colleen's name flashing at the top. I wanted answers, but at the same time, I didn't care to speak to her. I no longer carried the hatred I had a year ago, but that didn't mean I wanted to invite her back into my life. I only needed this answer for one thing, and one thing only. And it wasn't about her.

"I think things might get lost in translation over text, so I figured a call would be best. I hope that's all right with you. If not, I can go back to texting." Her voice didn't even sound familiar anymore. This was the woman I had been married to for six years, lived with, *loved*, yet I wouldn't have been able to recognize her by her voice if I had a gun to my head.

"This is fine. I just really need to know."

"Is it a girl?" Her question caught me by surprise. "Have you found someone else, and you're worried she'll do the same?"

"I'm not discussing this with you, Colleen. You said you would answer the question, but if it comes with strings or stipulations, then never mind. You don't have the right to ask me about my relationship status."

"Cash," she said, preventing me from carrying on with my tangent. "I'm sorry, okay? I'm sorry about it all."

I grew frustrated at the sound of her tears. This wasn't what I had in mind when I reached out. I only meant to ask a question, not give her the chance I'd been denying her for over a year. "Forget it. This was a mistake."

"Why can't you just let me fucking apologize?" Intense pain roared in her voice as she barked her demanding inquiry. When I didn't respond, too shocked to say anything, she continued, but this time, in a much softer tone. "That's all I've wanted, Cash. To say I'm sorry. I fucked up, and I can't take it back. I can't make it right or fix it. I hurt you, and there's not enough apologies in the world to make that better. I've never blamed you or made up excuses for my actions. All this time, I've only wanted a chance to say sorry and know you heard it."

Well, I definitely heard that, and it made me realize so much more. Even to this day, it seemed my ex had carried this guilt around with her, and all she needed to set it free was a moment of my time to own her mistake and apologize. It gave me even more hope that Jade and her mother would be able to work through everything, including the horrifying truth, as long as they chose to listen to one another.

"Thank you, Colleen."

"And thank *you* for giving me that chance. Now…you had a question. I feel the need to preface this by saying I'm fully aware that nothing you could've ever done would warrant what I did to you. All I can tell you is *why* it happened, and that I acknowledge it doesn't excuse my behavior."

"I know, Colleen." Although, I had to admit, it did feel good to hear her say these things. For so long, I assumed she felt no guilt, had let the blame fall on me in my absence, so listening to her sorrowful admission wiped away any lingering resentment I'd had toward her.

"You were gone all the time. Even when you were here, you were gone. When we first got married, I didn't think it would be a problem because that's what our entire relationship had been like. We were in our early twenties, so I had the time and space to see my friends and go out. I didn't have the responsibilities of dinner on the table when you got home from work, or cleaning up after someone else. I didn't have to answer to anyone about where I was going or if I bought a new outfit. But somewhere along the way, I must've...matured some."

I couldn't contain the incredulous, huffed laugh.

"What I *did* wasn't mature, and I'll be the first to admit it," she fought back, clearly defensive over my reaction. "But the things I *wanted* out of life had matured. This shouldn't come as a surprise because we used to argue about it. I wanted a family, time with my husband...things normal adult couples had. Our friends had started to get married and have babies, and I was the single one in the group—except I wasn't single. I just had a husband who was never around."

"Because I was working to pay the mortgage and car payments."

"I know that, Cash. And I knew it then, but in my head, all I could think about was how badly I missed being adored. You used to come home on Friday nights and lock me in the bedroom all weekend, like you couldn't get enough of me. But over time, things slowly stopped. At the end, you'd come home, decompress, and as soon as you'd gotten used to being there, you were heading out again. And I'm not saying this is your fault.

There were so many other ways I could've gone about it, but I didn't. Instead, I took the cowardly way out and ended up hurting you, someone I loved more than anything."

Her words actually sank in, something I hadn't expected. Honestly, I thought I would hear what she had to say, ignore the blame game, and hope there was enough left over to actually offer me something useful. But she'd given me more than that.

"It's easy to look back and say things would've been different if you had a normal career that didn't take you away from me five days a week, but there's really no way to know that. We'd never lived together the way most people do, so who's to say we would've even lasted the six years we had?"

When she paused, my chest constricted—not over her words, but what this all meant for Jade and me, and the relationship I'd do anything to have with her.

"If I may, I'd like to say something really quick before I lose the chance…if you *are* seeing someone, and that's what made you reach out, don't let her go. Something changed in our marriage in the last year to year and a half. I don't know what it was, nor do I think I'll ever figure it out, but in my opinion, it destroyed us. Maybe it was your job, the long days and weeks spent away from home, or the traveling to and from wherever you went. But you'd spend the weekends recovering, and during that time, I had already felt like I was missing something from my life, and I stupidly allowed myself to search for it without you."

"Thank you for that." My voice had nearly vanished, lost in the emotion our conversation filled me with. "And I'm sorry for never giving you the chance to apologize. That was unfair of me to do."

I didn't, nor would I ever, regret reaching out to her. She'd given me what I had asked for, and in turn, she had a chance to say what she'd held onto for so long. It was therapeutic in a way for both of us. However, that would change if this conversation progressed much further.

"Take care, Cash. I wish nothing but the best for you." And with that, our call ended.

⚓

I wasn't sure I'd make it through the first two weeks of suspension, let alone the third. Being at the house alone was miserable. Jade and I had talked every day, which helped ease some of the loneliness, but most of those calls were at night. Last week, I had met Cora and her son, Legend, during one of my walks on the beach. We had heard of each other, yet had never met in person. When she'd asked if I had any kids, I'd hesitated, and it sparked a conversation which led into a lengthy, and somewhat obscure, explanation about my relationship with Jade. It was nice to hear a female's opinion on the situation. Not to mention, she was right. Jade didn't need to worry about me while she was taking care of matters with her mother. I just had to be patient and wait for the right time.

I'd offered many times to drive over and help Jade out with Aria, to give Stevie a break, but she was adamantly against it. Every time I'd ask, she'd tell me she had too much going on, and if I were there, she'd feel obligated to spend time with me. No matter how many times I argued that I didn't need her to fit me into her schedule, she never gave in. And the few times I had asked if she'd thought any more about us, she told me she'd had too much on her mind to figure it out. So, I was stuck at home, alone, basically waiting by the phone for any word from Jade.

Halfway through the third week, just when I didn't think I'd make it one more day—hell, I worried I wouldn't last another hour, another minute, barely another second—Jade's name flashed across my cell. I couldn't answer it fast enough. Getting a call from her at eleven in the morning alarmed me. Ever since we'd started our daily communications, the earliest I had heard from her was maybe three or four in the afternoon, aside from a text here or there.

"Hey, is everything okay?" I tried to keep the concern out of my tone, but once I heard the pain and anxiety in hers when she whimpered my name, her voice heavy with tears, my body coiled tight. "Jade? Babe, what's going on? Are you hurt?"

"No, I'm fine." Her breathing shook and hiccupped while she attempted to control her emotions. "I just needed to hear your voice. I have no clue why I started to cry. I'm sorry for scaring you." Another shaky inhalation. "Do you have a minute to talk? I don't care about what, I just need you to take my mind off everything."

"Babe, I have all the time in the world for you, but I'm going to need you to tell me what has you so upset. I hate being this far away from you and not knowing what's going on."

"My mom is being released from the rehab center tomorrow."

"That's good news...right?"

"They're sending her home." She paused, probably waiting for her words to make sense to me. But they didn't. When I didn't respond, she offered more. "She's going back to her house, which means she'll need help. I had to tell them I couldn't and used Aria as my excuse, so she's being assigned to at-home care."

"You're upset because you can't help?" I was confused. I tried to comprehend, but I worried I'd further upset her. "I think she understands how difficult it would be for you to take on that responsibility with a toddler around."

"No...it's not that. I can't go to that house, Cash. I didn't want to go there last time, but I needed that book. But now...now it's even worse. I can't go back there. I just can't." Tears filled her words, and it broke me. My heart had been shattered and my soul completely demolished.

"You don't have to. She has help, so you're okay."

"What if she gets upset that I'm not there?"

I hesitated, aware of how sensitive this topic was for her. Ever since I'd mentioned the idea of using the therapist to help facilitate Jade's confession, she hadn't brought it up. And anytime

I did, she'd just brush over it like I'd asked about her hairstyle for the day. It'd been a week and a half, and I still didn't know what was going on. But after hearing her break down on the phone about being at her mom's house, I realized I couldn't continue to be passive.

"Have you spoken to Bryn yet? I know you wanted to wait until your mom processed the arrest, but that was almost two weeks ago. You said the other night she was handling it much better, and it had seemed like she wasn't as angry anymore. So does that mean you've brought it up to the therapist?"

"Cash…" This was her way of blowing me off, as if saying "I'm not ready to talk about it." But I didn't care, because *I* was ready. This was the woman I loved more than anything, and it was obvious her secret suffocated her. She needed space, I gave it to her. She asked for time to focus on her mom, I didn't argue. But if she thought I'd sit back and do nothing while her pain slowly extinguished the light inside of her…she was sadly mistaken.

"Jade…" I said her name the same way she had mine, except where her voice was desperate, pleading, mine was harder, more demanding. "Enough excuses. You can't wait until she leaves the rehab center, because by then, she'll be at her house, and it's clear you don't want to be there. You'll end up using that as an excuse to wait until she's all better. No more waiting, Jade. You've held this in for over six years. You deserve to heal as much as your mom does."

She released a long huff before saying, "You're right, but I just can't do it yet. Bryn's mentioned the idea of incorporating me into their talks, so I plan to bring it up then. This isn't something I can just blurt out. It'll kill her, and I can't handle hurting her right now…not after I finally got her back."

I understood where she was coming from, not because I'd ever been there before, but because it was easy to see the struggle she faced. It wasn't an easy decision, and I wished more than anything

I could've dealt with it all for her. But I couldn't. All I could do was support her and be there when she needed me.

"You don't have to do this alone." I hoped she believed that, but I felt the need to point it out just in case. "If you need me to hold your hand, I'll be there. If you just need to cry and get it out to shield your mother from your pain, I'll give you my shoulder, my ear. I'm a phone call away. I could be there in two hours."

"It's a three-hour drive, Cash."

"If you're going the speed limit." At least that earned me an unexpected laugh from her. "I'm not advocating that you tell her because I think she should be punished or deserves to feel guilt over what happened to you. I don't wish that at all. You say you finally got her back, and it's clear to me she feels the same way about you…but eventually, if you keep this bottled up, unable to even visit her at her house, she'll lose you all over again. You two will never truly have each other back in your lives for good if you don't face the reason you were apart to begin with."

"She just has so much recovery ahead of her, and she doesn't need any distractions."

"Why don't you come home…for the weekend? Take some time for yourself. Bring Aria, and we'll spend a few days together." Hope was a cruel emotion. It was like soaring to ten thousand feet, nothing beneath you, and then waiting for the imminent fall.

If you watched the moment hope bloomed inside someone, you'd see their eyes grow a little bit wider, and within them, you'd witness the spark. It was a light that burned in the center of their chest. The corners of their lips would twitch, and their breathing would accelerate just enough to be noticeable but not heard.

If you ever watched the moment when that hope died…you'd witness the light burning out. It wasn't like a flame at the bottom of a wick. It didn't slowly fade away. Instead, it was like a switch—on one second, off the next. And all you would be able to see was utter darkness.

I held my breath and waited for her answer, trying to rein in the hope.

"Don't you go back to work on Monday?" She sounded hesitant.

"Yeah, so? It's Thursday. We have plenty of time."

"My mom might get upset if I leave right now."

More excuses. "She's going home tomorrow, right? Tell her she needs time to settle in and get used to a new schedule with her therapists and nurses, and you don't want to be in the way. I don't care what the fuck you tell her, Jade. You need to take care of yourself, and Aria, too. And if that's coming here for three days, then you have to do it. Even if you don't come *here*, you need to get away. Take a break. Breathe. And stop worrying about things you can't control. She's your mom…she'll understand."

"Okay," she whispered.

"Yeah? You'll come home?" I completely failed at suppressing my excitement.

"For the weekend." She just had to clarify that part.

"And you'll bring Aria, too?"

"No, Cash…" The sarcasm hung so heavy in her tone I could've almost seen her eyes roll. "I'm going to leave her here with Stevie and Derek. They've been talking about getting a puppy, so I figured they could use the practice with my daughter."

"Good…maybe they'll train her to stop chewing my shoes."

Jade was quiet for a moment, as if debating the reality of my comment, and then she laughed. It was the sweetest sound I'd ever heard, and I couldn't wait to hear it while I held her in my arms.

CHAPTER 23

Jade

Cash quietly snored with his cheek resting on my stomach. I ran my fingers through his hair, absorbing all the time I could with him while he slept. We'd been apart for three weeks—aside from the thirty minutes I'd spent with him when I came home for clothes. Having him to talk to at night when I was with my mom had helped lessen how much I'd missed him, although it was never enough. I needed him. Only him. But I hadn't been in the right frame of mind to make that decision.

I still wasn't.

Even now, as I stroked his forehead and admired the way the lamp on the table behind me in the living room cast a soft glow over his resting features, I still couldn't decide what was best. I had a child to think about—a child who loved Cash more than anything. And he loved her, too. I never doubted that. I believed with my whole heart that he'd never hurt me or Aria, but that didn't help make things any easier. In fact, it made everything that much harder.

I loved him. Unequivocally, without a doubt, no two ways about it...I loved him. And because of that, anytime I thought about his job or what he did while he was gone, it was like I couldn't breathe. Ironically enough, my panic wasn't caused by *what* he did—that brought on a different set of emotions—but rather the chances of something happening that would cause him to never come home to me. I'd watched my mother grieve the loss of my father, and while I was fully aware I couldn't keep someone from dying, I could choose to walk away from those who frequently put their lives in danger. If I could help it, Aria would never know what it was like to bury a parent—biological or not.

Cash stirred and tightened the hold he had on me with his arms wrapped behind my back. I stilled, worried he'd wake up and my time admiring him would end. Since I hadn't been able to make up my mind about what I wanted, I didn't have many opportunities to drown in his presence without him knowing. I refused to let him believe I would stay if I hadn't decided to, and I couldn't do that until I had enough time to contemplate it. My mom's health had taken up so much of my days, and after talking to Cash at night, I'd close my eyes and crash.

Today had been the first time in weeks I'd even had a moment to myself. And it'd been amazing. Cash and I had taken Aria to the beach and actually walked the surf, something I had never done here. Aria pitched a fit because I wouldn't let her swim—cooler weather had set in and the water was too cold. However, the second Cash had lifted her in his arms, she was the happiest little girl in the world. She had missed him so much she practically glued herself to his leg ever since we arrived earlier today. And he'd missed her just as much, which was his excuse for letting her stay up past bedtime. By nine, I asserted my parental control and made her go to bed.

Then it was just the two of us.

Rather than curl into his side like I had done so many times in the past, I chose one end of the couch after he sat on the other—his usual spot. I could tell it bothered him that I'd added so much space between us, but I hadn't been ready to go there just yet. Apparently, he wouldn't let that stop him. With my body turned to face him, my back pressed against the armrest and feet propped on the center cushion, he found his way in…and took it. He'd parted my legs and wrapped his arms around me, fitting into the space between my back and the couch, and made himself comfortable on my stomach. No words were exchanged.

He'd claimed his spot, and I'd let him.

And it'd given me the last hour since he'd fallen asleep to figure out what I wanted. Unfortunately, I'd spent far more time admiring him and pretending we didn't have such a great divide between us, that I hadn't given anything else much thought.

Cash stirred again, and this time, he lifted his head, his sleepy gaze finding mine. I ran the tip of my finger along his smooth brow, down his cheek, and to his chin. The love in his eyes was undeniable, and I only hoped he could see it mirrored back at him. I needed him to recognize my feelings without having to utter the words. I knew once that happened, I'd never leave. And I'd spend every week in fear that he'd never return from his job.

"You should probably go to bed," I whispered while holding his stare.

"I don't want to. I've gone to bed alone for weeks, and I just got you back. I'm not willing to give this up just yet." His words were scratchy and slow, heavy with sleep. They nearly drove me insane with how sexy they sounded, how rough and masculine they were.

"Well, I can't stay like this all night." I tried to laugh, hoping to lighten the mood. "The armrest isn't terribly comfortable, neither is my posture, and soon, I'll need to pee."

"*Fine.*" He dragged out the word like one would expect a dramatic adolescent to do. "But if I'm exhausted tomorrow, you only have yourself to blame. This is vital sleep you're keeping me from."

The instant he pulled away from me, taking his body heat with him, I felt incomplete. Nevertheless, it was something that needed to be done. As much as I loved having him so close, I was well aware of the potential pain it could cause him if I didn't draw the line in the sand. He continued to tell me he loved me, though I never said it back. And he'd taken to calling me "babe." I loved the way that sounded, so I'd never asked him to stop.

"Night, babe." He lingered by his bedroom door, probably expecting me to follow.

But I didn't. I pulled myself off the couch and headed toward the back hall. "Night, Cash," I said over my shoulder, hoping it was enough to convince him that his puppy-dog eyes wouldn't change my mind. I needed to stay strong. I didn't have a choice.

While using the bathroom before bed, I told myself I needed to figure something out by the end of the weekend. As the warm water rinsed the soap from my hands, I tried to make a mental plan for how I'd spend my time here over the next two days, knowing it could be the last time. And after walking back down the hall toward my room, I realized I may never have the chance to fall asleep in his arms again.

My heart pounded with each step I took across the house. It practically leaped for joy when I twisted the knob to his room. And when I slid through the crack and closed the door behind me, it finally felt healed. The broken pieces had mended, and in that instant, everything felt…*right.*

He watched me in silence as I stomped around the bed, flung the covers back, and then threw myself onto the mattress. He snickered when I crossed my arms over my chest, sighed, and stared at the ceiling with a solid two feet of space stretched out between us.

"What are you doing, Jade?" Humor danced wildly in his voice.

I could feel his stare burning holes into the side of my face, but I refused to look at him. Walking into his room was like crossing the threshold from reality into the perfect alternate universe. In the darkness, we could be ourselves. No overthinking. No sick mother or dangerous job. We just were.

"You pitched such a fit about having to sleep alone, so I figured I'd come in here so you wouldn't be so exhausted tomorrow. I'd hate to be the reason you don't get any rest." I basked in the sound of his hushed amusement, and as soon as he settled onto his back again, eyes on the ceiling instead of on me, I sat up. "Fine. Have it your way."

No longer keeping quiet, a barking laugh erupted from his chest when I scooted closer to him. I lifted his arm so I could fit against his side, and with as much attitude as I could muster without cracking a smile, I laid my head on his shoulder and slung my hand across his waist.

"Gosh...you're so needy." The complaint would've been more convincing if I hadn't felt the beginnings of an infectious giggle reverberate in my chest. "Just having me in the same room isn't enough for you. *No.* You need me draped over your body." I then pulled my leg up and hooked it over one of his.

He tucked me against him with his arm across my back, his palm completely covering my shoulder. When he began to make feather-light figure eights on my skin with his fingertip, a chill ran down my spine. But nothing compared to what he did to me when his breath blew through the top of my hair. A fire ignited between my legs, and like a match dropped in a forest during a drought, it consumed my entire body in a split second.

I needed relief, the kind only Cash could offer. So I slid my hand up to his chest, then softly ran it down to his abs until I found the coarse hairs just beneath his navel. His arm flexed around me, which only spurred me on more. Turning my head the slightest bit, I was able to press my lips to his heated flesh. It seemed like every muscle in his body coiled tight when I kissed the smooth area just below his collarbone, but when my tongue snaked out and I ran the tip along his salty skin, a groan rumbled through the room.

"Jade..." His voice was husky and strained, yet it was full of desperation. It was obvious he was holding himself back, but the second I slipped my fingers beneath the elastic waistband on his shorts, he snapped. He grabbed my wrist—a little rougher than I was used to with him, but instead of filling me with fear, it turned me on—and then rolled into me, pushing me onto my back. In an instant, he had his hard, rigid body over mine, my hand pinned to the pillow over my head. "Don't..." he warned.

"Why not?" The desire ripping through me left me panting, my question breathless.

"Not until you decide to be with me."

The backs of my eyes stung with the presence of tears.

He hung his head, breaking our eye contact. Instead of saying anything else, he fell to the bed onto his side and hooked his arm around my waist. Twisting my body, he pulled my back to his front all in one move, and then curled himself against me. His hold around my waist locked me in place, secured me to him. It was enough to swathe me in comfort. Except it didn't. His flexed muscles and harsh breaths warned me of the agony I'd caused him. And because of that, my heart broke all over again.

I swallowed the lump in my throat and asked, "Have you ever watched the movie, 'Constipated'?"

"No." It was obvious he was confused by my random question.

"That's because it hasn't come out yet."

His chest rumbled just slightly. "Goodnight, babe," he whispered into my hair.

"Night, Cash."

I thought that was it, but then he added, "I love you," and I squeezed my eyes shut, giving in to the ache that tore through my chest. *I love you, too.*

As if he heard me, his body relaxed, his hold slackened, and he provided the consolation I so desperately needed.

"Jade, sweetheart," my mom said with pain flooding her voice. She sat on one couch and I sat on the other with Aria curled up next to me taking a nap. It wasn't until I heard her call my name that I realized I'd zoned out, lost in dark thoughts while staring into the kitchen. When I turned to look at her, she asked, "Could you please help me to bed? I need another pain pill and it'll make me sleepy, so I'd rather not be out here when it kicks in."

After three days with Cash, I hadn't wanted to come back here. But Mom needed help, and the at-home-care providers weren't with her all the time, so I didn't feel like I had much of a choice. When I woke up alone Monday morning, I knew my fantasy weekend had ended. Cash had gone back to work, and the knot in the pit of my stomach reminded me why I couldn't give him what he wanted. In order to stop obsessing over the worst-case scenarios that plagued me, I drove across the state to be there for my mom.

I kept telling myself this would get easier, but it never did. At first, I used Aria as an excuse why I couldn't stay long or had to leave. I made myself scarce when the nurses were with her. When she needed a ride to physical therapy, I'd met her at the door and had dropped her off the same way. But today, I couldn't avoid it any longer. The nurse had to leave unexpectedly, and my mom was still in pain—she hadn't been home for a full week yet.

But this…this proved to be more than I could handle.

Mom had taken the bedroom on the first floor since she couldn't climb the stairs. It had once been my room, where all my secrets were kept, but I hadn't been in it since the day I'd packed our belongings and left. Now she needed me to take her there, and I wasn't sure if I could.

She used the walker and took slow, cautious steps, and I followed behind, my throat growing tighter the closer we got. I tried to tell myself I was overreacting, that I had slept in that room for years, both during and long after *his* visits. But the longer I'd been away, the scarier those four walls became. I'd built it up to be this black hole with mold growing on the ceiling and dirt covering the floor. In my mind, rodents had taken over, bugs and insects living off the filth he'd left behind.

"Jade? Sweetheart?" Mom's voice caught my attention and I glanced up, expecting her to be right there. But she wasn't. She'd made it to the bedroom door and had turned to find me twenty feet behind her. I was frozen, unable to move. An invisible weight had pressed into my chest, making breathing almost impossible. "Jade?"

"I can't, Mom. I can't go in there." I took a step back, nearly tripping over my feet. "I-I have to go. I'm so sorry."

"Jade!" Her voice was filled with panic as she called after me. "Jade, please. I can't chase you. Talk to me."

I'd managed to grab Aria, find my purse and keys, and make it three steps from the front door by the time my mom reached the entrance to the living room. She called my name one more time, fear and anguish overpowering her weak voice.

It was enough to make me stop and face her.

"Baby, talk to me. Please," she begged, a sob catching in her words.

"I'm sorry, Mom." Tears blurred my vision and flooded my cheeks. "I love you. And I want to be here for you. But I can't be *here*. I can't go in there. I can't... I can't..."

She gasped and caught herself with the walker, using it to keep her from falling. Her eyes scanned the living room before she peered over her shoulder to the hallway, toward my old bedroom, and a deafening howl ripped through her.

I didn't need to say anything.

She already knew.

"Jade?" It was like she begged me to tell her it wasn't true, that she'd assumed the wrong thing. But I couldn't. And the moment she realized I wouldn't give her the words she desperately needed, she fell into the wall with her shoulder before sliding to the floor, distressing cries flooding the house.

I ran to her, worried she'd injured her hip again. Setting Aria on her feet, I kneeled next to my mother, who grabbed me and pulled me into her chest. Aria had no idea what was going on, but the chaos was enough to frighten her. Screaming in fear, she clung to me, until I pulled her closer and brought her into her grandmother's embrace. My mom took one look at her, then swung her questioning stare back to me, but rather than make me answer, she simply touched my face and cried, "I'm so sorry. So, so sorry."

After six years, that was all I needed to hear her say.

✦

"Where are you taking her?" Stevie's frantic voice filled my ear.

I glanced next to me and watched my mother sleep with the passenger seat fully reclined. "I'm taking her to Geneva Key. We weren't able to find anywhere she could stay that didn't involve stairs, and neither one of us could stand to be in that house a minute longer. What other choice do I have?"

"What's she going to do about her doctors' appointments and physical therapy? What about the at-home-care nurses? You can't just take her hours away this soon after hip surgery. And I'm pretty sure having her sit in a car for three hours is a horrible idea."

I couldn't help but smile at my friend through the phone. "Are you sad that I'm leaving?"

"Of course I am. This is all about me, Jade. How long have we been friends? You should know by now that I'm a selfish bitch, and I was secretly hoping you would just decide to stay here." Even though she was joking, she meant it on some small level.

"I'm not going across the country, Stevie."

"Country...state, same thing." She huffed dramatically. "Whatever. Enough about you. Back to your mom and her hip. What are you planning to do?"

"Well, right now, she's sound asleep, thanks to her painkillers. As far as her doctors and therapy, I've already made the calls. If I have to drive her back for appointments before we can get her transferred to someone over there, then so be it. I don't care."

"What about her house? A job? Now that she doesn't have his income, she'll need to work."

"Calm down. Those things don't matter—they're not important. You're missing the bigger picture here. My mom and I get to be together and sort through everything without a state between us. Without my fear of being in her home. We finally get to heal…and everything else will work out the way it's supposed to. The house will sell. She'll find a job if she has to."

"You're right."

I snickered. "I know I am."

"Have you talked to Cash about your plan?"

My chest grew tight. Things between us had felt strained Sunday night when he went to bed, closing himself off in his room, and I hadn't heard from him since. The few texts I'd sent him, along with the call I'd placed this afternoon, went unanswered. I had probably ruined everything, but I refused to give up. If he didn't want my mom or me there, then we'd leave and find somewhere else—*on* the island. For the first time in my life, I was ready to fight for what I wanted instead of waiting for it to happen.

Crying in my mother's arms did something to me. I wasn't sure if it was finally breaking down that wall of secrets between us, or if it came with the evidence of her love, but the tether that had held me back was snipped.

I was free.

And as soon as the idea of going to Geneva Key came up, there was no place else I wanted to be. This whole time, I couldn't make a decision because I'd been stuck in the grey space. But the second I had fully let my mom in, the colors began to shine, and I was finally free to live *my* life.

"Um…no. I tried to call him, but it went straight to voicemail."

"So you're just moving your mom into his house and hope he's okay with it?"

I truly believed Cash wouldn't have a problem with my mom living there, because it would mean I'd be there, too. Occasionally, when I started to panic that he'd given up on me, I worried that maybe he no longer desired a relationship. But in my heart, in my soul, deep within my core…I didn't believe that was true.

"Are you kidding? What man *wouldn't* be ecstatic to have his girlfriend's mom living with him?" And just like that, the lectures were over.

We stayed on the phone for the rest of the drive while Mom and Aria slept. When I pulled up to the house, I couldn't help the stabbing pain in my chest when I noticed all the lights off and his Range Rover missing from the back. Aware that he'd gone back to work, I hadn't expected him to be there on a Thursday night, but that didn't stop the hope from building on my way over.

"Mom..." I lightly touched her shoulder to stir her awake. "We're home."

CHAPTER 24

Jade

Light moved through the windows while I lay wide awake in Cash's bed. It was a Friday night, so I anticipated he'd come home, but I hadn't expected him quite this early. The low purr of a car pulling around the back of the house caused me to fling the covers off and jump to my feet, nervousness and excitement at war within me. But when I separated the slats of the blinds and saw Cash, relief washed over me in a soothing current.

He moved around the back of my car, his attention bouncing between it and the house, and then he took off in a sprint. By the time my unsteady legs carried me to his bedroom door, he'd already made it inside, only a few feet from where my mother was asleep in my bed.

"Cash," I whispered so I wouldn't wake anyone, but mostly because I couldn't find my voice. My fingers ached with how tightly I gripped the doorframe, needing it to steady myself. It was like I'd dreamt of this moment all day, and now that it was here, I was unsure of what to do.

Any fear I'd had that he'd changed his mind about us vanished the second he turned his head and took notice of me. In a heartbeat, he charged toward me, his long legs eating up the distance in record time. But when he stopped in front of me, he glanced over my shoulder into his room, then down my body, as if wondering why I'd be dressed in a sleepshirt in his bed.

Then his eyes found mine, and in them, I saw a man at the cusp of having everything he wanted, yet too scared to believe it all to be true. And it was proven in the way he appeared to hold himself back when he asked, "What are you doing here?"

"Aliens abducted me and when they brought me back, this was the only place I remembered." The only reason I was able to keep a straight face was the anxiety rolling through me—over his reaction, over what I had to say.

"Yeah? Did they steal your clothes, too?" He pointed to the shirt I had on, which happened to be his, and smirked.

"Yup. They beamed me back to Earth naked."

Slowly, he moved toward me, making me retreat into his room. "Damn...I miss all the good shit." But he stopped in the doorway with his grip on the frame, as if needing it to hold himself back.

Maybe two feet separated us, but I knew why he refused to come closer. He'd told me before that he wouldn't touch me until I gave him what he wanted. Little did he know, I wanted to give it to him more than anything else in the world.

"Really, Jade...why are you here? Did something happen?"

"Yeah. Something happened."

"What?" Concern filled his tone and his grip on the wood tightened.

"I fell..." When his body coiled tight, I added, "In love."

His posture visibly softened and he took a step toward me. "Oh yeah? When did that happen?"

"A while ago."

"He must be one lucky guy. What'd he do to deserve that?"

"He bought my daughter a sandbox."

That's all it took for him to swoop me into his arms. In a blur, he had the bedroom door closed with my back pressed against it, my body pinned between him and the cool wood behind me. He covered my mouth with his and rolled his hips into mine.

"Say it. I need to hear you say it, Jade."

"I love you." My words were nothing but breathless pants of air.

He didn't let me say anything else. His mouth took mine, his tongue parting my lips. In an instant, I was spun around. I tightened my legs around his waist, my ankles locked behind his back, and the next thing I knew, I was on the mattress with his body covering mine.

"Is this real?" he asked, gently kissing my neck.

"I'm not sure. But if it's not, I don't ever want to live in the real world."

His hands slid up my body, beneath my shirt. Then it was off, and I lay in front of him in nothing but panties. His hands and mouth explored every inch of skin, as if memorizing every curve, every scar, every mark. When he made it to the soft spot beneath my bellybutton, just above the lacy fabric around my hips, he paused and glanced up at me.

"You're here for good, right? You're not leaving on Monday? You're not packing your bags and taking Aria away from me? You're mine? Tell me…please." His desperation came out in panting breaths, begging for the words he needed to hear.

I ran my fingers through his thick hair and smiled. "I'm not going anywhere, Cash. I love you more than words can say." And just like that, he pulled himself up my body and returned my love with his lips.

Cash and I connected in a way I never thought possible. His sentiments of love flooded my ears while his fingertips dug into my hips. It was an intense mixture of slow and hard, care and desperation. The rougher his movements became, the higher my euphoria rose, until I dangled off the cliff with only his hands holding onto me.

"Are you with me?" His throaty question grazed my neck, his breath scorching my skin. Then he pressed his forehead to mine and said, "Open your eyes, babe. Look at me. Be in this with me. I need to know you're here."

"I *am* here," I argued, yet I still did as he said. He slowed the pace of his thrusts and searched my eyes for something. "What do you need, Cash? What do you need from me?"

"I need to know you're not thinking about anything other than you and me."

I smiled and said, "It's just me and you. I don't ever need anything else."

And then his mouth covered mine.

His body began to move again, bringing me back to the edge.

He held onto me like he was scared I'd disappear.

When he bucked into me, filling me completely, we both fell apart, while also putting each other back together. I wasn't whole without him. And I knew in my heart he felt the same. He needed me just as much as I needed him, and although I found that thought scary, it comforted me in ways I never imagined were possible.

"Why did you wait so long to tell me how you felt?" He lay on his side with his head on the pillow next to mine, his arm around my waist, holding me to him. "If you knew you loved me when I admitted it to you, why not tell me then? Why did you push me away and make me believe you weren't coming back?"

I turned my head to the side to look him in the eyes. It was dark, making it hard to see him, but I could feel his stare, and that was enough. "A lot happened that night, and I didn't want you to think I was saying it because you did. Then everything blew up, and honestly, it was just all so much. I couldn't handle dealing with my mom, worrying about Aria, *and* figuring this out with you. It was just easier to put it off…until I couldn't anymore."

"What changed your mind?"

"Nothing changed my mind, Cash. My feelings for you never went away. After that night in my mom's kitchen, but before you told me the truth, I was scared. I won't lie. All I could think about was how I'd brought my daughter into the home of a killer. It was strange, because I *knew* in my heart you'd never hurt either one of us, but I still felt guilty for putting her in that situation. Then you told me the truth, and while that made me feel better—you might've done bad things, but that didn't make you a bad person—it ended up leaving me worried about other things."

"Like what?"

"Like how dangerous your job is, and how I wasn't sure I could be strong enough to be what you needed. I hated Monday mornings when I thought you were just climbing cell towers, but after finding out that you basically put yourself in dangerous situations on a weekly basis…" I faced the ceiling again, needing a moment to clear away the pain burning the backs of my eyes. "For three weeks, I knew you were safe because you were here, but this week has been miserable. And I finally realized that I'd be giving up on so much time with you now, just to save myself the possible heartache of losing time with you later."

"That's why you stayed away?"

"Well, that and my mom. But it's the reason I've held back on fully committing to you. It was just easier to focus on her than it was to deal with my feelings toward you."

"How's your mom now?"

I laughed and wiped my eyes. "She's sound asleep in my room."

Cash pushed up on his elbow and stared at me. "*Here*?"

"Yeah." I added a shrug, hoping he'd find it cute and innocent.

"And you didn't bother to tell me that before we had sex?"

"I hate to break it to you, but my mom wasn't exactly on my mind when you had your hands on me. What did you want me to do, stop you mid-thrust and tell you she's across the house? Maybe offer to introduce you when we finish?"

His quiet chuckle drifted over my face. "You're right. I'm sorry. When did you get here?"

"Yesterday. I tried calling you, but your phone went straight to voicemail."

He dropped his head, bringing it closer to mine. "I was in Georgia at my parents' house, and they have horrible service. I tried texting you a few times but it kept bouncing back. Even their

Wi-Fi is slow as fuck, basically one grade above dial-up, and eventually, I just turned off my phone. It's in my suitcase somewhere. I hadn't thought to get it out before I left today."

"I thought you went back to work?"

He kissed me long and slow, our lips barely parting. When he pulled away, I could hear the smile in his words as he said, "I quit. I went in Monday and told Rhett I couldn't do it anymore. He actually said he was surprised I'd waited so long and had expected me to call him when I was on suspension, but I didn't feel that was something that should be done over the phone. From there, I flew in to see my parents. I couldn't handle being here without you."

"You quit?"

"Yeah, babe. I did."

"Why?"

"Because I don't ever want to spend another night without you again. And if I hadn't already made up my mind prior to last weekend, sleeping alone Sunday night reiterated it to me. I would do anything for you."

I wrapped myself around him and celebrated us being together all over again.

⚓

Cash set a piece of paper on the counter in front of me.

I started chopping the vegetables for dinner and glanced at his scrawled handwriting. "Oh my God, really? *Another* agreement? The first two weren't enough for you?" I teased and dismissed him.

"This one's different. The first is kind of null and void, don't you think? I mean, we both broke half the rules on it, and it was for roommates. Now that we're more than that, I figure a new one is in order."

"Oh, yeah? And what's this one say?"

"Read it and find out." He kissed my shoulder before popping a slice of bell pepper into his mouth. "Your mom's resting, so I'm going to take Aria out back to play in the sand."

I washed my hands, dried them, and snatched up the paper. At the top, in bold print, read, "More Than Roommates Agreement." And below that, in parentheses, it said, "take that, Sheldon Cooper." It made me snicker, but that immediately stopped when I began to read more.

The first line was from the honesty agreement he'd made a few weeks ago, including the amendment I had him add, as well as his rule that I couldn't color my hair green. But it was what followed that had sucked away all the humor from my chest.

I stormed down the hall and rushed through the back door, not giving any thought to my mother asleep in one of the rooms. "What the hell is this, Cash?"

He blinked surprised eyes at me, his mouth opening and closing. "Did you just curse? Out loud? Around *the child*?"

"Did you just suggest you stay home for two years and I go finish up my degree?" I shook the paper in the air and added, "On *your* dime?"

"I asked you first."

I huffed, which seemed to lessen my panic a little. The mirth in his eyes and the slight tug of his lips into a smile breathed calmness into me. "Yes. I cursed. Out loud. In front of *the child*. Happy now? Can we move on to more important things? Like you suggesting I go to school while you play the stay-at-home parent?"

He stood and walked over to me. With his hands on my shoulders and a grin brightening his face, he said, "I have money in savings, and you didn't get to finish college. I know it's been hard without having help with Aria, and I'd love to do that for you. I can afford to take time off."

"I'm not taking your money."

"Then look at it as a loan. I don't care what you have to tell yourself, as long as you do what *you* want." It was clear in the way he spoke and in his eyes that he genuinely aspired to give me this opportunity. It was overwhelming, and I wasn't sure how to handle it.

"Would it *really* be a loan?"

He wagged his brows, his grin growing larger. "I've got a loan with your name on it."

I dragged my gaze down his body to his pants and then back up to his face. "You're a little short."

As if he were holding himself back and my words snapped his restraint, he grabbed me, both palms gripping my backside, and hauled me against him. With a slow grind into me, he lowered his lips to my ear and said, "You weren't complaining last night."

I shoved against his chest, even though I didn't want to. "Cash...*the child*." I gestured behind him with a flick of my chin, as if reminding him of the toddler in the sandbox.

"For someone so small, she certainly gets in the way a lot." His eyes squinted with the wide grin plastered on his face, but he backed up regardless. "So...are you going to agree to finish college and let me be Tyke's manny?"

"I have no idea what I'd even go to school for."

"Then give it some thought." He smiled. "Did you read the rest of it?"

I glanced back at the paper, realizing there were several other lines I hadn't gotten to before running outside. By the fourth line, I had to stop and question him. "No panties in bed?"

"If you'd like, I can add that I'll sleep naked, too."

My smile stretched further, but I just shook my head and kept reading. "I don't think you can put babies on a roommate agreement."

He pinched the top of the page so his finger pointed to the header. "I believe it says '*more than*' on here. And babies should be on every agreement...one way or another. I'm not saying right now, but I thought you should know that when you're ready, I'm ready. And if it's not planned…I'm okay with that, too."

If it were possible to fall in love with him all over again, I would have. Right then and there.

I tipped my chin toward the little girl in the sandbox behind him. "I'm already a single mother. At this point in time, I don't care to add to that." But rather than say anything to me, he arched one brow and smirked.

Carrying on with the list, I ran my finger down the page to the spot where I'd left off. And the very next line made me gasp and cover my lips. Tears filled my eyes and my voice burrowed in my throat, creating a knot I couldn't swallow past. "You…you want to adopt Aria?"

"Yes. I'd love nothing more than to be her father. I already feel like she's mine. From the second she came into my life, I haven't been able to imagine my world without her in it. You either. And again, this doesn't have to happen right now. When you're ready, of course. I just needed to put it all out there for you. You deserve to know my intentions."

I couldn't think straight, and staring at him with tears in my eyes only made things awkward. So I went back to the paper in my hand, pretending to read the words he'd written. But once they actually made sense to me, I squeezed my eyes shut and released the salty rivers down my face.

On the very last line, he'd written: Marry me.

"I don't even know what to do with this, Cash." I waved the paper in front of him. "My mom still has so much work ahead of her—we both do. She has doctors' appointments and physical therapy. Then we have Bryn. Plus my mom's house and where she's going to live."

"Babe." His voice was so calm and even as he held my face in the palms of his hands. "You don't have to make any decisions right now. Think about it—all of it. Make changes, add whatever you think of, scratch off what you're not comfortable with. And once you have the agreement the way you want, give it back. Just because you agree to anything on here doesn't mean we have to go out tomorrow and make it happen. I just thought you have the right to know where my head's at. Where my heart's at. What I ultimately hope to have with you."

It wasn't that I *didn't* want these things, or that I was about to tell him no. In fact, if I could've shut my brain off long enough, I would've jumped into his arms and given him anything he asked for. But that was just it...I *couldn't* shut it off. Not only did I still have things with my mom to figure out, but I also had to deal with my own issues. I'd kept things inside for six years, buried it all way down deep, and now that they'd been dug up and brought into the light, there was no way I could ignore it any longer.

"Take care of your mom," he whispered, and pressed a chaste kiss to my forehead. "But promise me you'll think about this, too."

I nodded, assuring him I'd give his agreement thought, and then headed back inside.

And that's exactly what I did.

As I prepared dinner, I thought about it.

Lying next to him in bed, I couldn't stop thinking about it.

And every day since, it'd been on my mind.

But I still wasn't ready to give him back the revised agreement.

My mom had physical therapy Tuesdays and Thursdays, which Cash had offered to drive us to. Each time, he hauled us the almost-three hours there, and then three hours back. He helped facilitate the transition from her doctors on the east coast to a private practice on the island. And when he wasn't pitching in with either her or Aria, he was out scouting places for my mom to live.

"I feel like she doesn't want to move," he said one night in bed, two weeks after she'd come to stay in his house. "Everything I find, she has a problem with. I don't care if she stays here, but I figured she'd like a place of her own...I mean, she's mentioned it a dozen times."

ᵀʰᵉROOMMATE ᵈⁱˢAGREEMENT

I traced invisible lines on his chest with my head on his shoulder, our bare bodies wrapped together as one beneath the covers. "She's extremely appreciative of everything you're doing. I promise you that. But I'm pretty sure the thought of selling her house is causing mixed emotions."

"Why do you say that?"

"Just things I've gathered from her conversations with Bryn."

Her therapist had agreed to a more unconventional form of therapy—phone calls and occasional FaceTime sessions. And she'd even let me be a part of it. She truly was an amazing person who had her patients' best interests at heart, and it showed every time she was there for my mom—and when I'd needed it, for me as well. The amount of healing we'd been able to receive over the last two weeks was extraordinary, and I'd never be able to thank her enough for her patience and guidance.

"My dad bought that house for her when I was a baby, so there's sentimental value in it. But after finding out what took place there…" I instinctually tightened my hold on Cash. "She can't bear to hold onto it. So I think it's a struggle between the good and the bad it holds in her life."

"That makes sense. I just didn't want to step on toes or make her feel like I was trying to push her away. I'm trying to follow the lead here, but sometimes I feel lost, like I'm unsure where I'm needed." Cash had been so much help, and I loved having him around so much.

"Just keep doing what you're doing. Eventually, things will all fall into place."

"How are you holding up? I feel like everything has been about your mom or Aria."

I loved how he always made sure I was being taken care of, too. There'd been days I had barely eaten, and he'd pulled me aside to give me a sandwich or a bowl of fruit. Cash always made sure I took a break and focused on myself—even if it was only for five minutes. Then there were the nights in his bed, when he made sure everything centered around me. Even if we didn't make love, he still pampered me and let me know I was just as important as the woman with pins and a plate in her hip and the toddler who needed help with everything. To him, I was more than a mom, more than a caregiver, more than a driver or nurse or appointment keeper.

I was special.

I was loved.

I was *his*.

"Honestly…I've never felt better. There's still a long road ahead of us, and we all still have so much to figure out, but I feel hopeful about everything. Like nothing will stop us or get in our way."

It'd been five days since Cash had heard from his old boss, Rhett. I hadn't realized it until then, but I'd been holding my breath, waiting for the other shoe to drop. I trusted Cash, and I'd believed him when he promised I'd never have to worry about my stepdad again, but it wasn't until we'd learned that he'd been found dead in his cell that I could finally breathe. Apparently, he had a heart attack in the middle of the night. I didn't put it past Rhett or his team to have facilitated that. When I mentioned that theory to Cash, he simply kissed my forehead and told me it was over. I didn't ask any more questions.

An autopsy had been performed, proving the cause of death, but that didn't mean anything to me. Rhett had fabricated lab reports and DNA evidence from legitimate law enforcement officials, so I wouldn't put it past him to have the same done by a coroner. But either way, whether it was natural or induced, I didn't care. The devil was gone, and I never had to worry about him coming after me or my daughter again.

That remained a major topic of conversation with Bryn—for both my mom and myself. We even had a joint "session" where we both discussed our honest feelings about it, and I could hear how torn my mother was regarding his death. She was a good woman, so it hadn't come as a surprise that she felt sadness over it, but once we talked it out, I realized where the sorrow came from. She wasn't upset that he died, but rather hated how he never had to face the repercussions of his actions toward me. Without going into detail of what I'd walked into that night in her kitchen, I assured her that he didn't leave this earth without punishment.

"I'd love to find someone here, though," I whispered into the quiet room. "I love Bryn, and she's been so helpful. Not too many therapists would do what she's done for us. I don't want to give her up, but I feel it would be beneficial to have someone local to talk to. My mom loved the equine therapy she was in over there, but I haven't heard of anything like that here."

He kissed the top of my head and tightened his arm around me in a brief hug. "I'll look into that tomorrow. Maybe Bryn knows of someone. And even if it's not on the island, I'm sure we can make it work. There's got to be something around here that offers that."

"Have you given any thought to work?" I could've predicted his answer before I even asked the question. It was the same as it had always been—he refused to think about a job until I'd made a decision regarding college.

"Rhett said he had something for me when I was ready, but I told him I'm not looking right now. I don't need the income at the moment, and I can't bring myself to leave you quite yet."

That wasn't the answer I expected to come out of his mouth.

My body tensed. I worried about what kind of job his old boss would have for him, and why Cash hadn't immediately turned the offer down. "Did he tell you what kind of job it would be? Is it like what you used to do?"

He rolled into me, pushing me onto my back, and hovered above my face. "He did tell me...but until I know if I'll take him up on the offer, I'm keeping it to myself. You still haven't given me an answer about school, so I can't even entertain the idea of work until you've informed me of your plans. I told you I'd help with Aria, and I refuse to let a job interfere with that promise."

This was yet another topic of conversation with my mom and Bryn. I didn't complete my degree because of my responsibilities as a mother to Aria, but the more I delved into that, the more I realized I hadn't gone to school for the right reasons in the first place. I went to escape, to have an excuse to be away from home. The degree never mattered, and honestly, I'd never looked that far into the future to even figure out what I wanted to do with my life. And now that I finally had a real chance to complete what I started, I lacked the enthusiasm, because my reasons for attending no longer mattered.

"I would love to go back and graduate—if for nothing else but to show Aria that I did it. But I haven't been able to pull the trigger quite yet. There hasn't been a single reason big enough to push me forward. So you shouldn't let my choices interfere with yours. If anything, my mom will be here to help with Aria if I sign up for classes. Plus, if I *do* decide to attend, it will probably be on a part-time basis."

"Regardless...I'm not making that call until we have our agreement finalized."

I rolled my eyes and playfully shoved his chest. "I'm still working on it, okay?"

"Take all the time in the world, babe. Just know I'm here for you. I'll wait as long as you need. But please keep in mind I'm not a spring chicken anymore. My biological clock is ticking, and there's no telling how much longer I have to make babies with you."

"You don't seem to have much of a problem in that department." And he didn't. If I'd let him, he'd be inside me at least fifteen times a day. "But before we worry about that, there's so much more to figure out first."

"Speaking of...I know I brought it up last week, but you've been a bit busy, and I haven't wanted to pressure you into anything. Have you decided where you'd like to spend Thanksgiving?"

His parents had invited us to spend the holiday with them in Georgia. At first, Cash had turned down the offer, explaining how my mom was living with us and she was still recovering from a fractured hip. It'd been over six weeks since her surgery, and every day she became a little stronger—both mentally and physically. So I assumed his hesitancy was more about either bringing her with us or leaving her behind than it was her recovery. Which had been my main reason why I hadn't given him an answer yet. Even though his parents had included my mom, I still felt reluctant to agree. Now, Thanksgiving was a week away, so I had to make up my mind soon. I was running out of time.

"I'm not sure if my mom is up for that."

"Stop making excuses, Jade. I've talked to her, and she said she'd love to go. I think she's getting a little stir crazy here. I mean, the only time she gets to herself is when she's in her room." Cash had long since started referring to my old bedroom as my mom's, and his as ours. "She has all of us up her ass twenty-four-seven. Plus, she seems really excited to meet my parents."

"Do you want her to come with us? Or are you just saying this for my benefit? I know having her here can't be easy for you. You've been amazing over the last two weeks, but I'm scared you'll wake up and ask for your house back."

He laughed before lowering his mouth to mine. Whispering against my lips, he said, "I love *you*, Jade. And I love having your mother here. She's welcome to stay as long as she'd like. Nothing makes me happier than seeing Aria surrounded by people who love her unconditionally and getting to watch you heal."

My heart soared. "Okay. Then let's go to Georgia."

"What's the chances we'll have an agreement in place before we leave?"

I wanted nothing more than to give him the paper I'd scribbled on, adding my own desires and thoughts, but there was one thing holding me back, and it was something I wasn't ready to discuss with him yet. I needed to process it and possibly talk to Bryn or my mother first.

"I can't make any promises. But I can tell you that I've been working on it, and you'll get it as soon as I have everything sorted out."

"Can you at least tell me what parts are holding it up?" The worry in his tone weighed heavily on my chest, and I wanted more than anything to make it go away, to ease his mind and settle his heart.

"Most of it is the college part. But rest assured that I love you, and I'm not going anywhere. There's a lot on that list that I want more than my next breath...I need you to know that. My hesitation has nothing to do with being with you. I swear."

"So what you're saying is...you want to skip to all the good parts, like having babies and getting married," he teased, yet it was obvious he'd meant it. "I think we should practice a little more so you can fully wrap your mind around a future with me."

And with that, he filled me with all the love I could've ever dreamed of.

CHAPTER 25

Cash

Thanksgiving with my parents wasn't at all like I'd expected.

My mom monopolized Aria, spoiling her rotten—even more than I did—and she really took to Lindsey. They both seemed very fond of one another and created a familial bond over the three days we were there. My dad was smitten with Jade, and told me any chance he could that I needed to "lock her down" before she got away. In a rare show of openness, he talked about the early days with my mom, and how terrified he was that she'd wake up one day and realize there was someone better out there for her. Not that he thought I wasn't worthy of Jade, because he did. My dad thought the world of me and never gave me a reason to doubt how proud he was or how much he believed in me. Yet he saw something in Jade—probably the same thing I had from the very beginning—and knew how devastated I'd be if she wasn't in my life.

But Jade was quiet, soaking it all in. At first, it worried me, although the more I paid attention, the more I recognized the complete love, awe, and satisfaction in her eyes. She hadn't finished tweaking the agreement I'd proposed, nor had she told me what was holding her back from accepting it.

But after returning from Georgia, I surmised it had something to do with family—mine or hers, I still wasn't sure.

"So my mom really liked that condo you picked out." We were in the grocery store; I pushed the cart while Jade compared the labels. It had kind of become our thing. Aria was at the house with Lindsey, which gave the two of us a little bit of time alone. "I'm actually surprised. I didn't think she'd find anything she liked well enough to buy." She basically spoke to the shelf, not looking at me at all.

"Why? I picked out some damn good places for her."

Finally, Jade put the box of cereal into the cart and looked at me. "You did. But after spending the weekend in Georgia, I was convinced she'd start looking for places up there." She laughed beneath her breath, like she found it comical that our mothers had gotten along so well, but I could tell she was happy about it.

"That's funny you say that, because before we left, my mom had joked around about moving here. She said something about how it'd be cheaper to buy a house than airfare multiple times a year."

"I thought you said they hardly come here."

"Yeah, they don't. But I guess now that Mom has a kid to spoil rotten, she has more of a reason to come down. Because, you know, her son isn't enough." I feigned being offended at the rejection. But when Jade didn't laugh, didn't even crack a smile, I sensed something wasn't right. "What's wrong, babe?"

"I trust that you love Aria, and I can tell your parents are crazy about her...but do you think that'll change if we have our own kids?"

Abandoning my position at the front of the cart, I walked around it and took her hands in mine, making her look up at me. "Is that what you've been worried about? That us having children will somehow leave Aria out?"

She didn't have to answer; the tears shining in her eyes did that for her.

"Babe, no. Never. Aria *is* my daughter; don't you see that? We could have a dozen babies, and she'll still be my first. And I know my parents feel the same. My dad was adopted...don't forget that. There's no way in hell he'd ever treat her any differently than our next kid, or the one after that."

She closed her eyes and released a long sigh, and with that, the tension drained from her. "Thank you, Cash. I needed that. I kept telling myself I'd feel better once I saw your parents with her, but it just made my fear worse—because I saw how much they both doted on her."

"You've got nothing to stress about, babe. I promise."

Jade seemed lighter the rest of the trip, like a weight had been removed, and I wished she had mentioned her anxiety earlier rather than keeping it bottled up. But I couldn't dwell on that. Nothing between us had been easy, and I knew it would take time before she'd stop freaking out about everything. The only thing I could do was continue offering her my support and love, and wait for her to sort through her concerns and questions.

That night, after we'd gone back to our room, rather than crawl into bed with me after she washed her face, she sat on the edge of the mattress with a familiar piece of paper in her hand. The lamp on the table next to me glistened in her clear, excited eyes, and it made me sit straight up.

"So I've made all the changes I could think of in your agreement. I'm sure you'll have more to add, but I figured we should go over this first." Instead of handing the paper to me, she kept it in her tight grip, her eyes steady on mine. "I'd feel more comfortable with you going over it in front of me, so we can talk about the changes."

Well, that worried me.

When I nodded, she held it out, finally giving me the answers I'd spent damn near a month waiting for. But I couldn't get past the second article without stopping. "Why'd you cross out the college one?"

"Because I've decided I don't want to go back. My mom has been talking a lot about opening a place for equine therapy here on the island, and she told me today that Bryn is on board. The condo you found, the one she really loves, would leave her enough money after the sale of the house and the savings from when she was married to purchase land on the back side of the island. And I guess she's already spoken to some people about adding stables and buying horses."

"That's amazing, Jade."

She held her finger up, informing me she wasn't done. "And I would really love to help her with that. It'll take almost everything she has in the bank, but I can tell it's what she really wants to do, and I'd rather put the money you were going to loan me for college toward that, instead of a degree I'd never use. If that's okay with you."

"Are you kidding me? Of course it is." I held her by the back of the neck and pulled her mouth to mine, needing to feel her smile on my lips. I also wanted to disrupt any chance she'd have to mention the loan in more detail. I'd offered that as a way to get her to agree, never having a bit of intention of having her pay me back. And I knew if I told her that, she'd change her mind and find another way to get the money.

Then I released her and went back to the list, dropping all conversation of college.

She'd crossed out the line about having babies, and my heart sank. Slowly, I lifted my gaze to find hers, yet I couldn't sense any hesitation or worry coming from her. "No babies?" I asked in such a quiet voice it nearly went unheard.

"I'd like to discuss that with you once you're finished going through it."

My eyes continued to scan the list, but I couldn't take any of it in. My mind remained stuck on the black line running through "have babies together." I skipped over the amendment she'd added to adopting Aria, not really paying attention to her handwritten note, and kept skimming until I reached the end.

Marry me.

Just below it, she added: *Yes.*

"Really? You'll marry me?" Hope blossomed in my chest.

"Of course," she said, as if that had never been a question in her mind. "But this is what I was thinking—and hear me out before you go making any changes to that." My stomach twisted into knots waiting for her to explain. "Christmas is less than a month away, and I'd like it if my mom were here for that. I know you usually go to Georgia, but I was wondering if you could invite your parents here instead."

"Yeah...anything you want, Jade. But what does that have to do with you marrying me?"

"I'd marry you right now, but I need to get through the holidays and get my mom settled into her condo. I'd love to have the ranch in a good place, too, but that'll take more time than I'm willing to wait. So I was thinking, as long as you're okay with it, that we get married in February. That way, we can plan it and not have to rush or split our time between several things."

"Babe..." I pulled her closer until our foreheads touched. "All I care about is making you my wife. I don't give two shits when it happens. If you choose to wait two months, then we wait. If you decide to hold off for another year, then that's what we'll do—even though I'd probably bitch about it. All I need to know is that you're willing to spend the rest of your life with me."

A tear slipped down the side of her face just as she pecked my lips. "Anyway, that's why I put down on the line about adopting Aria that we should do it next year."

I glanced back at the paper, not even realizing she'd added that. And as soon as I found the one she'd crossed out, I couldn't hold back any longer. "Why don't you want to have kids with me?"

"I didn't say that."

"You crossed it off. If it's because you think Aria will somehow mean something different to me, you're wrong. I'm not sure how else to prove that to you."

"No, Cash." Her voice was smooth and filled with happiness. She covered my hand with hers and pulled me in with her promising gaze. "I crossed it out because it's already happened."

"I'm sure this won't come out right, but I need you to hear me, not the voice in your head, okay? The reason I want more kids with you isn't because I feel the need to have a biological child. I don't see the one we have as anything other than that. I just want *more* with you. A bigger family. We can adopt for all I care. As long as they're *our* kids, I don't give two shits where they come from."

She smiled and ran her fingertips along the edges of my face. "No...I don't mean it's already happened with Aria. I mean we already created a baby." And with that, she held my hand over her stomach.

I couldn't contain the emotions from consuming me. In an instant, I was on her, my mouth attacking hers, my hands all over her body. I never imagined I'd feel this excited to hear that kind of news. For so long, I'd convinced myself this wasn't what I wanted, that kids didn't have a place in my life. But Aria and Jade had proved me wrong.

And to think...an ad made out of desperation fulfilled something I hadn't realized I was missing.

"Wait." I pulled away to stare into her eyes. "You're sure?"

"Yes. I took a test before Thanksgiving."

"Have you seen a doctor?"

"No. I don't have insurance."

"Fuck that, Jade." I sat up, anger straightening my spine. "What were you going to do? Wait until February to get checked out? Do you even know how far along you are?"

"No, there's a clinic just over the bridge. I was going to see them, but I decided to talk to you first. And before I did that, I had to wrap my head around how Aria would be treated with another baby in the picture."

With her cheek against my palm, I settled down. "Then let's not wait two months. Let's do it now...this week, I mean. We can make it legal and then have the ceremony whenever you want. That way, we can wait until after the ranch is completed. Or we can still do it in a couple of months. I don't care, but I'm not going to let you go to a free clinic when I have insurance I can add you to."

She brushed me off. "They're real doctors, Cash."

"I don't care if they wrote the book on medicine…you need to be covered."

"And you need a job," she argued. "So now we're back to you. Last time it was brought up, you said something about Rhett offering you work, but you wouldn't tell me what it was. Now that I've given you my answer about school and what I plan to do, and now that you know we have a baby on the way…let's discuss this job offer."

It'd be a lie if I said I wasn't a little bit excited that she didn't need me home for the next two years. The position Rhett had brought up to me was for my dream job. "He said he can get me in with the DA as a detective."

"Don't you have to be a cop for that?"

I shook my head. "No. I'd work directly for the DA's office, making sure their cases are solid and ready for trial. I get to use my skills without the darkness of everything else. And the best part is I get to stay here. I wouldn't have to travel."

Her eyes lit up seconds before she leaped into my arms.

"Is this for real?" she asked against my lips.

"If it isn't, I don't want to live in reality."

EPILOGUE

Cash

It was six in the morning on a Monday, and I stood in front of the mirror in the bathroom. I'd done this five days a week for the last eight months, and I still couldn't believe this was my life. Somehow, in the pits of darkness, I'd found a light.

And her name was Jade.

"Your tie's crooked." My wife's voice flooded the room before her reflection appeared in the mirror. And once again, I questioned how I'd gotten so lucky. Her hair was wild from sleep, and it drove me crazy. In her arms, she carried our son, cradled to her chest. His thick head of raven hair was just as untamed as his mother's.

"Would you like to fix it for me?" I turned around and took the sleeping boy from her arms so she could straighten my tie. I could've done it myself, but every morning, I'd do it wrong just to make her adjust it. It was one of my favorite parts of the day. "Did Clay wake up, or did you get him up?" I asked as I smoothed his soft mane back.

"He was starting to stir, but my boobs were killing me, so I went ahead and got him up to empty them a little." Just the mention of her breasts had me staring at them, their fullness filling her shirt. It'd only been two weeks since she'd given birth to our son, and the thought of waiting another four before I could touch her again nearly drove me insane.

I'd already mentioned the idea of having more, but then she pointed out the need for a bigger house. And she wasn't ready to give up the ocean in our front yard. So I figured we'd keep practicing, and if we ended up needing something bigger, we'd discuss it then. Jade had laughed at me when after coming home from the hospital, I'd added to the bottom of our "More Than Roommates" agreement: **More babies**.

"You going to the ranch today?" Nothing—not even labor—kept her from at least visiting her mom's land and seeing the horses. Bryn and Lindsey had been an amazing team, and I knew they would be able to help so many.

"I think I'll stop by this afternoon. I hate leaving Clay behind for long."

"You know my mom loves it when you drop the kids off with her." Two months ago, my parents had bought a condo near Lindsey's. They hadn't made a permanent move just yet, but they liked the idea of having a place to stay when visiting. So far, they hadn't gone back home. It became a running joke with Jade that they never would.

She took Clay from me so I could leave for work. I bent down and pressed a kiss to his soft forehead, then to Jade's lips. I hated leaving them every morning, but I couldn't complain, because I got to come home to them every day.

I barely made it out of the bedroom before Aria ran to me. I picked her up and snarled into her neck, relishing in the giggles she gave. "You be a good girl for Mommy, okay?"

She nodded and then squeezed my neck. I squeezed her just as tight.

"Bye, Daddy," she said when I set her down.

Jade shook her head and laughed. "You do this every morning, and every morning your shirt gets wrinkled before you leave the house." She ran her palm down my work shirt to press it flat again.

"Maybe I do it just so you'll touch me."

She shoved me toward the back door. "Oh, and before I forget, at two o'clock this morning when I was feeding Clay, I added something to the agreement." The look on her face told me being late to work would be worth the detour to the kitchen.

Right in front of me, hanging on the fridge, was our paper. At the top, just beneath "More than Roommates," she'd added a subtitle: *Agree to "dis" Agreement*. Regardless of what it was called, it was ours. It'd been changed out over the last year for new ones, each list growing longer and longer as time passed. But on this one, at the very bottom, in her neat handwriting, I found: **I get to name our next kid**.

I glanced over my shoulder and found her smirking at me. "What's wrong with Clay?"

"Had I thought about it at the time, I would've realized what you'd done, *Cassius*."

I couldn't hide the grin. "Whatever do you mean?"

"Cassius Clay? Didn't we agree no oddball famous people's names?"

I didn't pick it because of that. Honestly, I liked how it sounded when our names were put together, like an unstoppable team.

I shrugged, feigning ignorance. "But if we have another girl, imagine how awesome it'd be to name her Ali." I winked, letting her know I was only kidding. My dad was the Muhammad Ali fan, not me. "Fine. If you'd like to name the next one, feel free."

That just meant she'd give me another. And I had it right here on the agreement. She wouldn't be able to argue with that.

"I love you, babe." I kissed her on the lips.

She mumbled back, "Love you, too," which was echoed by Aria.

"Love you, too, Tyke."

LEDDY'S NOTES

There's something about a man who steps up and not only takes care of a child who isn't biologically his, but *loves* it like it was, that just hits me straight in the heart. And so I've always wanted to write a book about a single mother and a man who comes into their lives. However, I never had the right story to tell, so the idea remained scribbled in a notebook.

That changed one fateful day when I decided to take a nap. This part is important because I never take naps. Ever. There's something about the sun being up that keeps me from actually falling asleep. Anyway, so I laid down and started to drift off when a random, almost forgotten thought filtered through the narrow gap of consciousness.

You may or may not remember it, but about two years ago, there was an ad that had been passed around Facebook about a man who was seeking a female to live with him. I can't remember too much about it, but I believe he said the rent was free, something about him being retired or whatnot. I just recall women commenting with "sign me up." Anyway, this is the memory that decided to cross my mind that day right before I fell asleep.

And when I woke up, I thought that would be a fun "roommates" book. It wasn't until the opening of chapter one when I realized this was also my "guy falls for woman with kid and loves the kid like his own" book.

Two birds.

One stone.

All made possible by a nap.

So, to conclude, the Leddy Harper Nap Foundations leaves you with this PSA: Take naps.

HEY YOU!!

Where to begin…

There is a certain man who deserves far more than a thank you for putting up with me when my fingers won't type as fast as the thoughts enter my brain…when taking a bathroom break is about as long as I can leave my computer. And of course, there are three incredible little girls who drive me (crazy) every single day. Without you four, I would be nothing. I love you more than you'll ever know.

Stephie… It's always so hard to come up with something at the end of a book for you because I tell you my thoughts on a daily basis. But since you love to hear how great you are, I'll say it again. You're a whorehole.

Kristie… My house needs decorating.

Marlo… I know I say this all the time, but I honestly don't think I could publish a book without you. Your creativity and thoughts, and just overall support, keep me steady in a windstorm. Love you, Lobs!

Angela… Holy cow you're never allowed to leave me. Ever. Got it? I have witnesses! You force me past my comfort zone and then hold my hand (and remind me of everything about a million times a day). I'd be lost without you!

Kristie… It'd be great if you could come over here. You know, to decorate my house.

Heidi… Or should I say, Mrs Axel?! LOL! Love you, C!

Stefanie… It may have taken us a while, but I think we finally found our groove!! I shall never ask you to beta after I finish writing again. From now on, you must be part of it from the beginning. You have no choice in the matter. "Debating" our opposite opinions gives my two-sided situations so much depth, and that's not possible if I've already written it. Thank you so much for walking through this journey with me and pointing me in the right direction (even when you don't know you're doing it).

Kristie… I'm waiting. So is my house.

Josie… As always, you didn't let me down! I honestly can't express how much I appreciate you. They say everything happens for a reason, and no matter how I feel about the whole Booktrope thing, I got you out of it. And if you ever try to leave, I'll lock you in my basement. Well, I don't have a basement, but I'll find one and lock you in it!

Judy… You're amazing! Thank you so much for everything you do! PS—I'm going to have to fire you because you're far too pretty to proofread my shit! Haha!

Robin… This cover. Let's not even talk about the headache that it started with, and only focus on the fabulous end product! Which, by the way, looks amazing on a blanket! Thank you so much for your patience and the many many hours you dedicate to me!

Emily… In a way, you're like my soul mate. You were there for me at the very beginning, like a high school sweetheart. And you continued to support me while I "found myself" with other people, like a college separation. And when it mattered the most, fate brought us both together with the help of a naked man. We're what books are written about! LMAO! Love you!!

Chris… You should tell your wife to come decorate my house.

TWOTs… You six keep me grounded, lift me up, and support me. You're like my gravity (Get it, Lauren?!)

Sarah… As always, I love you. Stop doubting it. What you can or do for me will never, ever ever ever, affect how I feel about you. I love you!

Canada… I have a bone to pick with you. You let Kristie out. If you wanna make it up to me, make her come decorate my house. Thanks in advance.

Readers… I don't have anything else to say but THANK YOU! To all the old and new, and those in between, thank you from the bottom of my heart for giving me a chance or sticking by me. Whether you loved or hated this book, or just liked it somewhat, you'll never know how grateful I am that you at least gave it shot.

Bloggers… You do this because you love it. For the love of the book, the love of the journey, the love of the author, or just plain old love of the escape a book can bring. There is not enough words to thank you for the time you give us, no matter how you feel about our particular book. Thank you isn't enough, so I'm gonna say this (read it in slow motion) thank you. (You totally read that with a deep voice and pictured a man running in slow-mo with his mouth wide open, didn't you?!)

Made in the
USA
Middletown, DE